OTHER LIFE

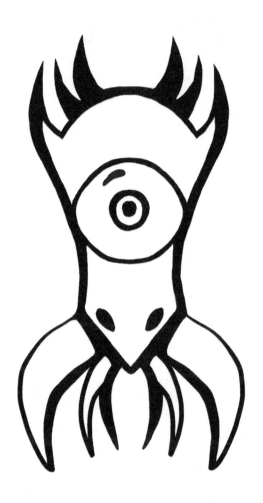

OTHER LIFE

AN ANTHOLOGY OF
NON-TERRESTRIAL BIOLOGY

Chad Arment, Editor

COACHWHIP PUBLICATIONS

Greenville, Ohio

ISBN 1-61646-327-9
ISBN-13 978-1-61646-327-4

Cover: Starfield, Pavlo Vakhrushev; Alien Jelly, Etienne van der Walt.
Frontispiece: Alien Squid, Alexander Kirichenkov

CoachwhipBooks.com

CONTENTS

THE WILLOWS
ALGERNON BLACKWOOD

I

AFTER LEAVING VIENNA, and long before you come to Buda-Pesth, the Danube enters a region of singular loneliness and desolation, where its waters spread away on all sides regardless of a main channel, and the country becomes a swamp for miles upon miles, covered by a vast sea of low willow-bushes. On the big maps this deserted area is painted in a fluffy blue, growing fainter in color as it leaves the banks, and across it may be seen in large straggling letters the word *Sümpfe*, meaning marshes.

In high flood this great acreage of sand, shingle-beds, and willow-grown islands is almost topped by the water, but in normal seasons the bushes bend and rustle in the free winds, showing their silver leaves to the sunshine in an ever-moving plain of bewildering beauty. These willows never attain to the dignity of trees; they have no rigid trunks; they remain humble bushes, with rounded tops and soft outline, swaying on slender stems that answer to the least pressure of the wind; supple as grasses, and so continually shifting that they somehow give the impression that the entire plain is moving and alive. For the wind sends waves rising and falling over the whole surface, waves of leaves instead of waves of water, green swells like the sea, too, until the branches turn and lift, and then silvery white as their underside turns to the sun.

Happy to slip beyond the control of the stern banks, the Danube here wanders about at will among the intricate network of channels intersecting the islands everywhere with broad avenues down which the waters pour with a shouting sound; making whirlpools, eddies, and foaming rapids; tearing at the sandy banks; carrying away masses of shore and willow-clumps; and forming new islands innumerably which shift daily in size and shape and possess at best an impermanent life, since the flood-time obliterates their very existence.

Properly speaking, this fascinating part of the river's life begins soon after leaving Pressburg, and we, in our Canadian canoe, with gipsy tent and frying-pan on board, reached it on the crest of a rising flood about mid-July. That very same morning, when the sky was reddening before sunrise, we had slipped swiftly through still-sleeping Vienna, leaving it a couple of hours later a mere patch of smoke against the blue hills of the Wienerwald on the horizon; we had breakfasted below Fischeramend under a grove of birch trees roaring in the wind; and had then swept on the tearing current past Orth, Hainburg, Petronell (the old Roman Carnuntum of Marcus Aurelius), and so under the frowning heights of Theben on a spur of the Carpathians, where the March steals in quietly from the left and the frontier is crossed between Austria and Hungary.

Racing along at twelve kilometers an hour soon took us well into Hungary, and the muddy waters—sure sign of flood—sent us aground on many a shingle-bed, and twisted us like a cork in many a sudden belching whirlpool before the towers of Pressburg (Hungarian, Poszóny) showed against the sky; and then the canoe, leaping like a spirited horse, flew at top speed under the grey walls, negotiated safely the sunken chain of the Fliegende Brücke ferry, turned the corner sharply to the left, and plunged on yellow foam into the wilderness of islands, sandbanks, and swamp-land beyond—the land of the willows.

The change came suddenly, as when a series of bioscope pictures snaps down on the streets of a town and shifts without warning into the scenery of lake and forest. We entered the land of desolation on wings, and in less than half an hour there was neither boat nor fishing-hut nor red roof, nor any single sign of human habitation and civilization within sight. The sense of remoteness from the world of humankind, the utter isolation, the fascination of this singular world of willows, winds, and waters, instantly laid its spell upon us both, so that we allowed laughingly to one another that we ought by rights to have held some special kind of passport to admit us, and that we had, somewhat audaciously, come without asking leave into a separate little kingdom of wonder and magic—a kingdom that was reserved for the use of others who had a right to it, with everywhere unwritten warnings to trespassers for those who had the imagination to discover them.

Though still early in the afternoon, the ceaseless buffetings of a most tempestuous wind made us feel weary, and we at once began casting about for a suitable camping-ground for the night. But the bewildering character of the islands made landing difficult; the swirling flood carried us in shore and then swept us out again; the willow branches tore our hands as we seized them to stop the canoe, and we pulled many a yard of sandy bank into the water before at length we shot with a great sideways blow from the wind into a backwater and managed to beach the bows in a cloud of spray. Then we lay panting and laughing after our exertions on the hot yellow sand, sheltered from the wind, and in the full blaze of a scorching sun, a cloudless blue sky above, and an immense army of dancing, shouting willow bushes, closing in from all sides, shining with spray and clapping their thousand little hands as though to applaud the success of our efforts.

"What a river!" I said to my companion, thinking of all the way we had traveled from the source in the Black Forest, and how we had often been obliged to wade and push in the upper shallows at the beginning of June.

"Won't stand much nonsense now, will it?" he said, pulling the canoe a little farther into safety up the sand, and then composing himself for a nap.

I lay by his side, happy and peaceful in the bath of the elements—water, wind, sand, and the great fire of the sun—thinking of the long journey that lay behind us, and of the great stretch before us to the Black Sea, and how lucky I was to have such a delightful and charming traveling companion as my friend, the Swede.

We had made many similar journeys together, but the Danube, more than any other river I knew, impressed us from the very beginning with its *aliveness*. From its tiny bubbling entry into the world among the pinewood gardens of Donaueschingen, until this moment when it began to play the great river-game of losing itself among the deserted swamps, unobserved, unrestrained, it had seemed to us like following the growth of some living creature. Sleepy at first, but later developing violent desires as it became conscious of its deep soul, it rolled, like some huge fluid being, through all the countries we had passed, holding our little craft on its mighty shoulders, playing roughly with us sometimes, yet always friendly and well-meaning, till at length we had come inevitably to regard it as a Great Personage.

How, indeed, could it be otherwise, since it told us so much of its secret life? At night we heard it singing to the moon as we lay in our tent, uttering that odd sibilant note peculiar to itself and said to be caused by the rapid tearing of the pebbles along its bed, so great is its hurrying speed. We knew, too, the voice of its gurgling whirlpools, suddenly bubbling up on a surface previously quite calm; the roar of its shallows and swift rapids; its constant steady thundering below all mere surface sounds; and that ceaseless tearing of its icy waters at the banks. How it stood up and shouted when the rains fell flat upon its face! And how its laughter roared out when the wind blew up-stream and tried to stop its growing speed! We knew all its sounds and voices, its tumblings and foamings, its unnecessary splashing against the bridges; that self-conscious chatter when there were hills to look on; the affected dignity of its speech when it passed through the little towns, far too important to laugh; and all these faint, sweet whisperings when the sun caught it fairly in some slow curve and poured down upon it till the steam rose.

It was full of tricks, too, in its early life before the great world knew it. There were places in the upper reaches among the Swabian forests, when yet the first whispers of its destiny had not reached it, where it elected to disappear through holes in the ground, to appear again on the other side of the porous limestone hills and start a new river with another name; leaving, too, so little water in its own bed that we had to climb out and wade and push the canoe through miles of shallows!

And a chief pleasure, in those early days of its irresponsible youth, was to lie low, like Brer Fox, just before the little turbulent tributaries came to join it from the Alps, and to refuse to acknowledge them when in, but to run for miles side by side, the dividing line well marked, the very levels different, the Danube utterly declining to recognize the newcomer. Below Passau, however, it gave up this particular trick, for there the Inn comes in with a thundering power impossible to ignore, and so pushes and incommodes the parent river that there is hardly room for them in the long twisting gorge that follows, and the Danube is shoved this way and that against the cliffs, and forced to hurry itself with great waves and much dashing to and fro in order to get through in time. And during the fight our canoe slipped down from its shoulder to its breast, and had the time of its life among the struggling waves. But the Inn taught the old river a lesson, and after Passau it no longer pretended to ignore new arrivals.

This was many days back, of course, and since then we had come to know other aspects of the great creature, and across the Bavarian wheat plain of Straubing she wandered so slowly under the blazing June sun that we could well imagine only the surface inches were water, while below there moved, concealed as by a silken mantle, a whole army of Undines, passing silently and unseen down to the sea, and very leisurely too, lest they be discovered.

Much, too, we forgave her because of her friendliness to the birds and animals that haunted the shores. Cormorants lined the banks in lonely places in rows like short black palings; grey crows crowded the shingle-beds; storks stood fishing in the vistas of shallower water that opened up between the islands, and hawks, swans, and marsh birds of all sorts filled the air with glinting wings and singing, petulant cries. It was impossible to feel annoyed with the river's vagaries after seeing a deer leap with a splash into the water at sunrise and swim past the bows of the canoe; and often we saw fawns peering at us from the underbrush, or looked straight into the brown eyes of a stag as we charged full tilt round a corner and entered another reach of the river. Foxes, too, everywhere haunted the banks, tripping daintily among the driftwood and disappearing so suddenly that it was impossible to see how they managed it.

But now, after leaving Pressburg, everything changed a little, and the Danube became more serious. It ceased trifling. It was halfway to the Black Sea, within seeming distance almost of other, stranger countries where no tricks would be permitted or understood. It became suddenly grown-up, and claimed our respect and even our awe. It broke out into three arms, for one thing, that only met again a hundred kilometers farther down, and for a canoe there were no indications which one was intended to be followed.

"If you take a side channel," said the Hungarian officer we met in the Pressburg shop while buying provisions, "you may find yourselves, when the flood subsides, forty miles from anywhere, high and dry, and you may easily starve. There are no people, no farms, no fishermen. I warn you not to continue. The river, too, is still rising, and this wind will increase."

The rising river did not alarm us in the least, but the matter of being left high and dry by a sudden subsidence of the waters might be serious, and we had consequently laid in an extra stock of provisions. For the rest, the officer's prophecy held true, and the wind, blowing down a perfectly clear sky, increased steadily till it reached the dignity of a westerly gale.

It was earlier than usual when we camped, for the sun was a good hour or two from the horizon, and leaving my friend still asleep on the hot sand, I wandered about in desultory examination of our hotel. The island, I found, was less than an acre in extent, a mere sandy bank standing some two or three feet above the level of the river. The far end, pointing into the sunset, was covered with flying spray which the tremendous wind drove off the crests of the broken waves. It was triangular in shape, with the apex up stream.

I stood there for several minutes, watching the impetuous crimson flood bearing down with a shouting roar, dashing in waves against the bank as though to sweep it bodily away, and then swirling by in two foaming streams on either side. The ground seemed to shake with the shock and rush, while the furious movement of the willow bushes as the wind poured over them increased the curious illusion that the island itself actually moved. Above, for a mile or two, I could see the great river descending upon me; it was like looking up the slope of a sliding hill, white with foam, and leaping up everywhere to show itself to the sun.

The rest of the island was too thickly grown with willows to make walking pleasant, but I made the tour, nevertheless. From the lower end the light, of course, changed, and the river looked dark and angry. Only the backs of the flying waves were visible, streaked with foam, and pushed forcibly by the great puffs of wind that fell upon them from behind. For a short mile it was visible, pouring in and out among the islands, and then disappearing with a huge sweep into the willows, which closed about it like a herd of monstrous antediluvian creatures crowding down to drink. They made me think of gigantic sponge-like growths that sucked the river up into themselves. They caused it to vanish from sight. They herded there together in such overpowering numbers.

Altogether it was an impressive scene, with its utter loneliness, its bizarre suggestion; and as I gazed, long and curiously, a singular emotion began to stir somewhere in the depths of me. Midway in my delight of the wild beauty, there crept, unbidden and unexplained, a curious feeling of disquietude, almost of alarm.

A rising river, perhaps, always suggests something of the ominous; many of the little islands I saw before me would probably have been swept away by the morning; this resistless, thundering flood of water touched the sense of awe. Yet I was aware that my uneasiness lay deeper far than the emotions of awe and wonder. It was not that I felt. Nor had it directly to do with the power of the driving wind—this shouting hurricane that might almost carry up a few acres of willows into the air and scatter them like so much chaff over the landscape. The wind was simply enjoying itself, for nothing rose out of the flat landscape to stop it, and I was conscious of sharing its great game with a kind of pleasurable excitement. Yet this novel emotion had nothing to do with the wind.

Indeed, so vague was the sense of distress I experienced, that it was impossible to trace it to its source and deal with it accordingly, though I was aware somehow that it had to do with my realization of our utter insignificance before this unrestrained power of the elements about me. The huge-grown river had something to do with it too—a vague, unpleasant idea that we had somehow trifled with these great elemental forces in whose power we lay helpless every hour of the day and night. For here, indeed, they were gigantically at play together, and the sight appealed to the imagination.

But my emotion, so far as I could understand it, seemed to attach itself more particularly to the willow bushes, to these acres and acres of willows, crowding, so thickly growing there, swarming everywhere the eye could reach, pressing upon the river as though to suffocate it, standing in dense array mile after mile beneath the sky, watching, waiting, listening. And, apart quite from the elements, the willows connected themselves subtly with my malaise, attacking the mind insidiously somehow by reason of their vast numbers, and contriving in some way or other to represent to the imagination a new and mighty power, a power, moreover, not altogether friendly to us.

Great revelations of nature, of course, never fail to impress in one way or another, and I was no stranger to moods of the kind. Mountains overawe and oceans terrify, while the mystery of great forests exercises a spell peculiarly its own. But all these, at one point or another, somewhere link on intimately with human life and human experience. They stir comprehensible, even if alarming, emotions. They tend on the whole to exalt.

With this multitude of willows, however, it was something far different, I felt. Some essence emanated from them that besieged the heart. A sense of awe awakened, true, but of awe touched somewhere by a vague terror. Their serried ranks, growing everywhere darker about me as the shadows deepened, moving furiously yet softly in the wind, woke in me the curious and unwelcome suggestion that we had trespassed here upon the borders of an alien world, a world where we were intruders, a world where we were not wanted or invited to remain—where we ran grave risks perhaps!

The feeling, however, though it refused to yield its meaning entirely to analysis, did not at the time trouble me by passing into menace. Yet it never left me quite, even during the very practical business of putting up the tent in a hurricane of wind and building a fire for the stew-pot. It remained, just enough to bother and per-plex, and to rob a most delightful camping-ground of a good por-tion of its charm. To my companion, however, I said nothing, for he was a man I considered devoid of imagination. In the first place, I could never have explained to him what I meant, and in the sec-ond, he would have laughed stupidly at me if I had.

There was a slight depression in the center of the island, and here we pitched the tent. The surrounding willows broke the wind a bit.

"A poor camp," observed the imperturbable Swede when at last the tent stood upright, "no stones and precious little firewood. I'm for moving on early tomorrow—eh? This sand won't hold anything."

But the experience of a collapsing tent at midnight had taught us many devices, and we made the cozy gipsy house as safe as pos-sible, and then set about collecting a store of wood to last till bed-time. Willow bushes drop no branches, and driftwood was our only source of supply. We hunted the shores pretty thoroughly. Every-where the banks were crumbling as the rising flood tore at them and carried away great portions with a splash and a gurgle.

"The island's much smaller than when we landed," said the accurate Swede. "It won't last long at this rate. We'd better drag the canoe close to the tent, and be ready to start at a moment's notice. *I* shall sleep in my clothes."

He was a little distance off, climbing along the bank, and I heard his rather jolly laugh as he spoke.

"By Jove!" I heard him call, a moment later, and turned to see what had caused his exclamation. But for the moment he was hid-den by the willows, and I could not find him.

"What in the world's this?" I heard him cry again, and this time his voice had become serious.

I ran up quickly and joined him on the bank. He was looking over the river, pointing at something in the water.

"Good heavens, it's a man's body!" he cried excitedly. "Look!"

A black thing, turning over and over in the foaming waves, swept rapidly past. It kept disappearing and coming up to the surface again. It was about twenty feet from the shore, and just as it was opposite to where we stood it lurched round and looked straight at us. We saw its eyes reflecting the sunset, and gleaming an odd yellow as the body turned over. Then it gave a swift, gulping plunge, and dived out of sight in a flash.

"An otter, by gad!" we exclaimed in the same breath, laughing.

It was an otter, alive, and out on the hunt; yet it had looked exactly like the body of a drowned man turning helplessly in the current. Far below it came to the surface once again, and we saw its black skin, wet and shining in the sunlight.

Then, too, just as we turned back, our arms full of driftwood, another thing happened to recall us to the river bank. This time it really was a man, and what was more, a man in a boat. Now a small boat on the Danube was an unusual sight at any time, but here in this deserted region, and at flood time, it was so unexpected as to constitute a real event. We stood and stared.

Whether it was due to the slanting sunlight, or the refraction from the wonderfully illumined water, I cannot say, but, whatever the cause, I found it difficult to focus my sight properly upon the flying apparition. It seemed, however, to be a man standing upright in a sort of flat-bottomed boat, steering with a long oar, and being carried down the opposite shore at a tremendous pace. He apparently was looking across in our direction, but the distance was too great and the light too uncertain for us to make out very plainly what he was about. It seemed to me that he was gesticulating and making signs at us. His voice came across the water to us shouting something furiously, but the wind drowned it so that no single word was audible. There was something curious about the whole appearance—man, boat, signs, voice—that made an impression on me out of all proportion to its cause.

"He's crossing himself!" I cried. "Look, he's making the sign of the Cross!"

"I believe you're right," the Swede said, shading his eyes with his hand and watching the man out of sight. He seemed to be gone in a moment, melting away down there into the sea of willows where the sun caught them in the bend of the river and turned them into a great crimson wall of beauty. Mist, too, had begun to ruse, so that the air was hazy.

"But what in the world is he doing at nightfall on this flooded river?" I said, half to myself. "Where is he going at such a time, and what did he mean by his signs and shouting? D'you think he wished to warn us about something?"

"He saw our smoke, and thought we were spirits probably," laughed my companion. "These Hungarians believe in all sorts of rubbish; you remember the shopwoman at Pressburg warning us that no one ever landed here because it belonged to some sort of beings outside man's world! I suppose they believe in fairies and elementals, possibly demons, too. That peasant in the boat saw people on the islands for the first time in his life," he added, after a slight pause, "and it scared him, that's all."

The Swede's tone of voice was not convincing, and his manner lacked something that was usually there. I noted the change instantly while he talked, though without being able to label it precisely.

"If they had enough imagination," I laughed loudly—I remember trying to make as much noise as I could—"they might well people a place like this with the old gods of antiquity. The Romans must have haunted all this region more or less with their shrines and sacred groves and elemental deities."

The subject dropped and we returned to our stew-pot, for my friend was not given to imaginative conversation as a rule. Moreover, just then I remember feeling distinctly glad that he was not imaginative; his stolid, practical nature suddenly seemed to me welcome and comforting. It was an admirable temperament, I felt; he could steer down rapids like a red Indian, shoot dangerous bridges and whirlpools better than any white man I ever saw in a canoe. He was a grand fellow for an adventurous trip, a tower of strength when untoward things happened. I looked at his strong face and light curly hair as he staggered along under his pile of driftwood (twice the size of mine!), and I experienced a feeling of relief. Yes, I was distinctly glad just then that the Swede was—what he was, and that he never made remarks that suggested more than they said.

"The river's still rising, though," he added, as if following out some thoughts of his own, and dropping his load with a gasp. "This island will be under water in two days if it goes on."

"I wish the *wind* would go down," I said. "I don't care a fig for the river."

The flood, indeed, had no terrors for us; we could get off at ten minutes' notice, and the more water the better we liked it. It meant an increasing current and the obliteration of the treacherous shingle-beds that so often threatened to tear the bottom out of our canoe.

Contrary to our expectations, the wind did not go down with the sun. It seemed to increase with the darkness, howling over-head and shaking the willows round us like straws. Curious sounds accompanied it sometimes, like the explosion of heavy guns, and it fell upon the water and the island in great flat blows of immense power. It made me think of the sounds a planet must make, could we only hear it, driving along through space.

But the sky kept wholly clear of clouds, and soon after supper the full moon rose up in the east and covered the river and the plain of shouting willows with a light like the day.

We lay on the sandy patch beside the fire, smoking, listening to the noises of the night round us, and talking happily of the jour-ney we had already made, and of our plans ahead. The map lay spread in the door of the tent, but the high wind made it hard to study, and presently we lowered the curtain and extinguished the lantern. The firelight was enough to smoke and see each other's faces by, and the sparks flew about overhead like fireworks. A few yards beyond, the river gurgled and hissed, and from time to time a heavy splash announced the falling away of further portions of the bank.

Our talk, I noticed, had to do with the faraway scenes and incidents of our first camps in the Black Forest, or of other subjects altogether remote from the present setting, for neither of us spoke of the actual moment more than was necessary—almost as though we had agreed tacitly to avoid discussion of the camp and its incidents. Neither the otter nor the boatman, for instance, received the honor of a single mention, though ordinarily these would have furnished discussion for the greater part of the evening. They were, of course, distinct events in such a place.

The scarcity of wood made it a business to keep the fire going, for the wind, that drove the smoke in our faces wherever we sat, helped at the same time to make a forced draught. We took it in turn to make some foraging expeditions into the darkness, and the quantity the Swede brought back always made me feel that he took an absurdly long time finding it; for the fact was I did not care much about being left alone, and yet it always seemed to be my turn to grub about among the bushes or scramble along the slippery banks in the moonlight. The long day's battle with wind and water—such wind and such water!—had tired us both, and an early bed was the obvious program. Yet neither of us made the move for the tent. We lay there, tending the fire, talking in desultory fashion, peering about us into the dense willow bushes, and listening to the thunder of wind and river. The loneliness of the place had entered our very bones, and silence seemed natural, for after a bit the sound of our voices became a trifle unreal and forced; whispering would have been the fitting mode of communication, I felt, and the human voice, always rather absurd amid the roar of the elements, now carried with it something almost illegitimate. It was like talking out loud in church, or in some place where it was not lawful, perhaps not quite *safe*, to be overheard.

The eeriness of this lonely island, set among a million willows, swept by a hurricane, and surrounded by hurrying deep waters, touched us both, I fancy. Untrodden by man, almost unknown to man, it lay there beneath the moon, remote from human influence, on the frontier of another world, an alien world, a world tenanted by willows only and the souls of willows. And we, in our rashness, had dared to invade it, even to make use of it! Something more than the power of its mystery stirred in me as I lay on the sand, feet to fire, and peered up through the leaves at the stars. For the last time I rose to get firewood.

"When this has burnt up," I said firmly, "I shall turn in," and my companion watched me lazily as I moved off into the surrounding shadows.

For an unimaginative man I thought he seemed unusually receptive that night, unusually open to suggestion of things other than sensory. He too was touched by the beauty and loneliness of the place. I was not altogether pleased, I remember, to recognize this slight change in him, and instead of immediately collecting sticks, I made my way to the far point of the island where the moonlight on plain and river could be seen to better advantage. The desire to be alone had come suddenly upon me; my former dread returned in force; there was a vague feeling in me I wished to face and probe to the bottom.

When I reached the point of sand jutting out among the waves, the spell of the place descended upon me with a positive shock. No mere "scenery" could have produced such an effect. There was something more here, something to alarm.

I gazed across the waste of wild waters; I watched the whispering willows; I heard the ceaseless beating of the tireless wind; and, one and all, each in its own way, stirred in me this sensation of a strange distress. But the *willows* especially; for ever they went on chattering and talking among themselves, laughing a little, shrilly crying out, sometimes sighing—but what it was they made so much to-do about belonged to the secret life of the great plain they inhabited. And it was utterly alien to the world I knew, or to that of the wild yet kindly elements. They made me think of a host of beings from another plane of life, another evolution altogether, perhaps, all discussing a mystery known only to themselves. I watched them moving busily together, oddly shaking their big bushy heads, twirling their myriad leaves even when there was no wind. They moved of their own will as though alive, and they touched, by some incalculable method, my own keen sense of the *horrible*.

There they stood in the moonlight, like a vast army surrounding our camp, shaking their innumerable silver spears defiantly, formed all ready for an attack.

The psychology of places, for some imaginations at least, is very vivid; for the wanderer, especially, camps have their "note" either of welcome or rejection. At first it may not always be apparent, because the busy preparations of tent and cooking prevent, but with the first pause—after supper usually—it comes and announces itself. And the note of this willow-camp now became unmistakably plain to me; we were interlopers, trespassers; we were not welcomed. The sense of unfamiliarity grew upon me as I stood there watching. We touched the frontier of a region where our presence was resented. For a night's lodging we might perhaps be tolerated; but for a prolonged and inquisitive stay—No! by all the gods of the trees and wilderness, no! We were the first human influences upon this island, and we were not wanted. *The willows were against us.*

Strange thoughts like these, bizarre fancies, borne I know not whence, found lodgment in my mind as I stood listening. What, I thought, if, after all, these crouching willows proved to be alive; if suddenly they should rise up, like a swarm of living creatures, marshaled by the gods whose territory we had invaded, sweep towards us off the vast swamps, booming overhead in the night—and then *settle down!* As I looked it was so easy to imagine they actually moved, crept nearer, retreated a little, huddled together in masses, hostile, waiting for the great wind that should finally start them a-running. I could have sworn their aspect changed a little, and their ranks deepened and pressed more closely together.

The melancholy shrill cry of a night-bird sounded overhead, and suddenly I nearly lost my balance as the piece of bank I stood upon fell with a great splash into the river, undermined by the flood. I stepped back just in time, and went on hunting for firewood again, half laughing at the odd fancies that crowded so thickly into my mind and cast their spell upon me. I recalled the Swede's remark about moving on next day, and I was just thinking that I

fully agreed with him, when I turned with a start and saw the subject of my thoughts standing immediately in front of me. He was
quite close. The roar of the elements had covered his approach.

"You've been gone so long," he shouted above the wind, "I
thought something must have happened to you."

But there was that in his tone, and a certain look in his face as
well, that conveyed to me more than his usual words, and in a flash
I understood the real reason for his coming. It was because the
spell of the place had entered his soul too, and he did not like
being alone.

"River still rising," he cried, pointing to the flood in the moonlight, "and the wind's simply awful."

He always said the same things, but it was the cry for compan-
ionship that gave the real importance to his words.

"Lucky," I cried back, "our tent's in the hollow. I think it'll hold
all right." I added something about the difficulty of finding wood,
in order to explain my absence, but the wind caught my words and
flung them across the river, so that he did not hear, but just looked
at me through the branches, nodding his head.

"Lucky if we get away without disaster!" he shouted, or words
to that effect; and I remember feeling half angry with him for putting the thought into words, for it was exactly what I felt myself.
There was disaster impending somewhere, and the sense of pre-
sentiment lay unpleasantly upon me.

We went back to the fire and made a final blaze, poking it up
with our feet. We took a last look round. But for the wind the heat
would have been unpleasant. I put this thought into words, and I
remember my friend's reply struck me oddly: that he would rather
have the heat, the ordinary July weather, than this "diabolical
wind."

Everything was snug for the night; the canoe lying turned over
beside the tent, with both yellow paddles beneath her; the provision
sack hanging from a willow-stem, and the washed-up dishes removed
to a safe distance from the fire, all ready for the morning meal.

We smothered the embers of the fire with sand, and then turned
in. The flap of the tent door was up, and I saw the branches and

the stars and the white moonlight. The shaking willows and the heavy buffetings of the wind against our taut little house were the last things I remembered as sleep came down and covered all with its soft and delicious forgetfulness.

II

Suddenly I found myself lying awake, peering from my sandy mattress through the door of the tent. I looked at my watch pinned against the canvas, and saw by the bright moonlight that it was past twelve o'clock—the threshold of a new day—and I had therefore slept a couple of hours. The Swede was asleep still beside me; the wind howled as before; something plucked at my heart and made me feel afraid. There was a sense of disturbance in my immediate neighborhood.

I sat up quickly and looked out. The trees were swaying violently to and fro as the gusts smote them, but our little bit of green canvas lay snugly safe in the hollow, for the wind passed over it without meeting enough resistance to make it vicious. The feeling of disquietude did not pass, however, and I crawled quietly out of the tent to see if our belongings were safe. I moved carefully so as not to waken my companion. A curious excitement was on me.

I was half-way out, kneeling on all fours, when my eye first took in that the tops of the bushes opposite, with their moving tracery of leaves, made shapes against the sky. I sat back on my haunches and stared. It was incredible, surely, but there, opposite and slightly above me, were shapes of some indeterminate sort among the willows, and as the branches swayed in the wind they seemed to group themselves about these shapes, forming a series of monstrous outlines that shifted rapidly beneath the moon. Close, about fifty feet in front of me, I saw these things.

My first instinct was to waken my companion, that he too might see them, but something made me hesitate—the sudden realization, probably, that I should not welcome corroboration; and meanwhile I crouched there staring in amazement with smarting eyes. I was wide awake. I remember saying to myself that I was *not* dreaming.

They first became properly visible, these huge figures, just within the tops of the bushes—immense, bronze-colored, moving, and wholly independent of the swaying of the branches. I saw them plainly and noted, now I came to examine them more calmly, that they were very much larger than human, and indeed that something in their appearance proclaimed them to be *not human* at all. Certainly they were not merely the moving tracery of the branches against the moonlight. They shifted independently. They rose upwards in a continuous stream from earth to sky, vanishing utterly as soon as they reached the dark of the sky. They were interlaced one with another, making a great column, and I saw their limbs and huge bodies melting in and out of each other, forming this serpentine line that bent and swayed and twisted spirally with the contortions of the wind-tossed trees. They were nude, fluid shapes, passing up the bushes, *within* the leaves almost—rising up in a living column into the heavens. Their faces I never could see. Unceasingly they poured upwards, swaying in great bending curves, with a hue of dull bronze upon their skins.

I stared, trying to force every atom of vision from my eyes. For a long time I thought they *must* every moment disappear and resolve themselves into the movements of the branches and prove to be an optical illusion. I searched everywhere for a proof of reality, when all the while I understood quite well that the standard of reality had changed. For the longer I looked the more certain I became that these figures were real and living, though perhaps not according to the standards that the camera and the biologist would insist upon.

Far from feeling fear, I was possessed with a sense of awe and wonder such as I have never known. I seemed to be gazing at the personified elemental forces of this haunted and primeval region. Our intrusion had stirred the powers of the place into activity. It was we who were the cause of the disturbance, and my brain filled to bursting with stories and legends of the spirits and deities of places that have been acknowledged and worshipped by men in all ages of the world's history. But, before I could arrive at any possible explanation, something impelled me to go farther out, and I crept forward on the sand and stood upright. I felt the ground still warm under my bare feet; the wind tore at my hair and face; and the sound of the river burst upon my ears with a sudden roar. These things, I knew, were real, and proved that my senses were acting normally. Yet the figures still rose from earth to heaven, silent, majestically, in a great spiral of grace and strength that overwhelmed me at length with a genuine deep emotion of worship. I felt that I must fall down and worship—absolutely worship.

Perhaps in another minute I might have done so, when a gust of wind swept against me with such force that it blew me sideways, and I nearly stumbled and fell. It seemed to shake the dream violently out of me. At least it gave me another point of view somehow. The figures still remained, still ascended into heaven from the heart of the night, but my reason at last began to assert itself. It must be a subjective experience, I argued—none the less real for that, but still subjective. The moonlight and the branches combined to work out these pictures upon the mirror of my imagination, and for some reason I projected them outwards and made them appear objective. I knew this must be the case, of course. I took courage, and began to move forward across the open patches of sand. By Jove, though, was it all hallucination? Was it merely subjective? Did not my reason argue in the old futile way from the little standard of the known?

I only know that great column of figures ascended darkly into the sky for what seemed a very long period of time, and with a very complete measure of reality as most men are accustomed to gauge reality. Then suddenly they were gone!

And, once they were gone and the immediate wonder of their great presence had passed, fear came down upon me with a cold rush. The esoteric meaning of this lonely and haunted region suddenly flamed up within me, and I began to tremble dreadfully. I took a quick look round—a look of horror that came near to panic—calculating vainly ways of escape; and then, realizing how helpless I was to achieve anything really effective, I crept back silently into the tent and lay down again upon my sandy mattress, first lowering the door-curtain to shut out the sight of the willows in the moonlight, and then burying my head as deeply as possible beneath the blankets to deaden the sound of the terrifying wind.

III

As though further to convince me that I had not been dreaming, I remember that it was a long time before I fell again into a troubled and restless sleep; and even then only the upper crust of me slept, and underneath there was something that never quite lost consciousness, but lay alert and on the watch.

But this second time I jumped up with a genuine start of terror. It was neither the wind nor the river that woke me, but the slow approach of something that caused the sleeping portion of me to grow smaller and smaller till at last it vanished altogether, and I found myself sitting bolt upright—listening.

Outside there was a sound of multitudinous little patterings. They had been coming, I was aware, for a long time, and in my sleep they had first become audible. I sat there nervously wide awake as though I had not slept at all. It seemed to me that my breathing came with difficulty, and that there was a great weight upon the surface of my body. In spite of the hot night, I felt clammy with cold and shivered. Something surely was pressing steadily against the sides of the tent and weighing down upon it from above. Was it the body of the wind? Was this the pattering rain, the dripping of the leaves? The spray blown from the river by the wind and gathering in big drops? I thought quickly of a dozen things.

Then suddenly the explanation leaped into my mind: a bough from the poplar, the only large tree on the island, had fallen with the wind. Still half caught by the other branches, it would fall with the next gust and crush us, and meanwhile its leaves brushed and tapped upon the tight canvas surface of the tent. I raised a loose flap and rushed out, calling to the Swede to follow.

But when I got out and stood upright I saw that the tent was free. There was no hanging bough; there was no rain or spray; nothing approached.

A cold, grey light filtered down through the bushes and lay on the faintly gleaming sand. Stars still crowded the sky directly overhead, and the wind howled magnificently, but the fire no longer gave out any glow, and I saw the east reddening in streaks through the trees. Several hours must have passed since I stood there before watching the ascending figures, and the memory of it now came back to me horribly, like an evil dream. Oh, how tired it made me feel, that ceaseless raging wind! Yet, though the deep lassitude of a sleepless night was on me, my nerves were tingling with the activity of an equally tireless apprehension, and all idea of repose was out of the question. The river I saw had risen further. Its thunder filled the air, and a fine spray made itself felt through my thin sleeping shirt.

Yet nowhere did I discover the slightest evidence of anything to cause alarm. This deep, prolonged disturbance in my heart remained wholly unaccounted for.

My companion had not stirred when I called him, and there was no need to waken him now. I looked about me carefully, noting everything; the turned-over canoe; the yellow paddles—two of them, I'm certain; the provision sack and the extra lantern hanging together from the tree; and, crowding everywhere about me, enveloping all, the willows, those endless, shaking willows. A bird uttered its morning cry, and a string of duck passed with whirring flight overhead in the twilight. The sand whirled, dry and stinging, about my bare feet in the wind.

I walked round the tent and then went out a little way into the bush, so that I could see across the river to the farther landscape, and the same profound yet indefinable emotion of distress seized upon me again as I saw the interminable sea of bushes stretching to the horizon, looking ghostly and unreal in the wan light of dawn. I walked softly here and there, still puzzling over that odd sound of infinite pattering, and of that pressure upon the tent that had wakened me. It must have been the wind, I reflected—the wind bearing upon the loose, hot sand, driving the dry particles smartly against the taut canvas—the wind dropping heavily upon our fragile roof.

Yet all the time my nervousness and malaise increased appreciably.

I crossed over to the farther shore and noted how the coastline had altered in the night, and what masses of sand the river had torn away. I dipped my hands and feet into the cool current, and bathed my forehead. Already there was a glow of sunrise in the sky and the exquisite freshness of coming day. On my way back I passed purposely beneath the very bushes where I had seen the column of figures rising into the air, and midway among the clumps I suddenly found myself overtaken by a sense of vast terror. From the shadows a large figure went swiftly by. Someone passed me, as sure as ever man did. . . .

It was a great staggering blow from the wind that helped me forward again, and once out in the more open space, the sense of terror diminished strangely. The winds were about and walking, I remember saying to myself, for the winds often move like great presences under the trees. And altogether the fear that hovered about me was such an unknown and immense kind of fear, so unlike anything I had ever felt before, that it woke a sense of awe and wonder in me that did much to counteract its worst effects; and when I reached a high point in the middle of the island from which I could see the wide stretch of river, crimson in the sunrise, the whole magical beauty of it all was so overpowering that a sort of wild yearning woke in me and almost brought a cry up into the throat.

But this cry found no expression, for as my eyes wandered from the plain beyond to the island round me and noted our little tent half hidden among the willows, a dreadful discovery leaped out at me, compared to which my terror of the walking winds seemed as nothing at all.

For a change, I thought, had somehow come about in the arrangement of the landscape. It was not that my point of vantage gave me a different view, but that an alteration had apparently been effected in the relation of the tent to the willows, and of the willows to the tent. Surely the bushes now crowded much closer— unnecessarily, unpleasantly close. *They had moved nearer.*

Creeping with silent feet over the shifting sands, drawing imperceptibly nearer by soft, unhurried movements, the willows had come closer during the night. But had the wind moved them, or had they moved of themselves? I recalled the sound of infinite small patterings and the pressure upon the tent and upon my own heart that caused me to wake in terror. I swayed for a moment in the wind like a tree, finding it hard to keep my upright position on the sandy hillock. There was a suggestion here of personal agency, of deliberate intention, of aggressive hostility, and it terrified me into a sort of rigidity.

Then the reaction followed quickly. The idea was so bizarre, so absurd, that I felt inclined to laugh. But the laughter came no more readily than the cry, for the knowledge that my mind was so receptive to such dangerous imaginings brought the additional terror that it was through our minds and not through our physical bodies that the attack would come, and was coming.

The wind buffeted me about, and, very quickly it seemed, the sun came up over the horizon, for it was after four o'clock, and I must have stood on that little pinnacle of sand longer than I knew, afraid to come down to close quarters with the willows. I returned quietly, creepily, to the tent, first taking another exhaustive look round and—yes, I confess it—making a few measurements. I paced out on the warm sand the distances between the willows and the tent, making a note of the shortest distance particularly.

I crawled stealthily into my blankets. My companion, to all appearances, still slept soundly, and I was glad that this was so. Provided my experiences were not corroborated, I could find strength somehow to deny them, perhaps. With the daylight I could persuade myself that it was all a subjective hallucination, a fantasy of the night, a projection of the excited imagination.

Nothing further came in to disturb me, and I fell asleep almost at once, utterly exhausted, yet still in dread of hearing again that weird sound of multitudinous pattering, or of feeling the pressure upon my heart that had made it difficult to breathe.

IV

The sun was high in the heavens when my companion woke me from a heavy sleep and announced that the porridge was cooked and there was just time to bathe. The grateful smell of frizzling bacon entered the tent door.

"River still rising," he said, "and several islands out in mid-stream have disappeared altogether. Our own island's much smaller."

"Any wood left?" I asked sleepily.

"The wood and the island will finish tomorrow in a dead heat," he laughed, "but there's enough to last us till then."

I plunged in from the point of the island, which had indeed altered a lot in size and shape during the night, and was swept down in a moment to the landing-place opposite the tent. The water was icy, and the banks flew by like the country from an express train. Bathing under such conditions was an exhilarating operation, and the terror of the night seemed cleansed out of me by a process of evaporation in the brain. The sun was blazing hot; not a cloud showed itself anywhere; the wind, however, had not abated one little jot.

Quite suddenly then the implied meaning of the Swede's words flashed across me, showing that he no longer wished to leave post-haste, and had changed his mind. "Enough to last till tomorrow"—he assumed we should stay on the island another night. It struck me as odd. The night before he was so positive the other way. How had the change come about?

Great crumblings of the banks occurred at breakfast, with heavy splashings and clouds of spray which the wind brought into our frying-pan, and my fellow-traveler talked incessantly about the difficulty the Vienna-Pesth steamers must have to find the channel in flood. But the state of his mind interested and impressed me far more than the state of the river or the difficulties of the steamers. He had changed somehow since the evening before. His manner was different—a trifle excited, a trifle shy, with a sort of suspicion about his voice and gestures. I hardly know how to describe it now in cold blood, but at the time I remember being quite certain of one thing—that he had become frightened!

He ate very little breakfast, and for once omitted to smoke his pipe. He had the map spread open beside him, and kept studying its markings.

"We'd better get off sharp in an hour," I said presently, feeling for an opening that must bring him indirectly to a partial confession at any rate. And his answer puzzled me uncomfortably: "Rather! If they'll let us."

"Who'll let us? The elements?" I asked quickly, with affected indifference.

"The powers of this awful place, whoever they are," he replied, keeping his eyes on the map. "The gods are here, if they are anywhere at all in the world."

"The elements are always the true immortals," I replied, laughing as naturally as I could manage, yet knowing quite well that my face reflected my true feelings when he looked up gravely at me and spoke across the smoke:

"We shall be fortunate if we get away without further disaster."

This was exactly what I had dreaded, and I screwed myself up to the point of the direct question. It was like agreeing to allow the dentist to extract the tooth; it *had* to come anyhow in the long run, and the rest was all pretence.

"Further disaster! Why, what's happened?"

"For one thing—the steering paddle's gone," he said quietly.

"The steering paddle gone!" I repeated, greatly excited, for this was our rudder, and the Danube in flood without a rudder was suicide. "But what—"

"And there's a tear in the bottom of the canoe," he added, with a genuine little tremor in his voice.

I continued staring at him, able only to repeat the words in his face somewhat foolishly. There, in the heat of the sun, and on this burning sand, I was aware of a freezing atmosphere descending round us. I got up to follow him, for he merely nodded his head gravely and led the way towards the tent a few yards on the other side of the fireplace. The canoe still lay there as I had last seen her in the night, ribs uppermost, the paddles, or rather, *the* paddle, on the sand beside her.

"There's only one," he said, stooping to pick it up. "And here's the rent in the base-board."

It was on the tip of my tongue to tell him that I had clearly noticed *two* paddles a few hours before, but a second impulse made me think better of it, and I said nothing. I approached to see.

There was a long, finely made tear in the bottom of the canoe where a little slither of wood had been neatly taken clean out; it looked as if the tooth of a sharp rock or snag had eaten down her length, and investigation showed that the hole went through. Had we launched out in her without observing it we must inevitably have foundered. At first the water would have made the wood swell so as to close the hole, but once out in mid-stream the water must have poured in, and the canoe, never more than two inches above the surface, would have filled and sunk very rapidly.

"There, you see an attempt to prepare a victim for the sacrifice," I heard him saying, more to himself than to me, "two victims rather," he added as he bent over and ran his fingers along the slit.

I began to whistle—a thing I always do unconsciously when utterly nonplussed—and purposely paid no attention to his words. I was determined to consider them foolish.

"It wasn't there last night," he said presently, straightening up from his examination and looking anywhere but at me.

"We must have scratched her in landing, of course," I stopped whistling to say. "The stones are very sharp."

I stopped abruptly, for at that moment he turned round and met my eye squarely. I knew just as well as he did how impossible my explanation was. There were no stones, to begin with.

"And then there's this to explain too," he added quietly, handing me the paddle and pointing to the blade.

A new and curious emotion spread freezingly over me as I took and examined it. The blade was scraped down all over, beautifully scraped, as though someone had sand-papered it with care, making it so thin that the first vigorous stroke must have snapped it off at the elbow.

"One of us walked in his sleep and did this thing," I said feebly, "or—or it has been filed by the constant stream of sand particles blown against it by the wind, perhaps."

"Ah," said the Swede, turning away, laughing a little, "you can explain everything."

"The same wind that caught the steering paddle and flung it so near the bank that it fell in with the next lump that crumbled," I called out after him, absolutely determined to find an explanation for everything he showed me.

"I see," he shouted back, turning his head to look at me before disappearing among the willow bushes.

Once alone with these perplexing evidences of personal agency, I think my first thoughts took the form of "One of us must have done this thing, and it certainly was not I." But my second thought decided how impossible it was to suppose, under all the circumstances, that either of us had done it. That my companion, the trusted friend of a dozen similar expeditions, could have knowingly had a hand in it, was a suggestion not to be entertained for a moment. Equally absurd seemed the explanation that this imperturbable and densely practical nature had suddenly become insane and was busied with insane purposes.

Yet the fact remained that what disturbed me most, and kept my fear actively alive even in this blaze of sunshine and wild beauty, was the clear certainty that some curious alteration had come about in his *mind*—that he was nervous, timid, suspicious, aware of goings on he did not speak about, watching a series of secret and hitherto unmentionable events—waiting, in a word, for a climax that he expected, and, I thought, expected very soon. This grew up in my mind intuitively—I hardly knew how.

I made a hurried examination of the tent and its surroundings, but the measurements of the night remained the same. There were deep hollows formed in the sand I now noticed for the first time, basin-shaped and of various depths and sizes, varying from that of a tea-cup to a large bowl. The wind, no doubt, was responsible for these miniature craters, just as it was for lifting the paddle and tossing it towards the water. The rent in the canoe was the only thing that seemed quite inexplicable; and, after all, it *was* conceivable that a sharp point had caught it when we landed. The examination I made of the shore did not assist this theory, but all the same I clung to it with that diminishing portion of my intelligence which I called my "reason." An explanation of some kind was an absolute necessity, just as some working explanation of the universe is necessary—however absurd—to the happiness of every individual who seeks to do his duty in the world and face the problems of life. The simile seemed to me at the time an exact parallel.

I at once set the pitch melting, and presently the Swede joined me at the work, though under the best conditions in the world the canoe could not be safe for traveling till the following day. I drew his attention casually to the hollows in the sand.

"Yes," he said, "I know. They're all over the island. But *you* can explain them, no doubt!"

"Wind, of course," I answered without hesitation. "Have you never watched those little whirlwinds in the street that twist and twirl everything into a circle? This sand's loose enough to yield, that's all."

He made no reply, and we worked on in silence for a bit. I watched him surreptitiously all the time, and I had an idea he was watching me. He seemed, too, to be always listening attentively to something I could not hear, or perhaps for something that he expected to hear, for he kept turning about and staring into the bushes, and up into the sky, and out across the water where it was visible through the openings among the willows. Sometimes he even put his hand to his ear and held it there for several minutes. He said nothing to me, however, about it, and I asked no questions. And meanwhile, as he mended that torn canoe with the skill and address of a red Indian, I was glad to notice his absorption in the work, for there was a vague dread in my heart that he would speak of the changed aspect of the willows. And, if he had noticed that, my imagination could no longer be held a sufficient explanation of it.

At length, after a long pause, he began to talk.

"Queer thing," he added in a hurried sort of voice, as though he wanted to say something and get it over. "Queer thing. I mean, about that otter last night."

I had expected something so totally different that he caught me with surprise, and I looked up sharply.

"Shows how lonely this place is. Otters are awfully shy things—"

"I don't mean that, of course," he interrupted. "I mean—do you think—did you think it really was an otter?"

"What else, in the name of Heaven, what else?"

"You know, I saw it before you did, and at first it seemed—so much *bigger* than an otter."

"The sunset as you looked up-stream magnified it, or something," I replied.

He looked at me absently a moment, as though his mind were busy with other thoughts.

"It had such extraordinary yellow eyes," he went on half to himself.

"That was the sun too," I laughed, a trifle boisterously. "I suppose you'll wonder next if that fellow in the boat—"

I suddenly decided not to finish the sentence. He was in the act again of listening, turning his head to the wind, and something in the expression of his face made me halt. The subject dropped, and we went on with our caulking. Apparently he had not noticed my unfinished sentence. Five minutes later, however, he looked at me across the canoe, the smoking pitch in his hand, his face exceedingly grave.

"I *did* rather wonder, if you want to know," he said slowly, "what that thing in the boat was. I remember thinking at the time it was not a man. The whole business seemed to rise quite suddenly out of the water."

I laughed again boisterously in his face, but this time there was impatience, and a strain of anger too, in my feeling.

"Look here now," I cried, "this place is quite queer enough without going out of our way to imagine things! That boat was an ordinary boat, and the man in it was an ordinary man, and they were both going down-stream as fast as they could lick. And that otter *was* an otter, so don't let's play the fool about it!"

He looked steadily at me with the same grave expression. He was not in the least annoyed. I took courage from his silence.

"And, for Heaven's sake," I went on, "don't keep pretending you hear things, because it only gives me the jumps, and there's nothing to hear but the river and this cursed old thundering wind."

"You *fool!*" he answered in a low, shocked voice, "you utter fool. That's just the way all victims talk. As if you didn't understand just as well as I do!" he sneered with scorn in his voice, and a sort of resignation. "The best thing you can do is to keep quiet and try to hold your mind as firm as possible. This feeble attempt at self-deception only makes the truth harder when you're forced to meet it."

My little effort was over, and I found nothing more to say, for I knew quite well his words were true, and that *I* was the fool, not *he*. Up to a certain stage in the adventure he kept ahead of me easily, and I think I felt annoyed to be out of it, to be thus proved less psychic, less sensitive than himself to these extraordinary happenings, and half ignorant all the time of what was going on under my very nose. *He knew* from the very beginning, apparently. But at the moment I wholly missed the point of his words about the necessity of there being a victim, and that we ourselves were destined to satisfy the want. I dropped all pretence thenceforward, but thenceforward likewise my fear increased steadily to the climax.

"But you're quite right about one thing," he added, before the subject passed, "and that is that we're wiser not to talk about it, or even to think about it, because what one *thinks* finds expression in words, and what one says, happens."

That afternoon, while the canoe dried and hardened, we spent trying to fish, testing the leak, collecting wood, and watching the enormous flood of rising water. Masses of driftwood swept near our shores sometimes, and we fished for them with long willow branches. The island grew perceptibly smaller as the banks were torn away with great gulps and splashes. The weather kept brilliantly fine till about four o'clock, and then for the first time for three days the wind showed signs of abating. Clouds began to gather in the south-west, spreading thence slowly over the sky.

This lessening of the wind came as a great relief, for the incessant roaring, banging, and thundering had irritated our nerves. Yet the silence that came about five o'clock with its sudden cessation was in a manner quite as oppressive. The booming of the river had everything in its own way then; it filled the air with deep murmurs, more musical than the wind noises, but infinitely more monotonous. The wind held many notes, rising, falling always beating out some sort of great elemental tune; whereas the river's song lay between three notes at most—dull pedal notes, that held a lugubrious quality foreign to the wind, and somehow seemed to me, in my then nervous state, to sound wonderfully well the music of doom.

It was extraordinary, too, how the withdrawal suddenly of bright sunlight took everything out of the landscape that made for cheerfulness; and since this particular landscape had already managed to convey the suggestion of something sinister, the change of course was all the more unwelcome and noticeable. For me, I know, the darkening outlook became distinctly more alarming, and I found myself more than once calculating how soon after sunset the full moon would get up in the east, and whether the gathering clouds would greatly interfere with her lighting of the little island.

With this general hush of the wind—though it still indulged in occasional brief gusts—the river seemed to me to grow blacker, the willows to stand more densely together. The latter, too, kept up a sort of independent movement of their own, rustling among themselves when no wind stirred, and shaking oddly from the roots upwards. When common objects in this way be come charged with the suggestion of horror, they stimulate the imagination far more than things of unusual appearance; and these bushes, crowding huddled about us, assumed for me in the darkness a bizarre *grotesquerie* of appearance that lent to them somehow the aspect of purposeful and living creatures. Their very ordinariness, I felt, masked what was malignant and hostile to us. The forces of the region drew nearer with the coming of night. They were focusing upon our island, and more particularly upon ourselves. For thus, somehow, in the terms of the imagination, did my really indescribable sensations in this extraordinary place present themselves.

I had slept a good deal in the early afternoon, and had thus recovered somewhat from the exhaustion of a disturbed night, but this only served apparently to render me more susceptible than before to the obsessing spell of the haunting. I fought against it, laughing at my feelings as absurd and childish, with very obvious physiological explanations, yet, in spite of every effort, they gained in strength upon me so that I dreaded the night as a child lost in a forest must dread the approach of darkness.

The canoe we had carefully covered with a waterproof sheet during the day, and the one remaining paddle had been securely tied by the Swede to the base of a tree, lest the wind should rob us of that too. From five o'clock onwards I busied myself with the stew-pot and preparations for dinner, it being my turn to cook that night. We had potatoes, onions, bits of bacon fat to add flavor, and a general thick residue from former stews at the bottom of the pot; with black bread broken up into it the result was most excellent, and it was followed by a stew of plums with sugar and a brew of strong tea with dried milk. A good pile of wood lay close at hand, and the absence of wind made my duties easy. My companion sat lazily watching me, dividing his attentions between cleaning his pipe and giving useless advice—an admitted privilege of the off-duty man. He had been very quiet all the afternoon, engaged in re-caulking the canoe, strengthening the tent ropes, and fishing for driftwood while I slept. No more talk about undesirable things had passed between us, and I think his only remarks had to do with the gradual destruction of the island, which he declared was not fully a third smaller than when we first landed.

The pot had just begun to bubble when I heard his voice calling to me from the bank, where he had wandered away without my noticing. I ran up.

"Come and listen," he said, "and see what you make of it." He held his hand cupwise to his ear, as so often before.

"*Now* do you hear anything?" he asked, watching me curiously.

We stood there, listening attentively together. At first I heard only the deep note of the water and the hissings rising from its turbulent surface. The willows, for once, were motionless and silent. Then a sound began to reach my ears faintly, a peculiar sound—something like the humming of a distant gong. It seemed to come across to us in the darkness from the waste of swamps and willows opposite. It was repeated at regular intervals, but it was certainly neither the sound of a bell nor the hooting of a distant steamer. I can liken it to nothing so much as to the sound of an immense gong, suspended far up in the sky, repeating incessantly its muffled metallic note, soft and musical, as it was repeatedly struck. My heart quickened as I listened.

"I've heard it all day," said my companion. "While you slept this afternoon it came all round the island. I hunted it down, but could never get near enough to see—to localize it correctly. Sometimes it was overhead, and sometimes it seemed under the water. Once or twice, too, I could have sworn it was not outside at all, but *within myself*—you know—the way a sound in the fourth dimension is supposed to come."

I was too much puzzled to pay much attention to his words. I listened carefully, striving to associate it with any known familiar sound I could think of, but without success. It changed in the direction, too, coming nearer, and then sinking utterly away into remote distance. I cannot say that it was ominous in quality, because to me it seemed distinctly musical, yet I must admit it set going a distressing feeling that made me wish I had never heard it.

"The wind blowing in those sand-funnels," I said determined to find an explanation, "or the bushes rubbing together after the storm perhaps."

"It comes off the whole swamp," my friend answered. "It comes from everywhere at once." He ignored my explanations. "It comes from the willow bushes somehow—"

"But now the wind has dropped," I objected. "The willows can hardly make a noise by themselves, can they?"

His answer frightened me, first because I had dreaded it, and secondly, because I knew intuitively it was true.

"It is *because* the wind has dropped we now hear it. It was drowned before. It is the cry, I believe, of the—"

I dashed back to my fire, warned by the sound of bubbling that the stew was in danger, but determined at the same time to escape further conversation. I was resolute, if possible, to avoid the exchanging of views. I dreaded, too, that he would begin about the gods, or the elemental forces, or something else disquieting, and I wanted to keep myself well in hand for what might happen later. There was another night to be faced before we escaped from this distressing place, and there was no knowing yet what it might bring forth.

"Come and cut up bread for the pot," I called to him, vigorously stirring the appetizing mixture. That stew-pot held sanity for us both, and the thought made me laugh.

He came over slowly and took the provision sack from the tree, fumbling in its mysterious depths, and then emptying the entire contents upon the ground-sheet at his feet.

"Hurry up!" I cried; "it's boiling."

The Swede burst out into a roar of laughter that startled me. It was forced laughter, not artificial exactly, but mirthless.

"There's nothing here!" he shouted, holding his sides.

"Bread, I mean."

"It's gone. There is no bread. They've taken it!"

I dropped the long spoon and ran up. Everything the sack had contained lay upon the ground-sheet, but there was no loaf.

The whole dead weight of my growing fear fell upon me and shook me. Then I burst out laughing too. It was the only thing to do: and the sound of my laughter also made me understand his. The stain of psychical pressure caused it—this explosion of unnatural laughter in both of us; it was an effort of repressed forces to seek relief; it was a temporary safety-valve. And with both of us it ceased quite suddenly.

"How criminally stupid of me!" I cried, still determined to be consistent and find an explanation. "I clean forgot to buy a loaf at Pressburg. That chattering woman put everything out of my head, and I must have left it lying on the counter or—"

"The oatmeal, too, is much less than it was this morning," the Swede interrupted.

Why in the world need he draw attention to it? I thought angrily.

"There's enough for tomorrow," I said, stirring vigorously, "and we can get lots more at Komorn or Gran. In twenty-four hours we shall be miles from here."

"I hope so—to God," he muttered, putting the things back into the sack, "unless we're claimed first as victims for the sacrifice," he added with a foolish laugh. He dragged the sack into the tent, for safety's sake, I suppose, and I heard him mumbling to himself, but so indistinctly that it seemed quite natural for me to ignore his words.

Our meal was beyond question a gloomy one, and we ate it almost in silence, avoiding one another's eyes, and keeping the fire bright. Then we washed up and prepared for the night, and, once smoking, our minds unoccupied with any definite duties, the apprehension I had felt all day long became more and more acute. It was not then active fear, I think, but the very vagueness of its origin distressed me far more that if I had been able to ticket and face it squarely. The curious sound I have likened to the note of a gong became now almost incessant, and filled the stillness of the night with a faint, continuous ringing rather than a series of distinct notes. At one time it was behind and at another time in front of us. Sometimes I fancied it came from the bushes on our left, and then again from the clumps on our right. More often it hovered directly overhead like the whirring of wings. It was really everywhere at once, behind, in front, at our sides and over our heads, completely surrounding us. The sound really defies description. But nothing within my knowledge is like that ceaseless muffled humming rising off the deserted world of swamps and willows.

We sat smoking in comparative silence, the strain growing every minute greater. The worst feature of the situation seemed to me that we did not know what to expect, and could therefore make no sort of preparation by way of defense. We could anticipate nothing. My explanations made in the sunshine, moreover, now came to haunt me with their foolish and wholly unsatisfactory nature, and it was more and more clear to us that some kind of plain talk with my companion was inevitable, whether I liked it or not. After all, we had to spend the night together, and to sleep in the same tent side by side. I saw that I could not get along much longer without the support of his mind, and for that, of course, plain talk was imperative. As long as possible, however, I postponed this little climax, and tried to ignore or laugh at the occasional sentences he flung into the emptiness.

Some of these sentences, moreover, were confoundedly disquieting to me, coming as they did to corroborate much that I felt myself; corroboration, too—which made it so much more convincing—from a totally different point of view. He composed such curious sentences, and hurled them at me in such an inconsequential sort of way, as though his main line of thought was secret to himself, and these fragments were mere bits he found it impossible to digest. He got rid of them by uttering them. Speech relieved him. It was like being sick.

"There are things about us, I'm sure, that make for disorder, disintegration, destruction, *our* destruction," he said once, while the fire blazed between us. "We've strayed out of a safe line somewhere."

And, another time, when the gong sounds had come nearer, ringing much louder than before, and directly over our heads, he said as though talking to himself:

"I don't think a gramophone would show any record of that. The sound doesn't come to me by the ears at all. The vibrations reach me in another manner altogether, and seem to be within me, which is precisely how a fourth dimensional sound might be supposed to make itself heard."

I purposely made no reply to this, but I sat up a little closer to the fire and peered about me into the darkness. The clouds were massed all over the sky, and no trace of moonlight came through. Very still, too, everything was, so that the river and the frogs had things all their own way.

"It has that about it," he went on, "which is utterly out of common experience. It is *unknown*. Only one thing describes it really; it is a non-human sound; I mean a sound outside humanity."

Having rid himself of this indigestible morsel, he lay quiet for a time, but he had so admirably expressed my own feeling that it was a relief to have the thought out, and to have confined it by the limitation of words from dangerous wandering to and fro in the mind.

The solitude of that Danube camping-place, can I ever forget it? The feeling of being utterly alone on an empty planet! My thoughts ran incessantly upon cities and the haunts of men. I would have given my soul, as the saying is, for the "feel" of those Bavarian villages we had passed through by the score; for the normal, human commonplaces; peasants drinking beer, tables beneath the trees, hot sunshine, and a ruined castle on the rocks behind the red-roofed church. Even the tourists would have been welcome.

Yet what I felt of dread was no ordinary ghostly fear. It was infinitely greater, stranger, and seemed to arise from some dim ancestral sense of terror more profoundly disturbing than anything I had known or dreamed of. We had "strayed," as the Swede put it, into some region or some set of conditions where the risks were great, yet unintelligible to us; where the frontiers of some unknown world lay close about us. It was a spot held by the dwellers in some outer space, a sort of peep-hole whence they could spy upon the earth, themselves unseen, a point where the veil between had worn a little thin. As the final result of too long a sojourn here, we should be carried over the border and deprived of what we called "our lives," yet by mental, not physical, processes. In that sense, as he said, we should be the victims of our adventure—a sacrifice.

It took us in different fashion, each according to the measure of his sensitiveness and powers of resistance. I translated it vaguely into a personification of the mightily disturbed elements, investing them with the horror of a deliberate and malefic purpose, resentful of our audacious intrusion into their breeding-place; whereas my friend threw it into the unoriginal form at first of a trespass on some ancient shrine, some place where the old gods still held sway, where the emotional forces of former worshippers still clung, and the ancestral portion of him yielded to the old pagan spell.

At any rate, here was a place unpolluted by men, kept clean by the winds from coarsening human influences, a place where spiritual agencies were within reach and aggressive. Never, before or since, have I been so attacked by indescribable suggestions of a "beyond region," of another scheme of life, another revolution not parallel to the human. And in the end our minds would succumb under the weight of the awful spell, and we should be drawn across the frontier into *their* world.

Small things testified to the amazing influence of the place, and now in the silence round the fire they allowed themselves to be noted by the mind. The very atmosphere had proved itself a magnifying medium to distort every indication: the otter rolling in the current, the hurrying boatman making signs, the shifting willows, one and all had been robbed of its natural character, and revealed in something of its other aspect—as it existed across the border to that other region. And this changed aspect I felt was new not merely to me, but to the race. The whole experience whose verge we touched was unknown to humanity at all. It was a new order of experience, and in the true sense of the word *unearthly*.

"It's the deliberate, calculating purpose that reduces one's courage to zero," the Swede said suddenly, as if he had been actually following my thoughts. "Otherwise imagination might count for much. But the paddle, the canoe, the lessening food—"

"Haven't I explained all that once?" I interrupted viciously.

"You have," he answered dryly; "you have indeed."

He made other remarks too, as usual, about what he called the "plain determination to provide a victim"; but, having now arranged my thoughts better, I recognized that this was simply the cry of his frightened soul against the knowledge that he was being attacked in a vital part, and that he would be somehow taken or destroyed. The situation called for a courage and calmness of reasoning that neither of us could compass, and I have never before been so clearly conscious of two persons in me—the one that explained everything, and the other that laughed at such foolish explanations, yet was horribly afraid.

Meanwhile, in the pitchy night the fire died down and the wood pile grew small. Neither of us moved to replenish the stock, and the darkness consequently came up very close to our faces. A few feet beyond the circle of firelight it was inky black. Occasionally a stray puff of wind set the willows shivering about us, but apart from this not very welcome sound a deep and depressing silence reigned, broken only by the gurgling of the river and the humming in the air overhead.

We both missed, I think, the shouting company of the winds.

At length, at a moment when a stray puff prolonged itself as though the wind were about to rise again, I reached the point for me of saturation, the point where it was absolutely necessary to find relief in plain speech, or else to betray myself by some hysterical extravagance that must have been far worse in its effect upon both of us. I kicked the fire into a blaze, and turned to my companion abruptly. He looked up with a start.

"I can't disguise it any longer," I said; "I don't like this place, and the darkness, and the noises, and the awful feelings I get. There's something here that beats me utterly. I'm in a blue funk, and that's the plain truth. If the other shore was—different, I swear I'd be inclined to swim for it!"

The Swede's face turned very white beneath the deep tan of sun and wind. He stared straight at me and answered quietly, but his voice betrayed his huge excitement by its unnatural calmness. For the moment, at any rate, he was the strong man of the two. He was more phlegmatic, for one thing.

"It's not a physical condition we can escape from by running away," he replied, in the tone of a doctor diagnosing some grave disease; "we must sit tight and wait. There are forces close here that could kill a herd of elephants in a second as easily as you or I could squash a fly. Our only chance is to keep perfectly still. Our insignificance perhaps may save us."

I put a dozen questions into my expression of face, but found no words. It was precisely like listening to an accurate description of a disease whose symptoms had puzzled me.

"I mean that so far, although aware of our disturbing presence, they have not *found* us—not 'located' us, as the Americans say," he went on. "They're blundering about like men hunting for a leak of gas. The paddle and canoe and provisions prove that. I think they *feel* us, but cannot actually see us. We must keep our minds quiet— it's our minds they feel. We must control our thoughts, or it's all up with us."

"Death, you mean?" I stammered, icy with the horror of his suggestion.

"Worse—by far," he said. "Death, according to one's belief, means either annihilation or release from the limitations of the senses, but it involves no change of character. *You* don't suddenly alter just because the body's gone. But this means a radical alteration, a complete change, a horrible loss of oneself by substitution—far worse than death, and not even annihilation. We happen

to have camped in a spot where their region touches ours, where
the veil between has worn thin"—horrors! he was using my very
own phrase, my actual words—"so that they are aware of our being
in their neighborhood."

"But *who* are aware?" I asked.

I forgot the shaking of the willows in the windless calm, the
humming overhead, everything except that I was waiting for an
answer that I dreaded more than I can possibly explain.

He lowered his voice at once to reply, leaning forward a little
over the fire, an indefinable change in his face that made me avoid
his eyes and look down upon the ground.

"All my life," he said, "I have been strangely, vividly conscious
of another region—not far removed from our own world in one
sense, yet wholly different in kind—where great things go on
unceasingly, where immense and terrible personalities hurry by,
intent on vast purposes compared to which earthly affairs, the rise
and fall of nations, the destinies of empires, the fate of armies and
continents, are all as dust in the balance; vast purposes, I mean,
that deal directly with the soul, and not indirectly with mere ex-
pressions of the soul—"

"I suggest just now—" I began, seeking to stop him, feeling as
though I was face to face with a madman. But he instantly over-
bore me with his torrent that *had* to come.

"You think," he said, "it is the spirit of the elements, and I
thought perhaps it was the old gods. But I tell you now it is—*neither*. These would be comprehensible entities, for they have rela-
tions with men, depending upon them for worship or sacrifice,
whereas these beings who are now about us have absolutely nothing to do with mankind, and it is mere chance that their space happens just at this spot to touch our own."

The mere conception, which his words somehow made so convincing, as I listened to them there in the dark stillness of that
lonely island, set me shaking a little all over. I found it impossible
to control my movements.

"And what do you propose?" I began again.

"A sacrifice, a victim, might save us by distracting them until we could get away," he went on, "just as the wolves stop to devour the dogs and give the sleigh another start. But—I see no chance of any other victim now."

I stared blankly at him. The gleam in his eye was dreadful. Presently he continued.

"It's the willows, of course. The willows *mask* the others, but the others are feeling about for us. If we let our minds betray our fear, we're lost, lost utterly." He looked at me with an expression so calm, so determined, so sincere, that I no longer had any doubts as to his sanity. He was as sane as any man ever was. "If we can hold out through the night," he added, "we may get off in the daylight unnoticed, or rather, *undiscovered*."

"But you really think a sacrifice would—"

That gong-like humming came down very close over our heads as I spoke, but it was my friend's scared face that really stopped my mouth.

"Hush!" he whispered, holding up his hand. "Do not mention them more than you can help. Do not refer to them *by name*. To name is to reveal; it is the inevitable clue, and our only hope lies in ignoring them, in order that they may ignore us."

"Even in thought?" He was extraordinarily agitated.

"Especially in thought. Our thoughts make spirals in their world. We must keep them *out of our minds* at all costs if possible."

I raked the fire together to prevent the darkness having everything its own way. I never longed for the sun as I longed for it then in the awful blackness of that summer night.

"Were you awake all last night?" he went on suddenly.

"I slept badly a little after dawn," I replied evasively, trying to follow his instructions, which I knew instinctively were true, "but the wind, of course—"

"I know. But the wind won't account for all the noises."

"Then you heard it too?"

"The multiplying countless little footsteps I heard," he said, adding, after a moment's hesitation, "and that other sound—"

"You mean above the tent, and the pressing down upon us of something tremendous, gigantic?"

He nodded significantly.

"It was like the beginning of a sort of inner suffocation?" I said.

"Partly, yes. It seemed to me that the weight of the atmosphere had been altered—had increased enormously, so that we should have been crushed."

"And *that*," I went on, determined to have it all out, pointing upwards where the gong-like note hummed ceaselessly, rising and falling like wind. "What do you make of that?"

"It's *their* sound," he whispered gravely. "It's the sound of their world, the humming in their region. The division here is so thin that it leaks through somehow. But, if you listen carefully, you'll find it's not above so much as around us. It's in the willows. It's the willows themselves humming, because here the willows have been made symbols of the forces that are against us."

I could not follow exactly what he meant by this, yet the thought and idea in my mind were beyond question the thought and idea in his. I realized what he realized, only with less power of analysis than his. It was on the tip of my tongue to tell him at last about my hallucination of the ascending figures and the moving bushes, when he suddenly thrust his face again close into mine across the fire-light and began to speak in a very earnest whisper. He amazed me by his calmness and pluck, his apparent control of the situation. This man I had for years deemed unimaginative, stolid!

"Now listen," he said. "The only thing for us to do is to go on as though nothing had happened, follow our usual habits, go to bed, and so forth; pretend we feel nothing and notice nothing. It is a question wholly of the mind, and the less we think about them the better our chance of escape. Above all, don't *think*, for what you think happens!"

"All right," I managed to reply, simply breathless with his words and the strangeness of it all; "all right, I'll try, but tell me one more thing first. Tell me what you make of those hollows in the ground all about us, those sand-funnels?"

"No!" he cried, forgetting to whisper in his excitement. "I dare not, simply dare not, put the thought into words. If you have not guessed I am glad. Don't try to. *They* have put it into my mind; try your hardest to prevent their putting it into yours."

He sank his voice again to a whisper before he finished, and I did not press him to explain. There was already just about as much horror in me as I could hold. The conversation came to an end, and we smoked our pipes busily in silence.

Then something happened, something unimportant apparently, as the way is when the nerves are in a very great state of tension, and this small thing for a brief space gave me an entirely different point of view. I chanced to look down at my sand-shoe—the sort we used for the canoe—and something to do with the hole at the toe suddenly recalled to me the London shop where I had bought them, the difficulty the man had in fitting me, and other details of the uninteresting but practical operation. At once, in its train, followed a wholesome view of the modern skeptical world I was accustomed to move in at home. I thought of roast beef, and ale, motor-cars, policemen, brass bands, and a dozen other things that proclaimed the soul of ordinariness or utility. The effect was immediate and astonishing even to myself. Psychologically, I suppose, it was simply a sudden and violent reaction after the strain of living in an atmosphere of things that to the normal consciousness must seem impossible and incredible. But, whatever the cause, it momentarily lifted the spell from my heart, and left me for the short space of a minute feeling free and utterly unafraid. I looked up at my friend opposite.

"You damned old pagan!" I cried, laughing aloud in his face. "You imaginative idiot! You superstitious idolater! You—"

I stopped in the middle, seized anew by the old horror. I tried to smother the sound of my voice as something sacrilegious. The Swede, of course, heard it too—the strange cry overhead in the darkness—and that sudden drop in the air as though something had come nearer.

He had turned ashen white under the tan. He stood bolt upright in front of the fire, stiff as a rod, staring at me.

"After that," he said in a sort of helpless, frantic way, "we must go! We can't stay now; we must strike camp this very instant and go on—down the river."

He was talking, I saw, quite wildly, his words dictated by abject terror—the terror he had resisted so long, but which had caught him at last.

"In the dark?" I exclaimed, shaking with fear after my hysterical outburst, but still realizing our position better than he did. "Sheer madness! The river's in flood, and we've only got a single paddle. Besides, we only go deeper into their country! There's nothing ahead for fifty miles but willows, willows, willows!"

He sat down again in a state of semi-collapse. The positions, by one of those kaleidoscopic changes nature loves, were suddenly reversed, and the control of our forces passed over into my hands. His mind at last had reached the point where it was beginning to weaken.

"What on earth possessed you to do such a thing?" he whispered with the awe of genuine terror in his voice and face.

I crossed round to his side of the fire. I took both his hands in mine, kneeling down beside him and looking straight into his frightened eyes.

"We'll make one more blaze," I said firmly, "and then turn in for the night. At sunrise we'll be off full speed for Komorn. Now, pull yourself together a bit, and remember your own advice about *not thinking fear!*"

He said no more, and I saw that he would agree and obey. In some measure, too, it was a sort of relief to get up and make an excursion into the darkness for more wood. We kept close together, almost touching, groping among the bushes and along the bank. The humming overhead never ceased, but seemed to me to grow louder as we increased our distance from the fire. It was shivery work!

We were grubbing away in the middle of a thickish clump of willows where some driftwood from a former flood had caught high among the branches, when my body was seized in a grip that made me half drop upon the sand. It was the Swede. He had fallen against me, and was clutching me for support. I heard his breath coming and going in short gasps.

"Look! By my soul!" he whispered, and for the first time in my experience I knew what it was to hear tears of terror in a human voice. He was pointing to the fire, some fifty feet away. I followed the direction of his finger, and I swear my heart missed a beat.

There, in front of the dim glow, *something was moving*.

I saw it through a veil that hung before my eyes like the gauze drop-curtain used at the back of a theater—hazily a little. It was neither a human figure nor an animal. To me it gave the strange impression of being as large as several animals grouped together, like horses, two or three, moving slowly. The Swede, too, got a similar result, though expressing it differently, for he thought it was shaped and sized like a clump of willow bushes, rounded at the top, and moving all over upon its surface—"coiling upon itself like smoke," he said afterwards.

"I watched it settle downwards through the bushes," he sobbed at me. "Look, by God! It's coming this way! Oh, oh!"—he gave a kind of whistling cry. "*They've found us.*"

I gave one terrified glance, which just enabled me to see that the shadowy form was swinging towards us through the bushes, and then I collapsed backwards with a crash into the branches. These failed, of course, to support my weight, so that with the Swede on top of me we fell in a struggling heap upon the sand. I really hardly knew what was happening. I was conscious only of a sort of enveloping sensation of icy fear that plucked the nerves out of their fleshly covering, twisted them this way and that, and re-placed them quivering. My eyes were tightly shut; something in my throat choked me; a feeling that my consciousness was expand-ing, extending out into space, swiftly gave way to another feeling that I was losing it altogether, and about to die.

An acute spasm of pain passed through me, and I was aware that the Swede had hold of me in such a way that he hurt me abomi-nably. It was the way he caught at me in falling.

But it was the pain, he declared afterwards, that saved me; it caused me to *forget them* and think of something else at the very instant when they were about to find me. It concealed my mind from them at the moment of discovery, yet just in time to evade their terrible seizing of me. He himself, he says, actually swooned at the same moment, and that was what saved him.

I only know that at a later date, how long or short is impossible to say, I found myself scrambling up out of the slippery network of willow branches, and saw my companion standing in front of me holding out a hand to assist me. I stared at him in a dazed way, rubbing the arm he had twisted for me. Nothing came to me to say, somehow.

"I lost consciousness for a moment or two," I heard him say. "That's what saved me. It made me stop thinking about them."

"You nearly broke my arm in two," I said, uttering my only connected thought at the moment. A numbness came over me.

"That's what saved *you!*" he replied. "Between us, we've managed to set them off on a false tack somewhere. The humming has ceased. It's gone—for the moment at any rate!"

A wave of hysterical laughter seized me again, and this time spread to my friend too—great healing gusts of shaking laughter that brought a tremendous sense of relief in their train. We made our way back to the fire and put the wood on so that it blazed at once. Then we saw that the tent had fallen over and lay in a tangled heap upon the ground.

We picked it up, and during the process tripped more than once and caught our feet in sand.

"It's those sand-funnels," exclaimed the Swede, when the tent was up again and the firelight lit up the ground for several yards about us. "And look at the size of them!"

All round the tent and about the fireplace where we had seen the moving shadows there were deep funnel-shaped hollows in the sand, exactly similar to the ones we had already found over the island, only far bigger and deeper, beautifully formed, and wide enough in some instances to admit the whole of my foot and leg.

Neither of us said a word. We both knew that sleep was the safest thing we could do, and to bed we went accordingly without further delay, having first thrown sand on the fire and taken the provision sack and the paddle inside the tent with us. The canoe, too, we propped in such a way at the end of the tent that our feet touched it, and the least motion would disturb and wake us.

In case of emergency, too, we again went to bed in our clothes, ready for a sudden start.

V

It was my firm intention to lie awake all night and watch, but the exhaustion of nerves and body decreed otherwise, and sleep after a while came over me with a welcome blanket of oblivion. The fact that my companion also slept quickened its approach. At first he fidgeted and constantly sat up, asking me if I "heard this" or "heard that." He tossed about on his cork mattress, and said the tent was moving and the river had risen over the point of the island, but each time I went out to look I returned with the report that all was well, and finally he grew calmer and lay still. Then at length his breathing became regular and I heard unmistakable sounds of snoring—the first and only time in my life when snoring has been a welcome and calming influence.

This, I remember, was the last thought in my mind before dozing off.

A difficulty in breathing woke me, and I found the blanket over my face. But something else besides the blanket was pressing upon me, and my first thought was that my companion had rolled off his mattress on to my own in his sleep. I called to him and sat up, and at the same moment it came to me that the tent was *surrounded*. That sound of multitudinous soft pattering was again audible outside, filling the night with horror.

I called again to him, louder than before. He did not answer, but I missed the sound of his snoring, and also noticed that the flap of the tent was down. This was the unpardonable sin. I crawled out in the darkness to hook it back securely, and it was then for the first time I realized positively that the Swede was not here. He had gone.

I dashed out in a mad run, seized by a dreadful agitation, and the moment I was out I plunged into a sort of torrent of humming that surrounded me completely and came out of every quarter of the heavens at once. It was that same familiar humming—gone mad! A swarm of great invisible bees might have been about me in the air. The sound seemed to thicken the very atmosphere, and I felt that my lungs worked with difficulty.

But my friend was in danger, and I could not hesitate.

The dawn was just about to break, and a faint whitish light spread upwards over the clouds from a thin strip of clear horizon. No wind stirred. I could just make out the bushes and river beyond, and the pale sandy patches. In my excitement I ran frantically to and fro about the island, calling him by name, shouting at the top of my voice the first words that came into my head. But the willows smothered my voice, and the humming muffled it, so that the sound only traveled a few feet round me. I plunged among the bushes, tripping headlong, tumbling over roots, and scraping my face as I tore this way and that among the preventing branches.

Then, quite unexpectedly, I came out upon the island's point and saw a dark figure outlined between the water and the sky. It was the Swede. And already he had one foot in the river! A moment more and he would have taken the plunge.

I threw myself upon him, flinging my arms about his waist and dragging him shorewards with all my strength. Of course he struggled furiously, making a noise all the time just like that cursed humming, and using the most outlandish phrases in his anger about "going *inside* to Them," and "taking the way of the water and the wind," and God only knows what more besides, that I tried in vain to recall afterwards, but which turned me sick with horror and amazement as I listened. But in the end I managed to get him into the comparative safety of the tent, and flung him breathless and cursing upon the mattress where I held him until the fit had passed.

I think the suddenness with which it all went and he grew calm, coinciding as it did with the equally abrupt cessation of the humming and pattering outside—I think this was almost the strangest part of the whole business perhaps. For he had just opened his eyes and turned his tired face up to me so that the dawn threw a pale light upon it through the doorway, and said, for all the world just like a frightened child:

"My life, old man—it's my life I owe you. But it's all over now anyhow. They've found a victim in our place!"

Then he dropped back upon his blankets and went to sleep literally under my eyes. He simply collapsed, and began to snore again as healthily as though nothing had happened and he had never tried to offer his own life as a sacrifice by drowning. And when the sunlight woke him three hours later—hours of ceaseless vigil for me—it became so clear to me that he remembered absolutely nothing of what he had attempted to do, that I deemed it wise to hold my peace and ask no dangerous questions.

He woke naturally and easily, as I have said, when the sun was already high in a windless hot sky, and he at once got up and set about the preparation of the fire for breakfast. I followed him anxiously at bathing, but he did not attempt to plunge in, merely dipping his head and making some remark about the extra coldness of the water.

"River's falling at last," he said, "and I'm glad of it."

"The humming has stopped too," I said.

He looked up at me quietly with his normal expression. Evidently he remembered everything except his own attempt at suicide.

"Everything has stopped," he said, "because—"

He hesitated. But I knew some reference to that remark he had made just before he fainted was in his mind, and I was determined to know it.

"Because 'They've found another victim'?" I said, forcing a little laugh.

"Exactly," he answered, "exactly! I feel as positive of it as though—as though—I feel quite safe again, I mean," he finished.

He began to look curiously about him. The sunlight lay in hot patches on the sand. There was no wind. The willows were motionless. He slowly rose to feet.

"Come," he said; "I think if we look, we shall find it."

He started off on a run, and I followed him. He kept to the banks, poking with a stick among the sandy bays and caves and little back-waters, myself always close on his heels.

"Ah!" he exclaimed presently, "ah!"

The tone of his voice somehow brought back to me a vivid sense of the horror of the last twenty-four hours, and I hurried up to join him. He was pointing with his stick at a large black object that lay half in the water and half on the sand. It appeared to be caught by some twisted willow roots so that the river could not sweep it away. A few hours before the spot must have been under water.

"See," he said quietly, "the victim that made our escape possible!"

And when I peered across his shoulder I saw that his stick rested on the body of a man. He turned it over. It was the corpse of a peasant, and the face was hidden in the sand. Clearly the man had been drowned, but a few hours before, and his body must have been swept down upon our island somewhere about the hour of the dawn—*at the very time the fit had passed.*

"We must give it a decent burial, you know."

"I suppose so," I replied. I shuddered a little in spite of myself, for there was something about the appearance of that poor drowned man that turned me cold.

The Swede glanced up sharply at me, an undecipherable expression on his face, and began clambering down the bank. I followed him more leisurely. The current, I noticed, had torn away much of the clothing from the body, so that the neck and part of the chest lay bare.

Halfway down the bank my companion suddenly stopped and held up his hand in warning; but either my foot slipped, or I had gained too much momentum to bring myself quickly to a halt, for I bumped into him and sent him forward with a sort of leap to save himself. We tumbled together on to the hard sand so that our feet splashed into the water. And, before anything could be done, we had collided a little heavily against the corpse.

The Swede uttered a sharp cry. And I sprang back as if I had been shot.

At the moment we touched the body there rose from its surface the loud sound of humming—the sound of several hummings—which passed with a vast commotion as of winged things in the air about us and disappeared upwards into the sky, growing fainter and fainter till they finally ceased in the distance. It was exactly as though we had disturbed some living yet invisible creatures at work.

My companion clutched me, and I think I clutched him, but before either of us had time properly to recover from the unexpected shock, we saw that a movement of the current was turning the corpse round so that it became released from the grip of the willow roots. A moment later it had turned completely over, the dead face uppermost, staring at the sky. It lay on the edge of the main stream. In another moment it would be swept away.

The Swede started to save it, shouting again something I did not catch about a "proper burial"—and then abruptly dropped upon his knees on the sand and covered his eyes with his hands. I was beside him in an instant.

I saw what he had seen.

For just as the body swung round to the current the face and the exposed chest turned full towards us, and showed plainly how the skin and flesh were indented with small hollows, beautifully formed, and exactly similar in shape and kind to the sand-funnels that we had found all over the island.

"Their mark!" I heard my companion mutter under his breath. "Their awful mark!"

And when I turned my eyes again from his ghastly face to the river, the current had done its work, and the body had been swept away into mid-stream and was already beyond our reach and almost out of sight, turning over and over on the waves like an otter.

THE GREEN SPLOTCHES
T. S. STRIBLING

(TRANSCRIBED FROM THE FIELD NOTES of James B. Standifer, Secretary DeLong Geographical Expedition to the Rio Infiernillo, Peru, with introductory note by J. B. S.)

SECRETARY'S NOTE

This strange, not to say sinister, record of the DeLong Geographical Expedition to the department of Ayacucho, Peru, is here given to the public in order that a wider circulation of the facts herein set forth may lead to some solution of the enigmas with which this narrative is laden.

These field notes have been privately circulated among the members of the DeLong Geographical Society, and the addenda to this account written by our president, Hilbert H. DeLong, have proved highly gratifying to the writer. No doubt this effort at publicity will bring forward another and equally interesting hypothesis.

It is hardly necessary to warn readers who devote themselves exclusively to fiction that this record is not for them.

Fiction deals in probabilities; geographical societies, unfortunately, are confined to facts. Fiction is a record of imaginary events, which, nevertheless, adheres to and explains human experience. Facts continually step outside of experience and offer riddles and monstrosities.

Thus, in a way, fiction is much truer than fact. Fiction is generalized truth; it is an international legal tender accredited everywhere;

fact is a very special truth, which passes current only with the most discerning—or with none.

Therefore, the writer wishes heartily to commend the great American scramble after fiction. It shows our enlightened public wishes to get at the real universal truths of Life, without wasting precious moments on such improbabilities as science, history, archeology, biography, invention and exploration.

To the last of this censored list these field notes unfortunately belong.

In conclusion the writer wishes to admit that he favors the Incan theory in explaining this narrative, and the reader is warned that this prejudice may color these notes. However, it has not been the writer's intention to do violence, through any twisting of fact, to the Bolshevik theory of Prof. Demetrius Z. Demetriovich, the Rumanian attaché to the expedition, or to the Jovian hypothesis of our esteemed president, the Hon. Gilbert H. DeLong, than whom, be it said, no man is more tolerant of the views of others.—James B. Standifer, Sec. DeL. Geo. Exp., Sept. 17, 1919.

TRANSCRIBER'S NOTE

The writer met the DeLong Geographical Expedition at Colon in June, 1919, on its way to New York. His curiosity was strongly aroused by the fact that every member of the party, even to the twenty-four-year-old secretary of the expedition, seemed to be suffering from some nervous complaint in the nature of shell shock.

At that time the writer was correspondent for the Associated Press and he naturally saw a "story" in the returning scientists. After some effort and persuasion, he obtained Mr. Standifer's field notes and photographs. The photographs were practically worthless on account of the deterioration of the films. And a single glance through the notes showed him that they were not practicable "A. P." material. After much consideration and many discussions with Mr. Standifer, the writer decided that the only possible form in which these strange memoranda could be placed before the public was in the guise of fiction.

Unfortunately this disguise is neither deep nor cleverly done. The crude outline of the actual occurrences destroys all approach to plot. Many of the incidents are irrelevant, but the only condition upon which Mr. Standifer would agree to this publication at all was that the record be given *in extenso*, "for the benefit," he stated, "of future and more studious generations."

In fact, throughout the writer's association with him, Mr. Standifer seemed of a sour, not to say misanthropic disposition. His sarcasm, which he hurls at the American fiction-reading public in his prefatory note, is based entirely, the writer believes, on the fact that Standifer wrote a book of travel called "Reindeer in Iceland," which he published at his own expense and which entirely failed to sell. That, no doubt, is enough to acidulate the sweetest disposition, but in a way it goes to prove that Standifer's notes on the Peruvian expedition are a painstaking and literal setting forth of genuine experiences, for a perusal of his book entitled, "Reindeer in Iceland," which the writer purchased from Mr. Standifer for fifty-four cents, shows its author has absolutely no imagination whatever.

It is hardly worth while to add that the explanatory note appended to this narrative by that distinguished scholar and author, the Right Honorable Gilbert H. DeLong, has not been touched by this pen.—T. S., Sept. 27, 1919.

Chapter I

Senor Ignacio Ramada, prefect of the department of Ayacucho, tapped his red lips under his mustache to discourage an overpowering yawn. It was mid *siesta*, high noon. He had been routed out of profound slumber by his *cholo*—boy—and presented with a long, impressive document with a red seal. Now he stood in the Salle des Armes of the governor's mansion, holding in his hand the letter of introduction from the *presidente* of the Lima Sociedad de Geográfico, very much impressed even amid his sleepiness by the red seal of the Sociedad and by the creaking new equipment of his callers.

"How, *senores*, can I assist in such a glorious undertaking?" he inquired in Spanish.

"We need guides," explained Prof. Demetriovich, who was the linguist of the party.

"Where does your journey carry you, *cabelleros?*" inquired the official, crackling the parchment in his hand.

"To the region beyond the Mantaro, called the Valley of the Rio Infiernillo."

Senor Ramada came out of his sleepiness with a sort of start. "No!"

"Yes."

The prefect looked at his guests.

"*Senores*, no one goes there."

Pethwick, the engineer, smiled.

"If the region were quite well known, Senor Ramada, it would hold little attraction for a geographical exploration party."

"Well, that's true," agreed the prefect after a moment's thought, "but it will be quite difficult to get a guide for that place; in fact—" here he swept his visitors with a charming smile—"the better a man knows that region, the farther he keeps away from it. Seriously, gentlemen, why not explore more hospitable locality, where one can find a comfortable inn at night and procure relays of llamas whenever necessary, for your baggage?"

Pethwick smiled friendlily.

"We did think of exploring the suburbs of Lima, but the street service was so bad—"

"Do you read novels?" inquired Standifer, the young secretary of the expedition.

"Why—yes," admitted the prefect, taken aback. "I am fond of Cisneros, Lavalle, Arestegui—"

The secretary pressed his lips together, nodded disdainfully and without further remark looked away through the entrance into the diamond-like brilliance of tropical sunshine in mountainous regions.

The prefect stared. "*Senor,*" he said rather sharply, "if you do not approve my literary taste—"

Pethwick stepped to the little Spaniard's side and whispered quickly:

"Overlook it, *senor*, overlook it. Literature is a tender point with him. He has lost one hundred and fifty-four dollars and forty-seven cents on an unprofitable literary venture. In fact, he is a young author."

He nodded confidentially at the prefect.

The official, with Latin delicacy, nodded back and patted Pethwick's arm to show that all was again well. Pethwick then said aloud:

"So we shall have to try to find our own way into the Valley de Rio Infiernillo?"

Ramada looked worried. Presently he slapped his hand on a mahogany sword cabinet that glowed warmly in the subdued light of the *salle.*

"*Senores!*" he cried, rattling the letter of introduction with his left hand. "It shall never be said that the prefect of the department of Ayacucho did not exert plenary powers to aid in disclosing to the world the enormous riches of his province and his native land!"

"So we may expect something?" inquired M. Demetriovich.

"I have the power to force some one to go with you," dramatically announced Ramada.

"Whom?" asked Standifer, looking around.

"Naturally my authority doesn't extend over freemen," conditioned the prefect.

"Your slaves?" inquired the secretary.

"Sir," announced the prefect, "wherever the Peruvian banner waves, Freedom smiles!"

"What at?" inquired the literal secretary.

As the governor was about to take new offense the old Rumanian hastily inquired:

"Whom do we get, *Senor* Ramada?"

"*Senores*, a garroting has been widely and I believe successfully advertised to take place on the fifth of August. If I may say it, *caballeros*, my political career depends in great measure on meeting fully and completely the thrills offered by the prospectuses.

The executions will be followed by a bull-fight. It was, gentlemen, if I may say it, it was to be the turning point of my political career, upon the prestige of which I meant to make my race for the presidency of our republic.

"Gentlemen, a time comes in the life of every statesman when he can sacrifice his country to his personal ambition, or his personal ambition to his country. That moment has now come in the life of Gonzales Pizarro Ramada. Gentlemen, I make it. Gentlemen, I am going to remit the extreme penalty placed by the *cortes* upon a murderer and a highwayman and permit them to go with you, gentlemen, as guides into the Valle de Rio Infiernillo."

Pethwick, who had been smiling with immense enjoyment at this rodomontade, straightened his face.

"A murderer and a highwayman!"

"Charming fellows," assured the prefect. "I often walk down to the *carcel* and converse with them. Such *chic!* Such original ideas on the confiscation of money—really very entertaining!"

The expedition looked at the eulogist a moment.

"Give us a minute to talk this over, *Senor* Ramada?" requested M. Demetriovich.

The prefect made the accentuated bow of a politician, adding that the republic would be proud to furnish chains and handcuffs to guarantee that her sons did their duty in the discharge of a patriotic function.

The three gentlemen of the DeLong Geographical Expedition spent an anxious five minutes in debate.

Presently Pethwick called:

"*Senor* Ramada, are you absolutely sure we cannot procure guides who are less—questionable for this journey?"

"Gentlemen, to be frank," said the prefect, who had also been studying over the matter, "I doubt very much whether either Cesare Ruano or Pablo Pasca would be willing to accompany you under those terms. I cannot force them. The law prohibits any unusual or cruel infliction of the death penalty and to send them to the Valley of the Rio Infiernillo would fall under that prohibition."

The four men stood meditating in the Salle des Armes. Professor Demetriovich stirred.

"Let's go have a talk with them," he suggested.

Contrary to Ramada's fears, Cesare Ruano, the man-killer, and Pablo Pasca, the road-agent, proved willing to escort the party to the Rio Infiernillo. So on the following day the expedition set forth with the legs of the convicts chained under their mules' bellies.

Ayacucho turned out en masse to watch the departure of so distinguished a cavalcade, and it might as well be admitted at once that none of the adventurers made so brave a showing or saluted the villagers with more graceful bows than did Cesare Ruano or Pablo Pasca. In fact, they divided the plaudits of the crowd about equally with the prefect, who kept murmuring to Pethwick:

"Not a bad stroke, *Senor* Pethwick, not a bad stroke."

The legs of the convicts were chained, naturally, to prevent any sudden leave-taking, but this plan held disadvantages. When one of the llama packs became loosened, either the scientists had to bungle the job themselves or take the leg-cuffs off their prisoners and allow them to dismount and do it for them. This entailed endless chaining and unchaining, which quickly grew monotonous and at length was abandoned after the geographers had exacted a solemn pledge of the two cutthroats not to run away. That much of the contract the guides kept to the letter. They never did run away, although the company lost them.

M. Demetriovich retained the manacles on the horn of his saddle, where, he told Pethwick, he hoped their jingle would have a great moral effect.

Oddly enough both the convicts were entirely innocent of the charges preferred against them, upon which they were convicted and so nearly executed.

Pablo Pasca told the whole circumstance to Pethwick. He, Pablo, did meet an old man one freezing July night in a mountain pass on the road to Ayacucho. They stopped and held some converse and Pablo had borrowed from him two hundred and forty-seven sols. Then what did this ingrate of a creditor do but beat his head against a tree, break an arm, go before a *magistrado* and charge Pasca with highway robbery.

Pablo's black eyes flashed as he related the incident. He had been amazed at such calumny, which he could not disprove. The jury believed the old wretch and sentenced Pablo to the garrote.

However, the One Who Ruled the Earth knew the truth, and Pasca prayed every night that he should not have his spinal cord snapped on such an unjust charge. So the One Who Ruled sent this society of fine gentlemen and scholars to fraternize with Pablo and to lift him to an exalted station. So he, Pablo, supposed now all the neighbors saw that his oath, as strange as it sounded, was true to the last jot and title. The padre in his visits to the *carcel* had taught Pablo a little verse which he should never forget: "Seest thou a man diligent in his profession—he shall sit before kings."

Cesare Ruano did not go so much into detail as did his fellow guide and friend, but he told Pethwick that the crime for which he was sentenced to the garrote was trivial and with a shrug of his shoulders let it go at that.

The trivial affair, however, had left a number of marks on Ruano's person, all of which the Ayacucho police had tabulated. A copy of this table was given M. Demetriovich in order that he might advertise for Cesare in case he should desert.

Pethwick read the inventory. It ran:

Cesare Ruano, a *cholo*, 27 years, reddish yellow, height 5ft. 7in., weight 84 kilos, (189 lbs), muscular, broad face, prominent cheek-bones, straight nose with wide nostrils, very white teeth, handsome. Scars: from right eyebrow through the right cheek to the lobe of ear; from left side of neck to the middle of chest bone; horizontal scar from nipple to nipple, rifle or pistol wound in right leg, two inches above knee; three buckshot in back, one in left buttock; little toe on left foot missing. Disposition uncommunicative, but of pleasant address and cheerful until irritated. A very handy man. Note: In case of arrest, officers are advised to shoot before accosting Ruano.

On the first few nights the travelers found lodgings at little mountain inns, whose red-peaked roofs of tiles were pulled down like caps over tiny eye-like windows. The tunnel-like entrance to such a hostelry always looked like a black mouth squared in horror at something it saw across the mountains.

This was much the same expression that the proprietor and guests wore when they learned the travelers were bound for the Rio Infiernillo.

Pablo Pasca always broke the news of their destination in rather dramatic style to the gamesters and hangers-on with which these centers of mountain life were crowded.

"*Senores,*" he would harangue, "you see before you a man sentenced to death; but because no garrote could affect his throat, so hard has it become from drinking gin, the prefect decided to send him on a journey to the Rio Infiernillo! Let us drink to our good fortune!"

This announcement usually brought roars of applause and laughter. Once a roisterer shouted:

"But your companions; what caused them to be sent?"

And Pablo answered with a droll gesture:

"One is a murderer; the rest are Americans!"

It made a great hit. The crowd invited Pablo to share its brandy.

However, after these introductions the landlord would presently stop laughing and after some questions invariably warn the scientists against their "mad undertaking." On two such occasions the proprietor became so earnest and excited that he begged the *senores* to walk out with him up the mountain-side to see for themselves the terrors that confronted them.

Pethwick never forgot his first glimpse of the mystery that colored his thoughts and dreams for the remainder of his life.

The night was clear but moonless. The party climbed uncertainly in darkness up a scarp of boulders and spurs of primitive rock. The landlord picked his way toward a clump of calisaya trees silhouetted against the sky. The chill air was shot with the fragrance of mountain violets. The climbers lent each other hands until the landlord reached a protruding root and then everybody scrambled up. Pethwick dropped down breathless at the foot of the tree, his heart beating heavily. At first he was faintly amused at his host's promise of a portent, but this amusement vanished presently amid the solemnity of night and the mountains.

The very stars above him wore the strange aspect of the Southern constellations. Against their glimmer the Andes heaved mighty shoulders. Peak beyond peak, they stood in cold blackness, made more chill and mysterious by the pallor of snow-fields.

The whole group shivered in silence for several minutes. At last M. Demetriovich asked with a shake in his Spanish:

"Well, *amigo*, what is there to see?"

"Wait," began the landlord.

At that moment a star shot far out against the blackness.

"*Alla!*" gasped the Peruvian.

Pethwick shivered and grinned. He had brought them up to see a shooting star.

"But wait!" begged their host, sensing the engineer's mirth.

Almost at once from where the star seemed to strike arose a faint, glowing haze as indefinite as the Milky Way. It must have been miles distant. In front of it two or three massifs were outlined and others, farther away, were dimly truncated by its radiance.

The *huésped* drew a long breath.

"Now there lies the Rio Infiernillo," he chattered. "It is a land from which no man returns alive. I have known many men to go, *senores*, thinking surely there must be great treasure where so much danger lay—and there may be, *senores*. No man can say. Every man has his opinion about the matter. I will tell frankly what mine is—"

He paused, evidently waiting for some one to urge his opinion.

Instead, Standifer spoke up:

"My opinion is it's a meteor and a phosphorescent display which sometimes follows."

The landlord laughed through the darkness with immense scorn of such a puerile opinion.

"What is yours?" inquired Pethwick.

"*Senores,*" defined the tavern-keeper solemnly, "that stream is called the Rio Infiernillo for a very good reason. For there every night comes the devil to dig gold to corrupt the priests, and—and, of course, the Protestants, too," he added charitably. "But he can never do it, *Senores.* Let him dig till he scoops down the mountains and reaches his own country, which is the source of the Rio Infiernillo— he will never do it!"

"Has any one ever seen where he has dug?" asked Pethwick, amused again.

"*Si, senor.*"

"I thought you said no one ever went over there and got back alive," observed Pethwick carelessly.

A slight pause; then the landlord explained:

"This man only lived a few minutes after he fell into my door. I saw him. His hair was white. He was burned. I heard his last words. No one else heard him."

This was uttered with such solemnity that Pethwick never knew whether it was an account of some weird tragedy of the mountains or whether it was cut out of whole cloth.

That night after Pethwick had gone to bed in the upper story of the hostelry, while the laughing and drinking flowed steadily below, it occurred to him that it was odd, after all, that the landlord should have led them on such a clamber to see a shooting star and a haze—and the two phenomena should have occurred so promptly.

On the following night another landlord led them out on the same mission and showed them the same set of wonders. His explanation was even more fantastic than the first.

Before the party retired that second night, Pethwick asked of M. Demetriovich:

"Professor, what is the probability that two meteors should perform the same evolutions in the same quarter of the sky and apparently strike in about the same place on two nights in succession?"

"I'd thought of that problem," returned the savant yawning. "In fact, I have set down some tentative figures on the subject." Here he referred to a little note-book. "It is roughly one chance in two-million."

"Small," observed Pethwick.

"That was for the stars alone. For two stars to fall in the same region, each time followed by a phosphorescence, diminishes the probability to one chance in eight trillion."

Pethwick whistled softly.

"In fact, it was not a meteorite we saw," concluded the professor, crawling into bed.

CHAPTER II

Pablo Pasca shouted something from perhaps a hundred yards up the trail. He was hidden from the string of toiling riders by a fold in the precipice. Pethwick looked ahead and saw two vultures launch themselves out over the abyss. One swung back down the face of the mountain and passed within forty feet of the party, its feathers whistling, its bald, whitish head turning for a look at the intruders and its odor momentarily tainting the cold wind.

A moment later the engineer saw the two guides had dismounted and their mules were snorting and jerking on the very edge of the precipice. The men themselves were staring at something and Pasca seemed almost as panic-stricken as the animals. The unquietness spread rapidly down the string of baggage-carriers.

Pethwick slid off his mount and hurried forward, slipping inside the llamas and dodging past the uncertain heels of the mules. He came out by the side of Pablo to a queer, not to say gruesome sight. In the air circled eight or ten vultures. They had been frightened from a row of skeletons, which evidently were articulated on wires and iron rods and stood before the travelers in the awkward postures such objects assume. Among the things, Pethwick recognized the whitened frames of snake, condor, sheep, vicuña, puma, monkey and at the end, standing upright, the bones of a man.

The specimens were accurately spaced around the end of the trail, for this was the last of the road. The skulls grinned fixedly at the DeLong Geographical Expedition. In the gusty wind the arms of the man swung and beat against his thigh bone in a grotesque travesty of mirth.

Something touched Pethwick from behind. He turned with a shudder and saw Standifer. The secretary of the expedition looked at the assemblage for a moment, then drew out his note-book and pen, gave the pen a fillip to start a flow of ink and methodically jotted down the list before him. When he had finished he glanced up inquiringly as he rescrewed the top on his writing instrument.

"Don't suppose any one is moving a museum, eh, Pethwick?"

"No," said the engineer, studying the figures.

"You don't think so?" Standifer snorted.

"Certainly not!"

"Huh!" Standifer drew forth his book again.

"Makes a sort of little mystery of it, doesn't it?"

And he jotted down this fact.

Prof. Demetriovich made his observation on the probable source of the objects before them.

"Standifer's hypothesis is not as bad as it sounds, Pethwick," observed the savant.

"You don't mean these really belong to some scientist?" cried the engineer.

"I think their arrangement proves it."

The engineer looked at the professor curiously.

"These skeletons are arranged in the order of their evolutionary development."

A glance showed this to be the case and it rather surprised Pethwick.

"Does that hold any significance?"

M. Demetriovich walked over to the frame of the puma and shook it slightly as he inspected it.

"It would suggest a scientist arranged these specimens. A savage or a rustic would have been more likely to have strung them out according to size, or else he would have mixed them higgledy-piggledy, and the probability that he would have hit on their evolutionary order would have been remote indeed." The professor gave the puma's bones another shake. "Besides that, this articulation is very cleverly done—too cleverly for unpracticed hands."

"But why should a scientist leave his specimens out like this?" demanded the engineer in amazement.

"To begin with, this seems to be the end of the trail—the shipping-point, so to speak, and for the further reason that water boils at a very low temperature at this altitude."

As the professor's fingers had touched some particles of flesh still adhering to the puma's vertebrae, he stepped across to a little patch of snow, stooped and washed his hands in it.

His two companions stared at him.

"Water boiling at a low temperature—altitude—what's that got to do with it?" interrogated the engineer.

The scientist smiled.

"I thought you would see that. If boiling water is too cool to clean the bones properly, here are some very trustworthy assistants above us."

M. Demetriovich indicated the vultures still soaring overhead.

The secretary, who had been scribbling rapidly during the last part of this discourse, now crossed out a few lines on a former page with the remark: "Well, there is no mystery to it after all."

"But look here!" exclaimed Pethwick. "We're scooped!"

"What do you mean—scooped?" asked the old Rumanian.

"Somebody has beaten us to this field. There are rival explorers in these mountains."

"Tut, tut," chided the old man. "You should say, my dear Pethwick, we have 'colleagues' instead of 'rivals,' I am charmed to believe they are here. We must get with them and try to be of assistance to them."

The kindly old scientist stared away among the great bluish peaks, speculating on where his "colleagues" would be.

"But look here," objected Standifer in alarm; "there will be another secretary with that expedition, grabbing all this literary material—"

"Lads, lads," reproached the old savant, "you have yet to learn the opulence of nature. She is inexhaustible. This party, another party, fifty parties toiling at the same time could never fathom all the marvels that lie under the sweep of our gaze. Why, gentlemen, for instance, in Bucharest I and a colleague worked for three years on the relation of the olfactory system of catarrhine monkeys with that of human beings. Our effort was to approximate in what epoch the sense of smell became of secondary importance to humanity. This, of course, would mark a great change in the mode of living among men.

"As I say, we spent three years on the two nervous systems and yet our discoveries were most dissimilar. Now, what are a few white nerve-threads to all this wilderness of snow and boulders? Your fears are quite baseless."

His two companions laughed, half ashamed of their jealousy, and then inspected the scene before them, which up till now had been lost in the grisly detail of the skeletons.

The mountain side on which they stood dropped away in an enormous declivity fully a mile and a half deep and led into a vast and sinister valley that stretched toward the northeast until its folds and twists were lost among the flashing peaks.

The extraordinary part of the scene was that instead of spreading the vivid green of the tropics below the tree-line this great depression looked black and burned. The ensemble recalled to Pethwick certain remarkable erosions he had seen in the West of the United States. Only here, the features were slashed out with a gigantism that dwarfed our western canyons and buttes.

And there was another striking difference. In the North American West the Grand Canyon and the Yosemite glow with a solemn beauty. The chasm looked like the raw and terrible wound of fire. Its blackened and twisted acclivities might have been the scars of some terrible torment.

A river lay through the center of this cicatrix, and although later it proved nearly half a mile wide, it was reduced to a mere rivulet amid such cyclopean setting. It twisted in and out, now lost to view, now shimmering in the distance, everywhere taking the color of its surroundings and looking for the world like one of those dull, spreading adders winding through the valley.

Pethwick now fully understood why the Indians had given the peculiar name to the river. It was a sobriquet any human being would have bestowed upon it at first glimpse. It required no guide to tell Pethwick he was looking down upon the Rio Infiernillo.

"This is the place, *senor*," said Pablo Pasca.

"Do we start back from here?"

Pethwick looked at him in surprise.

"We'll spend the next sixty days in this valley."

"I mean Cesare and myself, *senor*," explained the Zambo in hangdog fashion.

"You and Cesare!"

"We have shown you the Valley of the Rio Infiernillo—that was all we promised, *senor*," pursued Pablo doggedly.

Ruano glanced around. "Speak for yourself, Pablo!"

"You are not going into this den of Satan, are you?" cried Pablo to the murderer. "Past these— these"—he nodded at the skeletons.

Ruano grinned, showing two rows of big white teeth. "I'll go help make some more skeletons," he said carelessly.

Pethwick began to explain away Pasca's fears.

"Those are nothing but the specimens of a scientific expedition, Pablo."

"Do scientific expeditions collect skeletons?" shuddered the thief.

"Yes."

"Will you do that?"

"Very probably."

"And leave them for the birds to pick?"

"If we don't boil them." Pethwick grew more amused as the fears of his guide mounted.

"*Dios Mio!* What for?"

"To study them," laughed the engineer.

Pablo turned a grayish yellow.

"And you kill men and let the buzzards pick their bones—to study them?" aspirated the half-breed. "Will you kill me—and Ruano?"

"Certainly not!" ejaculated Pethwick, quite shocked. "What a silly idea!"

"But the other gang did, *senor*," cried the Zambo, nodding at the skeleton of the man at the end of the line, "and no doubt, senor, they told their guide that all was well, that everything was as it should be, until one fine day—*pang!*

"And here he stands, grinning at me, slapping his knee to see another big fool go down the scarp."

At such a hideous suspicion all three scientists began a shocked denial.

What did Pablo take them for—ghouls? They were civilized men, scientists, professors, engineers, authors.

"Then why did you choose for guides two men condemned to death unless it was to kill them and stay within the law?"

They reassured the robber so earnestly that he was half convinced, when unfortunately an extra gust of wind set the skeleton clapping his knee again.

The gruesome mirth set Pablo almost in a frenzy.

"*Ehue!* Yes! But how did the other party get their man? No doubt they found a dead man in this devil's country! Oh, yes, dead men are frequent in this place where men never go! They didn't kill their guide to study his bones. Oh, no! Not at all! Ha! No! He dropped dead. Very reasonable! Ho!"

With a yell he dropped his mule's rein and leaped for the mouth of the trail.

But Cesare Ruano was quicker than the thief. The murderer made one leap, caught the flying Zambo by the shoulder and brought him in a huddle on the stones.

The robber shrieked, screamed, began a chattering prayer.

"Oh, Holy Mary! Blessed Virgin! Receive my soul! I am to be killed! Blessed Queen!"

The words seemed to arouse some sort of anger in Cesare, for the big fellow shook Pablo till his teeth rattled.

"Shut up squeaking, you rabbit! Can't you tell when a man is about to murder you? These are gentlemen! You will stay with this party, coward! and do the work! You will help me! I will not leave them and neither will you. *Sabe?*"

As he accented this "*Sabe?*" with a violent shake, Pablo's head nodded vigorously whether he wanted it to or not.

Oddly enough the trouncing seemed to reassure Pasca more than all the arguments of the scientists.

"You are a shrewd man, Cesare," he gasped as soon as he was allowed to speak. "Are you sure they won't hurt us?"

Ruano laughed again, with a flash of teeth.

"They can't hurt me. I could mash these little men with my thumb. Whom are you afraid of, Pablo—the old gray man who can hardly walk?"

"Why, no," admitted the thief looking at M. Demetriovich.

"Or of that bean-pole boy, whose head is so weak he cannot remember the simplest thing without writing it in a book."

"Nor him either," agreed Pablo with a glance at Standifer.

"Or the engineer who cannot lift a hand without gasping for breath?"

"Anyway," argued Pasca, half convinced, "how did those other geographers manage to kill their guide? Perhaps they shot him when he was asleep."

"They were not geographers," snapped Ruano, "at least they were not like these men."

"How do you know?"

"Could another such a party be in the mountains and all the country not hear of it? Even in prison we heard the great American scientists were going to the Rio Infiernillo. Then take these men—would they tie all these bones together if they wanted to pack them on llamas to Ayacucho? You know they would not. They would take them apart and put them in sacks until they reached America."

"Why, that's a fact," agreed Pasca, staring at the skeletons with new interest. "Certainly no llama would carry one of these things." He stared a moment longer and added: "But perhaps these other scientists were also fools and did not think of that."

"Then they would not have had wit enough to kill their guide. It takes some wit to kill a man, Pablo, I assure you."

Naturally the geographers had been listening to this very candid opinion of their party. Now M. Demetriovich inquired, not without a certain respect in his voice:

"*Senor* Ruano, I may be wrong in my judgment. How do you think those skeletons came here?"

"*Senor*," returned the convict respectfully, "this is the Rio Infiernillo. I think the devil put them here to scare men away, so they cannot look into hell while they are alive. Because if they had a look, *senor*, it would be so horrible they would change their lives, become good men and go to heaven—and so the devil would lose patronage."

Standifer, who was chagrined with Ruano's description of himself, grunted out the word "barbarous." Pethwick shouted with laughter.

With a blush Standifer drew out his notebook. As he did so, he said to Cesare:

"These entries are made, not because I lack intelligence, as you seem to think, but because I am the official secretary of this expedition; besides I am an author. I wrote a book called 'Reindeer in Iceland.'"

A fit of coughing seized Pethwick.

"I meant nothing by what I said, *Senor* Standifer," explained Ruano, "except to hearten this rabbit. Think nothing of it." He turned to the crowd as a whole. "We will never get the mules and llamas past the skeletons, so we will have to remove the skeletons past the mules and llamas."

This plan recommended itself to the whole party and everybody set to work. The men lugged the things past the trembling animals and finally lined them up behind the cavalcade. They placed the human frame at the head of the troop, just as they had found it.

As Pethwick rode away he looked back at it. There it stood, representing the summit of creation, the masterpiece of life. It rattled its phalanges against its femur and grinned a long-toothed grin at the vast joke of existence—an evolutionary climb of a hundred-million years, a day or two of sunshine, a night or two of sleep, a little stirring, a little looking around, and poof! back it was where it had started a hundred million years ago. No wonder skeletons grin!

On the forward journey it transpired that Cesare Ruano had obtained a sort of moral ascendancy over the whole party.

He certainly had set the whole crowd straight about the skeletons. They had talked for an hour to decide where they came from and in half a dozen words Cesare proved to them they knew nothing about the matter whatsoever. Another thing that gave Cesare prestige was his abrupt quelling of Pasca's desertion. Without Cesare, the Zambo would have escaped. None of the scientists would have acted in time to stop his headlong flight.

Civilization has the unfortunate effect of slowing up men's mental operations in emergencies. Indeed, civilization places such a premium on foresight that a civilized man lacks ability to live from instant to instant. The ordinary American lives usually in next month or next year, but he is rarely at home in the "now" and "here."

This quality of concentration on the future is a splendid thing for developing inventions, building great businesses, painting great pictures, writing novels and philosophies, but it works badly indeed for guarding convicts, who invariably bolt in the present tense.

Cesare used his new authority to possess himself of a rifle.

"We don't know just who shot this skeleton," he explained very simply to M. Demetriovich, "and we don't know how many more skeletons the fellow may want. I prefer to keep mine. Now I have observed that you *senores* never glance about when you travel, but look straight into your mules' ears and think of a great many things, no doubt. But this fellow could collect your skeletons very easily. So I will take a rifle and ride before and shoot whoever it is before he shoots us."

Ruano chose Standifer's rifle for this task. The secretary was glad of it, for the weapon had been chafing his leg ever since the party left Ayacucho.

The immediate declivity leading into the Valley of the Rio Infiernillo was a field of boulders ranging in size from a man's head to a house. Far below them the tree line was marked by some small trees that had been tortured by the wind into grotesque shapes worked out by the Japanese in their dwarf trees. Here and there

patches of snow disguised their precarious footing into white
pitfalls.

The mules crept downward, exploring every step of the way with
their little hoofs, then easing their weight forward. It made a very
swaying, chafing ride. Pethwick's pommel worked against his stomach until he felt he had been sitting down a week, wrong side first.

After an endless jostle it seemed to the engineer that he was
not descending in the slightest, but was being shaken back and
forth, sticking in one place amid the cyclopean scenery. When he
looked back, the endless boulder-field slanted toward the sky; when
he looked down, it seemed as far as ever into the black and sinister valley where the river wound like an adder.

He looked to reaching the tree-line with a hope it would bring
him relief from the monotony. It did not. His saddle chafed, his
mule sagged and swayed. His fellow-scientists did as he was doing,
squirmed about on the torturing saddle-horns. The sameness drove
his mind in on itself. He began as Cesare had said, "to stare into
his mule's ears and think."

He wondered about the skeletons. He wondered what "trivial"
thing Cesare had done to get sentenced to the garrote. He wondered what that shooting star and the phosphorescent mist could
have been? Then he wondered about the skeletons again . . . about
Cesare . . .

A rifle-shot that sounded like a mere snap in the thin mountain air disturbed his reflections. He looked up and saw a faint wisp
of vapor float out of the .30-30 in Cesare's hands. The engineer
glanced anxiously to see if the murderer had shot any of his companions. They were all on their mules and all looking at each other
and at him. Every one in the crowd had felt instinctively that the
desperado had fired at some person—possibly at one of his own
party.

"What is it? " cried Standifer.

"A man yonder!" Pablo pointed.

"I don't know whether it was a man or not!" cried Ruano, jumping
from his slow mule and setting off down the declivity at a hazardous
run.

"Ruano!" shouted M. Demetriovich in horror. "Did you shoot at a human being like that? Drop that rifle, you bloodthirsty fellow. Drop it!"

Extraordinary to say, Cesare did drop his gun and as it struck the stones it fired again. The man plunged on downward at full tilt. It was an amazing flight. He took the boulders like a goat. The party stopped their mounts and sat watching the dash.

"Did you say it was a man?" asked the secretary shakily of Pablo.

"As sure as I am sitting here." At that moment, the flying Ruano swung in behind a large boulder.

"He was behind that!" cried Pablo sharply. Then he lifted his voice. "Did you get him, Cesare?" he shouted. "Was there any money on him?"

But almost immediately Pethwick glimpsed the murderer again, in fact saw him twice—or he may have caught a flash of two figures, one chasing the other.

Suddenly Pablo began yelling as if on a fox-course.

A shock of horror went through Pethwick. He knew too well what the convict would do if he caught the man. Nobody could waylay Cesare Ruano, even to look at him, in safety.

"Here, let's get down there!" cried the engineer in urgent tones. "Lord, we ought not to have given that brute a gun!"

"Maybe he hit him!" surmised Pablo in cheerful excitement.

"He's chasing him this minute somewhere behind those boulders." declared Standifer nervously.

M. Demetriovich dismounted, and from between two boulders recovered Standifer's rifle as they passed it.

Pethwick had screwed up his nerves for some dreadful sight behind the boulder, but there was nothing there. Nothing except a splotch of green liquid on the stones.

Smaller gouts of this green fluid led off down the boulder-field, making from one large boulder to another as if some dripping thing had tried to keep a covert between itself and the party of riders.

Pethwick dismounted and followed this trail perhaps a hundred yards, until it ceased. Then he stood looking about him in the cold sunshine. He could not hear the slightest sound. The blackened valley and the Infernal River lay far below him. High above him, at the end of the trail, the vultures wheeled against the sky.

CHAPTER III

From his headlong pursuit down the mountainside Cesare Ruano never returned.

What became of him none of his companions ever discovered. He dropped out of their lives as suddenly and completely as if he had dissolved into thin air.

A dozen possibilities besieged their brains. Perhaps he fell over a cliff. Or was drowned in the river. Or he may have deserted the expedition. Perhaps he was still wandering about, lost or crazed. Perhaps the man he pursued turned and killed him.

All these are pure conjectures, for they had not a clue upon which to base a rational hypothesis. The only hope for a suggestion, the green splotches on the boulders, proved to be a hopeless riddle itself.

The men picked up several of the smaller boulders and when camp was pitched Prof. Demetriovich made a chemical analysis of the stain. Its coloring matter was derived from chlorophyll. If Ruano's shot had penetrated the stomach of some running animal, it was barely possible for such a stain to have resulted—but it was improbable. This stain was free from cellular vegetal structure. In the mixture was no trace of the corpuscles or serum of blood.

On the afternoon of the second day following the incident, the men sat at the dinner-table discussing the matter.

In the tent beside the rude dining-table were cots and another table holding mineral and floral specimens and some insects. Two or three books were scattered on the cots and duffle-bags jammed the tent-corners.

Looking out through the flaps of their tent, the diners could see the eastern peaks and cliffs of the Infernal Valley turning orange under the sunset.

M. Demetriovich was talking.

"I consider the chlorophyll an added proof that there is another scientific expedition in this valley."

"What is your reasoning?" inquired Pethwick.

"Chlorophyll is a substance none but a chemist could, or rather would, procure. It serves no commercial purpose. Therefore it must be used experimentally."

"Why would a chemist want to experiment in this forsaken place?"

Standifer put in a question—

"Then you think Cesare shot a hole in a canister of chlorophyll solution?"

"When a man has a choice of improbabilities, all he can do is to choose the least improbable," explained M. Demetriovich friendlily.

"I wonder what Cesare would say about it?" speculated Pethwick.

"The green trail also suggests my theory," proceeded Prof. Demetriovich. "When Ruano shot the man behind the boulder, his victim evidently did not know that his can of solution had been punctured, for he sat hidden for perhaps a minute while his container leaked a large pool just behind the rock. Then Cesare charged, the fellow fled, losing small quantities as the liquid splashed out. At last the man observed the puncture and turned the can over and there the trail ended."

M. Demetriovich pushed his coffee cup toward Pablo without interrupting his deductions.

"I should say Cesare's bullet entered the can about an inch below the level of the liquid. That would explain why a continuous trail did not mark the fugitive."

"But why would one scientist be ambushing civilized men in a heaven-forsaken place like this?" cried Standifer in slightly supercilious tones. "And why should he carry a canister of chlorophyll around with him?"

Pethwick tapped the table with his fingers.

"It's unfair to demand the fellow's occupation, race, color and previous condition of servitude," he objected. Then after a moment: "I wish we could find Ruano—"

M. Demetriovich stirred his coffee and looked into it without drinking, a Latin habit he had formed in the Rumanian cafés.

"If I may be so bold, *senores*," put in Pablo Pasca, "a scientist—a lone scientist would go crazy in a place like this."

This remark, while as improbable as the other guesses, nevertheless spread its suggestion of tragedy over the situation.

"Nobody knows the action of chlorophyll exactly," brooded M. Demetriovich. "Somehow it crystallizes the energy in sunlight. If some man had developed a method to bottle the sun's energy directly, he would probably pursue his investigations in the tropics—"

"And he might desire secrecy," added Pethwick, "so much so that he would even—"

"You mean he would murder Cesare?" finished Standifer.

"A certain type of scientific mind might do that, gentlemen," agreed Demetriovich gravely.

"What sort, professor?"

"There are only a few countries in the world capable of producing a chemist who could experiment with chlorophyll and sunlight—"

The diners looked at the old scientist expectantly.

"Of these, I know only one country whose national creed is ruthlessness, only one whose chemists would kill an Indian on the bare possibility that the Indian might divulge his secret process—or his political affiliations."

"You mean he could be a German royalist?" queried Pethwick.

"If the Germans could synthesize the sun's energy and thus transform it directly into food, they would certainly be in a position to bid again for world dominion," stated M. Demetriovich positively. "It would annul a blockade of the seas. It would render unnecessary millions of men working in the fields and put them on the battlefront."

"But that's fantastic, professor!" cried Pethwick, "That's getting outside of probability."

"The green splotches themselves are outside of probability, Mr. Pethwick," stated the old savant gravely, "but they are here nevertheless."

"The moon is rising," observed Standifer casually.

The secretary's silly and trivial breaks into the conversation irritated Pethwick. He turned and said—

"Well, that doesn't bother me; does it you?"

"Oh, no," said Standifer, taking the rather tart remark in good faith. "I like to watch the moon rise. If I may say it, all my best literary ideas are evolved under the moonlight."

"Trot on out and see if you can't think up something good," suggested the engineer.

Standifer caught this sarcasm, flushed slightly but did get up and walk out through the tent entrance. A moment later the two men followed him, leaving the things to Pablo.

The rising moon centered their attention with the first glint of its disk between two peaks far down the valley. The last bronze twilight lingered in the west. The men shivered with the chill of coming night.

Despite Pethwick's jibe at the poetical influence of the moon as expressed by the secretary, the engineer felt it himself.

"It looks whiter, more silvery in this latitude," he observed after a continued silence.

"That mist about it looks like the veil of a bride," mused the author.

"May do it," said the engineer, who despised similes, "but it looks more like a mist around the moon."

"What's the matter with you, anyway, Pethwick?" snapped Standifer, wheeling around. "Just because you lack the gift of poetical expression is no reason why you should make an ass of yourself and bray every time I utter a well-turned phrase!"

"Was that what you were doing?" inquired the older man.

"It was, and if—" Standifer broke off suddenly and stared, then in amazement gasped—

"For Heaven's sake!"

"What is it?" Both the older men followed his gaze.

Standifer was staring into the fading sky utterly bewildered.

Pethwick shook him.

"What is it?"

The secretary pointed skyward.

They followed his finger and saw against the dull west the delicate silver crescent of a new moon.

It required half an instant for the incoherence of their two observations to burst upon them. The next impulse, all three turned.

The full moon they had seen rising in the east had disappeared. The mist, a phosphorescent mist, still hung about the peaks; indeed it seemed to settle on the distant crags and cliffs and glow faintly in the gathering darkness. It defined a sort of spectral mountain-scape. Then, before their astounded gaze, it faded into darkness.

A scratching sound caused Pethwick to shiver. It was Pablo striking a match inside the tent.

After his observation of what for want of a better name will have to be called the pseudo-moon, a curious mental apathy fell over Pethwick. Not that he failed to think of the extraordinary series of events that had befallen the expedition. He did think of them all the time. But he thought weakly, hopelessly. He picked up the problem in his brain without the slightest hope of finding the solution. He exhausted himself on the enigma, and yet he could not let it go.

He tried to forget it and center himself on his work. But little mysteries cropped out in his everyday toil. His principal duty with the expedition was map-making, the determination of the altitudes of the various observed peaks, and a mapping of the outcrops of the black micas, limonites, serpentines, pitchblendes, obsidians, and hornblendes. It was these dark-colored stones, he found, that gave the great chasm its look of incineration.

And this is what he did not understand. Here and there he found places where streams of lava sprang, apparently, out of the solid escarpment of the cliffs.

Now the whole Peruvian sierras are volcanic and these lava pockets did not surprise Pethwick. The inexplicable part was that no volcanic vent connected these little fumaroles with the interior of the mountain. They seemed to have burned from the outside. They looked as if some object of intense heat had branded the mountainside.

Ordinarily Pethwick's mind would have sprung like a terrier at such a problem; now, through sheer brain fag, he jotted the descriptions without comment. In this dull, soulless way he made the following extraordinary entry in his journal one morning:

> This morning, close to one of those burned pockets, or fumaroles, which I have before described, I found a roasted rabbit. The little animal was some twelve feet from the fumarole, sitting upright on its haunches and roasted. It looked as if its curiosity had been aroused, and it had been cooked instantly. As decomposition had not set in, it could not have been dead for more than a week.
>
> I wonder if this is a tab on the date of these fumaroles? If so, they must have been burned a few days ago, instead of being of geologic antiquity, as I at first assumed. If recent, they must be of artificial origin. Since they roast a rabbit before frightening it, they must occur with the abruptness of an explosion. Can these splotches be connected with the evil mystery surrounding this expedition? I cannot say, I have no theory whatever.

That evening at dinner Pethwick showed this entry to M. Demetriovich. The old Rumanian read it, and his only comment was a nod and a brief—

"Yes, I had discovered they were of recent origin myself."

Presently he suggested a game of chess to take their minds off the matter before they retired.

"You look strained, Pethwick," the old man said.

The engineer laughed briefly.

"I am strained. I'm jumpy every minute of the day and night."

The old savant considered his friend with concern.

"Wouldn't you better get out of here for a while, Herbert?"

"What's the use? I could think of nothing else."

"You would feel out of danger."

"I don't feel in danger."

"Yes, you do—all mystery connotes danger. It suggests it to us. That is why mystery is so stimulating and fascinating."

"Do you think we are in danger?"

"I am sure the man who killed Cesare would not hesitate over us."

Standifer, who was seated at the table began to smile in a superior manner at their fears.

Owing to the engineer's nervous condition this irritated Pethwick acutely. However, he said nothing about it, but remarked to M. Demetriovich—

"Tomorrow I am through with my work right around here."

"Then you'll take a rest, as I suggest."

"No, I'll take a pack, walk straight down this valley and find out what is making these fumaroles—and what became of Cesare."

At that moment, in the gathering blue of night, the eastern sky was lighted by the glare of the pseudo-moon. Its pallor poured in through the tent flaps and the shadows of the men's legs streaked the floor.

The mystery brought both the old men to the outside. They stared at the illumination in silence. The light was as noiseless as the aurora. As they watched it, Pethwick heard Standifer laughing inside the tent.

The secretary's idiocy almost snapped the engineer's control. He wanted to knock his empty head. At last the phenomenon died away and left its usual glimmer on the surrounding heights. In a few minutes this vanished and it was full night.

When the men reentered the tent, Standifer still smiled as if he enjoyed some immunity from their mystification and nervousness.

"Well, what's the joke?" asked Pethwick at last.

"The way you fellows go up in the air about this thing."

"You, I suppose, are on solid ground!" exploded Pethwick.

The author said nothing but continued his idiotic smile.

"I admit there are points here and there I don't understand," continued Pethwick after a moment. "No doubt we fail to understand it as thoroughly as you do."

"You do," agreed Standifer with such matter-of-factness the engineer was really surprised.

"What in the devil have you found out?" he asked irritably.

"Oh, the facts, the facts," said Standifer nonchalantly. "I'm a writer, you know, a trained observer; I dive to the bottom of things."

Pethwick stared, then laughed in a chattery fashion—

"Y-Yes, I see you diving to the bottom of this—"

The old professor, who had been studying the secretary, quietly interrupted—

"What do you know, James?"

The literary light hesitated a moment, then drew a handful of glittering metal out of his pocket and plunked it down on the table.

"I know all about it," he said and grinned in spite of himself.

The men stared. Pablo Pasca paused in his journeys to and from the kitchen tent to stare at the boy and the gold.

"Know all about what?" cut in Pethwick jumpily.

"The gold or the mystery?"

"Both."

Suddenly Pablo cried—

"I told you, *senores*, wealth lies where danger is so great!"

"Have you found a gold mine?" asked M. Demetriovich.

"No, I sold one of my books."

"Whom to—when—where—my Lord; who was the sucker?" Pethwick's questions almost exploded out of him.

"I had no idea my book had such a reputation," beamed the author.

"Youngster, if you'll cut the literary twaddle—" quavered Pethwick on edge.

"Well, I had a hunch there must be some very simple explanation of all this skull and cross-bone stuff you fellows were trying to pull. You know that doesn't go on in real life. It's only fiction, that resort of the mentally muddled—"

"Standifer! Spill it—if you know anything!"

"Go on, tell it your own way," encouraged Demetriovich. "You were saying 'mentally muddled.'"

"Sure—yes, well, nothing to it, you know. This life is very simple, once you get the key."

"Lord, doesn't that sound like 'Reindeer in Iceland'!" groaned the engineer.

"What was the light we saw just then, Mr. Standifer?" inquired the savant, who saw that the secretary would never get anywhere unaided.

"A new sort of portable furnace, sir, that extracts and reduces ores on the spot."

"Who runs it?"

"Indians."

"Have you seen any of them?"

"Saw one not three hours ago. Sold him a copy of 'Reindeer in Iceland.'"

Pethwick interrupted the catechism.

"Gave you that much gold for a copy of 'Reindeer in Iceland'! for the whole edition of 'Reindeer in Iceland'!"

"Did you enquire about Cesare?" proceeded M. Demetriovich.

"Yes, he's working for them."

"Did you think to ask about the chlorophyll?"

"That's used in a secret process of extracting gold."

"You say the men engaged in such a method of mining are *Indians?*"

"The man I saw was an Indian."

"Did you talk to him in English, Spanish, Quicha? What language?"

The secretary hesitated.

"Well—in English, but I had to explain the language to him. I think he knew it once but had forgotten it."

"A lot of South Americans are educated in the States," observed Pethwick, who by now was listening intently.

"Tell us what happened, Mr. Standifer," requested the Rumanian.

"Well, today I was about twelve miles down the valley. I had sat down to eat my lunch when I saw an Indian behind a rock staring at me as if his eyes would pop out of his head. I don't mind admitting it gave me a turn, after the way things have been happening around here. On second glance I thought it was Cesare. I was about to yell and ask when the fellow himself yelled at me—

"'Hey, Cesare, is that you?'

"Well, it nearly bowled me over. But I got a grip on my nerves and shouted back, 'No, I'm not Cesare!' And I was about to ask who the fellow was when he took it right out of my mouth and shouted to me, 'Who are you?'

"I told him my name and address, that I was an author and secretary of the De Long Geographical Expedition; then I asked him to come out and let's have a talk.

"The fellow came out all right, walking up to me, looking hard at me. He was an ordinary Indian with a big head and had on clothes about like Cesare's. In fact, you know it is hard to tell Indians apart. As he came up he asked me the very question I had in mind—

"'Do you know Cesare?'

"I said, 'Yes; where is he?'

"He stood looking at me and shook his head.

"I said, 'You don't know,' and he touched his mouth and laughed. Then I guessed that he didn't understand English very well, so I began explaining the language to him.

"He would point at something and say, 'Is that a bird? Is that a stone? Is that a river?' In each case he got it right, but there was always a hesitation, of about a second, perhaps, as if he were thinking like this: 'is that a—river?'"

Both the older men were staring intently at the boy as if they were trying to read something behind his words. Pethwick nodded impatiently.

"I am sure," continued Standifer, "the fellow once knew English and it was coming back to him."

"Undoubtedly," from Pethwick.

"Then he saw the corner of my book in my haversack, for I—I sometimes carry my book around to read when I'm lonely, and he said, 'What is that—'Reindeer in Iceland'?"

"That joggled me so, I said, 'Yes, how the deuce did you know that?'

"Well, at that he almost laughed himself to death and finally he said just about what was in my mind; 'That has a wider reputation than you imagine,' and he added, 'What is it for?'

"'What is what for?' says I.

"'Reindeer in Iceland,' says he.

"'To read,' says I. 'It contains facts,' says I. 'It's not like the rotten fiction you pick up.' And with that my whole spiel that I used to put up to the farmers in New York State when I sold my books from door to door came back to me. I thought what a lark it would be to try to sell a copy to an Indian in the Rio Infiernillo. 'If I do that,' I thought to myself, 'I'll be the star book-agent of both the Americas.' So I began:

"'It's not like the rotten fiction you buy,' says I. 'This volume gives you the truth about reindeer in Iceland; it tells you their food, their strength, their endurance, their value in all the different moneys of the world. It states where are the greatest herds. What reindeer hides are used for. How their meat, milk and cheese taste. How to prepare puddings from their blood. How the bulls fight. Their calls; their love-calls, danger-calls, hunger-calls. How their age may be calculated by the tines on their horns and the rings on their teeth and the set of their tails. In fact, sir,' said I, 'with this little volume in your pocket, it will be impossible for any man, no matter how dishonest he is, to palm off on you an old, decrepit reindeer under the specious representation that he or she is young, agile and tender.

"'The price of this invaluable compendium puts it within easy reach of one and all. It will prove of enormous practical and educational value to each and any. It makes little difference whether you mean to rear these graceful, docile animals or not; you need this volume, for as a means of intellectual culture it is unsurpassed. It contains facts, nothing but facts. You need it. Do you want it? Are you progressive? Its price is the only small thing about it— only fifty-four cents. Let me put you down.'

"With that, so strong is the force of habit, I whipped out an old envelope to take his order on.

"'What is fifty-four cents?' he asked, 'Have I got fifty-four cents?'

"'Just what I was wondering,' says I. 'Turn your pockets wrongside out and I'll see.'

"He turned 'em and spilled a lot of metals on the ground. I saw these pieces of gold and told him they would do. I told him I would give him all five of my volumes, for that is the number I brought on this trip, and I'm sorry now I didn't bring more.

"He just pushed the gold over to me without blinking an eye and we traded. I told him where we were camped and he said tomorrow he would call and get the other four volumes. And, gentlemen, that is all I know."

At the end of this tale, Standifer leaned back, smiling with pleasure at his sale. The two men sat studying him. At last Pethwick asked—

"You say he knew the title of your book?"

"Yes."

"Was the title showing?"

"No, just a little corner stuck out of the knapsack."

Pethwick considered a moment.

"You at first thought it was Cesare?"

"Yes."

"Did he have a scar on the side of his face?"

"No, I would have noticed that sure. Still his face was painted very thickly. I couldn't see any scar."

"You are sure it wasn't Cesare?"

"Absolutely sure."

Here M. Demetriovich took up what might be called the cross-examination.

"You say he didn't understand English at first—could he read the book you sold him?"

"No, that was the odd part. I had to tell him what the letters were and how they made words; how words made sentences. But he caught on the moment I showed him anything and never forgot at all. I tried him."

M. Demetriovich paused:

"You are sure it was an Indian?"

"Yes."

"But he didn't know the value of gold?"

"Well, I don't know about that," began Standifer.

"Did you say he gave you all that money for five dinky little books!" stormed Pethwick.

"Yes, but that doesn't say he doesn't understand—"

"A gold-miner," interrupted M. Demetriovich, "who is so highly scientific as to employ chlorophyll in a secret process of extracting gold and yet who—doesn't know the value of gold!"

The secretary caressed his glittering pile happily, yawned and slipped it back into his pocket.

"Anyway I wish I had a cartload of those books down here."

Pethwick sat on his stool clutching his knee to his breast, glaring at the author. Finally he gave a nervous laugh—

"I'm glad you've cleared up the mystery, Standifer."

"So am I," returned the secretary genially. "I was getting worried about it myself."

"I shouldn't think it would worry you, Standifer." Pethwick gave another shuddery laugh.

"I'm glad not to worry," agreed the secretary heartily.

The engineer sat moistening his dry lips with his tongue while little shivers played through him.

"By the way," he asked after a moment, "did you think to enquire about those skeletons? Is that—cleared up, too?"

"Yes, I did. He said he put them up there to keep the animals away. He said you never knew what sort of animals were about and he didn't want any in till he was ready. He said he put one of every species he could find because each animal was afraid of its own dead."

M. Demetriovich sat gazing at the boy. A grayness seemed to be gathering over the old man.

"That's a fact," he nodded. "I'd never thought of it before—each animal is afraid of its own dead. No skeleton shocks a human being except the skeleton of a man. I suppose it's true of the rest."

"Anyway, it's all cleared up now, Standifer," repeated the engineer with his chattering laugh. "It is as you say, Standifer; there are no mysteries outside of fiction."

He began laughing, shaking violently. His exclamations grew louder and wilder. M. Demetriovich jumped out of his seat, hurried over to his medicine-chest, fixed up a glass of something and with a trembling hand presented it to the engineer. Pethwick drank some and then the old man took a deep swallow himself.

"What's the matter?" asked the secretary, lifting a happy head.

"It's the reaction," shivered the engineer less violently. "You cleared up the mystery—so suddenly— Go on to sleep."

The boy dropped back to his pillow and was off instantly after his long walk.

The two older men sat staring at each other across the little table, their nerves calming somewhat under the influence of the sedative.

"Is it a lie," whispered Pethwick after long thought, "to cover the discovery of gold?"

M. Demetriovich shook his head.

"That boy hasn't enough imagination to concoct a fragment of his fantastic tale. The thing happened."

"Then in God's name, what is Cesare going to do to us tomorrow?"

"Cesare would never have given away all that gold," decided the old savant slowly.

"Unless—he means to recoup it all tomorrow."

M. Demetriovich shook his head.

"Cesare might have put on the paint—he could never have thought up such an elaborate mental disguise. That is far beyond him."

The two men brooded. At last the savant hazarded:

"It may be possible that the Bolsheviki have quit using gold. I believe there is a plan to use time-checks down in their socialistic program."

The engineer jumped another speculation, "The old Incans used gold as a common metal—the old Incans—sun-worshipers, who sacrifice living men to their deity—"

The two scientists sat in silence. From the icefields high above the chasm of the Rio Infiernillo came a great sighing wind. It breathed in on them out of the blackness; its cold breath chilled their necks, their hands, their wrists; it breathed on their ankles and spread up under their trousers, chilling their knees and loins.

The men shivered violently.

CHAPTER IV

Pethwick awoke out of some sort of nightmare about Incan sun-worshipers. He could hear the groans of victims about to be sacrificed and even after he had shuddered awake his sense of impending calamity persisted. He lifted himself on an elbow and stared about the tent. The sun shining straight into his face, no doubt, had caused his fantasy about the sun-worshipers.

He got to a sitting posture, yawning and blinking his eyes. Outside the day was perfectly still. A bird chirped querulously. In the corral he could hear the llamas snuffling. Then he heard repeated the groan that had disturbed him in his sleep. It came from the secretary's cot.

The engineer glanced across, then came fully awake. Instead of the young author, Pethwick saw an old, white-haired man lying in the cot with the back of his head showing past the blankets. The engineer stared at this thing blankly. A suspicion that Demetriovich had changed cots passed through his mind, but a glance showed him the old savant still asleep on his proper bed.

The engineer got up, stepped across and leaned over this uncanny changeling. It took him a full half-minute to recognize, in the drawn face and white hair of the sleeper, the boy Standifer.

A shock went over the engineer. He put his hand on the author's shoulder.

"Standifer!" he shouted. "Standifer!"

As Standifer did not move, Pethwick called to the professor with an edge of horror in his voice.

The old savant sprang up nervously. "What is it?"

"Here, look at this boy. See what has happened!"

The scientist stared from his cot, rubbed his eyes and peered.

"Is—is that Standifer?"

"Yes."

"What's happened to him?"

"I haven't the slightest idea, professor."

The scientist jabbed his feet into his slippers and came across the tent. He shook the sleeper gently at first, but gradually increased his energy till the cot squeaked and the strange white head bobbed on the pneumatic pillow.

"Standifer! Standifer!"

But the youth lay inert.

He stripped the covers and the underclothes of the young man.

Standifer lay before them naked in the cold morning air; his undeveloped physique looked bluish; then, on the groin of his right leg, Pethwick noticed an inflamed splotch that looked like a severe burn.

M. Demetriovich turned to his medicine-chest and handed Pethwick an ammonia bottle to hold under the boy's nose while he loaded a hypodermic with strychnine solution. A moment later he discharged it into the patient's arm.

A shudder ran through Standifer at the powerful stimulant. His breathing became better and after a bit he opened his eyes. He looked drowsily at the two bending over him and after a minute whispered—

"What's matter?"

"How do you feel?"

"Sleepy. Is it time to get up?"

"Do you ache—hurt?"

The secretary closed his eyes, evidently to take stock of his feelings.

"My head aches. My—my leg burns."

He reached down and touched the inflamed spot. As the strychnine took firmer hold the boy became alert enough to show surprise at his own state. He eased his sore leg to the floor and sat up on the edge of the cot. Both his companions began a series of questions.

Standifer had no idea what was the matter with him. He had not bruised either his head or his leg. Nothing had happened to him through the night, that he recalled, nor on the preceding day. After a bit, he remembered the sale of his books and drew from under his pillow the gold which he had received.

A thought crossed Pethwick's mind that Pablo Pasca had crept in during the night and had assaulted the sleeper. Demetriovich

took the bag and inspected it, smelled of it gingerly. Pethwick
watched him with some curiosity.

"How did you bring this home yesterday afternoon, James?"
queried the old man.

The secretary thought.

"In my pocket."

"In your right trousers pocket?"

Standifer made a movement to place his right and left sides
and said:

"Yes."

"Put on your trousers."

The youth did so, working his sore leg carefully inside.

"Put that gold in your pocket. Does it fall directly over the
burn?"

Standifer cringed and got the metal out as quickly as possible.

"I should say so."

M. Demetriovich nodded.

"And you slept with the gold under your pillow last night for
safe-keeping?"

"Yes."

"Then that did it," diagnosed the scientist.

"But how can gold—"

"The stuff must be poisoned somehow. I'll see if I can find how."

The savant moved to the table containing his chemicals and
test-tubes.

To Pethwick, the idea of poisoned gold sounded more like the
extravagance of the Middle Ages than a reality occurring in the
twentieth century. The engineer stood beside the table and watched
the professor pursue his reactions for vegetable and mineral poi-
sons. Standifer limped to the engineer's side. In the silver bowl of
an alcohol lamp, the boy caught a reflection of himself. He leaned
down and looked at the tiny image curiously. At length he asked:

"Pethwick, is there anything the matter with my hair?"

Then Pethwick realized that the boy did not know his hair was
white. And he found, to his surprise, that he hated to tell Standifer.
He continued watching the experiment as if he did not hear.

Standifer took up the lamp and by holding its bowl close he got a fair view of his head. He gave a faint gasp and looked for a mirror. At that instant Demetriovich took the only mirror on the table to condense a vapor floating out of a tube. The old man began talking quickly to the engineer:

"Pethwick, this is the cleverest destructive stroke that the Bolshevists have ever invented."

"What is it?"

"I still don't know, but they have poisoned this gold. They could probably do the same thing to silver. It makes the circulation of money deadly. It will perhaps cause the precious metals to be discarded as media of circulation."

The engineer looked incredulous.

"It's a fact. Do you recall how the report of ground glass in candies cut down the consumption of confectionery? If a large body of men should persistently poison every metal coin that passes through its hands—who would handle coins? Why, gentlemen," he continued as the enormity of the affair grew on him, "this will upset our whole commercial system. It will demonetize gold. No wonder that scoundrel offered our secretary so much gold for a book or two. He wanted to test his wares."

The old man's hand trembled as he poured a blue liquid from one test-tube to another.

"I am constrained to believe that in this Valley of the Infernal River we are confronted with the greatest malignant genius mankind has ever produced."

"Why should he want to demonetize gold?" interrupted Pethwick.

"It will force mankind to adopt a new standard of value and to use an artificial medium of exchange—'labor-hour checks,' perhaps, whose very installation will do more to socialize the world than any other single innovation."

The two friends stood watching him anxiously. "You can't find what they do it with?"

"Not a trace so far. It seems to defy analysis."

"Notice," observed Pethwick, "your electroscope is discharged."

M. Demetriovich glanced at the gold-leaf electroscope and saw that its tissue leaves were wilted.

Suddenly Standifer interrupted:

"Pethwick, is my hair white? Did that stuff turn my hair white?" He seized the mirror. "Look! Look!" he cried out of nervous shock and a profoundly wounded vanity.

The engineer turned with genuine sympathy for the author, but in turning he saw a man standing in the entrance watching the excitement with a slight smile.

The engineer paused abruptly, staring.

The stranger was a medium-sized Indian with an abnormally developed head and a thickly painted face. He wore the usual shirt and trousers of a *cholo* and for some reason gave Pethwick a strong impression of Cesare Ruano. Why he resembled Cesare, Pethwick could not state, even after he had inspected him closely. To judge from the Indian's faintly ironic expression, he must have been observing the scientists for several minutes.

M. Demetriovich first regained his self-possession.

"Are you the man who gave my boy this gold?" he asked sharply, indicating the metal with which he was experimenting.

The painted man looked at the heap.

"I gave a boy some gold for some books," he admitted.

"Well, that's the gold all right," snapped Pethwick.

"Did you know the gold you gave him was poisoned?" proceeded the savant severely.

"Poisoned? How was it poisoned?"

"That is for you to tell us."

"I don't know in the least. What effect did it have?"

The man's tones were completely casual, without fear, regret, or chagrin. "You see for yourself what it did."

The stranger looked at Standifer in astonishment and presently ejaculated:

"Is that the same boy?"

"You see you nearly killed him," stated the scientist grimly.

"It was quite accidental; I don't understand it myself. Let me look at his trouble."

He walked over with more curiosity than regret in his manner.

Pethwick watched the fellow with a sharp and extraordinary dislike. It was so sharp that it drove out of his mind the amazing fact of finding this sort of person in such a desolate valley.

Standifer exhibited the burn. The stranger looked at it, touched a spot here and there and finally said, more with the air of an instructor lecturing his inferiors than with that of an Indian talking to white men:

"This is the effect of a metal which I carried with the gold. A metal—I don't know what you call it in your language—possibly you may never have heard of it. Here is some."

He reached in his pocket and drew out a piece of silvery metal as large as a double eagle and dropped it on the table before M. Demetriovich. The old savant glanced at the metal, then looked more carefully.

"It's radium," he said in a puzzled voice. "It's the largest piece of radium I ever saw—it's the only piece of pure metallic radium I ever saw. It—it's worth quite a fortune—and owned by an Indian!"

Here M. Demetriovich breached his invariably good manners by staring blankly at his guest.

"So you are acquainted with it?" observed the stranger with interest.

"Not in its metallic form. I have extracted its bromides myself. And I've seen radium burns before. I might have known it was a radium burn, but I never dreamed of that metal."

"But that was gold that burned me," complained Standifer.

"That's true," agreed M. Demetriovich, "but, you see, the emanations of radium have the power of settling on any object and producing all the effects of radium itself. The gentleman carried those lumps of gold in his pockets along with about two million dollars' worth of radium." The old savant laughed briefly at the eeriness of the situation. "The gold became charged with radium, burned your leg and whitened your hair. It also affected my electrostat."

The three men turned to the stranger, who apparently carried fortunes of various metals jingling loose in his pocket.

"Sir," began the savant, "we must apologize to you for our unjust suspicions."

"Do you mean your suspicions were incorrect?" queried the red man.

"I mean," said the old savant with dignity, for this was no way to take an apology, "that we were morally culpable in attributing to you criminal motives without waiting for conclusive evidence."

The stranger smiled at this long sentence.

"I can understand your idea without your speaking each word of it. But the idea itself is very strange." He stroked his chin and some paint rubbed off on his fingers, showing a lighter yellowish skin beneath. Then he laughed. "If you should apologize for every incorrect idea you maintain, gentlemen, I should think your lives would be one long apology."

The superciliousness, the careless disdain in this observation, accented Pethwick's antipathy to the man.

At that moment the fellow asked—

"Do all your species live in cloth shelters such as these?"

Standifer, who seemed more kindly disposed toward the stranger than the others, explained that tents were temporary shelters and that houses were permanent.

The newcomer continued his smiling scrutiny of everything and at last asked:

"Can't you gentlemen even communicate with each other without using words and sentences?"

He paused then, as if to simplify what he had said, and went on—"Suppose you, Mr. Pethwick, desire to communicate with Mr.—" he made a gesture toward the scientist and added—"Mr. Demetriovich, would you be forced to articulate every word in the sentence?"

"How did you come to know my name?" asked the engineer, surprised. "Have we met before?"

The stranger laughed heartily. "I am sure we have not. I see you desire my name. Well, I have a number. In my country the citizens are numbered. I am sure when your own countries become densely populated, you, too, will adopt a numerical nomenclature."

"What is your number?" asked Standifer, quite astonished at this, as indeed were his companions.

"1753-12,657,109-654-3."

The secretary laughed.

"It sounds like a cross between a combination lock and a football game. Where do you come from, Mr.—Mr. Three?"

The painted man nodded down the valley casually.

"The name of my country is One, or First," he smiled. "Of course that is a very ancient and unscientific name, but notation must begin somewhere, and it usually begins at home. Now I dare say each one of you lives in a country called One—no, I see I am wrong." Then he repeated in a lower tone, "America—Rumania—Peru—very pretty names but unscientific."

By this time Mr. Three's remarkable feat of calling the men's names and then calling the countries of their birth made the explorers realize that they had encountered an amazing man indeed.

"Do you read our thoughts before we speak?" cried Standifer.

Mr. Three nodded easily.

"Certainly; without that all study of the lower animals would be a mere cataloguing of actions and habits."

Pethwick wondered if the fellow meant a very delicate insult to begin talking about the study of "lower animals" so promptly when the conversation naturally turned on himself and his companions. He said nothing, but Mr. Three smiled.

But M. Demetriovich was utterly charmed with the vistas of investigation the man's suggestion opened to him.

"Why, that would be wonderful, would it not!" he cried.

"Certainly, without mind-reading comparative psychology is impossible."

"We have professional mind-readers," cried M. Demetriovich with enthusiasm. "I wonder why the psychologists have never thought to have one try to read the minds—say of the higher simians!"

Mr. Three seemed to find all of this conversation funny, for he laughed again. But his words were quite serious.

"Besides, this 'mentage,' as we call mind-reading, enables one to converse with every other creature, just as I am talking to you. I take your language forms right out of your own minds and use them. If the creature has no language at all, you still receive its impressions."

By this time even Pethwick, who disliked the fellow almost to the point of hatred, realized that the stranger was wonderful indeed. The engineer decided Mr. Three came from some unknown country, which, he reluctantly admitted to himself, seemed to be more highly cultured than England or America. So, by accepting these facts, Pethwick, in a way, prepared himself not to be too surprised at anything.

"Do all your countrymen understand 'mentage' or mind-language?" enquired the engineer.

"It is our national mode of communication. I observe you move your hands when you talk—gestures, you call it. In One, we speak a word now and then to accent our thoughts—verbal gestures. Some of our population, who are nervous, sometimes speak several words, or even complete sentences. Often it is an affectation, unless, of course," he added politely as if to exempt his companions, "their minds are not strong enough to converse without words.

"On the other hand, a few well-placed words make speeches, and especially orations, very impressive. Still, some of our greatest orators never utter a sound. But I consider this too much repression, in fact rather an academic thing to do. What you would call a—a—a highbrow. Thank you, Mr. Standifer, for thinking me the term."

"It would be a great saving of time," mused Pethwick.

"Yes, indeed; in One, a person can present a whole thought, or a whole series of thoughts, in a single flash of the brain, if the thinker's brain is sufficiently strong. It is almost instantaneous."

Standifer smiled blissfully.

"Think of instantaneous sermons. Let's get to that place!"

Pethwick and the professor did not share in Standifer's badinage but sat amazed at this being whose name was a number. The engineer realized the futility of all the questions he could ask. Turn the idea about. Suppose Mr. Three should ask Pethwick to explain American civilization in a casual talk. It would be impossible. So it was impossible for Mr. Three to give Mr. Pethwick much idea of the land of One.

Mr. Demetriovich took up the questioning:

"Have you been using radium for a long time, Mr. Three?"

"For centuries. We are in the midst of a Radium Age. It was developed out of the Uranium Age. And that out of the Aluminum Age. All this arose out of a prehistoric Steel Age, a very heavy clumsy metal, I have heard archaeologists say."

"You don't mean your mechanical appliances are made out of radium?"

"No, radium is our source of power. It has changed our mechanics from molecular mechanics to atomic mechanics. The first men of One could utilize only molecular energy, such as steam and gasoline. With the aid of radium, we soon developed the enormous force that lies concentrated in the atom. This gives my countrymen unlimited power. It can be derived from any sort of matter, because all matter is composed of atoms and our force is generated through the destruction of atoms."

All this time Mr. Three's voice was growing weaker and weaker until finally he said—

"You will have to excuse me from any further conversation, gentlemen; my throat is not accustomed to much talking."

He tapped it with an apologetic smile. As he did so, he glanced about and his eyes lit on the chess-board and men which Pethwick and M. Demetriovich had been using the previous evening.

"What is that?"

"A game."

"Who plays it? Ah, M. Demetriovich and Mr. Pethwick. I would not object to a party if you feel disposed."

"Professor and I will try a consultation game against you," suggested Pethwick, moving a stool over to the table.

"I don't understand the game, but if you will just think how the pieces are moved," requested the mind-reader, "I dare say I will soon learn."

The engineer framed the demonstration in his mind and Mr. Three nodded.

"I see. It seems to be a sort of rudimentary stage of a game we call 'cube' in First. However, 'cube' is an entirely mental game, although young children are given material boards and pieces to assist them in focusing their attention.

"'Cube' has eight boards such as this, superimposed upon one another. Each board has thirty-two pieces on it, thus giving two-hundred and fifty-six pieces in all, each player controlling one hundred and twenty-eight. All the major pieces can move up or down, forward or backward, but the pawns can only advance, or go higher. As no real boards are used, the whole play must be kept in mind. The game becomes a contest of intricacy, that is, until one player grows confused, makes an incoherent move and is checkmated. It is a very pleasant amusement for persons who have nothing more serious to think about."

"I have seen mental chess-players in America," observed Standifer, "but they use only one board. I suppose more would complicate it. I don't play myself."

The chess-players made no answer to this remark, but set up the men. Mr. Three defeated the scientists' combined skill in a game of ten moves.

As this extraordinary party was brought to a conclusion, Pablo Pasca entered the tent with breakfast on a tray. When the thief saw the guest, he almost dropped the food, but after a moment came in and placed the dishes on the table. As he did so, he looked meaningly at Pethwick, nodded faintly and retired.

The engineer excused himself and followed the Indian. He found Pablo in the kitchen tent, shaken out of his ordinary stoicism.

"Do you know who he is, *senor?*" he asked in a low voice.

"His name is Three," said Pethwick, involuntarily guarding his own tone.

"No, I mean, do you know he is the man who murdered Cesare Ruano?" asked the thief earnestly.

The engineer nodded.

"I'd thought of that. How do you know he did?"

"How! *Dios Mio*—everything the man has on is Cesare's. Cesare's clothes! Cesare's shoes! On his finger is Cesare's ring— the ring Cesare was saving to be garroted in!"

"I thought somehow he resembled Cesare," nodded Pethwick, "and I knew it was not his face."

"*Ciertamente*, not Cesare, but his murderer," aspirated Pablo excitedly. "I saw this fellow behind this very boulder! This same fellow!"

Pethwick nodded in the sunlight, unaware that Pablo expected him to do anything. Indeed, the engineer was glad he had come out of the tent. Mr. Three's intelligence was oppressive. So now he stood breathing deeply, as if from some struggle. The cliffs, the sunshine, the river, the savor of the kitchen, almost made him doubt the existence in his tent of such a personage as Mr. Three from the Land of One. Where in Heaven's name was that land? Did there flourish over behind the Andes somewhere an unknown race of extraordinary arts and sciences who called themselves the First?

And there recurred to him his fancy that if such a nation existed, it must be an offshoot of the old Incan race. Perhaps fugitives flying before the old *conquistadores* found a haven in some spot and there had built up the most advanced civilization upon the face of the earth. The thought was utterly fantastic, and yet it was the only explanation of Mr. Three sitting there in the tent.

"Well?" said Pablo interrogatively.

The engineer came out of his reverie.

"Is that all you wanted to tell me?"

"All? Isn't that enough?"

"Oh, yes."

"Aren't you going to do anything?" demanded Pablo. "He is an Indian. I thought when Indians killed any one the white men garroted them. *Qwk!* Like that!" He pinched his throat and made a disagreeable sound.

"What am I to do?" inquired Pethwick blankly.

"Blessed Virgin! Does not the white man's law work in the Valley de Rio Infiernillo? I knock an old man on the head and barely save my neck. This *cholo* kills my good *camarada*, wears his clothes, steals the very ring Cesare meant to be garroted in, what happens to him? Why, he sits at the table with white men and plays! *Ehue!* A fine justice!"

The engineer hardly knew how to answer this. He stood looking at Pablo rather blankly. He felt sure an attempt to arrest Mr. Three would prove perilous indeed. On the other hand, Pablo's attitude demanded that Pethwick should act.

Isolated like this, Pethwick was the lone representative of the great Anglo-Saxon convention of justice. It is a strange convention that polices every clime and every tongue. Red, brown, black and yellow men refrain from violence because the white man says:

"Thou shalt not kill!"

Wherever a single unit of the white race is placed, that law inheres in him. Men of all colors come to him and say: "Murder has been done; now what will you do?"

And he must act.

He must deal out that strange Anglo-Saxon convention called justice, or he must die in the attempt.

That is what the white race means; it is what civilization means. It is not any one white man who has this power of judging and punishing; it is any white man. They are the knight-errants of the earth. Each one must fight, sit in judgment and administer justice to the best of his ability and conscience, so help him God.

It is the most amazing hegemony on the face of the earth, when one comes to think of it—and the most universally accepted.

Now Pablo was asking Pethwick an account of his stewardship.

Certainly the engineer did not think of the problem in just those terms. He was not conscious of his racial instinct. He thought, in rather loose American fashion, that since Pablo had put it up to him like this he would have to do something.

The Zambo began again.

"Look at what I did. I only knocked an old man on the head—"

Pethwick interrupted with a gesture:

"Pablo, get those handcuffs you and Cesare used to wear and bring 'em to the tent."

"*Si, senor*," hissed the half-breed gratefully.

Pethwick turned back toward the tent with thorough distaste for his commission. As he entered, Mr. Three glanced up with quizzical eyes and it suddenly flashed on the engineer with a sense of embarrassment that the man from One already knew what was in his thoughts.

This was soon proved. Mr. Three nodded his head smilingly.

"Yes," he said, "Pablo is quite right. Here is the ring."

He held up a hand and displayed an old silver ring engraved in the form of a snake.

M. Demetriovich glanced up at this extraordinary monologue.

"Then you did kill Cesare Ruano?" exclaimed the engineer.

Mr. Three paused for a moment, then answered:

"Yes, I did. There is no use going through a long catechism. I may also add, I knew the emanations of radium would have some effect on the boy, Standifer, but I did not know what."

The old savant stared at the man from One.

"Be careful what you say, Mr. Three. Your confession will place you in jeopardy of the law."

"Then you maintain laws in this country," observed Mr. Three. "What will be the nature of the instruction you will give me?"

"No instruction," said Pethwick; "punishment."

"A very antiquated custom. I should think anyone could see that criminals need instruction."

At that moment Pablo appeared in the entrance with the manacles.

"This is hardly the time to enter into an abstract discussion of punishment, Mr. Three," observed Pethwick brusquely. He held the manacles a moment a little self-consciously, then said, "You may consider yourself under arrest."

To Pethwick's surprise, the man from One offered no resistance, but peaceably allowed himself to be chained to the chair in which he sat. He watched the procedure with faintly amused expression and even leaned over to observe how the anklets were adjusted to his legs.

A certain air of politeness about the Incan at last constrained Pethwick to say:

"You understand, Mr. Three, we are forced to do this—it is the law."

"And you rather dislike me anyway, do you not, Mr. Pethwick?" added Three genially.

The engineer flushed, but kept his eyes steadily on Mr. Three's.

"I dislike you, but I dislike to do this more."

After the shackling the captors stood undecidedly. So they had captured the murderer of Cesare Ruano.

"We'll have to carry him before a magistrate," pondered M. Demetriovich. "It's very annoying."

"M. Demetriovich," said Mr. Three, still smiling in his chains, "you have studied physiology?

"Yes."

"And perhaps vivisection?"

"Certainly."

"Then why all this disturbance about killing a lower animal for scientific ends?"

The old Rumanian looked at Mr. Three steadfastly. "I cannot accept your point, Mr. Three. We are all human beings together, even if Cesare Ruano did not have the culture—"

The rather pointless proceedings were interrupted by a burst of snorting and braying from the corral. Pethwick hurried outside, for the pack animals were really of more importance than the prisoner. The engineer got out just in time to see Pablo go at full speed toward the enclosure. The Indian had a repeating rifle and no doubt feared the attack of a puma or jaguar.

On Pethwick's heels came both M. Demetriovich and the white-haired secretary. The valley was strewn with boulders big and little and the men had difficulty in running over broken ground. From a far off Pethwick saw that the down-river side of the corral had been knocked down, and all the llamas and mules came storming out, flying down toward the camp as if the fiends pursued them.

Pablo fired his rifle in the air in an effort to turn them. As he did so, the Zambo reeled as if he had received a mighty but invisible blow. Mules and llamas plunged straight past their staggering master and for a moment Pethwick was afraid they would run him down.

Next moment the engineer heard the secretary and the professor shouting at the top of their voices. He looked around and saw the comb of his tent on fire.

Thought of his prisoner likely to burn up, sent Pethwick sprinting breathless toward the tent. As the flames rushed over the oiled canvas Pethwick jerked up the ground-pins of the rear wall and shoved under.

Mr. Three still sat in the chair with arms and legs bound to the posts. He slumped queerly. His hat dropped down on his shirt. Half suffocated, the engineer grabbed up chair, manacles, man and all and rushed into the open.

Once outside, he dropped his burden and began to slap at the fire on his own clothes. The other men began to put out the fire on Mr. Three's garments. At their strokes the garments collapsed.

Inside Cesare Ruano's clothes was an empty human skin cut off at the neck. M. Demetriovich drew it out of the burning rags. It had a cicatrice across its breast from nipple to nipple. It had bullet wounds in legs and buttocks. It tallied exactly with the police description of the marks on the skin of Cesare Ruano.

With colorless faces the men stood studying the ghastly relic of the murderer in the brilliant sunshine.

The pack-animals were just disappearing down the river valley. A few remaining shreds of cloth burned where their tent once stood. About them the sinister landscape lay empty.

CHAPTER V

Prof. Demetriovich held up the gruesome relic.

"Gentlemen," he stated in his matter-of-fact voice, "somebody—something has been stalking us masked in this."

"But why masked?" Standifer's voice was tinged with horror.

"He was stalking us in a human skin, exactly as a hunter stalks a deer in a deer robe," returned M. Demetriovich.

"Then wasn't he a human being?" gasped the secretary.

"It certainly was the devil," gasped Pablo Pasca with a putty face. "The prefect told us not to come here."

"He knows he is a human being," accented Pethwick irritably, "but he doubts if we are. Did you notice his manner? Did you observe the supercilious, egotistical, conceited air of everything he did or said? He put us down as Darwin's connecting link. We are animals to him. He puts on one of our skins to hunt us down. Otherwise, he was afraid we would go scampering off from him like rabbits."

"Then he is a fool if he thought white men are animals," declared Pablo angrily.

"Well, he's not exactly a fool either," admitted Pethwick grudgingly, "but every single thing he said was a knock at us. I never heard—" The engineer's angry voice trailed off into angry silence.

The party stood puzzling over the extraordinary tactics of the man from One. As they buffeted the problem in their brains, a rabbit dashed almost under their feet bound down the valley. They paid no attention to it.

"I'll give you my guess," offered Pethwick. "I still believe we have encountered one of the ancient Incans. In Prescott's account of them, you notice the highest arts of civilization mingled with the grossest barbarities. A custom of wearing an enemy's skin may have grown up among them, just as our North American Indians used to take scalps. No doubt this fellow was spying on our number. I expect him to return soon with a band and attempt our capture."

"What a curious fate for the DeLong Geographical Expedition," mused the white-haired young secretary.

"Still," objected M. Demetriovich, "it might be a Bolshevist method of spreading terror."

"So, professor, you don't believe after all he put on Cesare's skin to stalk us?" queried Standifer.

"James, I don't know what to think," admitted the savant.

"The whole thing fits in better with my Incan theory," pressed the engineer. "The half-civilized Indians around here, like Pablo and Cesare, could very easily be afraid of some highly developed branch of the Incans, especially if the Incans were seeking victims to sacrifice to the sun. Under such circumstances it might be necessary to slip on the hide of a half-breed to get near the others."

"It would also explain why that man ambushed our party when we entered the valley," added the secretary.

"Thanks, Standifer, for helping me out," said Pethwick. "It would also show why the peons around here call this the Rio Infiernillo and give it such a wide berth."

M. Demetriovich pulled his chin.

"Your theory seems to hang together right now," he admitted. "If you are on the right track, we will have a marvel to report—if we ever get back."

"Then, too," went on Pethwick, encouraged, "since the prefect warned us against the valley, it suggests to me there has been something sinister here for years—long before Bolshevism became a power."

"These are queer theories," laughed Standifer, "one going to the extremely ancient and the other to the extremely modern."

During the latter part of this discussion, an *atok*, a sort of huge native rodent, slithered down the valley past the scientists, dodging from one boulder to another. Now a Peruvian fox whisked past.

The unusual animals passing within a few minutes proved sufficient to draw Pethwick's attention from the subject under discussion. The engineer looked up the stony stretch and a surprising sight filled his eyes.

The whole valley worked with glimpses of flying animals. Rats, hares, civets, what not, darted here and there from covert to covert. Along the edge of the river slunk a panther, making cat-like rushes between hiding-places. The shrill whistle of three frightened deer sounded down the valley.

It seemed as if a wave of fear were depopulating the whole Rio Infiernillo. All the engineer could see was innumerable furtive dodgings. From the dull surface of the river arose a loon, screaming, and it boomed down stream with fear-struck speed. Only one animal fled in the open, a huge black bear with a white muzzle, the *ucumari*. He was king of the Andes, as the grizzly reigns in the Rockies. He lunged down the middle of the canyon, taking the whole Infernal Valley for his course. He was afraid of nothing in the Sierras—except what was behind him.

The scientists hurried out from in front of the brute and let him lunge by unchallenged. They stared up the burnt valley, marveling at this exodus of animals.

Presently, far away against the blackish stones, Pethwick descried what seemed to be yellow fleas hopping among the boulders.

"That must be what made our pack-animals break loose!" cried the engineer.

"Wonder what they are?" from the author.

"I say it's the devil making a drive," answered Pablo, crossing himself with fervor.

The animals kept darting past. The distant fleas grew into bugs, then into some sort of animals and at last were defined against the charnel gulch as human beings.

"Jumping Jehosophat!" cried Standifer. "They are those Incans you were talking about, Pethwick. Scores of 'em! They've come for us!"

The secretary stepped around behind a large boulder that hid everything except his head. Others of the expedition followed suit, hardly knowing what to believe.

The approaching party were yellow men. Each one carried something in his hand that flashed like metal. They leaped from boulder to boulder in their chase with amazing activity. The very vicuñas themselves that skittered along the craggy sides of the valley did not exhibit a greater agility.

Pablo Pasca, notwithstanding his belief that all this was a great drive of the devil, nevertheless became excited at the passing game. As one speckled deer came shimmering down through the diamondlike sunshine, Pablo determined to beat Satan out of one carcass, so he leveled his rifle for a shot. The author saw it and put his fingers to his ears to dull the report.

At that moment a voice quite close to the party broke the silence with:

"Don't shoot. There must be no holes in the skins."

The word "skins" brought the party around with a start. They were nervous on the topic. The secretary, however, still stood with his fingers in his ears, watching deer.

On top of a large boulder, still wearing his look of condescension and amusement, sat the recent prisoner of the expedition, Mr. Three. Since he had flung off Cesare's clothes and skin, the weird creature was without apparel and sat naked in the cold vivid sunshine, his body of a clear yellowish complexion and his large head still painted a coppery red.

It was the most grotesque combination Pethwick could have imagined, but Mr. Three maintained a perfect composure, dignity—and condescension. His painted face had the faintly amused expression of a man watching the antics of, say, some pet goats.

The fellow's body suggested to Pethwick a ripe pear or yellow peach. His hands and feet were disagreeably small—sure sign of ancient and aristocratic blood. He must have slipped right through the manacles the moment his captors turned their backs. In one hand he held a small metallic rod.

Pethwick stared at the remarkable transformation and finally blurted out:

"Did you break loose from the handcuffs and set fire to our tent?"

"The fire was quite accidental," assured the man from One. "I did it with this focusing-rod when I got rid of your quaint old manacles."

"Focusing-rod," caught up Standifer, for, notwithstanding all he had suffered at the hands of Mr. Three, the pride of a flattered author and the remarkable sale of his books left him with a kindly feeling in his heart for the fellow.

"Yes, focusing-rod."

"What does it focus?"

"Wireless power."

"We have transmission of wireless power in America," observed the Professor, "but that is certainly the most compact terminal I ever saw."

Mr. Three glanced at the rod in his hand.

"Oh, yes, this is one of the primitive instruments. I fancy this came into use among thinking creatures along with fire, the keystone of the arch and the old-fashioned seventy-two-mile gun. They were important additions to human knowledge, but their discoverers and the dates of their discovery are lost in prehistoric eras."

For a moment Mr. Three sat pensively in the sunshine, his mind dwelling on that misty time in the land of One when some unrecorded genius found out how to focus wireless power with a little metal rod. No doubt to this mysterious man the principle of the rod appeared so simple that any rational creature would know it.

Presently he came out of his reverie and waved his focusing bar down the valley.

"You men," he directed, "will follow the rest of the quarry down the river—everything must go!"

For a moment the scientists stared at him, not understanding.

"What is it?" inquired Standifer.

"Follow the quarry down the valley and be quick about it," snapped the yellow man brusquely.

An indignant flush swept over Pethwick.

"You must be crazy, Three. We'll do as we please."

"Why should we go?"" inquired Demetriovich with his academic suavity.

Mr. Three tapped impatiently with his rod on the boulder.

"So our commander can select specimens to carry to One," he explained briefly.

"Oh, I see," cried Pethwick, somewhat mollified. "He wants us to help him select the animals, as we are naturalists."

For once in their intercourse, Mr. Three showed genuine surprise. He sprang to his feet and stared at them.

"You help him select! You!" The gnome broke into the most insulting of laughter. "You bunch of idiots, he is going to select one of you as a specimen to carry to One!" Here he threw off his brief tolerance of opposition and shouted, "Forward, march! I don't want to have to use force!"

For a moment the men stood almost paralyzed with amazement. Mr. Three evidently read the mental state, for he put a hand over his mouth to conceal his grin and to maintain his air of grim authority.

Pethwick first organized active resistance. Pablo Pasca still stood with his rifle at ready. Pethwick whispered sharply to the Indian:

"Get him!"

Almost by reflex action, the Zambo swung his rifle on Mr. Three and fired.

At the same moment Pablo staggered backward as if he had received a powerful blow out of the air. His rifle clattered to the stones. At the same instant Pethwick felt a sensation like a strong electric shock. Standifer grunted and clapped a hand to his already wounded leg.

At this act of war the party of scientists threw themselves flat behind boulders. Pethwick adjusted his rifle with hands shaking from his shock and then peered around his shelter for a glimpse of Mr. Three. He saw the yellow man still standing on the boulder. The engineer eased his rifle around unsteadily. The head of the gun wavered about the big painted head. With a determined effort the engineer settled it on his target. He was just squeezing the trigger when tingling knots rushed through his arms, legs and body, stiffening them, flashing fire in his brain, beating him with a thousand prickly hammers. It was an electric shock. He flattened under it, squirming and twisting.

The moment his thought of opposition vanished in pain the shock ceased.

All three white men and the Indian lay motionless. The only sound Pethwick could hear was an occasional groan from Standifer and the faint patter of passing animals.

A ray of sardonic amusement fluttered through the engineer's dizzy brain—the DeLong Geographical Expedition captured as a curious species of lower animals.

Sudden hearty laughter from the nearby boulder told the Engineer that Mr. Three had caught the jest and was enjoying it. Pethwick flushed angrily.

After this convincing contest with the focusing-rod the expedition abandoned resistance and surrendered themselves as prisoners of war, or perhaps it would be more accurate to say prisoners of science.

Although Pablo had shot at Mr. Three, the strange being regarded it no more than if a cat had scratched at him. Instead of being angry, he really tried to comfort the men. He told them only one of their number would be taken as a specimen to the land of One; the person chosen would be retained alive and, if he proved tractable, he would undoubtedly be allowed to run at large within certain limits and might be taught simple tricks wherewith to amuse the visitors at the zoo; such as playing a simple game of chess on one board.

This may or may not have been a sarcastic fling at the feeble game of chess which Pethwick had just played; at any rate the thought of playing endless games of chess through the bars of a zoological cage filled the engineer with nausea. No doubt on one side of him would be a monkey begging for peanuts and on the other a surly orang. For Pethwick did not doubt the specimen selected would be classed among the simians.

As they walked along the engineer thought up a new line of defense. He began to threaten Mr. Three with the American Army and Navy. He told the yellow man this expedition was American and their capture would be no small affair. They were a famous scientific body. They would be missed. Their abduction would mean a war between the land of One and the whole League of Nations.

At this Mr. Three interrupted incredulously:

"Do you creatures really compose a scientific body?"

Pethwick was so cut by the remark that he Stopped talking and walked along in silence.

The professor plied his captor with many questions. He discovered that the men from One had a portable furnace and were extracting radium from the outcrop of pitchblende in the valley. The mysterious burned places which Pethwick had noted in his journal were spots where the furnace had been operated. The strange lights which the expedition had seen on several occasions were the men moving the furnace from one place to another. Mr. Three explained that they always moved the furnace at night; it was difficult to do this during the day because the sun's rays created an etheric storm.

The yellow man's conversation entertained the white men notwithstanding their uncertain fate. Pablo Pasca, however, trembled on the verge of collapse. He knew he was in the hands of the imps of Satan. Now and then Pethwick heard him groan.

"Oh, Mother of Heaven! Oh, if I could get back to the garrote! Poor Cesare Ruano, in torment without his skin—or the ring he meant to be garroted in!"

Animals still rushed past the party and behind them came the yellow beaters, scaring up the game.

It was useless for anything to hide from these terrible men with their focusing-rods. Evidently they could sense an animal's fright and locate it as an ordinary man can locate a sound. As soon as they found something in a covert, a slight electric shock sent it headlong after the other animals.

For the first time in his life Pethwick felt some kinship for the lower animals. He, too, was in the *battue*, one with the foxes and rabbits that fluttered past him. For ages man had slaughtered the lower animals exactly as the men from One were doing now.

And just as man had annihilated the bison, the apteryx, the dodo, so no doubt this new and more powerful race from One would exterminate man and his cities, his works of art and his sciences. The vision of a charnel world painted itself on his depressed imagi-nation—a wiping out of existing races and a repeopling by these yellow Incans. Compared to such a conflict the late world war would be trivial.

Amid the day-dream of Armageddon, the engineer heard M. Demetriovich ejaculate to himself:

"So it is a German Bolshevist undertaking after all. There's a Zeppelin!"

Pethwick looked up suddenly. The prisoners had rounded a turn in the valley. Not more than three hundred yards distant rose an enormous structure in the shape of a Zeppelin. It required a sec-ond glance to observe this fact, as the huge creation stood on its end instead of lying horizontal as do the ordinary flying-ships.

Instead of being made of cloth, this Zeppelin had a skin of white metal, no doubt aluminum. Indeed, for the first time a dirigible had been constructed that had the staunchness and air-worthiness that deserved the name ship. This was no mere bubble of varnished cloth.

It was enormous. It rose some seven hundred and fifty feet high, an amazing skyscraper of silver whose fulgor was enhanced by the dark and melancholy background of the Infernal Valley.

The immense vessel rested on its stern which tapered down to perhaps four feet in diameter. It was shored up with long metal rods anchored in the earth. The rods, some hundred feet long, were inserted in the airship just where its great barrel began to taper to its stern.

Five hundred feet up the side of the cylinder Pethwick noticed the controlling planes, which looked exceedingly small for the vast bulk they were designed to pilot. When the engineer pointed these out to the professor, M. Demetriovich seemed surprised.

"Do you realize, Pethwick, what their small size indicates? The speed of this ship through the air must be prodigious if these tiny controls grip the air with sufficient leverage to direct this monster."

Then the old scientist went on to commend the novel idea of landing the dirigible on her stern. It did away with wide maneuvering to gain altitude. This aluminum dirigible could drop into a hole slightly larger than her own diameter and launch herself out of it straight at the sky. It was an admirable stroke.

Workmen dotted the vessel's side, scrubbing the bright skin as assiduously as a crew painting a man-of-war. Pethwick could distinguish this scrubbing force up for two or three hundred feet. Beyond that he caught only glimmers of moving dots amid the reflections of the sun.

The organization of the crew seemed cast along military lines. Small squads of men or soldiers marched in exact ranks and files over the valley to gather up the animals stunned by the focusing-rods.

At first Pethwick had not observed these animals, but a more careful look showed him a number of specimens that had been struck down as they passed the ship. The big-headed yellow men were collecting these in cages, evidently for exhibition purposes when they returned to the extraordinary land from which they came. The slaughter had not been wasteful. Only one member of each species had been taken.

The yellow men worked at top speed and were plainly under the continual barked orders of soldiery, but oddly enough not a sound was heard. The whole control was mental. The silence gave Pethwick the strange impression that he was looking at a gigantic cinema.

A movement behind the white men caused them to look around. A file of yellow soldiers was moving toward the dirigible, coming from the direction of their burned camp up the valley. These men bore the mounted skeletons which the DeLong Geographical Expedition had observed when they first entered the strange valley of the Rio Infiernillo.

The removal of these objects suggested to Pethwick that the men from One and their super-dirigible would soon sail from the valley. A great curiosity to see the departure seized the engineer. He looked for the big driving propellers which he thought must draw the ship, but he could see none.

At that moment four soldiers with a large metal cage approached the DeLong Geographical party. At the same time on one of the upper rounds of the airship, some seventy-five feet above the base, appeared a yellow man with a peculiar scintillating star fixed to his big yellow head. The personage looked directly toward the explorers but said nothing.

When he looked Mr. Three drew himself up and saluted in military fashion.

Then, evidently for the benefit of his captors, Mr. Three answered aloud the mental questions which his superior must have put to him. Here are the words of the one-sided conversation:

"Yes, sir."

"No, sir."

"Ordinary ruby-blooded mammals, sir, with intelligence somewhat higher than monkeys, sir.

"They communicate their simple thoughts exactly as monkeys do, sir—by chattering.

"They are absolutely insensible to all mental vibrations, sir, more completely so than the four-legged animals.

"I would suggest you take all five. They will prove very amusing, sir, in the national zoo. Their attempts to deceive each other and to deceive even me, sir, are as good as a farce. I believe you will find them much more humorous than chimpanzees or the ordinary monkeys, sir.

"Sorry you can't. In that case I suggest we take the brown one. His color is the nearest human. Then, too, he has the best physique. None of them have any minds to speak of.

"Very well, sir."

Here Mr. Three saluted stiffly and directed the four workmen with the cage toward Pablo Pasca.

As the laborers lowered their cage and started for the half-breed, Pablo's eyes almost started from his head. He whirled to run, but seemed to realize the hopelessness of trying to escape from the amazing agility of the men from One. Next moment he whipped out a knife and dashed into the midst of his assailants, slashing and stabbing like one possessed.

But the soldiers of One had feline agility. They dodged, whipped under his blows like game-cocks. One leaped straight over the heads of his comrades and landed headlong on the Zambo. It was an unfortunate leap. Pablo's blade caught him in the shoulder and a dark liquid spurted out.

In the instant of withdrawing the blade, the yellow men seized the half-breed's arms and legs. They went down with the Zambo in a struggling pile. Pablo kicked, bit, twisted his knife with a wrist movement, trying to cut something. But the yellow men worked swiftly and methodically.

"Quick!" commanded Mr. Three. "We must start in four minutes!" Then in answer to some question the yellow soldiers thought to him, "I can't use my focusing-rod. It might destroy what little mind he has."

A moment later the yellow men got to their feet with the ex-thief hanging between them by his legs and arms. The poor fellow turned an agonized face to Pethwick.

"*Senor! Senor!*" he screamed. "Save me! Save poor Pablo! Oh, Holy Mary! Sacred Mother! *Senor, Senor* Pethwick!"

His voice rose to a screech. Blood trickled from his nostrils. His face was white with fear.

Pethwick stared with wide eyes at the struggle. The injustice of this capture for scientific purposes thundered at the American's heart. Pethwick was a white man, of that race which deals justice among weaker men and carries out its judgments with its life.

At Pablo's shriek of despair something seemed to snap in Pethwick's head. He hesitated a second, then lunged into the victorious yellow men.

He never reached them. A wave of flame seemed to lap around him. Then came blackness.

When Pethwick revived, there were no more yellow men in sight. The great shining dirigible stood entirely closed and apparently lifeless. The sun was setting and its rays filled the great charnel valley with a bloody light. The dirigible looked like an enormous red water-stand. In a few minutes the lower half of the great ship was purple in shadow, while the upper half turned a deeper red. The silence was absolute. The three white men stood staring at the strange scene.

Quite suddenly from where the stern of the Zeppelin nested on the ground broke out a light of insufferable brilliancy. A luminous gas seemed to boil out in whirls of furious brightness. It spread everywhere, and in its radiance the great ship stood out in brilliant silver from stem to stern.

In that fulgor Pethwick saw the restraining rods cast off, and the dirigible from the land of One mounted straight into the green heart of the evening sky.

The moment it struck full sunlight at a height of five hundred yards it seemed caught in some tremendously strong wind, for it moved eastward with a velocity that increased by prodigious bounds. Within half a minute its light was reduced from the terrific glare of a furnace to the glow of a headlight, and then to a radiance like that of a shooting star against the darkening eastern sky.

As the watchers followed it with their eyes a strange thing happened. That white light turned to violet, then indigo blue, green, yellow, orange and red, and so faded out.

In the Valle de Rio Infiernillo lingered a phosphorescent mist that told of the first men's passing. It settled on the cliffs and crags and glowed with spectral luminosity. The men looked at each other; they too were covered with this shining stuff.

"Gentlemen," quavered M. Demetriovich, "I believe we have on us the residual emanations of radium. It will likely kill us. Let us go down to the river and wash it off."

The three men set out, stumbling through the darkness, guided somewhat by the faint light given off by their own bodies.

They waded into the black waters of the Infernal River, and began scrubbing each other furiously, trying to rid themselves of this dangerous luminosity. High above them it still shivered from cliff and crag. Presently this faded out and there reigned complete darkness and complete silence.

On the following morning, when the DeLong Geographical Expedition was about to start back for civilization they saw on the scene of the conflict between Pablo and the yellow soldiers, where the half-breed had stabbed his captors, a number of dark green stains.

On analysis this green also proved to be chlorophyll.

A COMMUNICATION FROM GILBERT DELONG, PRESIDENT OF THE DELONG GEOGRAPHICAL SOCIETY, TO THE TRUSTEES OF THE NOBEL PRIZE FOUNDATION, STOCKHOLM, SWEDEN:

Sirs: It is my privilege to bring to your attention the extraordinary journal of the DeLong Geographical Expedition into that unmapped region of Peru, in the department of Ayacucho, known as the Valle de Rio Infiernillo.

Enclosed with this journal is M. Demetriovich's able presentation of the theory that the dirigible observed in that valley was operated by the Bolshevist government of either Austria or Russia.

Also enclosed is the monograph of Mr. Herbert M. Pethwick, C.E., who presents a most interesting speculation tending to prove that the strange aircraft was a development made independently of the known civilized world by an offshoot of the ancient Incan race, depatriated by the Spaniards in 1553 A. D.

To my mind, both of these hypotheses, although brilliantly maintained, fail to take into consideration two highly significant facts which are set forth, but not greatly stressed in the record of the expedition as kept by Mr. James B. Standifer, Sec.

These two facts are, first, the serial number which served as a name of the man from One, and the other fact, that in both cases where a man from One was wounded he bled what for want of a better term must be called chlorophyllaceous blood.

From few other writers than Mr. Standifer would I accept so bizarre a statement of fact, but his power of exact and minute observation is so well attested by his well-known work, "Reindeer in Iceland," that I dare not question his strict adherence to truth.

The phenomena set forth in the journal happened. That is beyond cavil. The problem for the scientific world is their interpretation.

In handling this problem, I shall not only assume that the journal is accurate, but I shall still further assume that the being known in the record as Mr. Three told the precise truth in every statement ascribed to him.

I have every confidence in Mr. Three's probity for several reasons. First, he has no motive for prevarication. Second, a man who habitually communicates with his fellows by telepathy would not be accustomed to falsehood, since falsehood is physically impossible when a man's mind lies before his companions like an open book. Third, to a man habitually accustomed to truth, lying is a difficult and uncongenial labor. In brief, lying is like any other art; it requires practice to do it well.

In regard to the serial number, both of the above mentioned writers apparently fail to see the enormous problem it possesses. As for the chlorophyllaceous blood, our authors pass it with a vague surmise that somehow it is used in extracting gold, when the whole object of the expedition, according to Mr. Three, was not gold but radium.

Because my esteemed colleagues neglected these two critical points, their whole theories, as ably and ingeniously defended as they are, to my mind collapse into mere brilliant sophisms.

In the brief analysis herewith presented I shall touch on a number of points, among which the questions evoked by the serial number and the chlorophyll blood will be noticed in their proper places.

First, then, Mr. Three himself states that the object of the expedition was the extraction of radium from the pitchblende in the Infernal Valley. The use the men from One made of this radium was demonstrated at the departure of the dirigible, for that vessel must have been propelled by the emanations of radium. According to the description of Mr. Standifer, the ship used no screw propellers or tractors, but a powerful emanation of radium from under its stern shot the great metal cylinder upward exactly as powder propels a skyrocket.

That radium would possess such power is well known. It has been calculated that two pounds of radium would possess sufficient force to swing the earth out of its orbit.

With such power the airship would be capable of enormous speed. A high speed was guessed by M. Demetriovich when he observed the small controlling plane. However, the vastness of this speed was demonstrated by Mr. Standifer in the last paragraph of his account, by his curious observation that the airship, as seen against the evening sky, turned violet, indigo blue, green, yellow, orange, red and then was lost. In other words, it ran through the whole spectrum from the most rapid to the lowest vibrations per second and then vanished.

What is the meaning of this significant detail?

Allow me to recall an analogy in sound. The tone of a bell on a train departing at high speed becomes lower in pitch. This is because the vibrations reach the ear at longer intervals.

Apply that to the change of light observed on the airship. Then the vessel must have been withdrawing at such a speed that it lowered the "pitch" of light vibrations from white to red and finally cancelled its light in blackness.

The only conclusion to be drawn from this is that at the time of the light's extinction, the mysterious metal cylinder was hurtling through space at the speed of light itself; that is to say, at a speed of one hundred and eighty-six thousand miles per second.

Observe that I say, "space," not air. In the first place such a speed in air would fuse any metal. But there is another and a better reason.

It requires the average human eye one-twentieth of a second to perceive a color change. If Mr. Standifer had observed these color changes at the highest possible nerve rate, the operation would have acquired seven-twentieths of a second. Let us assume it required half a second. During that interval the cylinder would have traversed, at the speed of light, ninety-three thousand miles in a straight line. That is more than eleven times the diameter of this globe. Therefore it is far outside of our atmosphere. Also it proves the mysterious vessel was not bound for Austria or Russia. It was leaving the earth.

How was this velocity attained?

I submit by the reaction of radium upon sunlight.

As every schoolboy knows, the drift of a comet's tail is caused by the pressure of light. As soon as this airship arose to the height of about five hundred yards into sunlight, it began to drift eastward with a rapidly increasing velocity. In other words, the metal skin of the ship, which Mr. Pethwick took for aluminum, was probably a much lighter metal—a metal so light that it was capable of being buffeted along in the surf of sunlight. Now if the ship were propelled merely on the barbs of sunbeams, it would have attained the velocity of light. But the velocity of radium emanations is one-fifteenth that of light. So by running down the light current, and allowing the radium to react against the sunbeams, a speed of one and one-fifteenth the velocity of light may be generated; that is one-hundred and ninety-eight thousand miles per second.

Such speed would admit of interplanetary travel.

However, it is probable the men from One could accelerate the radiation from radium by electrical or chemical means. They may have learned to boil the metal as men boil water. In such case the pressure of its radiation would be vastly increased, and with it the possible speed of the ship. This gives an unknown and problematical power of transition far beyond the velocity of light. At such rate a journey even to one of the fixed stars would be within the realm of possibility.

We may therefore with prudence hypothesize that the mysterious ether ship observed in the Valley of the Rio Infiernillo was an interstellar voyager stopping by the earth as a coaling port to refuel with radium.

However, as it is improbable that the ether ship was going beyond the confines of our solar system, a speculation as to what planet the men from One were bound may be reached by noting the day and the hour the ship sailed from the earth.

As our earth swings around the ecliptic, it would be possible for interplanetary mariners to obtain a favorable current of sunlight in any direction. No doubt the navigator of the ether ship was bound for one of the planets in opposition to the sun at the time of the ship's departure. That is to say the yellow men were sailing for either Neptune or Jupiter.

That the men were returning to some planet much larger than the earth is suggested by their small size and extraordinary agility. No doubt these men found the gravitation of the earth slight compared with the attraction to which they were accustomed. This fact gave them extraordinary vigor.

Now let us consider the serial number that formed Mr. Three's name. It was 1753-12,657,109654-3.

This gives rise to a most interesting speculation:

The probable number of the units contained in a series, when any serial number is given, is computed by multiplying together the component parts of the serial number.

For instance, if one has two series of twelve each, the whole number of objects would be twenty-four. If one had six major series of two subseries of twelve each, the total number of units would be 144.

Applying this idea to Mr. Three's serial number, one would find the total probable population of Jupiter, or the land of One, by multiplying the component parts of this number together. This reached the enormous number product of 14,510,894,489,356. That is to say, fourteen and a half quadrillions.

This utterly quashes the Incan hypothesis. There is not room in South America for fourteen and a half quadrillion people—there is not room on the globe for such a number. That, in fact, is the probable population of either Neptune or Jupiter. For sake of simplicity, we will assume it is Jupiter.

No wonder, then, with such an inconceivable population, the inhabitants of Jupiter are militarized. No wonder they suggested Bolshevism to M. Demetriovich.

With such masses of life, all other species of animals are probably extinct. This would explain why the Jovians were so eager to capture specimens of fauna as well as radium.

The last point in the record, the chlorophyllaceous blood, has been to me the most difficult to find any analogy for in our terrestrial experience.

However, we must needs grasp the problem firmly and proceed with considered but ample steps toward any conclusion to which it leads.

Chlorophyll is the coloring matter in plants. It possesses the power of utilizing energy directly from sunlight. There is no reason to doubt that in the veins of the Jovians it still retains that peculiar power.

With such an extraordinary fluid in his veins, it might be possible for a Jovian to stand in the sunshine and to obtain from it energy and strength, just as a human being obtains energy and strength by eating vegetables that have stood in the sunshine.

In fact, the first method is no more amazing than the second. If, indeed, there be a difference, undoubtedly our human method is the more fantastic. The idea of obtaining energy from sunshine, not by standing in it, as any one would suppose, but by eating something else that has stood in it, is grotesque to the verge of madness.

Let us pursue that thought. No doubt in a concourse of fourteen and a half quadrillion inhabitants space would be so dear that there would be no vacant or tillable land. Therefore on Jupiter every man must absorb whatever sunshine he received. There would be no such thing as eating.

This accounts for the amazement of Mr. Three at seeing Standifer eat his lunch.

To put the same idea in another form—the crew of the ether ship were flora, not fauna.

This accounts for the yellow pear-like texture of their skins. No doubt the young Jovians are green in color. It would also explain why Mr. Three was entirely without anger when attacked and without pity for Pablo's pleadings, or for Standifer when he was burned, or for Ruano when he was murdered.

Anger, pity, love and hatred are the emotional traits of the mammalia. They have been developed through epochs of maternal protection. It is not developed in plants.

Mr. Three was a plant.

It would also explain why Mr. Three took only one animal of each species, instead of a male and a female. Sex is perhaps unknown on Jupiter. Mr. Three was perhaps expecting his animals to bud or sprout.

The last question to be broached is, How is it possible for plant life to possess mobility?

I wish to recall to the inquirer that here on our own globe the spores of the algae and other plants of that order have the power of swimming freely in the sea. Still, they are plants—plants just as mobile as fishes. They become stationary only at a later stage of their development.

Now, if for some reason these algae spores could retain their mobility, the result would be a walking, swimming or crawling plant.

The line between animal and plant life has never been so clearly drawn. It seems mere fortuity that the first forebear of animal life swam about and caught its sustenance by enveloping it in its gelatinous droplet, rather than by adhering to a reef and drawing its energy directly from the sun.

If that far-off protozoa had clung to the reef, the reader of this paragraph might have been a sycamore or a tamarind—he would not have been a man.

Now Mr. Three's forefather evidently crawled out of the sea into the sunshine but found nothing to envelop; therefore he followed the lip of the Jovian tide up and down, drawing his energy from the sun's rays. The result was a walking vegetable—in short, Mr. Three.

However, gentlemen of the Nobel Prize Foundation, it is not to press the views of the writer that this note was written, but to offer for your consideration as candidates for the fifty thousand dollar Nobel Prize for the year 1920 the names of:

Demetrios Z. Demetriovich, Herbert M. Pethwick and James B. Standifer.

One of the five prizes for 1920 will be awarded to the man or group who have done the greatest service for the advancement of human knowledge during the twelvemonth.

These men, by their observations, taken at the peril of their lives, have blazed new avenues for the use of radium. Their journal suggests the feasibility of the universal use of telepathy, a development now confined to a few adepts and belittled by the unthinking. Their discoveries reveal the possibility of interplanetary travel and the vast commercial emoluments such a trade would possess. Their journal suggests to the ambitious soul of man a step beyond world citizenship, and that is stellar citizenship. It is a great step and will profoundly modify human thought.

In the past, gentlemen, epoch-making discoveries have been too often rewarded by Bridewell or Bedlam; it is gratifying to know that we have reached a stage of civilization where the benefactors of their race receive instead honor and emolument.

> Gilbert H. DeLong.
> New York City,
> May, 1920.

Note by the Transcriber: It may interest the reader to know that the Nobel Prize was awarded to Dr. Gilbert H. DeLong, for the series of brilliant inductions set forth above.—T. S.

THE THING FROM—OUTSIDE
GEORGE ALLAN ENGLAND

THEY SAT ABOUT THEIR CAMP-FIRE, that little party of Americans re-treating southward from Hudson Bay before the on-coming men-ace of the great cold. Sat there, stolid under the awe of the North, under the uneasiness that the day's trek had laid upon their souls. The three men smoked. The two women huddled close to each other. Fireglow picked their faces from the gloom of night among the dwarf firs. A splashing murmur told of the Albany River's haste to escape from the wilderness, and reach the Bay.

"I don't see what there was in a mere circular print on a rock-ledge to make our guides desert," said Professor Thorburn. His voice was as dry as his whole personality. "Most extraordinary."

"*They* knew what it was, all right," answered Jandron, geolo-gist of the party. "So do I." He rubbed his cropped mustache. His eyes glinted grayly. "I've seen prints like that before. That was on the Labrador. And I've seen things happen, where they were."

"Something surely happened to our guides, before they'd got a mile into the bush," put in the Professor's wife; while Vivian, her sister, gazed into the fire that revealed her as a beauty, not to be spoiled even by a tam and a rough-knit sweater. "Men don't shoot wildly, and scream like that, unless—"

"They're all three dead now, anyhow," put in Jandron. "So *they're* out of harm's way. While we—well, we're two hundred and fifty wicked miles from the C.P.R. rails."

"Forget it, Jandy!" said Marr, the journalist. "We're just suf-fering from an attack of nerves, that's all. Give me a fill of 'baccy.

Thanks. We'll all be better in the morning. Ho-hum! Now, speaking of spooks and such—"

He launched into an account of how he had once exposed a fraudulent spiritualist, thus proving—to his own satisfaction—that nothing existed beyond the scope of mankind's everyday life. But nobody gave him much heed. And silence fell upon the little night-encampment in the wilds; a silence that was ominous.

Pale, cold stars watched down from spaces infinitely far beyond man's trivial world.

Next day, stopping for chow on a ledge miles upstream, Jandron discovered another of the prints. He cautiously summoned the other two men. They examined the print, while the women-folk were busy by the fire. A harmless thing the marking seemed; only a ring about four inches in diameter, a kind of cup-shaped depression with a raised center. A sort of glaze coated it, as if the granite had been fused by heat.

Jandron knelt, a well-knit figure in bright mackinaw and canvas leggings, and with a shaking finger explored the smooth curve of the print in the rock. His brows contracted as he studied it.

"We'd better get along out of this as quick as we can," said he in an unnatural voice. "You've got your wife to protect, Thorburn, and I,—well, I've got Vivian. And—"

"*You* have?" nipped Marr. The light of an evil jealously gleamed in his heavy-lidded look. "What you need is an alienist."

"Really, Jandron," the Professor admonished, "you mustn't let your imagination run away with you."

"I suppose it's imagination that keeps this print cold!" the geologist retorted. His breath made faint, swirling coils of vapor above it.

"Nothing but a pot-hole," judged Thorburn, bending his spare, angular body to examine the print. The Professor's vitality all seemed centered in his big-bulged skull that sheltered a marvellous thinking machine. Now he put his lean hand to the base of his brain, rubbing the back of his head as if it ached. Then, under what seemed some powerful compulsion, he ran his bony finger around the print in the rock.

"By Jove, but it *is* cold!" he admitted. "And looks as if it had been stamped right out of the stone. Extraordinary!"

"Dissolved out, you mean," corrected the geologist. "By cold."

The journalist laughed mockingly.

"Wait till I write this up!" he sneered. "'Noted Geologist Declares Frigid Ghost Dissolves Granite!'"

Jandron ignored him. He fetched a little water from the river and poured it into the print.

"Ice!" ejaculated the Professor. "Solid ice!"

"Frozen in a second," added Jandron, while Marr frankly stared. "And it'll never melt, either. I tell you, I've seen some of these rings before; and every time, horrible things have happened. Incredible things! Something burned this ring out of the stone—burned it out with the cold interstellar space. Something that can import cold as a permanent quality of matter. Something that can kill matter, and totally remove it."

"Of course that's all sheer poppycock," the journalist tried to laugh, but his brain felt numb.

"This something, this Thing," continued Jandron, "is a Thing that can't be killed by bullets. It's what caught our guides on the barrens, as they ran away—poor fools!"

A shadow fell across the print in the rock. Mrs. Thorburn had come up, was standing there. She had overheard a little of what Jandron had been saying.

"Nonsense!" she tried to exclaim, but she was shivering so she could hardly speak.

That night, after a long afternoon of paddling and portaging—laboring against inhibitions like those in a nightmare—they camped on shelving rocks that slanted to the river.

"After all," said the Professor, when supper was done, "we mustn't get into a panic. I know extraordinary things are reported from the wilderness, and more than one man has come out, raving. But we, by Jove! with our superior brains—we aren't going to let Nature play us any tricks!"

"And of course," added his wife, her arm about Vivian, "everything in the universe *is* a natural force. There's really no supernatural, at all."

"Admitted," Jandron replied. "But how about things *outside* the universe?"

"And they call you a scientist?" gibed Marr; but the Professor leaned forward, his brows knit.

"Hm!" he grunted. A little silence fell.

"You don't mean, really," asked Vivian, "that you think there's life and intelligence—Outside?"

Jandron looked at the girl. Her beauty, haloed with ruddy gold from the firelight, was a pain to him as he answered:

"Yes, I do. And dangerous life, too. I know what I've seen, in the North Country. I know what I've seen!"

Silence again, save for the crepitation of the flames, the fall of an ember, the murmur of the current. Darkness narrowed the wilderness to just that circle of flickering light ringed by the forest and the river, brooded over by the pale stars.

"Of course you can't expect a scientific man to take you seriously," commented the Professor.

"I know what I've seen! I tell you there's Something entirely outside man's knowledge."

"Poor fellow!" scoffed the journalist; but even as he spoke his hand pressed his forehead.

"There are Things at work," Jandron affirmed, with dogged persistence. He lighted his pipe with a blazing twig. Its flame revealed his face drawn, lined. "Things. Things that reckon with us no more than we do with ants. Less, perhaps."

The flame of the twig died. Night stood closer, watching.

"Suppose there are?" the girl asked. "What's that got to do with these prints in the rock?"

"*They*," answered Jandron, "are marks left by one of those Things. Footprints, maybe. That Thing is near us, here and now!"

Marr's laugh broke a long stillness.

"And you," he exclaimed, "with an A. M. and a B. S. to write after your name."

"If you knew more," retorted Jandron, "you'd know a devilish sight less. It's only ignorance that's cock-sure."

"But," dogmatized the Professor, "no scientist of any standing has ever admitted any outside interference with this planet."

"No, and for thousands of years nobody ever admitted that the world was round, either. What I've seen, I know."

"Well, what *have* you seen?" asked Mrs. Thorburn, shivering.

"You'll excuse me, please, for not going into that just now."

"You mean," the Professor demanded, dryly, "if the—hm!—this supposititious Thing wants to—?"

"It'll do any infernal thing it takes a fancy to, yes! If it happens to want us—"

"But what could Things like that want of us? Why should They come here, at all?"

"Oh, for various reasons. For inanimate objects, at times, and then again for living beings. They've come here lots of times, I tell you," Jandron asserted with strange irritation, "and got what They wanted, and then gone away to—Somewhere. If one of Them happens to want us, for any reason, It will take us, that's all. If It doesn't want us, It will ignore us, as we'd ignore gorillas in Africa if we were looking for gold. But if it was gorilla-fur we wanted, that would be different for the gorillas, wouldn't it?"

"What in the world," asked Vivian, "could a—well, a Thing from Outside want of *us?*"

"What do men want, say, of guinea-pigs? Men experiment with 'em, of course. Superior beings use inferior, for their own ends. To assume that man is the supreme product of evolution is gross self-conceit. Might not some superior Thing want to experiment with human beings?"

"But how?" demanded Mars.

"The human brain is the most highly-organized form of matter known to this planet. Suppose, now—"

"Nonsense!" interrupted the Professor. "All hands to the sleeping-bags, and no more of this. I've got a wretched headache. Let's anchor in Blanket Bay!"

He, and both the women, turned in. Jandron and Marr sat a while longer by the fire. They kept plenty of wood piled on it, too, for an unnatural chill transfixed the night-air. The fire burned strangely blue, with greenish flicks of flame.

At length, after vast acerbities of disagreement, the geologist and the newspaperman sought their sleeping-bags. The fire was a comfort. Not that a fire could avail a pin's weight against a Thing from interstellar space, but subjectively it was a comfort. The instincts of a million years, centering around protection by fire, cannot be obliterated.

After a time—worn out by a day of nerve-strain and of battling with swift currents, of flight from Something invisible, intangible—they all slept.

The depths of space, star-sprinkled, hung above them with vastness immeasurable, cold beyond all understanding of the human mind.

Jandron woke first, in a red dawn.

He blinked at the fire, as he crawled from his sleeping-bag. The fire was dead; and yet it had not burned out. Much wood remained unconsumed, charred over, as if some gigantic extinguisher had in the night been lowered over it.

"*Hmmm!*" growled Jandron. He glanced about him, on the ledge. "Prints, too. I might have known!"

He aroused Marr. Despite all the journalist's mocking hostility, Jandron felt more in common with this man of his own age than with the Professor, who was close on sixty.

"Look here, now!" said he. "*It* has been all around here. See? *It* put out our fire—maybe the fire annoyed *It*, some way—and *It* walked round us, everywhere." His gray eyes smouldered. "I guess, by gad, you've got to admit facts, now!"

The journalist could only shiver and stare.

"Lord, what a head I've got on me, this morning!" he chattered. He rubbed his forehead with a shaking hand, and started for the river. Most of his assurance had vanished. He looked badly done up.

"Well, what say?" demanded Jandron. "See these fresh prints?"

"Damn the prints!" retorted Mars, and fell to grumbling some unintelligible thing. He washed unsteadily, and remained crouching at the river's lip, inert, numbed.

Jandron, despite a gnawing at the base of his, brain, carefully examined the ledge. He found prints scattered everywhere, and some even on the river-bottom near the shore. Wherever water had collected in the prints on the rock, it had frozen hard. Each print in the river-bed, too, was white with ice. Ice that the rushing current could not melt.

"Well, by gad!" he exclaimed. He lighted his pipe and tried to think. Horribly afraid—yes, he felt horribly afraid, but determined. Presently, as a little power of concentration came back, he noticed that all the prints were in straight lines, each mark about two feet from the next.

"*It* was observing us while we slept," said Jandron.

"What nonsense are you talking, eh?" demanded Marr. His dark, heavy face sagged. "Fire, now, and grub!"

He got up and shuffled unsteadily away from the river. Then he stopped with a jerk, staring.

"Look! Look a' that axe!" he gulped, pointing.

Jandron picked up the axe, by the handle, taking good care not to touch the steel. The blade was white-furred with frost. And deep into it, punching out part of the edge, one of the prints was stamped.

"This metal," said he, "is clean gone. It's been absorbed. The Thing doesn't recognize any difference in materials. Water and steel and rock are all the same to It."

"You're crazy!" snarled the journalist. "How could a Thing travel on one leg, hopping along, making marks like that?"

"It could roll, if it was disk-shaped. And—"

A cry from the Professor turned them. Thorburn was stumbling toward them, hands out and tremulous.

"My wife—!" he choked.

Vivian was kneeling beside her sister, frightened, dazed.

"Something's happened!" stammered the Professor. "Here—come here—!"

Mrs. Thorburn was beyond any power of theirs, to help. She was still breathing; but her respirations were stertorous, and a complete paralysis had stricken her. Her eyes, half-open and expressionless, showed pupils startlingly dilated. No resources of the party's drug-kit produced the slightest effect on the woman.

The next half-hour was a confused panic, breaking camp, getting Mrs. Thorburn into a canoe, and leaving that accursed place, with a furious energy of terror that could no longer reason. Upstream, ever up against the swirl of the current the party fought, driven by horror. With no thought of food or drink, paying no heed to landmarks, lashed forward only by the mad desire to be gone, the three men and the girl flung every ounce of their energy into the paddles. Their panting breath mingled with the sound of swirling eddies. A mist-blurred sun brooded over the northern wilds. Unheeded, hosts of black-flies sang high-pitched keenings all about the fugitives. On either hand the forest waited, watched.

Only after two hours of sweating toil had brought exhaustion did they stop, in the shelter of a cove where black waters circled, foam-flecked. There they found the Professor's wife—she was dead.

Nothing remained to do but bury her. At first Thorburn would not hear of it. Like a madman he insisted that through all hazards he would fetch the body out. But no—impossible. So, after a terrible time, he yielded.

In spite of her grief, Vivian was admirable. She understood what must be done. It was her voice that said the prayers; her hand that—lacking flowers—laid the fir boughs on the cairn. The Professor was dazed past doing anything, saying anything.

Toward mid-afternoon, the party landed again, many miles upriver. Necessity forced them to eat. Fire would not burn. Every time they lighted it, it smouldered and went out with a heavy, greasy smoke. The fugitives ate cold food and drank water, then shoved off in two canoes and once more fled.

In the third canoe, hauled to the edge of the forest, lay all the rock-specimens, data and curios, scientific instruments. The party kept only Marr's diary, a compass, supplies, fire-arms and medicine-kit.

"We can find the things we've left—sometime," said Jandron, noting the place well. "Sometime—after It has gone."

"And bring the body out," added Thorburn. Tears, for the first time, wet his eyes. Vivian said nothing. Marr tried to light his pipe. He seemed to forget that nothing, not even tobacco, would burn now.

Vivian and Jandron occupied one canoe. The other carried the Professor and Marr. Thus the power of the two canoes was about the same. They kept well together, up-stream.

The fugitives paddled and portaged with a dumb, desperate energy. Toward evening they struck into what they believed to be the Mamattawan. A mile up this, as the blurred sun faded beyond a wilderness of ominous silence, they camped. Here they made determined efforts to kindle fire. Not even alcohol from the drug-kit would start it. Cold, they mumbled a little food; cold, they huddled into their sleeping-bags, there to lie with darkness leaden on their fear. After a long time, up over a world void of all sound save the river-flow, slid an amber moon notched by the ragged tops of the conifers. Even the wail of a timber-wolf would have come as welcome relief; but no wolf howled.

Silence and night enfolded them. And everywhere they felt that *It* was watching.

Foolishly enough, as a man will do foolish things in a crisis, Jandron laid his revolver outside his sleeping-bag, in easy reach. His thought—blurred by a strange, drawing headache—was:

"If *It* touches Vivian, I'll shoot!"

He realized the complete absurdity of trying to shoot a visitant from interstellar space; from the Fourth Dimension, maybe. But Jandron's ideas seemed tangled. Nothing would come right. He lay there, absorbed in a kind of waking nightmare. Now and then, rising on an elbow, he hearkened; all in vain. Nothing so much as stirred.

His thought drifted to better days, when all had been health, sanity, optimism; when nothing except jealousy of Marr, as concerned Vivian, had troubled him. Days when the sizzle of the frying-pan over friendly coals had made friendly wilderness music; when the wind and the northern star, the whirr of the reel, the whispering vortex of the paddle in clear water had all been things of joy. Yes, and when a certain happy moment had, through some word or look of the girl, seemed to promise his heart's desire. But now—

"Damn it, I'll save *her*, anyhow!" he swore with savage intensity, knowing all the while that what was to be, would be, unmitigably. Do ants, by any waving of antenna, stay the down-crushing foot of man?

Next morning, and the next, no sign of the Thing appeared. Hope revived that possibly It might have flitted away elsewhere; back, perhaps, to outer space. Many were the miles the urging paddles spurned behind. The fugitives calculated that a week more would bring them to the railroad. Fire burned again. Hot food and drink helped, wonderfully. But where were the fish?

"Most extraordinary," all at once said the Professor, at noon-day camp. He had become quite rational again. "Do you realize, Jandron, we've seen no traces of life in some time?"

The geologist nodded. Only too clearly he had noted just that, but he had been keeping still about it.

"That's so, too!" chimed in Marr, enjoying the smoke that some incomprehensible turn of events was letting him have. "Not a musk-rat or beaver. Not even a squirrel or bird."

"Not so much as a gnat or black-fly!" the Professor added. Jandron suddenly realized that he would have welcomed even those.

That afternoon, Marr fell into a suddenly vile temper. He mumbled curses against the guides, the current, the portages, everything. The Professor seemed more cheerful. Vivian complained of an oppressive headache. Jandron gave her the last of the aspirin tablets; and as he gave them, took her hand in his.

"I'll see *you* through, anyhow," said he. "I don't count, now. Nobody counts, only you!"

She gave him a long, silent look. He saw the sudden glint of tears in her eyes; felt the pressure of her hand, and knew they two had never been so near each other as in that moment under the shadow of the Unknown.

Next day—or it may have been two days later, for none of them could be quite sure about the passage of time—they came to a de-serted lumber-camp. Even more than two days might have passed; because now their bacon was all gone, and only coffee, tobacco, beef-cubes and pilot-bread remained. The lack of fish and game had cut alarmingly into the duffle-bag. That day—whatever day it may have been—all four of them suffered terribly from headache of an odd, ring-shaped kind, as if something circular were being pressed down about their heads. The Professor said it was the sun that made his head ache. Vivian laid it to the wind and the gleam of the swift water, while Marr claimed it was the heat. Jandron wondered at all this, inasmuch as he plainly saw that the river had almost stopped flowing, and the day had become still and overcast.

They dragged their canoes upon a rotting stage of fir-poles and explored the lumber-camp; a mournful place set back in an old "slash," now partly overgrown with scrub poplar, maple and birch. The log buildings, covered with tar-paper partly torn from the pole roofs, were of the usual North Country type. Obviously the place had not been used for years. Even the landing-stage where once logs had been rolled into the stream had sagged to decay.

"I don't quite get the idea of this," Marr exclaimed. "Where did the logs go to? Downstream, of course. But *that* would take 'em to Hudson Bay, and there's no market for spruce timber or pulpwood at Hudson Bay." He pointed down the current.

"You're entirely mistaken," put in the Professor. "Any fool could see this river runs the other way. A log thrown in here would go down toward the St. Lawrence!"

"But then," asked the girl, "why can't we drift back to civilization?"

The Professor retorted: "Just what we *have* been doing, all along! Extraordinary, that I have to explain the obvious!" He walked away in a huff.

"I don't know but he's right, at that," half admitted the journalist. "I've been thinking almost the same thing, myself, the past day or two—that is, ever since the sun shifted."

"What do you mean, shifted?" from Jandron.

"You haven't noticed it?"

"But there's been no sun at all, for at least two days!"

"Hanged if I'll waste time arguing with a lunatic!" Marr growled. He vouchsafed no explanation of what he meant by the sun's having "shifted," but wandered off, grumbling.

"What *are* we going to do?" the girl appealed to Jandron. The sight of her solemn, frightened eyes, of her palm-outward hands and (at last) her very feminine fear, constricted Jandron's heart.

"We're going through, you and I," he answered simply. "We've got to save them from themselves, you and I have."

Their hands met again, and for a moment held. Despite the dead calm, a fir-tip at the edge of the clearing suddenly flicked aside, shriveled as if frozen. But neither of them saw it.

The fugitives, badly spent, established themselves in the "barroom" or sleeping-shack of the camp. They wanted to feel a roof over them again, if only a broken one. The traces of men comforted them: a couple of broken peavies, a pair of snowshoes with the thongs all gnawed off, a cracked bit of mirror, a yellowed almanac dated 1899.

Jandron called the Professor's attention to this almanac, but the Professor thrust it aside.

"What do *I* want of a Canadian census-report?" he demanded, and fell to counting the bunks, over and over again. His big bulge of his forehead, that housed the massive brain of him, was oozing sweat. Marr cursed what he claimed was sunshine through the holes in the roof, though Jandron could see none; claimed the sunshine made his head ache.

"But it's not a bad place," he added. "We can make a blaze in that fireplace and be comfy. I don't like that window, though."

"What window?" asked Jandron. "Where?"

Marr laughed, and ignored him. Jandron turned to Vivian, who had sunk down on the "deacon-seat" and was staring at the stove.

"*Is* there a window here?" he demanded.

"Don't ask me," she whispered. "I—I don't know."

With a very thriving fear in his heart, Jandron peered at her a moment. He fell to muttering:

"I'm Wallace Jandron. Wallace Jandron, 37 Ware Street, Cambridge, Massachusetts. I'm quite sane. And I'm going to stay so. I'm going to save her! I know perfectly well what I'm doing. And I'm sane. Quite, quite sane!"

After a time of confused and purposeless wrangling, they got a fire going and made coffee. This, and cube bouillon with hardtack, helped considerably. The camp helped, too: A house, even a poor and broken one, is a wonderful barrier against a Thing from—Outside.

Presently darkness folded down. The men smoked, thankful that tobacco still held out. Vivian lay in a bunk that Jandron had piled with spruce boughs for her, and seemed to sleep. The Professor fretted like a child, over the blisters his paddle had made upon his hands. Marr laughed, now and then; though what he might be laughing at was not apparent. Suddenly he broke out:

"After all, what should *It* want of us?"

"Our brains, of course," the Professor answered, sharply.

"That lets Jandron out," the journalist mocked.

"But," added the Professor, "I can't imagine a Thing callously destroying human beings. And yet—"

He stopped short, with surging memories of his dead wife.

"What was it," Jandron asked, "that destroyed all those people in Valladolid, Spain, that time so many of 'em died in a few minutes after having been touched by an invisible Something that left a slight red mark on each? The newspapers were full of it."

"Piffle!" yawned Marr.

"I tell you," insisted Jandron, "there are forms of life as superior to us as we are to ants. We can't see 'em. No ant ever saw a man. And did any ant ever form the least conception of a man? These Things have left thousands of traces, all over the world. If I had my reference-books—"

"Tell that to the marines!"

"Charles Fort, the greatest authority in the world on unexplained phenomena," persisted Jandron, "gives innumerable cases of happenings that science can't explain, in his 'Book of the Damned.' He claims this earth was once a No-Man's land where all kinds of Things explored and colonized and fought for possession. And he says that now everybody's warned off, except the Owners. I happen to remember a few sentences of his: 'In the past, inhabitants of a host of worlds have dropped here, hopped here, wafted here, sailed, flown, motored, walked here; have come singly, have come in enormous numbers; have visited for hunting, trading, mining. They have been unable to stay here, have made colonies here, have been lost here.'"

"Poor fish, to believe that!" mocked the journalist, while the Professor blinked and rubbed his bulging forehead.

"I *do* believe it!" insisted Jandron. "The world is covered with relics of dead civilizations, that have mysteriously vanished, leaving nothing but their temples and monuments."

"Rubbish!"

"How about Easter Island? How about all the gigantic works there and in a thousand other places—Peru, Yucatan and so on—which certainly no primitive race ever built?"

"That's thousands of years ago," said Marr, "and I'm sleepy. For heaven's sake, can it!"

"Oh, all right. But *how* explain things, then!"

"What the devil could one of those Things want of our brains?" suddenly put in the Professor. "After all, what?"

"Well, what do we want of lower forms of life? Sometimes food. Again, some product or other. Or just information. Maybe *It* is just experimenting with us, the way we poke an ant-hill. There's always this to remember, that the human brain-tissue is the most highly-organized form of matter in this world."

"Yes," admitted the Professor, "but what—?"

"*It* might want brain-tissue for food, for experimental purposes, for lubricant—how do *I* know?"

Jandron fancied he was still explaining things; but all at once he found himself waking up in one of the bunks. He felt terribly cold, stiff, sore. A sift of snow lay here and there on the camp floor, where it had fallen through holes in the roof.

"Vivian!" he croaked hoarsely. "Thorburn! Marr!"

Nobody answered. There was nobody to answer. Jandron crawled with immense pain out of his bunk, and blinked round with bleary eyes. All of a sudden he saw the Professor, and gulped.

The Professor was lying stiff and straight in another bunk, on his back. His waxen face made a mask of horror. The open, staring eyes, with pupils immensely dilated, sent Jandron shuddering back. A livid ring marked the forehead, that now sagged inward as if empty.

"*Vivian!*" croaked Jandron, staggering away from the body. He fumbled to the bunk where the girl had lain. The bunk was quite deserted.

On the stove, in which lay half-charred wood—wood smothered out as if by some noxious gas—still stood the coffee-pot. The liquid in it was frozen solid. Of Vivian and the journalist, no trace remained.

Along one of the sagging beams that supported the roof, Jandron's horror-blasted gaze perceived a straight line of frosted prints, ring-shaped, bitten deep.

"Vivian! Vivian!"

No answer.

Shaking, sick, gray, half-blind with a horror not of this world, Jandron peered slowly around. The duffle-bag and supplies were gone. Nothing was left but that coffee-pot and the revolver at Jandron's hip.

Jandron turned, then. A-stare, his skull feeling empty as a burst drum, he crept lamely to the door and out—out into the snow.

Snow. It came slanting down. From a gray sky it steadily filtered. The trees showed no leaf. Birches, poplars, rock-maples all stood naked. Only the conifers drooped sickly-green. In a little shallow across the river snow lay white on thin ice.

Ice? Snow? Rapt with terror, Jandron stared. Why, then, he must have been unconscious three or four weeks? But how—?

Suddenly, all along the upper branches of trees that edged the clearing, puffs of snow flicked down. The geologist shuffled after two half-obliterated sets of footprints that wavered toward the landing.

His body was leaden. He wheezed, as he reached the river. The light, dim as it was, hurt his eyes. He blinked in a confusion that could just perceive one canoe was gone. He pressed a hand to his head, where an iron band seemed screwed up tight, tighter.

"Vivian! Marr! Halloooo!"

Not even an echo. Silence clamped the world; silence, and a cold that gnawed. Everything had gone a sinister gray.

After a certain time—though time now possessed neither reality nor duration—Jandron dragged himself back to the camp and stumbled in. Heedless of the staring corpse he crumpled down by the stove and tried to think, but his brain had been emptied of power. Everything blent to a gray blur. Snow kept slithering in through the roof.

"Well, why don't you come and get me, Thing?" suddenly snarled Jandron. "Here I am. Damn you, come and get me!"

Voices. Suddenly he heard voices. Yes, somebody was outside, there. Singularly aggrieved, he got up and limped to the door. He squinted out into the gray; saw two figures down by the landing. With numb indifference he recognized the girl and Marr.

"Why should they bother me again?" he nebulously wondered. "Can't they go away and leave me alone?" He felt peevish irritation.

Then, a modicum of reason returning, he sensed that they were arguing. Vivian, beside a canoe freshly dragged from thin ice, was pointing; Marr was gesticulating. All at once Marr snarled, turned from her, plodded with bent back toward the camp.

"But listen!" she called, her rough-knit sweater all powdered with snow. "*That's* the way!" She gestured downstream.

"I'm not going either way!" Marr retorted. "I'm going to stay right here!" He came on, bareheaded. Snow grayed his stubble of beard; but on his head it melted as it fell, as if some fever there had raised the brain-stuff to improbable temperatures. "I'm going to stay right here, all summer." His heavy lids sagged. Puffy and evil, his lips showed a glint of teeth. "Let me alone!"

Vivian lagged after him, kicking up the ash-like snow. With indifference, Jandron watched them. Trivial human creatures!

Suddenly Marr saw him in the doorway and stopped short. He drew his gun; he aimed at Jandron.

"*You* get out!" he mouthed. "Why in — can't you stay dead?"

"Put that gun down, you idiot!" Jandron managed to retort. The girl stopped and seemed trying to understand. "We can get away yet, if we all stick together."

"Are you going to get out and leave me alone?" demanded the journalist, holding his gun steadily enough.

Jandron, wholly indifferent, watched the muzzle. Vague curiosity possessed him. Just what, he wondered, did it feel like to be shot?

Marr pulled trigger.

Snap!

The cartridge missed fire. Not even powder would burn.

Marr laughed, horribly, and shambled forward.

"Serves him right!" he mouthed. "He'd better not come back again!"

Jandron understood that Marr had seen him fall. But still he felt himself standing there, alive. He shuffled away from the door. No matter whether he was alive or dead, there was always Vivian to be saved.

The journalist came to the door, paused, looked down, grunted and passed into the camp. He shut the door. Jandron heard the rotten wooden bar of the latch drop. From within echoed a laugh, monstrous in its brutality.

Then quivering, the geologist felt a touch on his arm.

"Why did you desert us like that?" he heard Vivian's reproach. "Why?"

He turned, hardly able to see her at all.

"Listen," he said, thickly. "I'll admit anything. It's all right. But just forget it, for now. We've got to get out o' here. The Professor is dead, in there, and Marr's gone mad and barricaded himself in there. So there's no use staying. There's a. chance for us yet. Come along!"

He took her by the arm and tried to draw her toward the river, but she held back. The hate in her face sickened him. He shook in the grip of a mighty chill.

"Go, with—you?" she demanded.

"Yes, by God!" he retorted, in a swift blaze of anger, "or I'll kill you where you stand. *It* shan't get you, anyhow!"

Swiftly piercing, a greater cold smote to his inner marrows. A long row of the cup-shaped prints had just appeared in the snow beside the camp. And from these marks wafted a faint, bluish vapor of unthinkable cold.

"What are you staring at?" the girl demanded.

"Those prints! In the snow, there—see?" He pointed a shaking finger.

"How can there be snow at this season?"

He could have wept for the pity of her, the love of her. On her red tam, her tangle of rebel hair, her sweater, the snow came steadily drifting; yet there she stood before him and prated of summer. Jandron heaved himself out of a very slough of down-dragging lassitudes. He whipped himself into action.

"Summer, winter—no matter!" he flung at her. "You're coming along with me!" He seized her arm with the brutality of desperation that must hurt, to save. And murder, too, lay in his soul. He knew that he would strangle her with his naked hands, if need were, before he would ever leave her there, for *It* to work Its horrible will upon.

"You come with me," he mouthed, "or by the Almighty—!"

Marr's scream in the camp, whirled him toward the door. That scream rose higher, higher, even more and more piercing, just like the screams of the runaway Indian guides in what now appeared the infinitely long ago. It seemed to last hours; and always it rose, rose, as if being wrung out of a human body by some kind of agony not conceivable in this world. Higher, higher—

Then it stopped.

Jandron hurled himself against the plank door. The bar smashed; the door shivered inward.

With a cry, Jandron recoiled. He covered his eyes with a hand that quivered, claw-like.

"Go away, Vivian! Don't come here—don't look—"

He stumbled away, babbling.

Out of the door crept something like a man. A queer, broken, bent over thing; a thing crippled, shrunken and flabby, that whined.

This thing—yes, it was still Marr—crouched down at one side, quivering, whimpering. It moved its hands as a crushed ant moves its antennae, jerkily, without significance.

All at once Jandron no longer felt afraid. He walked quite steadily to Marr, who was breathing in little gasps. From the camp issued an odor unlike anything terrestrial. A thin, grayish grease covered the sill.

Jandron caught hold of the crumpling journalist's arm. Marr's eyes leered, filmed, unseeing. He gave the impression of a creature whose back has been broken, whose whole essence and energy have been wrenched asunder, yet in which life somehow clings, palpitant. A creature vivisected.

Away through the snow Jandron dragged him. Marr made no resistance; just let himself be led, whining a little, palsied, rickety, shattered. The girl, her face whitely cold as the snow that fell on it, came after.

Thus they reached the landing at the river.

"Come, now, let's get away!" Jandron made shift to articulate. Marr said nothing. But when Jandron tried to bundle him into a canoe, something in the journalist revived with swift, mad hatefulness. That something lashed him into a spasm of wiry, incredibly venomous resistance. Slavers of blood and foam streaked Marr's lips. He made horrid noises, like an animal. He howled dismally, and bit, clawed, writhed and groveled! he tried to sink his teeth into Jandron's leg. He fought appallingly, as men must have fought in the inconceivably remote days even before the Stone Age. And Vivian helped him. Her fury was a tiger-cat's.

Between the pair of them, they almost did him in. They almost dragged Jandron down—and themselves, too—into the black river that ran swiftly sucking under the ice. Not till Jandron had quite flung off all vague notions and restraints of gallantry; not until he struck from the shoulder—to kill, if need were—did he best them.

He beat the pair of them unconscious, trussed them hand and foot with the painters of the canoes, rolled them into the larger canoe, and shoved off.

After that, the blankness of a measureless oblivion descended.

Only from what he was told, weeks after, in the Royal Victoria Hospital at Montreal, did Jandron ever learn how and when a field-squad of Dominion Foresters had found them drifting in Lake

Moosawamkeag. And that knowledge filtered slowly into his brain during a period inchoate as Iceland fogs. That Marr was dead and the girl alive—that much, at all events, was solid. He could hold to that; he could climb back, with that, to the real world again.

Jandron climbed back, came back. Time healed him, as it healed the girl. After a long, long while, they had speech together. Cautiously he sounded her wells of memory. He saw that she recalled nothing. So he told her white lies about capsized canoes and the sad death—in realistically-described rapids—of all the party except herself and him.

Vivian believed. Fate, Jandron knew, was being very kind to both of them.

But Vivian could never understand in the least why her husband, not very long after marriage, asked her not to wear a wedding-ring or any ring whatever.

"Men are so queer!" covers a multitude of psychic agonies.

Life, for Jandron—life, softened by Vivian—knit itself up into some reasonable semblance of a normal pattern. But when, at lengthening intervals, memories even now awake—memories crawling amid the slime of cosmic mysteries that it is madness to approach—or when at certain times Jandron sees a ring of any sort, his heart chills with a cold that reeks of the horrors of Infinity.

And from shadows past the boundaries of our universe seem to beckon Things that, God grant, can never till the end of time be known on earth.

SPAWN OF THE COMET
OTIS ADELBERT KLINE

FOREWORD

AS THE COMING of that singular visitor from sidereal space known as the "great comet of 1847" or "Green's comet," has been duly recorded by those whose duty it is to chronicle such events, I will merely mention it in passing. But mention it I must, as it is so unmistakably linked with that menace to all terrestrial life which immediately followed its departure for the cosmic vastnesses, and which came so near to terminating the tenure of mankind on the earth.

It was called "Green's comet," after Sir George Green, the eminent English astronomer who discovered it. Long before it had reached the outer limits of the solar system it blazed with a light that marked it as no ordinary visitor from the interstellar voids.

Indeed, it appeared to have so large and compact a nucleus that scientists feared the entire solar system would be upset by its visit. But when it passed the orbits of the outer planets and relative perturbations were computed, it was found that despite its great size, its mass was not so formidable as to be alarming.

Because it did not develop a tail as it neared the sun, its immense coma—the nebulosity or head, surrounding the nucleus—was thought to consist of millions of small meteoroids, while what had previously been mistaken for the outside surface of a solid nucleus was spectrascopically proven to be the outer limit of an atmosphere quite like our own, but so filled with clouds of vapor that it was impossible to see the nucleus itself.

It was believed that the comet's atmosphere was warmed and the coma made incandescent by the friction of the meteoroids as they passed through its upper atmosphere, and also by the countless thousands of collisions which took place among them.

There was one thing, however, that caused considerable apprehension. Although the earth, so I am informed, once passed through the tail of a comet without injury, astronomers had computed that on its return journey from its circuit of the sun the head of this comet would pass quite near the earth—might even collide with it.

In consequence, certain religious leaders became vociferous in their prophecies regarding the immediate end of the world with attendant fire, brimstone and such fearsome accessories. The tailless comet, surrounded by that bright, nebulous, translucent coma of huge dimensions, was an exceedingly striking and brilliant spectacle. These prophets of destruction could nightly point to it and thereby gain many followers who garbed themselves in nightgowns and congregated on roof tops, singing psalms and waiting for the fiery chariot to come and taxi them up through the pearly gates.

But, strange to say, though on its return journey from the sun, the comet came within half a million miles of the earth—a very short distance as cosmic space is figured—and for a time looked larger and brighter than the full moon, there were no other signs of its immediate proximity than a few extra storms, earthquakes, tidal waves, volcanic eruptions, and a protracted and exceedingly brilliant meteoric shower.

It was that which followed this sudden and unexpected call of our bright visitor from the silent, star-strewn solitudes, which came so near to causing the end of the world, which, for the human race, amounts to the same thing.

And it is this calamity which I have set myself the task of chronicling in order that future generations may know the truth of the matter from at least one eyewitness.

Richard Perry.

Chapter I

Threads of Death

I was spending the week-end in the country with Sue.

To me, Dick Perry, one of the cave-dwelling desk slaves in Chicago's busy Loop, that was the height of bliss. Sue Davis, the eminent biologist and biochemist, was my fiancée. We were at the Davis country home.

The comet had come and gone, and the earth, as well as all earthly creatures, had settled down to its former more or less well-ordered existence.

It was Saturday forenoon—one of those drowsy, peaceful, pleasant mornings in late July so characteristic of the verdant Mississippi Valley. Sue and I had gone for a stroll on the farm, had crossed a field of nodding, fragrant clover, and had paused where a single huge hackberry tree cast its speckled shade over a small grass plot.

I was lying on my back in the grass and gazing dreamily up into the clear blue sky, while Sue, seated beside me, wove a garland of clover blossoms. Feeling poetic—I was but twenty-two and Sue nineteen—I began to compare the blue eyes with that of the heavens, and the spun gold of her hair with the sunbeams that danced down through the gently waving hackberry leaves, and to compose a verse suited to my mood. But there came a droning sound, louder than that made by the thousands of bees in the clover.

"The mail plane is coming in," said Sue. "Sit up, lazybones, and watch it land. The field is only a mile from here."

As I sat up the unmistakable droning of an airplane grew louder. Looking skyward, I could not see it at first. But I did see something which I had not noticed before—a small, wispy white cloud scudding rapidly northward. Then I saw the plane coming from the west.

It appeared to me that cloud and plane were traveling at about the same speed, and if either changed its velocity or direction, they would meet. Nothing phenomenal in that, of course. I have often seen planes fly through the clouds. But here were the only cloud and the only plane in sight, and it would be interesting, I thought, if they should meet when each had so much open space in which to travel.

As they drew closer together I saw that the cloud was considerably higher than the plane.

"They won't meet, after all," I said, half to myself, half to my fair companion.

But scarcely had the words left my lips ere a strange thing happened. It appeared to me that the cloud, which was roughly disk-shaped with a few ragged streamers beneath, tilted and glided downward toward the level of the plane.

It came to me in the next instant that from our viewpoint the motions of all heavenly objects near the zenith must necessarily be relative—that the plane might have ascended toward the cloud. And yet this would not account for the apparent tilting of the cirrus disk.

Plane and cloud met. For a moment the airplane was completely concealed. But as it emerged once more into view I noticed that it was beginning a steep climb.

"He must be going to loop the loop," I said, but the words had scarcely left my lips when the motor died. It appeared that the pilot had misjudged the amount of speed necessary for the climb and had not opened the throttle enough. The plane appeared to stop for a moment—then fell backward and downward, went into a sideslip, and hurtled groundward, out of control.

Sue gripped my arm and uttered a little scream of terror. We both leaped to our feet just as the ship crashed in a pasture not more than a half mile from where we stood, and about an equal distance from the landing field.

"Oh, how terrible!" Sue exclaimed. "Let's run over and see what we can do. The pilot may not be dead."

"Not one chance in a thousand for that," I answered, "the way he crashed. But we'll hurry over anyway."

We ran across the clover field and climbed the pasture fence.

As we neared the wreck we saw three men, evidently from the airport, coming from the other direction. They arrived at the spot when we did.

The plane had struck with one wing down. That wing was partly crumpled by the shock of the collision. The nose was buried in the soft, boggy ground of the pasture, and the fuselage was a twisted wreck. Hanging about it like an invisible aura was a sickening, musty odor—a revolting, charnel scent, as if some ancient grave had been desecrated.

Fearing the effect on Sue of the horrible sight which I felt positive would be revealed, I suggested to her that she look the other way when two of the men from the airport went into the wreck for the remains of the pilot.

But the cries of horror which I expected to hear from the two men did not materialize. Instead, they uttered exclamations of astonishment.

The man who was standing outside the wreck called to one of them:

"What's the matter, Bill?"

"We can't find no sign of a body here," was the reply. "This crate must have been flying without a pilot."

"Maybe Jackson fell out before the crack-up," said the man outside.

"Must have been a long time before, if he did," was the answer, "because I was watching the ship come in, and I'd have seen him if he fell out. Besides, she behaved all right until she passed through the cloud:"

"He might have fallen out in the cloud," said the man outside.

"And then flew away with it? Don't talk foolish."

"Well, anyway, he's not here. Whew! What a smell! Notice it?"

"Notice it! I'm strangling!"

The three men dragged out the mail sacks, shouldered them, and moved off in the direction of the landing field.

Sue and I were turning to go when my attention was attracted by several long, silky bits of what appeared to be hair or thread, caught in the rudder. Puzzled by the presence of material of this sort in so unusual a place, I walked closer to examine it. On nearer inspection it appeared like glossy blond hair of rather coarse texture.

I touched a strand of it with an inquisitive forefinger, and an astounding thing happened. With lightning-like rapidity that part of it which dangled beyond my finger and the rudder to which it was attached, assumed the shape of a spiral spring and jerked my finger toward the rudder.

Automatically I attempted to jerk my finger away. But the effort was unavailing. Despite the apparent flimsiness of the strand which held it, it was bound as tightly to that rudder as if it had been held by a length of piano wire.

The strand, I observed, was caught in a cleft where the wood had split. I had been pulling downward from this point. I pulled a second time, this time upward, and the strand instantly came free, but it was no sooner freed from the crotch than it wrapped its remaining coils around my finger.

"What are you doing?" asked Sue.

"I have discovered something very strange," I replied, showing her my tightly wrapped finger.

"Why, it's nothing but a hair," she said, and attempted to pull it from my finger, which was already beginning to show signs of congested circulation. But she could neither stretch nor break it. And the two ends had, twisted about each other, forming a splice that was as tight and immovable as the other loops.

"Don't touch it!" I warned her, withdrawing my finger. "It's not a hair."

"Then what is it?" she asked, surprised.

"I don't know," I responded, "but something more sinister than you imagine. There are two more hanging on the rudder. Don't go near them. I'll try to get them and take them to your father for examination. Whatever they are, they seem to be endowed with life and an unbelievable amount of strength."

I obtained a dry weed-stalk near by and touched one of the remaining strands with it. To my surprise it did not move, but hung as limp and lifeless as if it had been what it appeared to be—a hair or thread.

Breaking the stalk in two, I caught the two strands between the two pieces of weed-stalk, and turned them until I had enough purchase to pull them from the cleft. I continued to turn them until they were wound around the stalks. Then Sue and I left for the house.

The walk of a mile and a half to the Davis home occupied only twenty-five minutes. But before we had traversed half that distance my finger, which had turned blue and begun to throb unmercifully, started to bleed where the strands surrounded it. These strands, which I was unable to pull off, continued to sink deeper into my flesh as if they slowly contracted, and I was conscious of a burning sensation, as if some powerful corrosive were searing the wound.

Upon entering the house we found Sue's father, Professor Absolom Davis, working in small but excellently equipped experimental laboratory.

A small man with a pointed, iron gray beard, he is scarcely taller than his daughter, who is five feet two. Yet he has always appeared to me as a man of concentrated, dynamic energy. Despite the fact that we had apparently interrupted some intensely engrossing experiment as we burst unceremoniously into his laboratory, he beamed cordially at us through his large, thick-lensed glasses, and exclaimed:

"Well, well! Back so soon? Did you have a pleasant stroll?"

I briefly related to him the incidents that had just taken place—showed him the strands I had wrapped around the sticks, after warning him not to touch them, and also exhibited my tightly wrapped finger.

After examining it for a moment, he poured some alcohol into a test tube and plunged the numbed digit into it. There was no result except an increased burning sensation where the strands had broken through the skin.

Wrinkling his brow in puzzlement, he put some alcohol into a second test tube, and into this dropped a small quantity of clear, pungent-smelling liquid. I was ordered to plunge my finger into this, but the result was no different than before, except that the burning was slightly intensified.

After watching it for a moment, the professor prepared a third solution, using distilled water instead of alcohol, and dropping into it something with a peculiar, almond-like odor. Almost instantly the two spliced tendrils uncurled, and upon removing my finger from the test tube I was able to unwind the coils as easily as if they had been common thread.

Directing me to thoroughly wash my hands at once, the professor took a pair of surgical scissors and cut off a piece of the substance which had been wrapped around my finger.

The stuff seemed difficult to cut, and snapped like a piece of steel wire when severed. Then he put it under a compound microscope and examined it. The experiment which he had previously been conducting seemed completely forgotten in the excitement of this new investigation.

"What is it?" I asked, after washing my hands.

He continued to peer through the microscope, slightly moving various adjustments. Without replying to my question, he took the piece he had been examining and immersed it in a blue solution. Again he slid it under the microscope. Then he snipped off a second piece, immersed it in a pink solution, and carefully examined it.

Presently he looked up. Apparently the question which I had asked some minutes before had just broken through his preoccupation.

"I don't know what it is," he said, "except that it is organic and apparently constructed of thousands of long, thin, and extremely tough contractile fibres in a clear plasmic substance which is interlaced with chains of fatty cells that indicate the presence of some sort of a nervous system. This, to judge from the way the strands behave, is both motor and sensory. There are also waxy cells which evidently contain the corrosive digestive fluid which cut through your skin so readily. Here, look for yourself."

I peered through the microscope, but to my untrained eye it appeared that a thin cable, partly pink and partly translucent, crossed the round field. There were specks, blotches, and chains of tiny globules, but they meant nothing to me.

While Sue was looking at it, the professor prepared a slide by coating it with some sticky substance. Then he carefully snipped off a small piece of one of the strands I had brought in on the two stalks, so it fell on and stuck to the slide.

This done, he removed the slide containing the pink-stained fragment, and put the sticky slide in its place.

After examining it for some time in silence, he took down a large glass mortar from a shelf. Holding the two sticks containing the wound strands over this, he snipped off a piece about two inches in length, letting it fall into the mortar.

Then he went outdoors. A few minutes later he returned with an earthworm about six inches in length wriggling in his fingers.

"In the interests of science," he said, and dropped the worm into the mortar. It fell on the strand which he had previously placed there, and which, at the touch of the worm, seemed instantly galvanized into life. With amazing speed it coiled itself around the squirming creature. Then the coils slowly tightened, the worm becoming more convulsive in its movements, and leaving little streaks of slime on the smooth surface of the mortar as it lashed about in all directions.

Presently the worm was cut in two. Between the severed halves lay a small, slime-smeared coil of what looked like hair. Slowly this coil opened until it had reached its previous length of about two inches. The head end of the worm, more active than the tail, again blundered against the threadlike thing. Once again it was seized in the thin, powerful coils, then slowly cut in two.

"What is it, professor?" I asked.

Continuing to stare at the contents of the mortar through his thick glasses, he replied:

"At present I can only say that it is, without a doubt, a clue to the disappearance—the almost certain death—of Jackson, the aviator. Beyond that I can tell you nothing definite—not unless further experiments reveal something which I have not yet discovered. Run along, now, you and Sue. I must be alone. There is important work to be done. There are investigations to be made which may be of incalculable benefit to the human race—may even save humanity from the worst menace by which it has ever been confronted!"

CHAPTER II

Bleached Bones

Sue and I lunched together, served by Wong, the efficient Chinese butler. The professor never took lunch, and Mrs. Davis had driven to Sterling, a near-by town, for the purpose of doing some shopping. Late that afternoon she returned.

A small, sweet-faced, white-haired woman, Mrs. Davis is rarely perturbed. Sue and I were consequently amazed to hear her talking excitedly to the professor in the laboratory. Then both of them came into the drawing-room where we were seated.

"Some strange things have been happening to-day," she said as she greeted us. "Banker Crolius, of Sterling, while driving home from the country club in his roadster, suddenly disappeared. A farm hand who saw him in the car only a moment before his disappearance, describes a strange cloud which was mingled with the dust thrown up by his car, but which separated from it and sailed away as soon as the car overturned in the ditch. The motorcycle policeman who found the empty car reported that there was a nauseating odor around it, but no sign of Crolius."

"He must have shared the fate of Jackson," I said.

"Without a doubt," said the professor. "But that is not all. Look at this; it's positively ghastly."

He passed me a copy of the evening paper which his wife had just brought from Sterling. Together, Sue and I scanned the glaring headlines, and read the article which followed:

TAMPICO CITIZEN BADLY INJURED BY FALLING SKULL
BELIEVED TO BE THAT OF MISSING AVIATOR, JACKSON

William Aldrich, a citizen of Tampico, was seriously injured today while walking on the main street of his home town, when a human skull which had apparently fallen from the sky struck him on the right shoulder. It fell with such force that he was knocked down. Examination by a physician revealed two broken bones beneath a very painful bruise. Near the fallen skull the metal frames and broken glass of an aviator's goggles were found.

A moment later a number of other bones, which Dr. Brown of Tampico pronounced those of a human being, fell nearly a block from where Mr. Aldrich had been struck down. These bones were so white and dry that the doctor declared they must have been exposed to the weather for a long period of time.

Among these bones were found a cigarette lighter, some coins, a bunch of keys, several buttons and buckles, and a wrist watch on an aviator's identification bracelet. Despite the fact that Pilot Jackson disappeared not more than two hours before this happened, it is thought that he has been murdered in some mysterious way, and his bones dehydrated and dropped, for the bracelet is his, and descriptions of the other articles tally with those he was known to have carried.

"Do you think they were really Jackson's bones?" I asked the professor.

"I think it highly probable that they were," he replied.

"But how—"

"Come into my laboratory, Dick," he said. "I have something to show you."

As Professor Davis led me into his laboratory, his eyes sparkled with excitement behind his thick-lensed glasses. He bent over the mortar into which he had dropped the mysterious fragment of hair-like substance and the earthworm, earlier in the afternoon. Then a look of amazement came over his features.

"Really," he said, "this is most remarkable! Look here, Dick. The creature has grown more swiftly than I thought possible."

I, too, looked into the mortar.

To my surprise I saw that the two-inch piece of the odd material had a mushroom-like growth on one end. This end was raised nearly an inch above the bottom of the bowl as if the mushroom growth were a little balloon, gradually lifting the hairlike strand. But this was not all, for sprouting beneath the cap were many other hairs, shorter than the original one, but of the same diameter and evidently growing at an astonishing rate of speed.

"Do you know what it is?" I asked.

"I believe," said the professor, "that we are confronted by a creature unknown to science, and up to the present day, entirely outside the experience of mankind. Unless other similar incidents have occurred recently, the strange fates of Jackson and Crolius are unique in the annals of the world. Without a doubt, Crolius and Jackson met the same fate—were attacked either by the same creature or by one like it. And this"—pointing to the thing in the mortar—"is perhaps a reproduction of that creature. I say 'perhaps' because even among the creatures known and classified by science we find numerous instances of offspring which, in certain stages of their existence, bear very little resemblance to their parents."

"Do you mean to tell me," I said, "that the hairlike strand was an egg or spore from which this creature in the mortar is developing?"

"Not precisely that," replied the professor. "It seems that we have to do, here, with a creature that reproduces itself by fission or subdivision—or at least a creature which has the power to do so, even though it may normally reproduce its kind by spores, spawn or eggs.

"I think that we can safely assume, in this case, that the division was accidental so far as the intention of the creature itself is taken into account. The hairlike tentacle was caught in the airplane rudder when creature and plane were both traveling swiftly at right angles to each other's courses. As a result three of these tentacles caught in the splintered rudder were torn loose and carried down with the ship. With my scissors I farther divided the tentacle before placing it in the mortar.

"You will observe that those tentacles which are still coiled around the sticks on which you brought them have neither moved nor shown any signs of growth. Our experience shows that they will not move unless touched by living organic matter—food. And food, which I supplied in the form of an earthworm, is undoubtedly the reason the piece in the mortar was enabled to grow.

"I have been watching this one closely, and have learned something more. The tentacles themselves, as we have learned before, are not stimulated to action except when touched by organic food, but once the umbrella-like crown has grown above them, they are led to the food by the crown's perception of motion. The worm, as you will observe, has all been devoured, or rather, absorbed, except a few segments from the posterior extremity. These segments are quite near the original and longest tentacle, but they are motionless. The growth of the creature has ceased for a lack of food, with this food quite near it, yet I saw it travel toward and capture the wriggling anterior end again and again until it had consumed all of it.

"We have here an analogy with the two tragedies which took place to-day. Swift movement, apparently, had attracted the parent of this creature to its prey, both in the case of Jackson and that of Crolius—assuming, of course, that both men were taken by the same monster."

"Then," I said, "you are of the opinion that this little creature in the mortar is a miniature replica of the thing that took Jackson?"

"That," said the professor, "is only problematical. It may be of an entirely different form. To draw an analogy from a creature well known to science, and probably the one most closely resembling this creature with which we have to deal, take the chrysaora, a kind of jellyfish. In one state of its existence it is a minute, flat, worm-like affair. This eventually settles down on the sea bottom and turns into a hydra—a tube-like organism with threads. The hydra not only reproduces many other hydras, but eventually turns into the segmented strobila, like a stack of saucers. This, in turn, produces the free-swimming disk-shaped medusa, which is the adult jellyfish.

"But while the jellyfish is in the hydra stage, many strange monsters, entirely different in appearance from any of these creatures, have been produced by artificial division. For that reason it is possible that the individual we have here is nothing like the parent from which it sprang. The fact that the creature more nearly resembles a jellyfish than any other earthly creature—that it is in fact a sort of medusa of the air—makes this analogy all the more plausible."

He pushed the few remaining posterior segments of the earthworm into contact with the trailing tentacle, then watched reflectively while the creature, drawing its umbrella-like cap down to the morsel, slowly consumed it.

Scarcely had the last trace of the earthworm disappeared, ere the creature rose once more, but this time it was able to lift the weight of the tentacle, and started to float upward like a toy balloon dragging the string to which it is attached.

Galvanized into action by this unexpected development, the professor jumped for a butterfly net which was hanging on a hook near-by. His swift motion evidently attracted the creature, for it darted after him, its long original tentacle as well as the shorter ones it was developing, outstretching toward him. But despite his age, the professor was as dexterous through long practice with a butterfly net as is many a younger man with a racquet or foil, and with a quick movement he brought it down over his quarry.

On a table in one corner of the room was a large, finely meshed cage. This cage contained a half dozen cocoons and three large, brightly colored cecropia moths which had just emerged, and which the professor had confined for later observation.

Opening the door of the cage, the professor pushed in the butterfly net, permitting his captive to float up out of the meshes. Then, removing the net, he closed the door and watched the thing floating about in the air near the top of the cage, while he mopped from his brow the perspiration which his sudden and unaccustomed exertions had engendered.

"I suppose the thing will eat my cecropias," he said, "but in the meantime we may learn something more of the habits of this medusa of the air."

Scarcely had he spoken, ere one of the cecropias spread its newly opened wings and started to fly across the cage. With a quick dart, the medusa pounced upon it, and its tentacles wound themselves around the fat, soft body. For a few seconds, the moth fluttered helplessly—then it fell to the floor of the cage, while the wiry tentacles of its remorseless enemy sank deeper and deeper into its yielding thorax and abdomen.

It was the professor who first noticed that the medusa—for such we had begun to call it—no longer depended on its tentacles for the absorption of its food, but had developed a number of small, slightly projecting sucker mouths which all but covered the under surface of the cap. With these it was able to assimilate much more rapidly than before.

In an incredibly short space of time the cecropia had completely disappeared, while the medusa, its cap now doubled in size and its tentacles uniformly about three inches in length, slowly floated about the cage, the frilled edges of its cap rippling like thin fabric stirred by a breeze, but actually doing the work of propelling the creature through the air.

"What do you suppose makes it float?" I asked.

"I've been wondering," replied the professor. "Possibly it has the power to generate a gas lighter than air, which keeps it up. It might, for example, have the power to separate the pure hydrogen gas from the moisture in the air. By Jove! If that is it—"

The professor hastily secured a large test tube, a razor-sharp scalpel, and his butterfly net. Cautiously opening the door of the cage, he inserted the net and soon had the medusa in its folds. Immersing the creature in a large pan of water, he held the inverted, water-filled test tube down over it, and sliding the scalpel under the edge, inserted it in the creature's cap. A tiny bubble arose in the tube.

The professor plunged the scalpel into a different spot, and another bubble traveled to the top of the tube, the creature's arms writhing meanwhile like a nest of snakes. Again and again he pricked the cap until about a half inch of water in the test tube was displaced by gas.

Permitting the rest of the water to run out of the tube, and tossing the medusa back into the cage, where it no longer floated about in the air, but lay writhing and squirming on the floor, the professor carried the tube, still inverted, to a nearby table.

"If this is hydrogen, Dick," he said, "I've found a way to rid the world of this menace."

"How is that?"

"By fire," he answered. "A spark, a shell, a rocket, or an explosive bullet will turn each creature into a roaring furnace of flame."

Standing the inverted tube on the table for a moment, he picked it up with a test tube holder. Then he lighted a taper and held the flame in the mouth of the tube. Nothing happened. He thrust the flame still higher. It sputtered and went out.

"No use, Dick," he said. "Had that been hydrogen, we should have had a small explosion. It's something else. I'll have to make further tests."

Still keeping the tube inverted, he inserted a rubber stopper in the mouth. Then he stood it upside down on the table.

At this moment Sue entered through the door which led to the drawing room.

"Mother and I just heard fearful news on the radio," she said. "Thirty-six airplanes in various parts of the country have crashed. The occupants have not been found. More than a hundred people have disappeared while driving their automobiles, and most of the machines have been wrecked as a consequence. Recognizing the fact that something in the air must have snatched these people from their machines, the government has sent scout and combat planes to investigate. Similar reports have been received from Canada and Mexico, and the air forces of these two countries are patrolling the skies in an effort to learn the cause of the mystery. What does it mean? What can we do?"

"It means," said the professor soberly, "that I must get in touch with the War Department at once and tell them what little I know. Then I must, somehow, continue my experiments."

CHAPTER III

The Thing in the Laboratory

After dinner the professor and I returned to his laboratory. He had called the War Department, and supplied them with such information as he had.

We found the caged medusa more than doubled in size, float-ing about as if searching for more prey. The cecropias had all been devoured. The punctures made by the professor's scalpel had disappeared, and the cells which he had deflated were not only increased in size proportionately to the animal's growth, but completely filled out with gas once more.

While I watched it moving about, the professor tested the gas which he had confined in the tube. Presently he called to me:

"I've found it, Dick. It's helium. How the creature obtains it so rapidly is a mystery to me, as there are only four parts to every million parts of air, and proportions in its organic food must be very slight. But it is unmistakably helium, so fire will only be effective against it in such local areas as it can reach directly."

"But what about explosive shells?" I asked.

"The monsters could be blown into fragments, of course," he replied, "but remember, each fragment would become a new mon-ster. Fighting these giant medusae of the skies with shells would simply mean multiplying them."

"Then what can we do?" I asked.

"That," he replied, "is what we must find out as quickly as pos-sible. In order to do this we must take some risks. We must ex-periment and observe until we can find the weak spot in this creature's defense. I am about to sacrifice to-morrow's roast for the good of the cause."

So saying, he went out, and I heard him talking to the cook in the kitchen. A moment later he returned with a raw leg of lamb which he thrust into the cage.

The medusa, evidently attracted by the movement, soared downward, tentacles extended, as we had previously seen it do when attracted by the motion of organic matter. A tentacle touched the raw meat and in a moment the creature had settled down over the roast to feed.

The professor sighed.

"My favorite food," he said, "but it is going in a good cause. And we have, so the cook tells me, a smoked ham which will go well with some fresh eggs."

The medusa fed noiselessly, but with apparent voracity. As the meat dwindled in bulk, the body of the medusa increased in size, its tentacles lengthened proportionately.

Almost before we realized it, the body of the creature was more than a foot in diameter, while the tentacles had reached a length of nearly eighteen inches, yet the roast was not more than half consumed. Then a queer thing happened. The cage began to fill with vapor—silvery white like a cirrus cloud on which the sun is shining. And I began to grow increasingly conscious of a sickening, musty odor like that I had noticed at the wreck of Jackson's plane.

The professor, alert scientist that he was, seized a glass tube and a rubber plug for each end. Then he rushed out into the kitchen. A few moments later he returned with the tube packed full of crushed ice. He wiped it thoroughly with a towel, then opened the door of the cage and thrust the tube into the densest part of the vapor.

When he withdrew it, it was covered with large drops of moisture.

These he scraped into a test tube which he held up to the light for a moment, shaking it slightly as if to note its viscosity. Then he went to the table, put it in a test tube rack, and quickly prepared a number of solutions in other tubes. Into each of these he dropped a minute quantity of the liquid he had collected—pausing in each instance to note the result.

In watching him, I had forgotten to keep an eye on the cage. Presently I thought of it once more and turned to look at it. To my surprise I saw that it was completely hidden by a dense cloud of vapor—a disk-shaped cloud that was a perfect miniature copy of that into which Pilot Jackson had plunged, never to emerge.

The professor looked up from his experiments.

"Water, Dick," he said, "nothing but water. The mystery is, how is it able to collect and hold a cloud symmetrically around it? I rather suspect—"

He paused in amazement as he suddenly noticed how large and dense the cloud had become around the cage.

"Why, this is astounding, Dick," he said. "I had no idea it could grow so huge on a few pounds of meat. Perhaps we had better—"

He was interrupted this time by a rending crash, which came from the interior of the cloud. Then it rose toward the ceiling, and on the table our startled eyes saw the remains of the cage with its four sides bulged out, its top tilted back, and its frame splintered. Lying on the bottom of the cage, as white as if it had been kiln-dried, was the leg bone which had been in the roast.

The disk-shaped cloud, now nearly four feet in diameter, was floating around the edges of the ceiling, evidently looking for a means of egress from the room. Beneath it trailed more than a hundred squirming, wriggling tentacles, partly concealed by several little ragged streamers of vapor.

"Don't move, Dick," said the professor softly. "We are both in deadly peril. I have a plan."

Slowly, cautiously, he reached beneath the table. He groped there for a moment, then brought out a gasoline blowtorch. Turning a valve, he filled the generator. Then he struck a match and ignited it.

I noticed that when he made the quick motion necessary for the lighting of the match, the tentacles of the creature floating above us suddenly extended toward him as if attracted by the movement.

The professor noted this, also, and worked the air pump of the torch slowly and carefully, while he kept an eye on the medusa. The creature had halted, its tentacles still extended toward him, as if undecided whether to attack or not. Presently it began to float slowly in his direction.

Knowing that he would be unable to get his torch going in time to use it effectively, I looked about for a weapon. Across the room, at a distance of about ten feet from me, was the professor's golf bag. The driver and brassie reared their heads invitingly above the other clubs. If I could but get one of them!

The medusa drew nearer and nearer to the professor, who coolly continued to work the pressure pump. The torch began to roar, but I knew it would not be in operation for at least another half minute, and the exploring tentacles were now less than a foot from the scientist.

Had I been content to move slowly, I might have averted that which followed. But I arose with rash haste and leaped toward the golf clubs.

Before I could make a second move, with a suddenness that was appalling, the monster pounced on me. At the first touch of those wiry tentacles I felt a terrific shock, as if a powerful electric current had passed through my body. Every muscle was numbed, stiffened. I was unable to move a finger.

A second shock followed—a third. There was a roaring in my ears; there rose a penetrating stench like that of burning feathers. I could feel the wiry tentacles biting into my flesh, yet the numbing waves that came from them rendered the wounds almost painless.

The roaring sound increased. I heard a horrible, wailing shriek. Then things went black before my eyes and I lost consciousness.

When I came to my senses once more, I was lying on a davenport in the drawing-room. The professor was holding a phial of some pungent aromatic beneath my nostrils, while Sue and Mrs. Davis chafed my hands.

I blinked, sat up, and tried to remember what had happened. Then it all came back to me—the grip of wiry tentacles, the roaring sound, the numbing shocks, the sickening stench, and that horrible shriek. I remembered it as sounding something between the wail of a steam siren and the scream of a woman.

"Better lie down for a while, Dick," cautioned the professor. "You've had a narrow escape. If that animated galvanic battery had been just a little more powerful you could never have recovered from those shocks."

I leaned back on the cushions, for it made me giddy to sit up.

"I passed out when the thing screamed, or at least I thought it screamed," I said. "What followed?"

"When you thought it screamed," said the professor, "you were right. It screamed not once, but again and again. It roared before it screamed. Didn't you hear it roar?"

"I heard a roaring sound," I replied. "I didn't know whether it was made by the torch or the creature."

"Possibly it was both," said the professor. "The roaring of the monster sounded very like the roaring of the torch, except that it was louder. It began to roar as soon as its tentacles touched you. I could tell by the spasmodic jerking of your muscles that it was sending an electric current through your body, and quite a powerful one.

"There are a few animals already known to science which have this power. Some of them are deep-sea creatures, but the electric eel of Brazil is the most striking example. This eel, when its electrical organs are fully charged, is said to be capable of rendering a man or a large animal unconscious from electric shock. So it is not surprising that this creature, so many times larger than the largest electric eel, was able to do the same for you with a number of shocks.

"My torch began to function just as the creature attacked you, and I first tried to rescue you by burning off the wiry tentacles. But it had so many of these in reserve that the task seemed endless. I, too, was attacked and had the creature's store of electrical energy not been depleted by the shocks it had sent through your body, it is probable that both of us would have been rendered unconscious and ultimately devoured. As it was, I was rapidly becoming helplessly entangled in the tentacles, so I turned the torch on the monster's body. It was then that it shrieked—not once, but many times. The volume of its terrible voice was astounding; its weird tones were horrible to hear!

"But the torch finally won. All the tentacles let go except those which had been burned off, and the thing, after bumping around on the walls for a time, flew against the window screen with such force that it was ripped from the frame. Then it disappeared, still screaming weirdly, into the night.

"I made a very weak solution of prussic acid and painted the remaining tentacles with this. There were quite a few around your arms, legs and body. One also was tightly bound around your forehead. All relaxed instantly when the solution was applied. I then used it on the tentacles which still clung to me, after which Wong and I carried you here."

"Was it prussic acid solution you used on my finger this morning?" I asked. "That stuff that had a bitter almond odor?"

"That was it," replied the professor. "Prussic acid has a paralyzing effect on the nervous system. It is a good thing that I learned, this morning, that it will cause the tentacles of these creatures to relax. It would have been dangerous to have had to experiment with the longer tentacles in the position they had gripped you this evening."

"I have always thought," I said, "that the touch of prussic acid to the human skin was poisonous, particularly to a cut surface, and that one whiff of the fumes was usually deadly."

"So it is," replied the professor. "In a sufficiently strong solution it would be deadly to apply it to an abraded skin, and one whiff of prussic or hydrocyanic acid gas is usually lethal. But the solution I used was diluted sufficiently to make it safe for application to the human skin, or even to an open wound. I purposely made a weak solution this morning, intending to make it a little stronger if necessary, but as you saw, it worked."

At this moment, Wong entered with a tea tray and a steaming pot of fragrant Darjeeling.

I sat up for my cup of tea, and we discussed the strange incidents of the day.

Then Mrs. Davis ordered us all to bed with a firmness that would not be gainsaid.

Early the next morning Wong awakened me with a gentle knock at my door, and upon my bidding him enter, brought me a demitasse and cigarettes.

"Plofessey Davis like see you along lab'toly plenty quick," he said.

"Tell him I'll be right down," I replied.

I dressed and hurried downstairs. The professor was waiting in his laboratory.

"Dick," he said, "something has happened since last evening that has, it seems to me, a rather sinister significance. I haven't told my wife or Sue, as I don't wish to alarm them."

"What has happened?" I asked.

"Come with me," he replied. "I told my wife you and I were going for a walk, so we can go out without arousing her suspicion. Sue, I believe, is still sleeping. The poor child is exhausted after the ordeal of yesterday."

After threading our way among the various outbuildings, we entered the lane between a corn and wheat field which led to the pasture. Traversing the lane, we came to the pasture itself. Sue and I had crossed it only the day before, and it had revealed at that time, only the undulating, blue grass.

But overnight there had sprouted, near its center, a colony of gray-white growths, varying in height from three to nearly twelve feet. They were roughly cylindrical in shape, and their tops were fringed with squirming, wiry tentacles, some of which reached nearly to the ground, while others stood at various angles at or near the horizontal, and still others reached skyward.

That the movements of the tentacles were not due to the morning breeze was quite evident from the fact that they moved in all directions. The cylindrical stalks, also, bent in various directions from time to time, almost as if they were bowing to each other, and those that bent toward us revealed cavernous openings at their tops, greatly resembling the mouths of anemones.

The wind, blowing from them to us, carried the revolting charnel smell that had become so familiar to us.

"What are they?" I asked.

"You know as much as I," replied the professor. "They may be one of the life phases of the cloud-medusae. From the similarity of their tentacles, and the analogy we have in our submarine medusae, as well as the similar, I might say identical stench that emanates from them, I am inclined to think this is the case. Yet they might be a totally different race of creatures, which have traveled to us simultaneously with the medusae, from the space wanderer which we believe is responsible for this unprecedented invasion. Only a careful observation of them will tell."

While we were talking, Jake Smith, the professor's farm hand, approached, driving a herd of cattle before him with the assistance of a young collie. The racket they made—the clatter of hoofs, the bawling of cattle and calves, the barking of the dog, and the shouts of the man—seemed to have a magnetic effect on the strange growths before us, for instantly all bent toward the herd, mouths gaping and tentacles wriggling menacingly.

With the herd were three calves which showed a tendency to wander. While the collie was bringing in one of these strays another got away and scampered straight toward the mysterious growths. As it drew near them, all bent toward it, and when it would have run between two of the tallest, the nearer, arching its cylindrical stem like a striking serpent, suddenly pounced upon it and bore it struggling and bawling, aloft, hopelessly entangled in the myriad tentacles.

Then the mother cow, evidently attracted by the cries of distress of her doomed offspring, dashed after it. By the time she reached the thing that held her calf aloft, the little creature's cries had ceased. She ran helplessly around the stem for a moment, then backed up as if about to charge it head on. But she backed within range of the tentacles of three more of the horrible monstrosities, which instantly bent over and seized her, holding her helpless.

The farm hand and dog rushed after her, but the man was warned off by the professor, and he succeeded in calling off the dog before it was too late.

"Go back to the house, Dick," said the professor. "Bring my blowtorch as quickly as you can. Also my twelve-gauge pump gun and twelve-gauge double barrel, with as many shells as you can carry. I'll stay here and watch. Hurry!"

As fast as my legs would carry me, I dashed toward the house. I found the professor's blowtorch in the laboratory where he had left it the night before; and having gone shooting with him many times, I knew where to find the weapons.

Slipping into a hunting coat, I loaded the game pockets with the torch and all the ammunition they would safely bear. Then, taking the two guns, I hurried back to the pasture.

The professor had approached to within fifty feet of the outer line of monsters. One of these, the one which had captured the calf, had grown considerably taller. Whereas it had been about twelve feet in height before, it was now nearer eighteen and still growing. The remains of the calf, still clutched to the mouth-like opening at the top, were barely visible as a rounded, dark mass showing here and there in the wilderness of tentacles which surrounded it.

The three creatures that had captured the cow had also increased in size, and what we could see of the helpless bovine had dwindled tremendously. They continued their arched position over the carcass, feeding noiselessly, and apparently without any competition among themselves, unless it was one of speed.

"Quick!" said the professor. "Give me the torch. I can be generating it while you load the gun."

I handed him the torch and proceeded to load the two shotguns.

"What can we do with shotguns against these monsters?" I asked.

"Nothing, at present," he replied, lighting the generator of the torch and working the pressure pump, "but if a certain theory of mine is correct we will soon have considerable use for them."

"Which gun do you want?" I asked.

"The double barrel," he replied. "When you start you will probably have to shoot straight and often. I only want the double barrel in case of an emergency, as I plan to use the torch. Give me about a dozen extra shells."

I handed him the shells, and he put them in his pockets after looking at the wadded ends.

"Number fours," he said. "About as good as any, I guess. Did you bring nothing but fours?"

"I also brought a dozen loads of buckshot," I replied, "and one box of number twos."

"We'll try the fours first, at any rate," he said. "Now I want you to watch the creature that captured the calf."

I looked, and saw that it had now reached a height of about twenty feet. Its victim seemed entirely consumed. But the startling thing I noticed was the strange metamorphosis that was taking place in the shape of the creature itself. The cylindrical body seemed to be separating into a number of disk-shaped segments, piled one on top of the other like stacked dishes. Tentacles were beginning to branch out from the top of each segment.

"If I am not mistaken," said the professor, "the top segment will presently arise and sail away, or rather attempt to sail away, for as soon as it flies clear of the others, I want you to shoot it down. If it is far enough from them to make it safe for me to approach it, I can then destroy it with the torch."

It was not long before a dense cloud of vapor formed around the top segment. Suddenly it rose and turned over, dropping the whitened bones of the calf. Then it sailed slowly away over the heads of its fellows, its wiry tentacles trailing below. As soon as it was beyond range of their tentacles, I fired into the most dense part of the cloud. It dipped slightly. Again I fired, and it slowly sank to the ground.

"Watch the next one," shouted the professor, running to the one I had brought down, torch in one hand and shotgun in the other. "Don't let any of them get away."

As he turned his torch on the writhing, squirming mass that lay on the ground, it gave vent to a shriek similar to the one which had rung in my ears the night before. Again and again it shrieked under the relentless flame. The noise distracted my attention for a moment and I looked back at the monster I was supposed to be watching, just in time to see a second cloud-covered medusa sail away. Two shots brought this one to the ground as they had the former. Meanwhile the shrieks of the first creature ceased and the professor moved on to the second to start another pandemonium with his searing torch.

Pushing four more shells into the magazine, I waited for the next medusa to arise. The farm hand had, meanwhile, come up with another blowtorch and a double-barreled shotgun.

"The professor told me to pen up the cows and bring these," he said.

"Light your torch," I told him. "As soon as you get it going you can help the professor."

"What in tarnation's he burnin'?" asked Smith, priming his own torch. "Smells like feathers or old shoes, or somethin'."

"It's worse than either," I replied. "When you get your torch going I'll show you what to do."

Before the farm hand succeeded in getting his torch to roaring, two more medusae arose, and I brought them down. But, unfortunately, I fired at one too soon and it fell among its treelike fellows where the professor did not dare to approach it.

The professor was searing his fourth medusa when I shot down the sixth, telling Smith to watch the professor, then imitate him.

Before the seventh arose, the fifth, which I had shot down among the others, got up once more, thus affording me a demonstration of the marvelous recuperative powers of these creatures. Although I must have riddled and emptied practically every helium-filled cell in its body, it had closed the rent and refilled them in this marvelously short space of time. This time I was careful not to shoot until it had cleared its treelike fellows.

Twenty flying medusae in all arose from the stalk that had devoured the calf. When I had shot down the last one, I saw that the three creatures that had seized the cow had relinquished her dry bones, and were also forming into segments. It was evident that I would have to do some fast shooting when these segments started to fly.

Before the first one arose, Sue came cantering up on Blue Streak, her favorite saddle horse. It was her custom to ride each morning before breakfast, and hearing the shooting, she had ridden out to investigate.

"What are these things, and what in the world are you doing?" she asked.

"They are medusae passing through one of their life stages," I replied, "and I'm shooting them down as fast as they start to fly, while your father and the hired man kill them with the torches."

"Can't I help you?" she asked. "Please let me do something."

"My supply of shells is running low," I said. "You might dash back to the house and get me as many as you can carry—fours, twos, and threes."

"Splendid!" she replied, wheeling her mount. "I'll bring my gun, too, and help you."

I had thought to keep her out of danger for the time being by sending her back to the house, but to my horror, the first three disks from the three monsters that had devoured the cow, rose, turned over, and sailed after her, evidently attracted by the rapid movement of her mount.

I brought down the foremost with two quick shots, but in my haste and anxiety I missed the second, so I was forced to waste two more charges on it. I fired my last shot at the third, causing it to sag slightly, then pushed another shell into the magazine and quickly pumped it into the chamber. But to my horror I saw that I dared not fire again. The medusa was now so close to Sue that to fire would mean that she and her mount must surely be struck.

Shouting to the others to attract their attention, I started after Sue on the run. But before I had taken a dozen steps I groaned in anguish as I saw the monster dart downward, its tentacles encircling horse and rider. The roaring sound which it made as it attacked was punctuated by screams of pain and terror from girl and horse as the electrically charged tentacles seized them.

"Turn your horse, Sue!" I shouted. "Ride this way!"

But Sue was by this time enveloped in the dense cloud which surrounded the monster's disk-like body.

CHAPTER IV

Besieged World

The medusa was clinging tenaciously to horse and rider when I shouted to Sue to turn her mount. She must have heard me, for the horse suddenly wheeled and came galloping in my direction.

I could not see Sue, who was completely enveloped by the cloud which surrounded her attacker, but knew that she must be struggling frantically in its clutches, from the way it moved.

Calling to Blue Streak, I seized his bridle, but he was so terrified he dragged me fully a hundred feet before I could bring him to a stop.

In the meantime the professor and Smith arrived with their guns and torches. They started in at once, burning the writhing tentacles first. This frightened the horse still more, and he pranced while I clung to the bridle.

It only took the two men a few minutes to get Sue out of the saddle and destroy the shrieking creature that had attacked her, but to me those minutes seemed like hours. She was unconscious, apparently from the electrical shocks. Giving Smith the reins to hold, I helped the professor as he bent over her, painting the tentacles that still encircled her body and arms with diluted prussic acid from the bottle he had in his pocket.

As I was chafing her hands, I saw the last of the medusae rise and sail away, avoiding us—probably because of the smell of its burned comrade. They had all escaped while we were fighting to save Sue. We took her to the house, where we left her under her mother's care.

That afternoon I drove to Sterling in the professor's sedan to get some oxyacetylene torches which we planned to use as weapons of defense. As I sped along over the smooth concrete pavement I was surprised and horrified at the number of colonies of stalk medusae that had sprung up overnight. Some of the cornfields were nearly obliterated by them. And in a few of the pastures I saw individuals undergoing the metamorphosis which indicated that they had been well fed.

Upon my arrival in Sterling, I stopped at a garage which I knew did welding, and tried to buy an outfit from them. They had only one, which was not for sale, but referred me to a wholesaler who would sell me as many outfits as I wanted.

I repaired to the office of the wholesaler, and bought three outfits with extra drums of gas, which I loaded into the back of the sedan. The wholesaler told me that the government had issued a warning to use only closed automobiles and airships. Several medusae, he said, had been shot down with anti-aircraft guns, but no means had been devised of dispatching them after they fell, and they had eventually escaped. Machine gun bullets fired from airplanes, he said, had proved ineffective, although some of the medusae thus attacked had been noticed to fly erratically or sink slightly for a time.

The medusae, he said, had spread to every continent of the world, and an international conference was being held for the purpose of devising a method of combating this menace to humanity.

I stopped at a grocery store and filled every available space in the car with bacon, ham, flour, and canned goods. Then, after buying all the papers I could get containing news of the latest developments of the medusae invasion, I took to the highway.

I got back to the farmhouse without incident, but the proximity of the stalk medusae to the edges of the road made it evident that another such trip would soon be out of the question.

Smith and the professor met me as I drove up. The latter looked into the tonneau.

"Got three outfits, I see, and a supply of groceries. Good boy! We'll need them. Let Smith have the car, now, and come up to the house."

I got out, glad to stretch my cramped limbs, and turned the wheel over to Smith.

As the professor and I walked to the house together, he said:

"I've been watching these stalk medusae, and have not only learned something about their feeding habits, but how they begin life on our earth."

"Really!" I replied. "That's important. Tell me about it."

"Yes. They begin life as microscopic, ribbon-like spores—the probable form in which they left Green's comet to colonize our earth. The weight of one of these spores, even in proportion to its minute size, is so infinitesimal that it can float for great distances in even the slightest air currents. It seems, also, to have some electromagnetic faculty which enables it to seize and utilize magnetic lines of force, thus making it possible for it to travel in interplanetary and interstellar space. Its presence here seems to indicate that it has this power, and I have found it is unharmed by liquid air, which approaches the cold of space.

"As the creature reproduces by division, a single spore arriving on any stellar body where life and growth are possible can quickly colonize that body.

"Having arrived on earth, I find that a spore immediately sends roots into the soil like a plant, but that it also extends its tentacles in the air in search of animal food. It thus feeds above and below the soil, becoming the stalk medusa so horribly familiar to us. When it reaches a certain size, each stalk turns into twenty saucer-shaped disks, which soon become flying medusae.

"At my suggestion, the government is now experimenting with flame throwers as a means for combating the menace. They are efficient for short distances, and in such limited areas as can be covered by them, but they are far from being the solution of our problem. We must find some other, swifter way. I have ordered some supplies sent from Washington for the purpose of experimenting along these lines. They are being shipped to our local airport. But it will be difficult, if not impossible, to get them, as the roads are now blocked by the medusae, as well as the fields and pastures."

"Can't they fly over us and drop them?" I asked.

"As the shipment will contain some very powerful explosives, I'm afraid that wouldn't be practical," said the professor.

At this juncture Smith came in to report that the oxyacetylene outfits were ready to use, and that quite a number of stalk medusae were springing up around the house.

The professor and I went out and found that Smith had rigged up the outfits quite ingeniously. Each one was installed on a wheelbarrow with the nozzle fastened on the end of a twelve-foot bamboo pole. This pole was laid across a rack which Smith had built on the front of the vehicle, enabling a man to move the outfit about without having to hold onto the pole or turn out the gas.

Each of us took one of the outfits and immediately began the war of extermination against the stalk medusae surrounding the house and other buildings. It was slow work, as there were thousands of them. But after several hours of strenuous endeavor, we had spaces cleared around the buildings wide enough to forestall any immediate attacks from the creatures.

We then turned our weapons over to the three remaining farm hands, who, under Smith's supervision, began widening the clear space we had made. The professor and I returned to the house.

Scarcely had we entered the drawing room when the voice of a very excellent soprano who was singing over the radio was suddenly stilled, and an announcer cut in:

"Sorry to have to interrupt the program," he said, "but I have just received an important announcement by telephone. The Chicago air scouts report that an immense number of the flying, cloud-hidden monsters that are menacing the world are congregating far out over Lake Michigan. The attention of the scout fleet was first drawn to them by hideous, howling noises, so loud that even at a distance of a mile they were easily audible above the roaring of the airplane propellers. Upon investigating, the scouts saw the monsters forming in a long line not more than two hundred feet above the lake.

"These strange creatures appeared to be carrying on an intelligent conversation with each other by means of terrific howls, and at times, seemed to be silenced by a leader, which addressed them all collectively. They are now bearing down on the City of Chicago, and every person is warned to stay within doors, keeping all doors and windows closed.

"Regardless of the heat, fires should be immediately kindled in all furnaces, boilers, stoves and fireplaces as a measure of defense. It is thought that the smoke, cinders and sparks may be distasteful to the monsters, and the fire will keep them from reaching down chimneys with their deadly tentacles. Our air force is trying to break up the line by dropping bombs on it, but as fast as a gap is opened the creatures close it once more. Take heed, everybody, on peril of your lives! Stay inside. Keep doors and windows locked. Build fires."

"Just as I feared," said the professor. "These creatures from another world, perhaps from another universe are more intelligent than they at first appeared to be. They are beginning, now, to work in groups—to exercise their intelligence as well as their instinct for the capture of food. Man has proved a wily and elusive food morsel, so they are uniting forces and trawling for him. Think of it, Dick! A group of monsters from outside space trawling for men, exactly as men trawl for fish! Seems absolutely incredible, doesn't it?"

"It does," I answered. "It also seems impossible that they should have suddenly begun talking to each other. So far we have heard, none of these creatures talked to each other before."

"I don't see anything so surprising about that," said the professor. "We discovered that they had voices, and powerful ones, when I burned the one that attacked you. It is quite possible that, although endowed with voices as soon as they reach the flying stage, they do not actually learn to converse until they reach a certain stage of development. This is true of all creatures with voices— true of man himself.

"A peculiarity of the flying medusae is that they make no sound when cut or blown to pieces. Cutting, puncturing or tearing them evidently does not hurt them. They seem to know, instinctively, that it will not kill them, but that it works actually as a form of artificial reproduction by fission, as each fragment will eventually become a new individual. Burning, however, is different. Burning destroys the living tissues beyond repair. And when they are burned, they shriek. They evidently know that burning means death."

The professor paused, then spoke very solemnly: "Dick, we have a greater menace in the medusae than even I, who recognized their extremely dangerous character from the first, ever thought possible. There is no telling how intelligent they are, or what faculties they can develop in adapting themselves to terrestrial environment. It is evident that the adults, at least, have auditory organs. They could not converse vocally without them.

"They apparently have a sense of smell, also, by which they locate their prey. The swift motion of the prey evidently aids this sense, just as waving a bottle of perfume beneath the nostrils makes the aroma more rapidly perceptible than when it is held still.

"They have, I have concluded, no organs of sight—or only imperfectly developed ones. No doubt the comet on which we believe they came has been away from the sun for so many thousands of years that its surface was constantly in darkness. The light from the meteoroids of the coma, when they are made incandescent by passage through the upper regions of the comet's atmosphere, could scarcely penetrate the thick clouds which our astronomers observed any better than they could penetrate an exceedingly dim twilight. Under the circumstances, organs of sight would have been useless, and would probably have atrophied had the creatures originally possessed them.

"It may be that under the conditions which they find on our planet, these monsters will be able to develop their organs of sight. Nor have we plumbed the limit of their intelligence. They may, for all we know, be as intelligent as man himself, or more so."

At this moment Wong entered, and bowed obsequiously.

"Captain Felton like make talk Plofessey Davis a long telumphone," he announced.

"Excuse me," said the professor. "It's probably news of the supplies from Washington."

He went to the writing desk and picked up the receiver-transmitter.

"Yes, captain? They are here, you say? I don't know how I'll be able to get them. . . . All right, captain."

Putting down the phone, he turned to me.

"Don't be foolhardy, Dick," he said. "You can't go to that airport on the ground, and you have no means of flying there. Why, the attempt would be suicidal!"

"Nevertheless," I replied, "I have a plan for getting through, and I believe I can make it work."

My plans for making the trip to the airport did not include the use of either the automobile or the road. The land leading to the highway was now almost a solid mass of stalk medusae, and the highway itself had been declared impassable, blocked as it was by the interlacing tentacles which grew clear up to the edge of the concrete. I did have a plan however, which I thought quite capable of being carried into effect.

Among the farm implements was a powerful caterpillar tractor. When I told the professor that I intended to use it and take a short cut across the fields, he was dumbfounded.

"Why, Dick, that would be fatal. There isn't even a cab over it for protection. I can't think of permitting it."

"What if I turn it into a tank first?" I asked.

"Into a tank? How?"

"There are plenty of materials and tools. The old chicken house you tore down had a sheet metal roof. Fastened on two-by-fours and well braced, this will make a cab that will be as good a protection as a closed automobile. And with a few lights of glass from your greenhouse we can make a windshield that will answer our purpose. With one man driving and another using an acetylene torch, we can go through almost anything short of a stone wall. The torch will not only burn any medusae that may impede our progress, but will cut through the wire fences."

"By Jove!" exclaimed the professor. "It sounds feasible enough. Get Smith to help you build that tank. I suppose it will take several days, but the thing will be almost invincible, once it is constructed."

"I don't think it will take two of us long to build," I answered. "We should have it ready for the trip by tomorrow afternoon."

"If you do, so much the better," said the professor. "Go ahead, and while you are at it, I'll do some more experimenting."

Smith and I set to work on our tank shortly thereafter. The other farm hands, reinforced at times by the professor, kept after the stalk medusae that continued to sprout near the buildings, using the acetylene torches. But just outside the little circle kept cleared around the buildings was a solid forest of stalk medusae that stretched as far as the eye could see in every direction. And the air was heavy with the sickening, musty stench that exuded from their silver-gray bodies and deadly tentacles.

While Smith and I worked on our tank, Sue came out from time to time to tell us of the latest developments as announced on the radio. Once she brought us lemonade, and again, tea, sandwiches and cakes.

According to the latest reports, the medusae had adopted their trawling tactics everywhere. Yet they appeared to be aware that their intended prey was thickest in the cities, and swooped down on them in great numbers.

Some cities were approached during fogs or rainstorms when the coming of the medusae went unnoticed, and as a result, thousands of people perished. Even the smallest towns and villages had their lookouts posted, and when a suspicious cloud was sighted whistles were blown, bells rung, and shots fired, in order that everyone might seek cover.

Thousands of stalk medusae were sprouting in city lawns and parks, and as a result every fire-making apparatus that could be secured was pressed into use.

It was not until after dinner that night that we heard for the first time of individual medusae attacking closed houses, insinuating their fine tentacles through crevices around windows and doors, keyholes, or any other openings, until they were able to find and kill the inmates by terrific electrical shocks; after absorbing them through the tentacles alone, they would move on again in search of other prey.

Householders were warned to keep torches ready, to have fires going at all times, and to keep soldering irons, pokers, tongs and shovels red-hot, to be used in case of attack. They were warned, also, that when touching a tentacle with a metal object they should wear rubbers and either insulate the grip of the weapon they were using or wear rubber gloves.

That night we took turns watching, the professor, Smith, Wong, and I, with the furnace going full blast and every window and door tightly closed. As it was unusually warm we made a most uncomfortable night of it.

It was three o'clock on the following afternoon before Smith and I were ready to start across the fields to the airport in our tank.

Smith, who had handled tractors for many years, was to do the driving, while I managed the torch. In addition to these weapons and the pump-gun, we carried a bottle of dilute prussic acid solution and a small brush to be used for removing any tentacles that might wrap themselves around us. My right arm, which projected from the side of the cab through a hole cut especially for the purpose, was protected by sheet metal armor, and my hand, with which I grasped the pole to which the nozzle was fastened, was covered by a heavy leather gauntlet to which Sue had stitched tiny overlapping plates of metal.

Sue, Mrs. Davis, the professor, and the entire entourage were present to see us off.

Farewells and godspeeds were said, and we lumbered off across the barnyard and into the pasture lane.

At the mouth of the lane we encountered our first stalk medusae. They bent down to receive us, and their writhing tentacles whipped menacingly around us. But the tractor knocked the stalks down and trundled over them, almost as if they had not been there, while the spurting acetylene flame instantly severed every tentacle it touched.

We made slow but steady progress, leaving a writhing, squirming, stinking trail of crushed and scorched medusae behind us. After we crossed the pasture we cut our first fence with the acetylene torch, and entered what had been the clover field.

As I looked at the weird, unearthly landscape, I was struck by its contrast with the pleasant scene it had presented two days before, when I had lain in the speckled shade of the hackberry tree listening to the bees droning in the sweet-scented clover while Sue wove a garland of blossoms.

Where the clover had been, the ground was dry and bare between the ugly, tentacle-crowned, silver-gray stalks. The hackberry tree, stripped of its leaves and drained of its sap, stood a gaunt, lifeless skeleton, its bare limbs stretched heavenward as if in a plea for vengeance on its merciless destroyers.

The droning of the bees, the chirping of the crickets, and singing of birds—all were stilled, to be replaced by one monotonous and sinister sound—the rustling of countless millions of writhing, squirming tentacles. And the pleasant fragrance of clover and wildflowers had given away to the disgusting decay-smell of the medusae.

We lumbered slowly across the former clover field, cut a second fence, and entered the pasture in which Pilot Jackson had crashed two days before. Here we found more and larger medusae than we had previously encountered, and our progress was for a time considerably retarded But we got across at last, cut a third fence, and entered what had once been a cornfield. Like the other fields we had crossed, it was completely denuded of vegetation by the rankly growing crop of the invaders from the moon.

As we approached the airport we saw with relief that the landing field had been kept clear of medusae. A squad of men using a flame thrower were kept busy destroying such sprouts as cropped up from time to time.

The surface of the entire field was blackened by the repeated burning to which it had been subjected.

When we cut our last fence and entered the landing field, we were greeted by a loud cheer from a group in front of the airport, and they crowded curiously around us as we approached.

Captain Felton, in charge of the port, greeted us cordially, and ordered the munitions loaded for us. They consisted of several cases of hand grenades, a trench mortar with ammunition, an anti-aircraft gun with ammunition, a machine gun with ammunition, and a number of unloaded shells with material for loading them. As we knew very little about these weapons we detailed a corporal named Ole Hansen to go with us and show us how to assemble and use them.

In a few minutes a sergeant reported that our cargo was loaded. After we had taken leave of the captain and stowed Ole Hansen among the munitions, Smith climbed into the driver's seat. I lighted my torch and took my position beside him.

The men at the airport cheered us and wished us luck as we trundled off over the scorched field.

Soon we were smashing and burning our way back over the path by which we had come. We made much better time than before as the medusae over which we had previously passed were badly crippled, and those on either side had many of their tentacles burned away.

It was not until we were on the last lap of our journey, crashing through the lane that led to the cattle pens, that Smith noticed something amiss at the Davis house.

"Mr. Perry!" he cried in horror. "Look! Look over there toward the house!"

I looked, and the blood froze in my veins, for where the house should have been plainly visible, I could see only a dense, silver-gray cloud. As we approached it there came plainly to our ears above the sound of our motor the roaring sound which a giant medusa makes when it attacks.

CHAPTER V

The Attacking Medusa

"That sure must be a big one from the size of the cloud," said Smith, as he urged the tractor forward to where the huge medusa was attacking the house.

"Ay tank we ban going to have one hal of a fight pretty quick," said Ole, as he loosened the lid of a case of hand grenades.

Smith stopped our tank about a hundred feet from the house. Then we all got out and stepped behind it, using it for a breastwork. Ole tore the lid off his case of grenades, took one out, and setting the timer, hurled it with an expert overhand throw so it exploded just above the top of the cloud. The sound it made was barely audible above the terrific roaring of the giant medusa.

A group of squirming, twisted tentacles reached out at us from the cloud mass as if in reprisal, but I burned them off with the torch.

Smith seized the shotgun, and fired six charges into the portion of the cloud where he thought the disk-like body of the monster was located, and Corporal Hansen continued his bombardment with hand grenades. But neither seemed to have any effect on the medusa.

"If the damned thing would only get mad and chase us," shouted Smith, "we could lure it away with the tank."

"Perhaps I can make it mad with the torch," I said, and started toward the house.

But Smith seized my arm.

"Hold on there," he said. "Do you want to commit suicide? One jolt from the batteries of that thing and I reckon you'll be through for keeps. Besides, you might set the house afire."

By this time Ole had used up his box of grenades. Instead of getting more, he dragged out the machine gun and began assembling it.

"Damn' grenades don't work so gude," he said, "but I bet you dis baby will give it hal."

I handed the torch to Smith, and, reloading the pump gun, began a bombardment of the upper part of the cloud. I doubt whether it had much effect on the huge medusa, but it was all that I could do, and it relieved by feelings somewhat, for I was badly worried. We had found nobody about the place, and, for all we knew, Sue and her parents had already been killed by the monster. It might merely be lingering to absorb their bodies through its tentacles before leaving. There was no way of communicating with them if they were alive, because of the terrific roaring sound made by the attacking medusa.

I was reloading the gun for the third time, and Ole had just finished assembling his machine gun, when the sound made by the monster suddenly changed. At first I thought the professor had succeeded in burning it, causing it to shriek, but this sound was not a shriek. It was not exactly like a howl, but sounded more like a moan—a groaning, unearthly sound so loud that it nearly split my eardrums.

Petrified into inactivity for a moment by this new development, the three of us stood spellbound, watching for the creature's next move. There was a terrific agitation which lasted for some time, accompanied by the unearthly moaning and groaning in ever increasing crescendo. From time to time we could see the ends of writhing tentacles projecting beyond the periphery of the cloud mass, squirming as if the creature were in horrible agony.

"Ay tank dot teeng ban purty damn sick," said Ole, coolly loading his machine gun. "What say we give him some more hal?"

"Wait, Ole," I said. "Something has happened that we don't know anything about."

Scarcely had I spoken ere the writhing and groaning of the monster suddenly ceased and the cloud around it began slowly to dissolve.

Then, to my intense relief, I heard the voice of Professor Davis.

"Dick! Smith! Don't do any more shooting. The thing is dead, and we are all safe in the house."

As the cloud dissolved it revealed a most astounding and hideous spectacle. Sprawled over the roof, and almost completely hiding it, was the limp, sagging body of the medusa. It lay there like an immense slimy silver-gray pancake with frilled edges, its tentacles trailing limply to the ground in all directions. The body was fully thirty feet in diameter, and the tentacles were at least thirty-five feet long.

The professor opened the door of his laboratory. In his hand was a pair of scissors. He snipped off an end of one of the tentacles which hung in front of the door—then gingerly touched it with his finger tip. It remained motionless. He touched another tentacle, and it did not move. Then he pushed them all aside and leaped out, running toward us and shouting like a schoolboy:

"Eureka! I've found it! I've found it!"

"Found what?" I asked.

"The very thing that I used in the first place to make the tentacles relax—prussic acid," he replied. "Prussic acid or some of its derivatives will do the trick."

With his scissors the professor snipped the remaining tentacles from before the door. Then he held it open for us to enter.

Sue and her mother were waiting there to greet us, and were as relieved to know that I was still alive as I was to learn that they had escaped death. They both shed tears of joy, and I must confess that, as I kissed them, my own eyes were moist.

The professor put in a call for Washington, and the imperturbable Wong brought tea.

"After you and Smith left," the professor told me, "I was busy in my laboratory, when Sievers, one of the farm hands, came rushing in, shouting that a big cloud was coming toward the house. I went out to observe it, and one look through my binoculars convinced me that it was a flying medusa. I told Sievers to bring the other two men into the house at once, and that all of them should bring their rubber boots and raincoats from their quarters.

"As swiftly as possible we closed every window and door, and started a fire in the furnace and one in the grate in the living room. Then I distributed rubber gloves—luckily I have a good supply on hand at all times for laboratory work. In the meantime Sue primed and lighted the two blowtorches for me, and we had two of the portable oxyacetylene outfits for use, one on the first floor and one on the second.

"It suddenly grew so dark outside that we were forced to turn on the lights. I knew then that the monster had settled on the roof to begin its attack. Stationing Sievers and the other two men on the second floor, two to manage the acetylene outfit, and one to use the blowtorch, I remained on the first floor with my wife and daughter, Nora the cook, and Wong. Mrs. Davis and Nora stayed in the center of the living room, Sue guarding them with a blowtorch, while Wong and I patrolled the lower floors with the portable acetylene outfit." The professor paused for breath.

"Almost immediately," he resumed, "the long, deadly tentacles began worming themselves in around doors and windows and through keyholes. Wong and I were busy, hurrying from one place to another and burning them off, and I could tell from the sounds upstairs that the men stationed there were equally busy.

"Although the roaring of the monster made it difficult for us to distinguish what was going on outside, I faintly heard your shots and the explosions of the grenades. Sue had turned the radio on to top-volume so I might hear the latest reports while working in my laboratory, and it added its raucous notes to the bedlam of sounds.

"Most of the announcements had to do with the war against the medusae, and one of them was being made just at an instant when I was looking into the drawing room to see how the ladies were getting along. It stated that a nurseryman near Plano, Illinois, had reported that a number of stalk medusae which had grown in a grove of cherry laurel at his nursery had collapsed as if dead, and were beginning to give off a most abominable odor.

"The statement of this fact set me to thinking. I remembered that prussic acid had apparently paralyzed the tentacles on which I first experimented. Prussic, or as it is technically known, hydrocyanic acid, is present in the cherry laurel in considerable quantities. In this case it was evident that the acid had not only paralyzed but had killed the medusae.

"Leaving Wong to patrol alone for a few moments, I rushed into my laboratory. Unfortunately, my supply of prussic acid was reduced to about a minimum—not enough even to begin with. Then I remembered that most of the cyanides have similar toxic effects to those of hydrocyanic acid; and I was well supplied with potassium cyanide, which I use for dispatching insects. The next question was, how to poison the medusa with potassium cyanide.

"I finally decided to try shooting it through the crystals. Accordingly I removed the shot loads from two shells and replaced them with potassium cyanide. Each shell held nearly a half ounce of the crystals. Wadding and crimping them once more, I loaded my shotgun with them. Then I saturated a handkerchief with a neutralizing solution, making an emergency gas mask, and went to the door of the laboratory, I cocked both barrels, opened the door a little way, and pushing the gun out, muzzle upward, discharged them both. I instantly jerked the door shut, expecting a hundred tentacles to dart after me, but not one appeared. Then I heard the struggles and groans of the monster and knew that my shot had told.

"After the medusa had ceased to groan and writhe, I was reasonably certain that it was dead. I did not, however, know whether or not life still remained in the tentacles. So I snipped one off and investigated. You know the rest."

At this point the telephone rang, and the professor communicated his important tidings to the Secretary of War.

That afternoon was a rather busy one for all of us. We treated machine gun bullets with potassium cyanide solution, and dropped the crystals into shotgun shells. We coated hand grenades with potassium cyanide, mixed with a flour and water paste. Then we began our war of extermination.

The machine gun, we soon found, was the most efficient weapon. After we had exhausted our other munitions, we left the shooting to the skillful corporal, while we performed the disagreeable task of removing the immense, stinking carcass of the giant medusa from the roof. We had to cut it and drag it away in sections, and this nauseating work occupied most of the afternoon.

It was soon learned that even in minute quantities prussic acid, and most of the cyanides, were deadly to the medusae. Their remarkable powers of absorption and assimilation which made their rapid growth possible acted for their destruction when the one poison that had proved so deadly to them was introduced.

It was found that if a single attached tentacle of a stalk medusa were touched with a small quantity of potassium cyanide or prussic acid solution, the entire animal would be poisoned fatally in less than ten minutes.

Airplanes armed with machine guns, the bullets of which were coated with potassium cyanide or other prussic acid derivatives, applied over a thin coating of wax to prevent any chemical action, cruised the skies in search of the flying medusae, and brought them down by the hundreds.

Such products as oil of cherry laurel, technical oil of bitter almonds, and other commercial products containing prussic acid, were found efficient as coatings for bullets.

Closely following on the heels of the first day's prussic acid warfare, a new problem presented itself. The bodies of the dead monsters seemed to putrefy almost as rapidly as they had been able to grow, and not only contaminated the air with a horrible odor, but constituted a menace to public health.

It was Professor Davis who suggested that they be used to fertilize the ground which they had so lately despoiled not only of organic life but of many of its life-maintaining elements. In the country this was done chiefly by cutting them up with sharp disk harrows, then plowing them under.

More than a year passed before the medusae were no longer counted a menace, but in two years it was generally believed that they had been totally exterminated.

As I write the final page of this strange chronicle I am seated at the edge of a certain clover field—the field beside which I was lying in the mottled shade of the hackberry tree nearly three years ago, while Sue wove a garland of clover blossoms—the field which I later saw denuded of all life save the hideous, tentacled stalk medusae.

Above us towers a gaunt specter—the only visible reminder of that terrible scourge that visited the earth three years ago. The dead hackberry still extends its naked limbs heavenward, but now as if in thanksgiving for the vengeance that has been consummated.

The bees are humming busily in the fragrant clover once more. The mail plane is winging its swift way, undisturbed, to the airport. And Sue, my wife, is weaving a garland of clover blossoms.

THE PLANETOID OF PERIL
PAUL ERNST

HARLEY 2Q14N20 STOPPED for a moment outside the great dome of the Celestial Developments Company. Moodily he stared at their asteroid development chart. It showed, as was to be expected, the pick of the latest asteroid subdivision projects: the Celestial Developments Company, established far back in 2045, would handle none but the very best. Small chance of his finding anything here!

However, as he gazed at the chart, hope came suddenly to his face, and his heart beat high under his sapphire blue tunic. There was an asteroid left for sale there—one blank space among the myriad, pink-lettered Sold symbols. Could it be that here was the chance he had been hunting so desperately?

He bent closer, to read the description of the sphere, and the hope faded gradually from his countenance. According to its orbit and location, and the spectroscopic table of its mineral resources, it was a choice planetoid indeed. Of course such a rich little sphere, listed for sale by the luxurious Celestial Developments Company, would cost far more than he could ever rake together to pay for an asteroid.

Shaking his head, he adjusted his gravity regulator to give him about a pound and a half of weight, and started to float on. Then, his lips twisting at his own absurd hopefulness, he stopped again; and after another moment of indecision turned into the archway that led to the concern's great main office. After all, it wouldn't hurt to inquire the price, even though he knew in advance it would be beyond his humble means.

A youngster in the pale green of the one-bar neophyte in business promptly glided toward him.

"Something for you to-day, sir?" he asked politely.

"Yes," said Harley. "I'm looking around for a planetoid; want to get a place of my own out a way from Earth. Something, you understand, that may turn out to be a profitable investment as well as furnishing an exclusive home-site. I see on your chart that you have a sphere left for sale, in the Red Belt, so I came in to ask about it."

"Ah, you mean asteroid Z-40," said the youngster, gazing with envious respect at the ten-bar insignia, with the crossed Sco drills, that proclaimed Harley to be a mining engineer of the highest rank. "Yes, that is still for sale. A splendid sphere, sir; and listed at a remarkably low figure. Half a million dollars."

"Half a million dollars!" exclaimed Harley. It was an incredibly small sum: scarcely the yearly salary of an unskilled laborer. "Are you sure that's right?"

"Yes, that's the correct figure. Down payment of a third, and the remaining two thirds to be paid out of the exploitation profits—"

Here the conversation was interrupted by an elderly, grey-haired man with the six-bar dollar-mark insignia of a business executive on his purple tunic. He had been standing nearby, and at the mention of asteroid Z-40 had looked up alertly. He glided to the two with a frown on his forehead, and spoke a few curt words to the neophyte, who slunk away.

"Sorry, sir," he said to Harley. "Z-40 isn't for sale."

"But your young man just told me that it was," replied Hartley, loath to give up what had begun to look like an almost unbelievable bargain.

"He was mistaken. It's not on the market. It isn't habitable, you see."

"What's wrong—hasn't it an atmosphere?"

"Oh, yes. One that is exceptionally rich in oxygen, as is true of all the spheres we handle. With a late model oxygen concentrator, one would have no trouble at all existing there."

"Is its speed of revolution too great?"

"Not at all. The days are nearly three hours long: annoying till you get used to it, but nothing like the inferior asteroids of the Mars Company where days and nights are less than ten minutes in duration."

"Well, is it barren, then? No minerals of value? No vegetation?"

"The spectroscope shows plenty of metals, including heavy radium deposits. The vegetation is as luxuriant as that of semi-tropic Earth."

"Then why in the name of Betelguese," said Harley, exasperated, "won't you sell the place to me? It's exactly what I've been looking for, and what I'd despaired of finding at my price."

"I'm forbidden to tell why it isn't for sale," said the executive, starting to float off. "It might hurt our business reputation if the truth about that bit of our celestial properties became widely known— Oh, disintegrate it all! Why wasn't the thing erased from the chart weeks ago!"

"Wait a minute." Harley caught his arm and detained him. "You've gone too far to back out now. I'm too eager to find some such place as your Z-40 to be thrown off the subject like a child. *Why* isn't it for sale?"

The man tightened his lips as though to refuse to answer, then shrugged.

"I'll tell you," he said at last. "But I beg of you to keep it confidential. If some of our investors on neighboring asteroids ever found out about the peril adjoining them on Z-40, they'd probably insist on having their money back."

He led the way to a more secluded spot under the big dome, and spoke in a low tone, with many a glance over his shoulder to see if anyone were within earshot.

"Z-40 is an exceptionally fine bit of property. It is commodious; about twenty miles in diameter. Its internal heat is such that it has a delightful climate in spite of the extreme rarity of atmosphere common to even the best of asteroids. It has a small lake; in fact it has about everything a man could want. Yet, as I said, it is uninhabitable."

His voice sank still lower.

"You see, sir, there's already a tenant on that sphere, a tenant that was in possession long before the Celestial Developments Company was organized. And it's a tenant that can't be bought off or reasoned with. It's some sort of beast, powerful, ferocious, that makes it certain death for a man to try to land there."

"A beast?" echoed Harley. "What kind of a beast?"

"We don't know. In fact we hardly even know what it looks like. But from what little has been seen of it, it's clear that it is like no other specimen known to universal science. It's something enormous, some freak of animal creation that seems invulnerable to man's smaller weapons. And that is why we can't offer the place for sale. It would be suicide for anyone to try to make a home there."

"*Has* anyone ever tried it?" asked Harley. "Any competent adventurer, I mean?"

"Yes. Twice we sold Z-40 before we realized that there was something terribly wrong with it. Both buyers were hardy, intrepid men. The first was never heard of after thirty-six hours on the asteroid. The second man managed to escape in his Blinco Dart, and came back to Earth to tell of a vast creature that had attacked him during one of the three-hour nights. His hair was white from the sight of it, and he's still in a sanitarium, slowly recovering from the nervous shock."

Harley frowned thoughtfully. "If this thing is more than a match for one man, why don't you send an armed band with heavy atomic guns and clear the asteroid by main force?"

"My dear sir, don't you suppose we've tried that? Twice we sent expensive expeditions to Z-40 to blow the animal off the face of the sphere, but neither expedition was able to find the thing, whatever it is. Possibly it has intelligence enough to hide if faced by overwhelming force. When the second expedition failed, we gave it up. Poor business to go further. Already, Z-40 has cost us more than we could clear from the sale of half a dozen planetoids."

For a long time Harley was silent. The Company was a hard-headed, cold-blooded concern. Anything that kept them from selling an asteroid must be terrible indeed.

His jaw set in a hard line. "You've been honest with me," he said at length. "I appreciate it. Just the same—I still want to buy Z-40. Maybe I can oust the present tenant. I'm pretty good with a ray-pistol."

"It would be poor policy for us to sell the asteroid. We don't want to become known as a firm that trades in globes on which it is fatal to land."

"Surely my fate is none of your worry?" urged Harley.

"The asteroid," began the executive with an air of finality, "is not for—"

"Man, it's *got* to be!" cried Harley. Then, with a perceptible effort he composed himself. "There's a reason. The reason is a girl. I'm a poor man, and she's heiress to fabulous— Well, frankly, she's the daughter of 3W28W12 himself!" The executive started at mention of that universally known number. "I don't want to be known as a fortune hunter; and my best bet is to find a potentially rich asteroid, cheap, and develop it—incidentally getting an exclusive estate for my bride and myself far out in space, away from the smoke and bustle of urban Earth. Z-40, save for the menace you say now has possession of it, seems to be just what I want. If I can clear it, it means the fulfillment of all my dreams. With that in view, do you think I'd hesitate to risk my neck?"

"No," said the executive slowly, looking at the younger man's powerful shoulders and square-set chin and resolute eyes. "I don't think you would. Well, so be it. I'd greatly prefer not to sell you Z-40. But if you want to sign an agreement that we're released of all blame or responsibility in case of your death, you can buy it."

"I'll sign any agreement you please," snapped Harley. "Here is a down payment of a hundred and seventy thousand dollars. My name is Harley; sign 2Q14N20; unmarried—though I hope to change that soon, if I live—occupation, mining engineer, ten-bar degree; age, thirty-four. Now draw me up a deed for Z-40, and see that I'm given a stellar call number on the switchboard of the Radi-vision Corporation. I'll drop around there later and get a receiving unit. Good day." And, adjusting his gravity regulator to lighten his weight to less than a pound, he catapulted out the archway.

Behind him a prosaic business executive snatched a moment from a busy day to indulge in a sentimental flight of fancy. He had read once of curious old-time beings called knights, who had undertaken to fight and slay fire-eating things called dragons for the sake of an almost outmoded emotion referred to as love. It occurred to him that this brusque man of action might be compared to just such a being. He was undertaking to slay a dragon and win a castle for the daughter of 3W28W12—

The romantic thought was abruptly broken up by the numeral. It jarred so, somehow, that modern use of numbers instead of names, when thinking of sentimental passages of long ago. "The rose is fair; but in all the world there is no rose as fair as thou, my princess 3W28W12. . . ." No, it wouldn't do.

Cursing himself for a soft-headed fool, he went to deliver a stinging rebuke to somebody for not having blocked Z-40 off the asteroid chart weeks before.

"Harley 2Q14N20," recited the control assistant at Landon Field. "Destination, asteroid Z-40. Red Belt, arc 31.3470. Sights corrected, flight period twelve minutes, forty-eight seconds past nine o'clock. All set, sir?"

Harley nodded. He stepped inside the double shell of his new Blinco Dart—that small but excellent quantity-production craft that had entirely replaced the cumbersome space ships of a decade ago—and screwed down the man-hole lid. Then, with his hand on the gravity bar, he gazed out the rear panel, ready to throw the lever at the control assistant's signal.

The move was unthinkingly, mechanically made. Too many times had he gone through this process of being aimed by astronomical calculation, and launched into the heavens, to be much stirred by the wonder of it. The journey to Z-40 in the Dart was no more disquieting than, a century and a half ago, before the United States had fused together into one vast city, a journey from Chicago to Florida would have been in one of the inefficient gasoline-driven vehicles of that day.

All his thoughts were on his destination, and on a wonder as to what could be the nature of the thing that dwelt there.

He had just come from the sanitarium where the man who'd bought Z-40 before him was recovering from nervous exhaustion. He'd gone there to try to get first hand information about the creature the executive at the Celestial Developments Company had talked so vaguely of. And the tale the convalescent had told him of the thing on the asteroid was as fantastic as it was sketchy.

A tremendous, weirdly manlike creature looming in the dim night—a thing that seemed a part of the planetoid itself, fashioned from the very dirt and rock from which it had risen—a thing immune to the ray-pistol, that latest and deadliest of man-made small-arms—a thing that moved like a walking mountain and stared with terrible, stony eyes at its prey! That was what the fellow said he had faintly made out in the darkness before his nerves had finally given way.

He had impressed Harley as being a capable kind of a person, too; not at all the sort to distort facts, nor to see imaginary figures in the night.

There was that matter of the stone splinter, however, which certainly argued that the wan, prematurely white-haired fellow was a little unbalanced, and hence not to be believed too implicitly. He'd handed it to Harley, and gravely declared it to be a bit of the monster's flesh.

"Why, it's only a piece of rock!" Harley had exclaimed before he could check himself.

"Did you ever see rock like it before?"

Turning it over in his hands, Harley had been forced to admit that he never had. It was of the texture and roughness of granite, but more heavily shot with quartz, or tridymite than any other granite he'd ever seen. It had a dull opalescent sheen, too. But it was rock, all right.

"It's a piece of the thing's hide," the man had told him. "It flaked off when it tried to pry open the man-hole cover of my Dart. A moment after that I got Radivision arc directions from London

Field, aimed my sights, and shot for Earth. It was a miracle I escaped."

"But surely your ray-pistol—" Harley had begun, preserving a discreet silence about the man's delusion concerning the stone splinter.

"I tell you it was useless as a toy! Never before have I seen any form of life that could stand up against a ray-gun. But *this* thing *did!*"

This was another statement Harley had accepted with a good deal of reservation. He had felt sure the weapon the man had used had a leak in the power chamber, or was in need of recharging, or something of the kind. For it had been conclusively proved that all organic matter withered and burned away under the impact of the Randchron ray.

Nevertheless, discounting heavily the convalescent's wild story, only a fool would have clung to a conviction that the menace on Z-40 was a trivial one. There was *something* on that asteroid, something larger and more deadly than Harley had ever heard of before in all his planetary wanderings.

He squared his shoulders. Whatever it was, he was about to face it, man against animal. He was reasonably certain his ray-gun would down anything on two legs or ten. If it didn't—well, there was nothing else that could; and he'd certainly provide a meal for the creature, assuming it ate human flesh. . . .

A mechanic tapped against the rear view panel to recall his wandering attention. The control assistant held up his hands, fingers outspread, to indicate that there were ten seconds left.

Harley's hand went to his throat, where was hung a locket—a lovely but useless trinket of the kind once much worn by Earth women—and his fingers tightened tenderly on it. It had belonged to Beatrice 3W28W12's great-great-grandmother, and Beatrice had given it to him as a token.

"With luck, my dear," he whispered aloud. "With luck. . . ."

There was a slight vibration. He threw the gravity bar over to the first notch. Earth dropped, plummet-like, away from him. He

pushed the bar to the limit leg; and, at a rate of hundreds of miles
a second, was repelled from Earth toward Z-40, and the thing that
skulked there.

With a scarcely perceptible jar, he landed on the small sphere
that, he hoped, was to be his future home. Before opening his man-
hole lid, he went from panel to panel of the Dart and cautiously
reconnoitered. He had elected to land beside the little lake that
was set like a three hundred-acre gem on the surface of Z-40, and
it was more than possible that the enemy had its den nearby.

However, a careful survey of the curved landscape in all directions failed to reveal a glimpse of anything remotely threatening.
He donned his oxygen concentrator—in appearance a simple tube
of a thing, projecting about six inches above his forehead, and set
in a light metal band that encircled his head. Adjusting his gravity
regulator so he wouldn't inadvertently walk clear off into empty
space—he calculated his weight would be less than a twentieth of
an ounce here—he stepped out of the Dart and gazed around at the
little world.

Before him was the tiny lake, of an emerald green hue in the
flashing sunlight. Around its shores, and covering the adjacent,
softly rolling countryside as far as eye could reach, was a thick
growth of carmine-tinted vegetation: squat, enormous-leaved
bushes; low, sturdy trees, webbed together by innumerable vines.
To left and right, miniature mountains reared ragged crests over
the abbreviated horizon, making the spot he was in a peaceful,
lovely valley.

He sighed. There was everything here a man could wish for—
provided he could win it! Loosening his ray-pistol in its holster,
he started to walk slowly around the lake to choose a site for the
house he intended to build. On the opposite shore he found a place
that looked suitable.

A few yards back from the water's edge, curling in a thick crescent like a giant sleeping on its side, was a precipitous outcropping of rock; curious stuff, rather like granite, that gleamed with

dull opalescence in the brilliant sunlight. With that as a sort of natural buttress behind the house, and with the beautiful lake as his front dooryard, he'd have a location that any man might envy.

He returned to his Dart, hopped back across the lake in it, and unloaded his Sco drill.[1] With this he planned to sink a shaft that would serve in the future as the cellar for his villa, and in the present as an entrenchment against danger.

But now the swift night of Z-40 was almost upon him. The low slant of the descending sun warned him that he had less than ten minutes of light left, until the next three-hour day should break over the eastern rim. He placed the drums and the flexible hose of the Sco drill so that he could begin operations with it as soon as the dawn broke, and started to walk toward the precipitous outcropping of quartziferous stone immediately behind the home-site he had picked. He would climb to the top of this for a short look around, and then return to the Dart—in which double-hulled, metal fortress he thought he would be safe from anything.

He had almost reached the rock outcropping when the peculiarities of its outline struck him anew. He'd already observed that the craggy mound rather resembled a sleeping, formless giant. The closer he got to it the more the resemblance was heightened and the greater grew his perplexity.

It sprang straight up from the carmine underbrush, like a separate heap of stone cast there by some mighty hand. One end of it tapered down in a thick ridge; and this ridge had a deep, horizontal

[1] This implement, invented by Blansco 9X247A in 2052, is not so much a "drill" as a compressor. It is somewhat superficially defined in the Universal Dictionary, 2061 edition, as "a portable mechanism which, by alternating gaseous blasts of extreme heat and cold, breaks down the atoms of inorganic matter, causing them to collapse together in dense compression." Thus a cubic yard of earth can be reduced in size, in a few moments, to a pebble no larger than a pea; which pebble would weigh, on Earth, close to a ton.

cleft running along it which made it appear as though it were divided into two leglike members. In the center the mound swelled to resemble a paunchy trunk with sagging shoulders. This was topped by a huge, nearly round ball that looked for all the world like a head. There were even rudimentary features. It was grotesque—one of those freak sculptures of nature, Harley reflected, that made it seem as though the Old Girl had a mind and artistic talent of her own.

He scrambled through the brush till he reached that part of the long mound that looked like a head. There, as the sun began to stream the red lines of its descent over the sky, he prepared to ascend for his view of the surrounding landscape.

He'd got within twenty feet of the irregular ball, and had adjusted his gravity regulator to enable him to leap to its top, when he stopped as abruptly as though he had been suddenly paralyzed. Over the two deep pits that resembled nostrils in the grotesque mask of a face he thought he had observed a quiver. The illusion had occurred in just the proper place for an eyelid. It was startling, to say the least.

"I'm getting imaginative," said Harley. He spoke aloud as a man tends to do when he is alone and uneasy. "I'd better get a tighter grip on my nerves, or—good God!"

Coincident with the sound of his voice in the thin, quiet air, the huge stumps that looked like legs stirred slightly. A tremor ran through the entire mass of rock. And directly in front of Harley, less than twenty feet from where he stood, a sort of half-moon-shaped curtain of rock slid slowly up to reveal an enormous, staring eye.

Frozen with a terror such as he had never felt before in a life filled with adventure, scarce breathing, Harley glared at the monstrous spectacle transpiring before him. A hill was coming to life. A granite cliff was growing animate. It was impossible, but it was happening.

The half-moon curtains of rock that so eerily resembled eyelids, blinked heavily. He could hear a faint rasping like the rustle of sandpaper, as they did so. One of the great leg stumps moved distinctly, independent of the other one. Three columnar masses of rock—arms, or tentacles, with a dozen hinging joints in each—slowly moved away from the parent mass near the base of the head, and extended toward the Earth man.

Still in his trance, with his heart pounding in his throat till he thought it would burst, Harley watched the further awful developments. The eyelids remained opened, disclosing two great, dull eyes like poorly polished agates, which stared expressionlessly at him. There was a convulsion like a minor earthquake, and the mass shortened and heightened its bulk, raising itself to a sitting posture. The three hinged, irregular arms suddenly extended themselves to the full in a thrust that barely missed him. They were tipped, those arms, with immense claws, like interlocking, rough-hewn stone fingers. They crashed emptily together within a few feet of Harley. Then, and not till then, did the paralysis of horror loose its grip on the human.

He tore his ray-pistol from its holster and pointed it at the incredible body. An angry, blue-green cone of light leaped from the muzzle, and played over the mighty torso. Nothing happened. He squeezed the trigger back to the guard. The blue-green beam increased in intensity, and a crackling noise was audible. Under that awful power the monster should have disappeared, dissolved to a greasy mist. But it didn't.

The light beam from the ray-gun died away. The power was exhausted. It was only good for about ten seconds of such an emergency, full-force discharge, after which it must be re-charged again. The ten seconds were up. And the gigantic creature against which it had been directed had apparently felt no injury from a beam that would have annihilated ten thousand men.

The now useless ray-pistol slipped from his limp fingers. Stupefied with horror at the futility of the deadly Randchron ray against this terrible adversary, he stood rooted to the spot. Then the thing reached for him again; and his muscles were galvanized to action—to instinctive, stupid, reasonless action.

Screaming incoherently, mad with horror of the stone claws that had clutched at him, he turned and ran. In great leaps he bounded away from the accursed lake and made for the taller trees and thicker vegetation at a distance from the shore. It was the worst thing he could have done. There was a chance that he could have reached his Dart, had he thought of it, and soared aloft out of reach. But he thought of nothing. All he wanted to do, in that abysmal fear that can still make a mindless animal out of a civilized man, was to run and hide—to get away from the fearful monster that had risen up to glare at him with those stony, pitiless eyes, and to reach for him with two-fingered hands like grinding rock vises.

Just as the sun fell below the rim of the asteroid, plunging it into a darkness only faintly relieved by the light of the stars, he crashed into the deeper underbrush. A trailing creeper tripped him in his mad flight. He fell headlong, to lie panting, sobbing for breath, in the thick carpet of blood-colored moss.

Behind him, from the direction of the lake, he heard a sudden clangor as of rock beating against metal. This endured only a short time. Then the solid ground beneath him shook slightly, and an appalling crash of trees and underbrush to the rear told him that the stone colossus was on his trail.

He leaped to his feet and continued his great bounds over the sharply curved surface of the asteroid, banging against tree trunks, bruising himself against stones, falling in the darkness to rise again and flee as before in a mad attempt to distance the crashing sound of pursuit behind him.

Then he felt himself writhing in thin air as his flying course took him over the edge of a cliff. Down, down he fell, to land in a dense bed of foliage far below. Something hit his head with terrific force. Pinwheels of light flashed before his eyes, to fade into velvety nothingness. . . .

Slowly, uncertainly he wavered back to consciousness. For a moment he was aware of nothing save that he was lying on some surface that was jagged and uncomfortable, and that it was broad daylight. He opened his eyes, and saw that he was reclining, across a springy bed formed of the top of a tree. Ahead of him loomed a cliff about a hundred feet high.

Remembrance suddenly came to him. The unreasoning rush through the underbrush. The nightmare creature lumbering swiftly after him. The fall over the cliff into the top of this tree.

With a cry, he sat up, expecting to see the stone giant nearby and poised to leap. But it was nowhere in sight; nor, listen as intently as he would, could he hear the sounds of its crashing path through the brush. Somehow, for the moment at least, he had been saved. Perhaps his disappearance over the cliff edge had thrown it off his track.

He became aware of the fact that it was difficult for him to breathe. His lungs were heaving in a vain effort to suck in more oxygen, and his tongue felt thick as though he were being strangled. Then he saw that his oxygen concentrator had been knocked from his head when he fell, and was dangling from a limb several feet away. It was almost out of breathing range. Had it fallen on through the branches to the ground he would have died, in his unconsciousness, in the rarified atmosphere. He reached for it; settled the band around his head again.

After once more listening and peering around to make sure the rock colossus was not about, he descended the tree that had saved his life, and began to walk in the direction he judged the lake to be. He would get into his Dart, cruise aloft out of harm's way, and perhaps think up some effective course of action.

He was thinking clearly, now. And, in the glare of daylight, no longer an unreasoning animal fleeing blindly over a dim-lit foreign sphere, he was unable to understand his panic of the night. Afraid? Of course he had been afraid! What man wouldn't have been at sight of that monstrous thing? But that he, Harley 2Q14-N2o, should have lost his head completely and gone plunging off into the brush like that, seemed unbelievable. To the depths of his soul he felt ashamed. And to his own soul he made the promise that he would wipe out, in action, that hour of cowardice.

As he wound his way through the squat, carmine forest, he tried to figure out the nature of the thing that had crashed balefully after him in the black hours.

It had seemed made of rock—a giant, primitive stone statue imbued with life. But it was impossible that it should really be fashioned of rock. At least it ought to be impossible. Rock is inorganic, inanimate. It simply couldn't have the spark of life in it. Harley had seen many strange creations, on many strange planets, but never had he seen inorganic mineral matter endowed with animation. Nor had anyone else.

Yet the thing *looked* as though made of stone. Of some peculiar, quartz-suffused granite—proving that the wan, white-haired man he had talked to in the sanitarium had not been mad at all, but only too terribly sane. The creature's very eyes had had a stony look. Its eyelids had rasped like stone curtains rubbing together. Its awful, two-fingered hands, or claws, had ground together like stones rubbing.

Was it akin to the lizards, the cold-blooded life of Earth? Was this rocky exterior merely a horny shell like that of a turtle? No. Horn is horn and rock is rock. The two can't be confused.

The only theory Harley could form was that the great beast was in some strange way a link between the animal and the mineral kingdoms. Its skeletal structure, perhaps, was silicate in substance, extending to provide an outside covering that had hardened into actual stone, while forming an interior support to flesh that was half organic, half inorganic matter. Some such silicate construction was to be found in the sponge, of Earth. Could this be a gigantic relative of that lowly creature? He did not know, and couldn't guess. He wasn't a zoologist. All he knew was that the thing appeared to be formed of living, impregnable stone. He knew, also, that this fabulous creature was bent on destroying him.

At this point in his reflections, the glint of water came to his eyes between the tree trunks ahead of him. He had come back to the lake.

For moments he stood behind one of the larger trees on the fringe and searched around the shore for sight of the rock giant. It was nowhere in evidence. Rapidly he advanced from the forest and ran for the Dart. From a distance it appeared to be all right: but as he drew near a cry rose involuntarily to his lips.

In a dozen places the double hull of the little space craft was battered in. The man-hole lid was torn from its braces and bent double. The glass panels, unbreakable in themselves, had been shoved clear into the cabin; their empty sash frames gaped at Harley like blinded eyes. Never again would that Blinco Dart speed through the heavens!

He went to the spot where he had left his Sco drill, and a further evidence of the thing's cold blooded ferocity was revealed. The intricate mechanism had been wrenched into twisted pieces. The drums were battered in and the flexible hose lengths torn apart in shreds. The inventor himself couldn't have put it in working order again.

He was hopelessly trapped. He had no means of fighting the colossus. He had no way of escaping into space, nor of returning to Earth and trying to raise a loan that would allow him to come back here with men and atomic guns. He hadn't even a way of intrenching himself in the ground against the next attack.

For an instant his hair prickled in a flash of the blind panic that had seized him a few hours before. With a tremendous effort of will he fought it down. This—the destruction of his precious Dart and drill—was the result of one siege of insensate fear. If he succumbed to another one he might well dash straight into the arms of death. He sank to the ground and rested his chin on his fist, concentrating all his intellect on the hopeless problem that faced him.

The surface of Z-40 was many square miles in extent. But, if he tried to hide himself, he knew it was only a question of time before he would be hunted down. The asteroid was too tiny to give him indefinite concealment. Flight, then, was futile.

But if he didn't try to conceal himself in the sparse forest lands, it meant that he must stay to face the monster at once—which was insanity. What could he do, bare-handed, against that thirty-foot, three-tentacled, silicate mass of incredible life!

It was useless to run, and it was madness to stay and confront the thing. What, then, could he do? The sun had slid down the sky and the red of another swift dusk was heralding the short night before he shook his head somberly and gave the fatal riddle up.

He rose to his feet, intending to make his way back to the concealment—such as it was—of the forest. It might be that he could find safety in some lofty treetop till day dawned again. Then he stopped, and listened. What was that?

From far away to the left he could hear faint sounds of some gargantuan stirring. And, coincident with the flickering out of the last scrap of sunlight, a distant crashing came to his ears as an enormous body smashed like an armored ship through trees and thorn bushes and trailing vines. The rock thing had found his trail and was after him again.

A second time Harley fled through the dim-lighted night, stumbling over boulders and tripping on creepers. But this time his flight was not that of panic. Frightened enough, he was; but his mind was working clearly as he leaped through the forest away from the source of the crashing.

The first thing he noted was that though—as far as his ears could inform him—he was managing to keep his lead, he wasn't outdistancing his horrible pursuer by a yard. Dark though the night was, and far away as he contrived to keep himself, the colossus seemed to cling to his trail as easily as though following a well-blazed path.

He climbed a tree, faced at right angles to the course he had pursued, and swung for the next tree. It was a long jump. But desperation lent abnormal power to his muscles, and the gravity regulator adjusted to extremely low pitch, was a great help. He made it safely. Another swinging leap into the dark, to land sprawling in a second tree; a third; a fourth. Finally he crouched in a tangle of boughs, and listened. He was a quarter of a mile from the point where he had turned from his first direction. Perhaps this deviation would throw the rock terror off.

It didn't. He heard the steady smashing noise stop. For an instant there was a silence in the darkness of the asteroid that was painful. Then the crashing was resumed, this time drawing straight toward where he was hidden. Somehow the thing had learned of his change of direction.

He continued his flight into the night, his eyes staring glassily into the darkness, his expression the ghastly one of a condemned man. And as he fled the crashing behind him told how he was followed—easily, infallibly, in spite of all his twisting and turning and efforts at concealment. What hellish intelligence the monster must possess!

He ran for eternities. He ran till his chest was on fire, and the sobbing agony of his breathing could be heard for yards. He ran till spots of fire floated before his eyes and the blood, throbbing in his brain, cut out the noise of the devilish pursuit behind him. At long last his legs buckled under him, and he fell, to rise no more.

He was done. He knew it. His was the position of the hunted animal that lies panting, every muscle paralyzed with absolute exhaustion, and glares in an agony of helplessness at the hunter whose approach spells death.

The crashing grew louder. The tremor of the ground grew more pronounced as the vast pursuer pounded along with its tons and tons of weight. Harley gazed into the blackness back along the way he had come, his eyes sunk deep in the hollows fatigue had carved in his face, and waited for the end. The dark night darkened still more with the approach of another swift, inexorable dawn.

There was a terrific rending of tree trunks and webbed creepers. Dimly in the darkness he could see something that towered on a level with the tallest trees, something that moved as rapidly and steadily as though driven by machinery. Fear so great that it nauseated him, swept over him in waves; but he could not move.

The first grey smear of dawn appeared in the sky. In the ghostly greyness he got a clearer and clearer sight of the monster. He groaned and cowered there while it approached him—more slowly now, eyeing him with staring, stony orbs in which there was no expression of any kind, of rage or hate, of curiosity or triumph.

Great stumps of legs, with no joints in them, on which the co-lossus stalked like a moving stone tower—a body resembling an enormous boulder carved by an amateurish hand to portray the trunk of a human being—a craggy sphere of rock for a head, set directly atop the deeply riven shoulders—a face like the horrible mask of an embryonic gargoyle—a mouth that was simply a lipless chasm that opened and closed with the sound of rocks grinding together in a slow-moving glacier—the whole veiled thinly by trail-ing lengths of snapped vines, great shattered tree boughs, bushes, all uprooted in its stumping march through the forest! Harley closed his eyes to shut out the sight. But in spite of himself they flashed open again and stared on, as though hypnotized by the spectacle they witnessed.

The grey of dawn lightened to the first rose tint of the rising sun. As though stung to action by the breaking of day, the thing hastened its ground-shaking pace. With one last stride, it came to Harley's side and loomed far above, the unwinking eyes glaring down at him.

The three arms, hinged at equidistant points at the base of the horrible head, slowly lowered toward his prostrate form. There was a grating noise as the creature hinged in the middle and bent low, bringing its enormous, staring eyes within two yards of his face.

One of its hands closed over his leg, tentatively, experimen-tally, as though to ascertain of what substance he was made. He cried aloud as the rock vise, like a gigantic lobster claw, squeezed tight. The thing drew back abruptly. Then the chasm of its mouth opened a little, for all the world as though giving vent to sound-less, demoniac laughter. All three of the vise-like hands clamped over him—lightly enough, considering their vast size, and intimat-ing that the colossus did not mean to kill him for a moment or two—but so cruelly that his senses swam with the pain of it.

He felt the grip relax. The vast stone pincers were lifted from him; slithered to the ground beside him.

The first blinding rays of the sun were beating straight on the colossal figure, which glittered fantastically, like a huge splintered opal, in their brilliance.

It glared down at Harley. The abyss of a mouth opened as though again giving vent to silent, infernal laughter. Then, with the noise of a landslide, the giant form settled slowly to the ground. The rock half-moons of curtains dropped over the expressionless, dull eyes. The whole great figure quivered, and grew still. It lay without movement, stretched along the ground like a craggy, opalescent hill.

Dazed, stunned by such fantastic behavior, Harley struggled wearily to his feet. He had been a dead man as surely as though shot with a ray-gun. One twitch of those terrible rock pincers would have broken him in two pieces. It had seemed as though that deadly twitch were surely forthcoming. And then the thing had released him—and had lain down to go to sleep! Or was it asleep?

He took a few slow steps away from it, expecting to see the three great tentacles flash out to capture him as a cat claws at a mouse that thinks it is escaping. The arms didn't move. Astounding as it was, Harley was free to run away if he chose. Why was that?

A hint of a clue to the creature's action began to unfold in his mind. When he had first laid eyes on it, in daylight, it was asleep. It had not pursued him during the preceding day, which argued that again it was asleep. And now, with the first touch of dawn, it was once more quiet, immobile.

The answer seemed to be that it was entirely nocturnal; that for some obscure, unguessable reason sunlight induced in it a state of suspended animation. It seemed an insane theory, but no other surmise was remotely reasonable.

But if it were invariably sunk in a coma during daylight, why had it delayed killing him just a moment ago? Its every act indicated that it possessed intelligence of a high order. It was more than probable that it realized its limitation—why hadn't it acted in accordance with that realization?

On thinking it over, he believed he had the answer to that, too. He remembered the way the gaping mouth had seemed to express devilish mirth. The thing was playing with him. That was all. It had saved him for another night of hopeless flight and infallible trailing through the forests of Z-40.

He gazed at the monster in a frenzy of impotent rage and fear. If only he could kill it somehow in its sleep! But he couldn't. In no way could he harm it. Secure in its silicate covering, it was impervious to his wildest attempts at destruction. And it knew it, too; hadn't it laughed just before sinking down to slumber through the asteroidal day?

With his Sco drill he might have pierced that silicon dioxide armor till he reached the creature's gritty flesh. Then he could have used his ray-pistol, possibly disintegrating all its vitals and leaving only an empty rock shell sprawling hugely there in the trampled underbrush.

But he had neither drill nor pistol. The one had been wrecked by the monster; the other he had dropped in his madness of fright, after completely exhausting its power chamber.

Half crazed by the hopelessness of his plight, he paced up and down beside the great length of animated stone. Trapped on an asteroid—utterly unarmed—alone with the most pitiless, invulnerable creation Nature had placed in a varied universe! Could Hell itself have devised a more terrible fate?

Shuddering, he turned away. He had some two and a half hours of grace, before the sun should set again and darkness release the colossus from its torpor. There was only one thing he could do: place the diameter of the sphere between the thing and himself, and try to exist through another night of terror.

His hands went to his belt to adjust the gravity regulator strapped about his waist. By reducing his weight to an ounce or two, he could make the long journey possible for his fatigue-numbed muscles—

His hands clenched into fists, and his breath whistled between his set teeth as a wild hope came to him. The touch of the regulator had brought inspiration. A way to defeat the gigantic creature stretched on the ground beside him! A way to banish it forever from the surface of this lovely little world where all was perfect but the monstrous thing with which it was cursed!

Trembling with the reaction wrought in him by the faint glow of hope, he began to race toward the lake and his wrecked Blinco

Dart. It wasn't hard to find the way; the rock giant had left a trail as broad as a road; trees broken off like celery stalks, bushes smashed flat, tracks that looked like shallow wells sunk into the firm ground. Fifty yards to a step, he leaped along this path, praying that one object, just one bit of machinery in the Dart had escaped the general wreckage.

Arrived at the little shell at last, he was forced to pause a moment and compose himself before he could step into the battered interior. Everything hinged on this one final chance!

Drawing a long breath, he entered the cabin and made his way to the stern repellor. A groan escaped his lips. It was ruined. Evidently the thing had reached in the man-hole opening with one of its three mighty tentacles, and, with sure instinct, had fastened its stone claws on the repellor housing. At any rate, it was ground to bits. But—there was the bow repellor.

He went to that, and the flame of hope came back to his eyes. It was untouched! He threw back the housing to make sure. Yes, the inter-sliding series of plates, that reversed or neutralized gravitational attraction at a touch, were in alignment.

He bent to the task of disconnecting it from the heavy bed-plate to which it was bolted, his fingers flying frenziedly. Then back to the torpid colossus he hurried, clutching the precious repellor tight in his arms lest he should drop it, walking carefully lest he should fall with it.

There he was faced by a new difficulty that at first seemed insurmountable. How could he fasten the repellor to that great, impenetrable, opalescent bulk?

A second time he bounded back toward the Dart, to return with the heavy bow and stern bed-plates from its hull.

Once more the orange ball of the sun was sinking low. The terrible brevity of those three-hour days! He had less than ten minutes, Earth time, in which to work.

One of the thing's arms, or tentacles, was pointing out away from the parent mass. It was twice the diameter of his body, and was ponderously heavy; but by rigging a fulcrum and lever device, with a stone as the fulcrum and a tough log as the lever, he managed to raise it high enough to thrust one of the bed-plates under it. The other massive metal sheet he laid across the top.

The lower rim of the sun touched the horizon. A tremor ran through the colossus. In frantic haste, racing against the flying seconds, Harley clamped the two plates tight against the columnar tentacle with four long hull-bolts from the Dart. He set the repellor in position on the top bed-plate, and began to fasten it down.

He felt another tremor run through the stone column on which he was squatting. With a rasping sound, one of the half-moon rock-curtains the thing had for eyelids blinked open and shut. He shot the last bolt into place and tightened it.

The stone claws, just behind which he had fastened the repellor, ground savagely shut. The great tentacle began to lift, and carried him with it—toward the chasm of a mouth. That chasm opened wide. . . .

Harley straightened up and jumped for the ground. As he jumped, he kicked the repellor control bar hard over.

There was a shrieking of wind as though all the hurricanes in the universe were battling each other. He felt himself turned over and over, buffeted, torn at, in a mad aerial whirlpool. The whirlpool calmed as the abruptly created vacuum, caused by the monster's rapid drive upward, passed after it into space. Far overhead there was one fleeting glimpse of a pinpoint of dull opalescence reflecting the rays of the dying sun. Then the pinpoint disappeared in fathomless space. With his gravity regulator adjusted to the point where it almost neutralized his weight, he fell slowly back toward the ground. . . .

Almost immediately after he had landed in the darkness that blanketed the surface of the planetoid, a big space yacht settled down near him. A searchlight bored a hole in the blackness, to bathe him in cold light. Down the beam came a band of men from Earth, pushing atomic cannon and gazing apprehensively about them. In the lead was an elderly man with the six-bar dollar-mark insignia of a business executive on his purple tunic.

He hastened to Harley's side. Harley only dimly heard what he said. Something to the effect that the man had been worried after selling the fatal asteroid. Had got in touch with the Radivision Corporation and learned that this call number was dead. Had come with men and big guns to rescue him, if it wasn't too late, and take him back to Earth. Had cruised for half an hour before locating him. "I've been calling myself a murderer ever since I let you have Z-40, Mr. 2Q14N20," he concluded. "I was sure we'd get here only to find you'd been killed. But I see you've managed to escape from the creature so far—though by the look of you, it must have been a narrow shave."

At this Harley shook off some of the gathering dizziness that hazed his mind. He threw back his shoulders. "Managed to *escape*? I did better than that. I got rid of the thing forever! Yes, I'll return to Earth with you, but only because I need a new Blinco Dart. I'm coming back to Z-40 at once. Perfect little paradise, now that I've got rid of that—animated—rock pile—"

The belated rescuers caught him as he collapsed.

HUNT THE HUNTER
KRIS NEVILLE

"We're somewhat to the south, I think," Ri said, bending over the crude field map, "That ridge," he pointed, "on our left, is right here." He drew a finger down the map. "It was over here," he moved the finger, "over the ridge, north of here, that we sighted them."

Extrone asked, "Is there a pass?"

Ri looked up, studying the terrain. He moved his shoulders, "I don't know, but maybe they range this far. Maybe they're on this side of the ridge, too."

Delicately, Extrone raised a hand to his beard. "I'd hate to lose a day crossing the ridge," he said.

"Yes, sir," Ri said. Suddenly he threw back his head. "Listen!"

"Eh?" Extrone said.

"Hear it? That cough? I think that's one, from over there. Right up ahead of us."

Extrone raised his eyebrows.

This time, the coughing roar was more distant, but distinct.

"It is!" Ri said. "It's a farn beast, all right!"

Extrone smiled, almost pointed teeth showing through the beard. "I'm glad we won't have to cross the ridge."

Ri wiped his forehead on the back of his sleeve. "Yes, sir."

"We'll pitch camp right here, then," Extrone said. "We'll go after it tomorrow." He looked at the sky. "Have the bearers hurry."

"Yes, sir."

Ri moved away, his pulse gradually slowing. "You, there!" he called. "Pitch camp, here!"

He crossed to Mia, who, along with him, had been pressed into
Extrone's party as guides. Once more, Ri addressed the bearers,
"Be quick, now!" And to Mia, "God almighty, he was getting mad."
He ran a hand under his collar. "It's a good thing that farn beast
sounded off when it did. I'd hate to think of making him climb that
ridge."

Mia glanced nervously over his shoulder. "It's that damned
pilot's fault for setting us down on this side. I told him it was the
other side. I told him so."

Ri shrugged hopelessly.

Mia said, "I don't think he even saw a blast area over here. I
think he wanted to get us in trouble."

"There shouldn't be one. There shouldn't be a blast area on this
side of the ridge, too."

"That's what I mean. The pilot don't like businessmen. He had
it in for us."

Ri cleared his throat nervously. "Maybe you're right."

"It's the Hunting Club he don't like."

"I wish to God I'd never heard of a farn beast," Ri said. "At
least, then, I wouldn't be one of his guides. Why didn't he hire
somebody else?"

Mia looked at his companion. He spat. "What hurts most, he
pays us for it. I could buy half this planet, and he makes me his
guide—at less than I pay my secretary."

"Well, anyway, we won't have to cross that ridge."

"Hey, you!" Extrone called.

The two of them turned immediately.

"You two scout ahead," Extrone said. "See if you can pick up
some tracks."

"Yes, sir," Ri said, and instantly the two of them readjusted their
shoulder straps and started off.

Shortly they were inside of the scrub forest, safe from sight.
"Let's wait here," Mia said.

"No, we better go on. He may have sent a spy in."

They pushed on, being careful to blaze the trees, because they
were not professional guides.

"We don't want to get too near," Ri said after toiling through the forest for many minutes. "Without guns, we don't want to get near enough for the farn beast to charge us."

They stopped. The forest was dense, the vines clinging.

"He'll want the bearers to hack a path for him," Mia said. "But we go it alone. Damn him."

Ri twisted his mouth into a sour frown. He wiped at his forehead, "Hot. By God, It's hot. I didn't think it was this hot, the first time we were here."

Mia said, "The first time, we weren't guides. We didn't notice it so much then."

They fought a few yards more into the forest.

Then it ended. Or, rather, there was a wide gap. Before them lay a blast area, unmistakable. The grass was beginning to grow again, but the tree stumps were roasted from the rocket breath.

"This isn't ours!" Ri said. "This looks like it was made nearly a year ago!"

Mia's eyes narrowed. "The military from Xnile?"

"No," Ri said. "They don't have any rockets this small. And I don't think there's another cargo rocket on this planet outside of the one we leased from the Club. Except the one *he* brought."

"The ones who discovered the farn beasts in the first place?" Mia asked. "You think it's their blast?"

"So?" Ri said. "But who are they?"

It was Mia's turn to shrug. "Whoever they were, they couldn't have been hunters. They'd have kept the secret better."

"We didn't do so damned well."

"We didn't have a chance," Mia objected. "Everybody and his brother had heard the rumor that farn beasts were somewhere around here. It wasn't our fault Extrone found out."

"I wish we hadn't shot our guide, then. I wish he was here instead of us."

Mia shook perspiration out of his eyes. "We should have shot our pilot, too. That was our mistake. The pilot must have been the one who told Extrone we'd hunted this area."

"I didn't think a Club pilot would do that."

"After Extrone said he'd hunt farn beasts, even if it meant going to the alien system? Listen, you don't know . . . Wait a minute."

There was perspiration on Ri's upper lip.

"*I* didn't tell Extrone, if that's what you're thinking," Mia said.

Ri's mouth twisted, "I didn't say you did."

"Listen," Mia said in a hoarse whisper. "I just thought. Listen. To hell with how he found out. Here's the point. Maybe he'll shoot us, too, when the hunt's over."

Ri licked his lips. "No. He wouldn't do that. "We're not—not just anybody. He couldn't kill us like that. Not even *him*. And besides, why would he want to do that? It wouldn't do any good to shoot us. Too many people already know about the farn beasts. You said that yourself."

Mia said, "I hope you're right." They stood side by side, studying the blast area in silence. Finally, Mia said, "We better be getting back."

"What'll we tell him?"

"That we saw tracks. What else can we tell him?"

They turned back along their trail, stumbling over vines.

"It gets hotter at sunset," Ri said nervously.

"The breeze dies down."

"It's screwy. I didn't think farn beasts had this wide a range. There must be a lot of them, to be on both sides of the ridge like this."

"There may be a pass," Mia said, pushing a vine away.

Ri wrinkled his brow, panting. "I guess that's it. If there were a lot of them, we'd have heard something before we did. But even so, it's damned funny, when you think about it."

Mia looked up at the darkening sky. "We better hurry," he said.

When it came over the hastily established camp, the rocket was low, obviously looking for a landing site. It was a military craft, from the outpost on the near moon, and forward, near the nose, there was the blazoned emblem of the Ninth Fleet. The rocket roared directly over Extrone's tent, turned slowly, spouting fuel expensively, and settled into the scrub forest, turning the vegetation beneath it sere by its blasts.

Extrone sat on an upholstered stool before his tent and spat disgustedly and combed his beard with his blunt fingers.

Shortly, from the direction of the rocket, a group of four high-ranking officers came out of the forest, heading toward him. They were spruce, the officers, with military discipline holding their waists in and knees almost stiff.

"What in hell do you want?" Extrone asked.

They stopped a respectful distance away. "Sir . . ." one began.

"Haven't I told you gentlemen that rockets frighten the game?" Extrone demanded, ominously not raising his voice.

"Sir." the lead officer said, "it's another alien ship. It was sighted a few hours ago, off this very planet, sir."

Extrone's face looked much too innocent. "How did it get there, gentlemen? Why wasn't it destroyed?"

"We lost it again, sir. Temporarily, sir."

"So?" Extrone mocked.

"We thought you ought to return to a safer planet, sir. Until we could locate and destroy it."

Extreme stared at them for a space. Then, indifferently, he turned away, in the direction of a resting bearer. "You!" he said. "Hey! Bring me a drink!" He faced the officers again. He smiled maliciously. "I'm staying here."

The lead officer licked his firm lower lip. "But, sir . . ."

Extrone toyed with his beard, "About a year ago, gentlemen, there was an alien ship around here then, wasn't there? And you destroyed it, didn't you?"

"Yes, sir. When we located it, Sir."

"You'll destroy this one, too," Extrone said.

"We have a tight patrol, sir. It can't slip through. But it might try a long range bombardment, sir."

Extrone said, "To begin with, they probably don't even know I'm here. And they probably couldn't hit this area if they did know. And you can't afford to let them get a shot at me, anyway."

"That's why we'd like you to return to an inner planet, sir."

Extrone plucked at his right ear lobe, half closing his eyes. "You'll lose a fleet before you'll dare let anything happen to me, gentlemen. I'm quite safe here, I think."

The bearer brought Extrone his drink.

"Get off," Extrone said quietly to the four officers.

Again they turned reluctantly. This time, he did not call them back. Instead, with amusement, he watched until they disappeared into the tangle of forest.

Dusk was falling. The takeoff blast of the rocket illuminated the area, casting weird shadows on the gently swaying grasses; there was a hot breath of dry air and the rocket dwindled toward the stars.

Extrone stood up lazily, stretching. He tossed the empty glass away, listened for it to shatter. He reached out, parted the heavy flap to his tent.

"Sir?" Ri said, hurrying toward him in the gathering darkness.

"Eh?" Extrone said, turning, startled. "Oh, you. Well?"

"We . . . located signs of the farn beast, sir. To the east."

Extrone nodded. After a moment he said, "You killed one, I believe, on your trip?"

Ri shifted. "Yes, sir."

Extrone held back the flap of the tent. "Won't you come in?" he asked without any politeness whatever.

Ri obeyed the order.

The inside of the tent was luxurious. The bed was of bulky feathers, costly of transport space, the sleep curtains of silken gauze. The floor, heavy, portable tile blocks, not the hollow kind, were neatly and smoothly inset into the ground. Hanging from the center, to the left of the slender, hand-carved center pole, was a chain of crystals. They tinkled lightly when Extrone dropped the flap. The light was electric from a portable dynamo. Extrone flipped it on. He crossed to the bed, sat down.

"You were, I believe, the first ever to kill a farn beast?" he said.

"I . . . No, sir. There must have been previous hunters, sir."

Extrone narrowed his eyes. "I see by your eyes that you are envious—that is the word, isn't it?—of my tent."

Ri looked away from his face.

"Perhaps I'm envious of your reputation as a hunter. You see, I have never killed a farn beast. In fact, I haven't *seen* a farn beast."

Ri glanced nervously around the tent, his sharp eyes avoiding Extrone's glittering ones. "Few people have seen them, sir."

"Oh?" Extrone questioned mildly. "I wouldn't say that. I understand that the aliens hunt them quite extensively . . . on some of their planets."

"I meant in our system, sir."

"Of course you did." Extrone said, lazily tracing the crease of his sleeve with his forefinger. "I imagine these are the only farn beasts in our system."

Ri waited uneasily, not answering.

"Yes," Extrone said, "I imagine they are. It would have been a shame if you had killed the last one. Don't you think so?"

Ri's hands worried the sides of his outer garment. "Yes, sir. It would have been."

Extrone pursed his lips. "It wouldn't have been very considerate of you to— But, still, you gained valuable experience. I'm glad you agreed to come along as my guide."

"It was an honor, sir."

Extrone's lip twisted in wry amusement. "If I had waited until it was safe for me to hunt on an alien planet, I would not have been able to find such an illustrious guide."

". . . I'm flattered, sir."

"Of course," Extrone said. "But you should have spoken to me about it, when you discovered the farn beast in our own system."

"I realize that, sir. That is, I had intended at the first opportunity, sir . . ."

"Of course," Extrone said dryly. "Like all of my subjects," he waved his hand in a broad gesture, "the highest as well as the lowest slave, know me and love me. I know your intentions were the best."

226

OTHER LIFEOTHER LIFE

Ri squirmed, his face pale. "We do indeed love you, sir."

Extrone bent forward. "*Know* me and love me."

"Yes, sir. *Know* you and love you, sir." Ri said.

"Get out!" Extrone said.

"It's frightening," Ri said, "to be that close to him."

Mia nodded.

The two of them, beneath the leaf-swollen branches of the gnarled tree, were seated on their sleeping bags. The moon was clear and cold and bright in a cloudless sky; a small moon, smooth-surfaced, except for a central mountain ridge that bisected it into almost twin hemispheres.

"To think of him. As flesh and blood. Not like the—well, that—what we've read about."

Mia glanced suspiciously around him at the shadows. "You begin to understand a lot of things, after seeing him."

Ri picked nervously at the cover of his sleeping bag.

"It makes you think," Mia added. He twitched. "I'm afraid, I'm afraid he'll . . . Listen, we'll talk. When we get back to civilization. You, me, the bearers. About him. He can't let that happen. He'll kill us first."

Ri looked up at the moon, shivering. "No. We have friends. We have influence. He couldn't just like that—"

"He could say it was an accident."

"No," Ri said stubbornly.

"He can say anything," Mia insisted. "He can make people believe anything. Whatever he says. There's no way to check on it."

"It's getting cold," Ri said.

"Listen," Mia pleaded.

"No," Ri said. "Even if we tried to tell them, they wouldn't listen. Everybody would know we were lying. Everything they've come to believe would tell them we were lying. Everything they've read, every picture they've seen. They wouldn't believe us. *He* knows that."

"Listen," Mia repeated intently. "This is important. Right now he couldn't afford to let us talk. Not right now. Because the Army is not against him. Some officers were here, just before we came back. A bearer overheard them talking. They don't *want* to overthrow him!"

Ri's teeth, suddenly, were chattering.

"That's another lie," Mia continued. "That he protects the people from the Army. That's a lie. I don't believe they were ever plotting against him. Not even at first. I think they *helped* him, don't you see?"

Ri whined nervously.

"It's like this," Mia said. "I see it like this. The Army *put* him in power when the people were in rebellion against military rule."

Ri swallowed. "We couldn't make the people believe that."

"No?" Mia challenged. "Couldn't we? Not today, but what about tomorrow? You'll see. Because I think the Army is getting ready to invade the alien system!"

"The people won't support them," Ri answered woodenly.

"*Think.* If he tells them to, they will. They trust him."

Ri looked around, at the shadows.

"That explains a lot of things," Mia said, "I think the Army's been preparing for this for a long time. From the first, maybe. That's why Extrone cut off our trade with the aliens. Partly to keep them from learning that he was getting ready to invade them, but more to keep them from exposing *him* to the people. The aliens wouldn't be fooled like we were, so easy."

"No!" Ri snapped. "It was to keep the natural economic balance."

"You know that's not right."

Ri lay down on his bed roll. "Don't talk about it. It's not good to talk like this. I don't even want to listen."

"When the invasion starts, he'll have to command all their loyalties. To keep them from revolt again. They'd be ready to believe us, then. He'll have a hard enough time without people running around trying to tell the truth."

"You're wrong. He's not like that. I know you're wrong."

Mia smiled twistedly. "How many has he already killed? How can we even guess?"

Ri swallowed sickly.

"Remember our guide? To keep our hunting territory a secret?"

Ri shuddered. "That's different. Don't you see? This is not at all like that."

With morning came birds' songs, came dew, came breakfast smells. The air was sweet with cooking, and it was nostalgic, childhoodlike, uncontaminated.

And Extrone stepped out of the tent, fully dressed, surly, letting the flap slap loudly behind him. He stretched hungrily and stared around the camp, his eyes still vacant-mean with sleep.

"Breakfast!" he shouted, and two bearers came running with a folding table and chair. Behind them, a third bearer, carrying a tray of various foods; and yet behind him, a fourth, with a steaming pitcher and a drinking mug.

Extrone ate hugely, with none of the delicacy sometimes affected in his conversational gestures. When he had finished, he washed his mouth with water and spat on the ground.

"Lin!" he said.

His personal bearer came loping toward him.

"Have you read that manual I gave you?"

Lin nodded, "Yes."

Extrone pushed the table away. He smacked his lips wetly. "Very ludicrous, Lin. Have you noticed that I have two businessmen for guides? It occurred to me when I got up. They would have spat on me, twenty years ago, damn them."

Lin waited.

"Now I can spit on them, which pleases me."

"The farn beasts are dangerous, sir," Lin said.

"Eh? Oh, yes. Those. What did the manual say about them?"

"I believe they're carnivorous, sir."

"An alien manual. That's ludicrous, too. That we have the only information on our newly discovered fauna from an alien manual—and, of course, two businessmen."

"They have very long, sharp fangs, and, when enraged, are capable of tearing a man—"

"An alien?" Extrone corrected.

"There's not enough difference between us to matter, sir. Of tearing an alien to pieces, sir."

Extrone laughed harshly. "It's 'sir' whenever you contradict me?"

Lin's face remained impassive. "I guess it seems that way. Sir."

"Damned few people would dare go as far as you do," Extrone said. "But you're afraid of me, too, in your own way, aren't you?"

Lin shrugged. "Maybe."

"I can see you are. Even my wives are, I wonder if anyone can know how wonderful it feels to have people *all* afraid of you."

"The farn beasts, according to the manual . . ."

"You are very insistent on one subject."

". . . It's the only thing I know anything about. The farn beast, as I was saying, sir, is the particular enemy of men. Or if you like, of aliens. Sir."

"All right," Extrone said, annoyed. "I'll be careful."

In the distance, a farn beast coughed.

Instantly alert, Extrone said, "Get the bearers! Have some of them cut a path through that damn thicket! And tell those two businessmen to get the hell over here!"

Lin smiled, his eyes suddenly afire with the excitement of the hunt.

Four hours later, they were well into the scrub forest. Extrone walked leisurely, well back of the cutters, who hacked away, methodically, at the vines and branches which might impede his forward progress. Their sharp, awkward knives snickered rhythmically to the rasp of their heavy breathing.

Occasionally, Extrone halted, motioned for his water carrier, and drank deeply of the icy water- to allay the heat of the forest, a heat made oppressive by the press of foliage against the outside air.

Ranging out, on both sides of the central body, the two businessmen fought independently against the wild growth, each scouting the flanks for farn beasts, and ahead, beyond the cutters, Lin flittered among the tree trunks, sometimes far, sometimes near.

Extrone carried the only weapon, slung easily over his shoulder, a powerful blast rifle, capable of piercing medium armor in sustained fire. To his rear, the water carrier was trailed by a man bearing a folding stool, and behind him, a man carrying the heavy, high-powered two-way communication set.

Once Extrone unslung his blast rifle and triggered a burst at a tiny, arboreal mammal, which, upon the impact, shattered asunder, to Extrone's satisfied chuckle, in a burst of blood and fur.

When the sun stood high and heat exhaustion made the near-naked bearers slump, Extrone permitted a rest. While waiting for the march to resume, he sat on the stool with his back against an ancient tree and patted, reflectively, the blast rifle, lying across his legs.

"For you, sir," the communications man said, interrupting his reverie.

"Damn," Extrone muttered. His face twisted in anger. "It better be important." He took the head-set and mike and nodded to the bearer. The bearer twiddled the dials.

"Extrone. Eh? . . . Oh, you got their ship. Well, why in hell bother me? . . . All right, so they found out I was here. You got them, didn't you?"

"Blasted them right out of space," the voice crackled excitedly. "Right in the middle of a radio broadcast, sir."

"I don't want to listen to your gabbling when I'm hunting!" Extrone tore off the head-set and handed it to the bearer. "If they call back, find out what they want, first. I don't want to be bothered unless it's important."

"Yes, sir."

Extrone squinted up at the sun; his eyes crinkled under the glare, and perspiration stood in little droplets on the back of his hands.

Lin, returning to the column, threaded his way among reclining bearers. He stopped before Extrone and tossed his hair out of his eyes, "I located a spoor," he said, suppressed eagerness in his voice. "About a quarter ahead. It looks fresh."

Extrone's eyes lit with passion.

Lin's face was red with heat and grimy with sweat, "There were two, I think."

"Two?" Extrone grinned, petting the rifle. "You and I better go forward and look at the spoor."

Lin said, "We ought to take protection, if you're going, too."

Extrone laughed. "This is enough." He gestured with the rifle and stood up.

"I wish you had let me bring a gun along, sir," Lin said.

"One is enough in *my* camp."

The two of them went forward, alone, into the forest. Extrone moved agilely through the tangle, following Lin closely. When they came to the tracks, heavily pressed into drying mud around a small watering hole, Extrone nodded his head in satisfaction.

"This way." Lin said, pointing, and once more the two of them started off.

They went a good distance through the forest, Extrone becoming more alert with each additional foot. Finally, Lin stopped him with a restraining hand. "They may be quite a way ahead. Hadn't we ought to bring up the column?"

The farn beast, somewhere beyond a ragged clump of bushes, coughed. Extrone clenched the blast rifle convulsively.

The farn beast coughed again, more distant this time.

"They're moving away," Lin said.

"Damn!" Extrone said.

"It's a good thing the wind's right, or they'd be coming back, and fast, too."

"Eh?" Extrone said.

"They charge on scent, sight, or sound. I understand they will track down a man for as long as a day."

"Wait," Extrone said, combing his beard. "Wait a minute."

"Yes?"

"Look," Extrone said. "If that's the case, why do we bother tracking them? Why not make them come to us?"

"They're too unpredictable. It wouldn't be safe. I'd rather have surprise on our side."

"You don't seem to see what I mean," Extrone said. "We won't be the—ah—the bait."

"Oh?"

"Let's get back to the column."

"Extrone wants to see you," Lin said.

Ri twisted at the grass shoot, broke it off, worried and unhappy. "What's he want to see me for?"

"I don't know," Lin said curtly.

Ri got to his feet. One of his hands reached out, plucked nervously at Lin's bare forearm. "Look," he whispered. "You know him, I have—a little money. If you were able to . . . if he wants," Ri gulped, "to *do* anything to me—I'd pay you, if you could . . ."

"You better come along," Lin said, turning.

Ri rubbed his hands along his thighs; he sighed, a tiny sound, ineffectual. He followed Lin beyond an outcropping of shale to where Extrone was seated, petting his rifle.

Extrone nodded genially. "The farn beast hunter, eh?"

"Yes, sir."

Extrone drummed his fingers on the stock of the blast rifle. "Tell me what they look like," he said suddenly.

"Well, sir, they're . . . uh . . ."

"Pretty frightening?"

"No, sir . . . Well, in a way, sir."

"But *you* weren't afraid of them, were you?"

"No, sir. No, because . . ."

Extrone was smiling innocently. "Good. I want you to do something for me."

"I . . . I . . ." Ri glanced nervously at Lin out of the tail of his eye, Lin's face was impassive.

"Of *course* you will," Extrone said genially. "Get me a rope, Lin. A good, long, strong rope."

"What are you going to do?" Ri asked, terrified.

"Why, I'm going to tie the rope around your waist and stake you out as bait."

"No!"

"Oh, come now. When the farn beast hears you scream—you can scream, by the way?"

Ri swallowed

"We could find a way to make you."

There was perspiration trickling down Ri's forehead, a single drop, creeping toward his nose.

"You'll be safe." Extrone said, studying his face with amusement. "I'll shoot the animal before it reaches you."

Ri gulped for air. "But . . . if there should be more than one?"

Extrone shrugged.

"I— Look, sir. Listen to me," Ri's lips were bloodless and his hands were trembling. "It's not me you want to do this to. It's Mia, sir. *He* killed a farn beast before *I* did, sir. And last night—last night, he—"

"He what?" Extrone demanded, leaning forward intently.

Ri breathed with a gurgling sound. "He said he ought to kill you, sir. That's what he said. I heard him, sir. He said he ought to kill you. He's the one you ought to use for bait. Then if there was an accident, sir, it wouldn't matter, because he said he ought to kill you. I wouldn't . . ."

Extrone said, "Which one is he?"

"That one. Right over there."

"The one with his back to me?"

"Yes, sir. That's him. That's him, sir.

Extrone aimed carefully and fired, full charge, then lowered the rifle and said, "Here comes Lin with the rope I see."

Ri was greenish. "You . . . you . . ."

Extrone turned to Lin. "Tie one end around his waist."

"Wait," Ri begged, fighting off the rope with his hands. "You don't want to use me, sir. Not after I told you . . . Please, sir. If anything should happen to me . . . Please, sir. Don't do it."

"Tie it," Extrone ordered.

"No, sir. Please. Oh, please don't, sir."

"Tie it," Extrone said inexorably.

Lin bent with the rope; his face was colorless.

They were at the watering hole—Extrone, Lin, two bearers, and Ri.

Since the hole was drying, the left, partially exposed bank was steep toward the muddy water. Upon it was green, new grass, tender-tuffed, half mashed in places by heavy animal treads. It was there that they staked him out, tying the free end of the rope tightly around the base of a scaling tree.

"You will scream," Extrone instructed. With his rifle, he pointed across the water hole. "The farn beast will come from this direction, I imagine."

Ri was almost slobbering in fear.

"Let me hear you scream," Extrone said.

Ri moaned weakly.

"You'll have to do better than that." Extrone inclined his head toward a bearer, who used something Ri couldn't see.

Ri screamed.

"See that you keep it up that way," Extrone said. "That's the way I want you to sound." He turned toward Lin. "We can climb this tree, I think."

Slowly, aided by the bearers, the two men climbed the tree, bark peeling away from under their rough boots. Ri watched them hopelessly.

Once at the crotch, Extrone settled down, holding the rifle at alert. Lin moved to the left, out on the main branch, rested in a smaller crotch.

Looking down, Extrone said, "Scream!" Then, to Lin, "You feel the excitement? It's always in the air like this at a hunt."

"I feel it," Lin said.

Extrone chuckled. "You were with me on Meizque?"

"Yes."

"That was something, that time." He ran his hand along the stock of the weapon.

The sun headed west, veiling itself with trees; a large insect circled Extrone's head. He slapped at it, angry. The forest was quiet, underlined by an occasional piping call, something like a whistle. Ri's screams were shrill, echoing away, shiveringly. Lin sat quiet, hunched.

Extrone's eyes narrowed, and he began to pet the gun stock with quick, jerky movements. Lin licked his lips, keeping his eyes on Extrone's face. The sun seemed stuck in the sky, and the heat squeezed against them, sucking at their breath like a vacuum. The insect went away. Still, endless, hopeless, monotonous, Ri screamed.

A farn beast coughed, far in the matted forest.

Extrone laughed nervously, "He must have heard."

"We're lucky to rouse one so fast," Lin said.

Extrone dug his boot cleats into the tree, braced himself. "I like this. There's more excitement in waiting like this than in anything I know."

Lin nodded.

"The waiting, itself, is a lot. The suspense. It's not only the killing that matters."

"It's not only the killing," Lin echoed.

"You understand?" Extrone said. "How it is to wait, knowing in just a minute something is going to come out of the forest, and you're going to kill it?"

"I know," Lin said.

"But it's not *only* the killing. It's the waiting, too."

The farn beast coughed again; nearer.

"It's a different one," Lin said.

"How do you know?"

"Hear the lower pitch, the more of a roar?"

"Hey!" Extrone shouted, "You, down there. There are two coming. Now let's hear you really scream!"

Ri, below, whimpered childishly and began to retreat toward the tether tree, his eyes wide.

"There's a lot of satisfaction in fooling them, too," Extrone said. "Making them come to your bait, where you can get at them." He opened his right hand. "Choose your ground, set your trap. Bait it." He snapped his hand into a fist, held the fist up before his eyes, imprisoning the idea. "Spring the trip when the quarry is inside. Clever. That makes the waiting more interesting. Waiting to see if they really will come to your bait."

Lin shifted, staring toward the forest.

"I've always liked to hunt," Extrone said. "More than anything else, I think."

Lin spat toward the ground. "People should hunt because they have to. For food. For safety."

"No," Extrone argued. "People should hunt for the love of hunting."

"Killing?"

"Hunting," Extrone repeated harshly.

The farn beast coughed. Another answered. They were very near, and there was a noise of crackling underbrush.

"He's good bait," Extrone said. "He's fat enough and he knows how to scream good."

Ri had stopped screaming; he was huddled against the tree, fearfully eying the forest across from the watering hole.

Extrone began to tremble with excitement. "Here they come!"

The forest sprang apart. Extrone bent forward, the gun still across his lap.

The farn beast, its tiny eyes red with hate, stepped out on the bank, swinging its head wildly, its nostrils flaring in anger. It coughed. Its mate appeared beside it. Their tails thrashed against the scrubs behind them, rattling leaves.

"Shoot!" Lin hissed. "For God's sake, shoot!"

"Wait," Extrone said. "Let's see what they do." He had not moved the rifle. He was tense, bent forward, his eyes slitted, his breath beginning to sound like an asthmatic pump.

The lead farn beast sighted Ri. It lowered its head.

"Look!" Extrone cried excitedly. "Here it comes!"

Ri began to scream again.

Still Extrone did not lift his blast rifle. He was laughing. Lin waited, frozen, his eyes staring at the farn beast in fascination.

The farn beast plunged into the water, which was shallow, and, throwing a sheet of it to either side, headed across toward Ri.

"Watch! Watch!" Extrone cried gleefully.

And then the aliens sprang their trap.

TREE, SPARE THAT WOODMAN
DAVE DRYFOOS

STIFF WITH SHOCK, Naomi Heckscher stood just inside the door to Cappy's one-room cabin, where she'd happened to be when her husband discovered the old man's body.

Her nearest neighbor—old Cappy—dead. After all his wire-pulling to get into the First Group, and his slaving to make a farm on this alien planet, dead in bed!

Naomi's mind circled frantically, contrasting her happy anticipations with this shocking actuality. She'd come to call on a friend, she reminded herself, a beloved friend—round, white-haired, rosy-cheeked; lonely because he'd recently become a widower. To her little boy, Cappy was a combination Grandpa and Santa Claus; to herself, a sort of newly met Old Beau.

Her mouth had been set for a sip of his home brew, her eyes had pictured the delight he'd take in and give to her little boy.

She'd walked over with son and husband, expecting nothing more shocking than an ostentatiously stolen kiss. She'd found a corpse. And to have let Cappy die alone, in this strange world . . .

She and Ted could at least have been with him, if they'd known.

But they'd been laughing and singing in their own cabin only a mile away, celebrating Richard's fifth birthday. She'd been annoyed when Cappy failed to show up with the present he'd promised Richard. Annoyed—while the old man pulled a blanket over his head, turned his round face to the wall, and died.

Watching compassionately, Naomi was suddenly struck by the matter-of-fact way Ted examined the body. Ted wasn't surprised.

"Why did you tell Richard to stay outside, just now?" she demanded. "How did you know what we'd find here? And why didn't you tell me, so I could keep Richard at home?"

She saw Ted start, scalded by the splash of her self-directed anger, saw him try to convert his wince into a shrug.

"You insisted on coming," he reminded her gently. "I couldn't have kept you home without—without saying too much, worrying you—with the Earth-ship still a year away. Besides, I didn't know for sure, till we saw the tree-things around the cabin."

The tree-things. The trees-that-were-not. Gnarled blue trunks, half-hidden by yellow leaf-needles stretching twenty feet into the sky. Something like the hoary mountain hemlocks she and Ted had been forever photographing on their Sierra honeymoon, seven life-long years ago.

Three of those tree-things had swayed over Cappy's spring for a far longer time than Man had occupied this dreadful planet. Until just now . . .

The three of them had topped the rise that hid Cappy's farm from their own. Richard was running ahead like a happily inquisitive puppy. Suddenly he'd stopped, pointing with a finger she distinctly recalled as needing thorough soapy scrubbing.

"Look, Mommie!" he'd said. "Cappy's trees have moved. They're around the cabin, now."

He'd been interested, not surprised. In the past year, Mazda had become Richard's home; only Earth could surprise him.

But, Ted, come to think of it, had seemed withdrawn, his face a careful blank. And she?

"Very pretty," she'd said, and stuffed the tag-end of fear back into the jammed, untidy mental pigeon-hole she used for all unpleasant thoughts. "Don't run too far ahead, dear."

But now she had to know what Ted knew.

"Tell me!" she said.

"These tree-things—"

"There've been *other* deaths! How many?"

"Sixteen. But I didn't want to tell you. Orders were to leave women and children home when we had that last Meeting, remember."

"What did they say at the Meeting? Out with it, Ted!"

"That—that the tree-things think!"

"But that's ridiculous!"

"Well, unfortunately, no. Look, I'm not trying to tell you that terrestrial trees think, too, nor even that they have a nervous system. They don't. But—well, on Earth, if you've ever touched a lighted match to the leaf of a sensitive plant like the mimosa, say— and I have—you've been struck by the speed with which *other* leaves close up and droop. I mean, sure, we know that the leaves droop because certain cells exude water and nearby leaves feel the heat of the match. But the others don't, yet they droop, too. Nobody knows how it works . . ."

"But *that's* just defensive!"

"Sure. But *that's* just on Earth!"

"All right, dear. I won't argue any more. But I still don't understand. Go on about the Meeting."

"Well, they said these tree-things both create and respond to the patterned electrical impulses of the mind. It's something like the way a doctor creates fantasies by applying a mild electric current to the right places on a patient's brain. In the year we've been here, the trees—or some of them—have learned to read from and transmit to our minds. The range, they say, is around fifty feet. But you have to be receptive—"

"Receptive?"

"Fearful. That's the condition. So I didn't want to tell you because you *must not* let yourself become afraid, Naomi. We're clearing trees from the land, in certain areas. And it's their planet, after all. Fear is their weapon and fear can kill!"

"You still—all you men—should have let us women know! What do you think we are? Besides, I don't really believe you. How can fear kill?"

"Haven't you ever heard of a savage who gets in bad with his witch-doctor and is killed by magic? The savage is convinced, having seen or heard of other cases, that he *can* be killed. The witch-doctor sees to it he's told he *will* be killed. And sometimes the savage actually dies—"

"From poison, I've always thought."

"The poison of fear. The physical changes that accompany fear, magnified beyond belief by belief itself."

"But how in the world could all this have affected Cappy? He wasn't a savage. And he was elderly, Ted. A bad heart, maybe. A stroke. Anything."

"He passed his pre-flight physical only a year ago. And—well, he lived all alone. He was careful not to let you see it, but I know he worried about these three trees on his place. And I know he got back from the Meeting in a worried state of mind. Then, obviously, the trees moved—grouped themselves around his cabin within easy range. But don't be afraid of them, Naomi. So long as you're not, they can't hurt you. They're not bothering us now."

"No. But where's Richard?"

Naomi's eyes swept past Ted, encompassing the cabin. No Richard! He'd been left outside . . .

Glass tinkled and crashed as she flung back the cabin door. "Richard! Richard!"

Her child was not in sight. Nor within earshot, it seemed.

"Richard Heckscher! Where are you?" Sanity returned with the conventional primness. And it brought her answer.

"Here I am, Mommie! Look-ut!"

He was in a tree! He was fifteen feet off the ground, high in the branches of a tree-thing, swaying—

For an instant, dread flowed through Naomi as if in her bloodstream and something was cutting off her breath. Then, as the hands over mouth and throat withdrew, she saw they were Ted's. She let him drag her into the cabin and close the broken door.

"Better not scare Richard," he said quietly, shoving her gently into a chair. "He might fall."

Dumbly she caught her breath, waiting for the bawling out she'd earned.

But Ted said, "Richard keeps us safe. So long as we fear for him, and not ourselves—"

That was easy to do. Outside, she heard a piping call: "Look at me now, Mommie!"

"Showing off!" she gasped. In a flashing vision, Richard was half boy, half vulture, flapping to the ground with a broken wing.

"Here," said Ted, picking up a notebook that had been on the table. "Here's Cappy's present. A homemade picture book. Bait."

"Let *me* use it!" she said. "Richard may have seen I was scared just now."

Outside again, under the tree, she called, "Here's Cappy's present, Richard. He's gone away and left it for you."

Would he notice how her voice had gone up half an octave, become flat and shrill?

"I'm coming down," Richard said. "Let me down, tree."

He seemed to be struggling. The branches were cagelike. He was caught!

Naomi's struggle was with her voice. "How did you *ever* get up there?" she called.

"The tree let me up, Mommie," Richard explained solemnly, "but he won't let me down!" He whimpered a little.

He must *not* become frightened! "You tell that tree you've got to come right down this instant!" she ordered.

She leaned against the cabin for support. Ted came out and slipped his arm around her.

"Break off a few leaves, Richard," he suggested. "That'll show your tree who's boss!"

Standing close against her husband, Naomi tried to stop shaking. But she lacked firm support, for Ted shook, too.

His advice to Richard was sound, though. What had been a trap became, through grudging movement of the branches, a ladder. Richard climbed down, scolding at the tree like an angry squirrel.

Naomi thought she'd succeeded in shutting her mind. But when her little boy slid down the final bit of trunk and came for his present, Naomi broke. Like a startled animal, she thrust the book into his hands, picked him up and ran. Her mind was a jelly, red and quaking.

She stopped momentarily after running fifty yards. "Burn the trees!" she screamed over her shoulder. "Burn the cabin! Burn it all!" She ran on, Ted's answering shouts beyond her comprehension.

Fatigue halted her. At the top of the rise between Cappy's farm and their own, pain and dizziness began flowing over her in waves. She set Richard down on the mauve soil and collapsed beside him.

When she sat up, Richard squatted just out of reach, watching curiously. She made an effort at casualness: "Let's see what Daddy's doing back there."

"He's doing just what you said to, Mommie!" Richard answered indignantly.

Her men were standing together, Naomi realized. She laughed. After a moment, Richard joined her. Then he looked for his book, found it a few paces away, and brought it to her.

"Read to me, Mommie."

"At home," she said.

Activity at Cappy's interested her now. Wisps of smoke were licking around the trees. A tongue of flame lapped at one while she watched. Branches writhed. The trees were too slow-moving to escape . . .

But where was Ted? What had she exposed him to, with her hysterical orders? She held her breath till he moved within sight, standing quietly by a pile of salvaged tools. Behind him the cabin began to smoke.

Ted wasn't afraid, then. He understood what he faced. And Richard wasn't afraid, either, because he didn't understand.

But she? Surreptitiously Naomi pinched her hip till it felt black and blue. That was for being such a fool. She must *not* be afraid!

"Daddy seems to be staying there," she said. "Let's wait for him at home, Richard."

"Are you going to make Daddy burn *our* tree?"

She jumped as if stung. Then, consciously womanlike, she sought relief in talk.

"What do *you* think we should do, dear?"

"Oh, I *like* the tree, Mommie. It's cool under there. And the tree plays with me."

"How, Richard?"

"If I'm pilot, he's navigator. Or ship, maybe. But he's so dumb, Mommie! I always have to tell him everything. Doesn't know what a fairy is, or Goldilocks, or anything!"

He clutched his book affectionately, rubbing his face on it. "Hurry up, Mommie. It'll be bedtime before you ever read to me!"

She touched his head briefly. "You can look at the book while I fix your supper."

But to explain Cappy's pictures—crudely crayoned cartoons, really—she had to fill in the story they illustrated. She told it while Richard ate: how the intrepid Spaceman gallantly used his ray gun against the villainous Martians to aid the green-haired Princess. Richard spooned up the thrills with his mush, gazing fascinated at Cappy's colorful and fantastic pictures, propped before him on the table. Had Ted been home, the scene might almost have been blissful.

It might have been . . . if their own tree hadn't reminded her of Cappy's. Still, she'd almost managed to stuff her fear back into that mental pigeon-hole before their own tree. It was unbelievable, but she'd been glancing out the window every few minutes, so she saw it start. Their own tree began to walk.

Down the hill it came—right there!—framed in the window behind Richard's head, moving slowly but inexorably on a root system that writhed along the surface. Like some ancient sculpture of Serpents Supporting the Tree of Life. Except that it brought death . . .

"Are you sick, Mommie?"

No, not sick. Just something the matter with her throat, preventing a quick answer, leaving no way to keep Richard from turning to look out the window.

"I think our tree is coming to play with me, Mommie."

No, no! Not Richard!

"Remember how you used to say that about Cappy? When he was really coming to see your daddy?"

"But Daddy isn't home!"

"He'll get here, dear. Now eat your supper."

A lot to ask of an excited little boy. And the tree *was* his friend, it seemed. Cappy's tree had even followed the child's orders. Richard might intercede—

No! Expose him to such danger? How could she think of it?

"Had enough to eat, dear? Wash your hands and face at the pump, and you can stay out and play till Daddy gets home. I—I want— I may have to see your friend, the tree, by myself . . ."

"But you haven't finished my story!"

"I will when Daddy gets home. And if I'm not here, you tell Daddy to do it."

"Where are you going, Mommie?"

"I might see Cappy, dear. Now go and wash, please!"

"Sure, Mommie. Don't cry."

Accept his kiss, even if it *is* from a mouth rimmed with supper. And don't rub it off till he's gone out, you damned fool. You frightened fool. You shaking, sweating, terror-stricken fool.

Who's he going to kiss when you're not here?

The tree has stopped. Our little tree is having its supper. How nice. Sucking sustenance direct from soil with aid of sun and air in true plant fashion—but exhausting our mineral resources.

(How wise of Ted to make you go to those lectures! You wouldn't want to die in ignorance, would you?)

The lecture—come on, let's go back to the lecture! Let's free our soil from every tree or we'll not hold the joint in fee. No, not joint. A vulgarism, teacher would say. Methinks the times are out of joint. Aroint thee, tree!

Now a pinch. Pinch yourself hard in the same old place so it'll hurt real bad. Then straighten your face and go stick your head out the window. Your son is talking—your son, your sun.

Can your son be eclipsed by a tree? A matter of special spatial relationships, and the space is shrinking, friend. The tree is only a few hundred feet from the house. It has finished its little supper and is now running around. Like Richard. *With* Richard! Congenial, what?

Smile, stupid. Your son speaks. Answer him.

"What, dear?"

"I see Daddy! He just came over the hill. He's running! Can I go meet him, Mommie?"

"No, dear. It's too far."

Too far. Far too far.

"Did you say something to me, Richard?"

"No. I was talking to the tree. I'm the Spaceman and he's the Martian. But he doesn't want to be the Martian!"

Richard plays. Let us play. Let us play.

You're close enough to get into the game, surely. A hundred and fifty feet, maybe. Effective range, fifty feet. Rate of motion? Projected time-interval? Depends on which system you observe it from. Richard has a system.

"He doesn't want to play, Mommie. He wants to see you!"

"You tell that tree your Mommie *never* sees strangers when Daddy isn't home!"

"I'll *make* him wait!"

Stoutly your pot-bellied little protector prevents his protective mother from going to pot.

"If he won't play, I'll use my ray gun on him!"

Obviously, the tree won't play. Watch your son lift empty hands, arm himself with a weapon yet to be invented, and open fire on the advancing foe.

"Aa-aa-aa!"

So *that's* how a ray gun sounds!

"You're dead, tree! You're dead! Now you *can't* play with me any more. You're dead!"

Seeing it happen, then, watching the tree accept the little boy's fantasy as fact, Naomi wondered why she'd never thought of that herself.

So the tree was a treacherous medicine-man, was it? A true-believing witch-doctor? And who could be more susceptible to the poisoning of fear than a witch-doctor who has made fear work—and believes it's being used against him?

It was all over. She and the tree bit the dust together. But the tree was dead, and Naomi merely fainting, and Ted would soon be home . . .

IN THE FOREST
LESLIE PERRI

THERE WAS A WIND. It blew through the topmost branches of the tall trees in a silent, autumnal forest. Dry leaves trembled nervously as the dark tree trunks stirred in a thrust of the wind. A scarlet maple leaf lay unmoving on the inky surface of a cold spring. Behind an interlacing of nakedly white birches a young deer stood still with wide lacquered eyes fixed on him. Its tar-black nostrils shone in a quivering of fright and then like the wind it rustled momentarily on the forest floor of crackling leaves and disappeared.

He breathed heavily with disappointment. He had transmitted fear, his own apprehensions, again.

He moved from the protection of an overhanging rock. The ease with which he moved delighted him sensuously. This sportive exhilaration had to be curbed; it made him less sensitive to the problem at hand. He had to communicate.

There were obviously lower orders, mainly the winged beings. Some were tiny and fragile. They would approach and light on him with the unwariness of the naive, trusting to their speed to escape from danger. From them he had no consciousness of intelligence. They buzzed and swarmed and hummed with monotonous idiocy. The larger winged beings were more interesting but they wore the drabness of the forest on their sleek wings. They would not come close but made inquiring sounds and swooped away at his approach.

246

He had learned to move silently through the silent forest. He felt almost weightless and infinitely agile and this delight he had to renounce for the time. He could walk erect, or run with incredible rapidity. And when he stood erect his body attained a new vitality and with his head above the lower woody vegetable growths he experienced a new dignity and regality. He was no petitioning refugee from the pitiless vise of unending cold. Here in this autumnal forest was the warmth and promise of spring, for him.

Excitement made him warmer and more jubilant still. He had to communicate. But with whom? With which of these beings could he share his unbelievable adventure? He ran down a sloping floor of the forest and ran and ran, slipping and sliding on the leaves until he was breathless. And came to halt in a marshy spot with the spikes of dried vegetation towering about him. His heart beat with transcendental joy. He ached to babble of his happiness and then to relive his adventure in the telling of it to another intelligence the equal of his.

He breathed more slowly and more slowly yet. Above the trees, caught in the web of branches, a brilliant blue sky gleamed and virgin cloud forms of purest white drifted slowly above the trap of the forest. And there, lower than the clouds, was the magnificence of a burning sun, a brilliance whose golden shadow warmed the tree trunks, the faces of the dry leaves, the soft, sucking black earth of the marsh and—him. In this warmth he luxuriated, with every sensibility in his being. His body had starved for warmth.

And while he stood thus, a long slithering form passed before him, describing in its movement across the moss and rocks and black leaf-moulded earth resilient, graceful curves. It passed him without notice, conveying nothing, an impenetrable life form.

And then, as suddenly, his muscles tightened and he withdrew reluctantly from the warmth of the sun.

He moved closer into the dried, tassel-topped grasses, feeling the scrape of sharp seed-bearing burrs as they clung to him. In a closely woven burrow, hidden from the sun and the reach of the wind, he heard a new sound, a louder, sharper crackle in the forest. A new scent crowded into the burrow and overpowered him with a new sensation, a suffocating awareness of danger.

He was cold again, and taut. The shadow from which he had escaped enclosed him again. This same deadly shadow of fear sapped his new vitality and destroyed his sensuous joy.

There was that sharper sound, a baying shrillness that resounded through the forest quiet and hammered at the tree trunks and unresisting vegetation with an unreasoning insistence. The echo of this new, insane voice of danger stirred him.

He moved cautiously and quickly from the burrow and through the marsh. He was not erect now, but low and rapid-moving. He thought desperately of survival now, not communication. This howling, yapping being had found him out, scented him in the forest and he knew only that he had to escape.

The forest floor rose gradually to greater and greater heights. He recognized the terrain and the character of this part of the forest. There was, at the summit, a sudden drop down a face of irregular outcroppings of stone. And at the base of this lay a vast body of water in which he could hide. He could manage the tall face of stone, hiding and blending into its cold greyness.

The baying and yapping was closer and he moved even more rapidly. The chase seemed directed to him, not purposeless. Behind the baying and shrill crying of this hunter was yet another will. And this chilled him with hopeless horror. He felt instinctively that he could communicate with *this* will, that this was the intelligence he sought. But between it and him was this unleashed agent for his destruction.

He ran more quickly and with a new sensation of weariness as the slope mounted. The vegetation was green here, and somewhat sparser. There were fewer places of refuge. At times he ran without the protection of any covering, only the moss and green ground vines underfoot.

As he reached the summit he heard a new sound, a sharp undecipherable crack and whine overhead. When he had reached the top of the sharp rise, he stood erect for a moment, seeking the surest path for his descent of the sharp rock face. The body of water below gleamed warmly blue. The sun was a glorious, almost perfectly round entity, low in the sky. His body straightened involuntarily, rose up in the warmth of the sun, darkly and strangely outlined against the unbroken blue of the sky. And then as the crack and whine of the gun sounded in the evening quiet, not once but twice, and inexpertly a third time, his shape crumbled against the sky and he toppled from the cliff edge into the still blue of the lake below.

The man breathed heavily as he came up the hill. He was red-faced from exertion and frustration. He was heavy and clumsy in the perfection Abercrombie and Fitch had tailored into his hunting clothes. He held his rifle, an expensive and aesthetically beautiful instrument of destruction, like a blunt, ugly club.

He stood at the edge of the cliff and looked down. There was nothing. Only the serenity of the early evening, the unanswering quiet of the lake, the ridge of mountains, the darkening sky.

"Now what in the hell was that?" the man muttered.

The dog, beside him, shivered and sat down suddenly. Its howl was unbidden, undirected, and it filled the forest with unrest.

THE ANGLERS OF ARZ
ROGER DEE

THE THIRD NIGHT of the *Marco Four's* landfall on the moonless Altarian planet was a repetition of the two before it, a nine-hour intermission of drowsy, pastoral peace. Navigator Arthur Farrell— it was his turn to stand watch—was sitting at an open-side port with a magnoscanner ready; but in spite of his vigilance he had not exposed a film when the inevitable pre-dawn rainbow began to shimmer over the eastern ocean.

Sunrise brought him alert with a jerk, frowning at sight of two pinkish, bipedal Arzian fishermen posted on the tiny coral islet a quarter-mile offshore, their blank triangular faces turned stolidly toward the beach.

"They're at it again," Farrell called, and dropped to the mossy turf outside. "Roll out on the double! I'm going to magnofilm this!"

Stryker and Gibson came out of their sleeping cubicles reluctantly, belting on the loose shorts which all three wore in the balmy Arzian climate. Stryker blinked and yawned as he let himself through the port, his fringe of white hair tousled and his naked paunch sweating. He looked, Farrell thought for the thousandth time, more like a retired cook than like the veteran commander of a Terran Colonies expedition.

Gibson followed, stretching his powerfully-muscled body like a wrestler to throw off the effects of sleep. Gibson was linguist-ethnologist of the crew, a blocky man in his early thirties with thick black hair and heavy brows that shaded a square, humorless face.

"Any sign of the squids yet?" he asked.

"They won't show up until the dragons come," Farrell said. He adjusted the light filter of the magnoscanner and scowled at Stryker. "Lee, I wish you'd let me break up the show this time with a dis-beam. This butchery gets on my nerves."

Stryker shielded his eyes with his hands against the glare of sun on water. "You know I can't do that, Arthur. These Arzians may turn out to be Fifth Order beings or higher, and under Terran Regulations our tampering with what may be a basic culture-pattern would amount to armed invasion. We'll have to crack that cackle-and-grunt language of theirs and learn something of their mores before we can interfere."

Farrell turned an irritable stare on the incurious group of Arzians gathering, nets and fishing spears in hand, at the edge of the sheltering bramble forest.

"What stumps me is their motivation," he said. "Why do the fools go out to that islet every night, when they must know damned well what will happen next morning?"

Gibson answered him with an older problem, his square face puzzled. "For that matter, what became of the city I saw when we came in through the stratosphere? It must be a tremendous thing, yet we've searched the entire globe in the scouter and found nothing but water and a scattering of little islands like this one, all covered with bramble. It wasn't a city these pink fishers could have built, either. The architecture was beyond them by a million years."

Stryker and Farrell traded baffled looks. The city had become something of a fixation with Gibson, and his dogged insistence—coupled with an irritating habit of being right—had worn their patience thin.

"There never was a city here, Gib," Stryker said. "You dozed off while we were making planetfall, that's all."

Gibson stiffened resentfully, but Farrell's voice cut his protest short. "Get set! Here they come!"

Out of the morning rainbow dropped a swarm of winged lizards, twenty feet in length and a glistening chlorophyll green in the early light. They stooped like hawks upon the islet offshore, burying the two Arzian fishers instantly under their snapping, threshing bodies. Then around the outcrop the sea boiled whitely, churned to foam by a sudden uprushing of black, octopoid shapes.

"The squids," Stryker grunted. "Right on schedule. Two seconds too late, as usual, to stop the slaughter."

A barrage of barbed tentacles lashed out of the foam and drove into the melee of winged lizards. The lizards took the air at once, leaving behind three of their number who disappeared under the surface like harpooned seals. No trace remained of the two Arzian natives.

"A neat example of dog eat dog," Farrell said, snapping off the magnoscanner. "Do any of those beauties look like city-builders, Gib?"

Chattering pink natives straggled past from the shelter of the thorn forest, ignoring the Earthmen, and lined the casting ledges along the beach to begin their day's fishing.

"Nothing we've seen yet could've built that city," Gibson said stubbornly. "But it's here somewhere, and I'm going to find it. Will either of you be using the scouter today?"

Stryker threw up his hands. "I've a mountain of data to collate, and Arthur is off duty after standing watch last night. Help yourself, but you won't find anything."

The scouter was a speeding dot on the horizon when Farrell crawled into his sleeping cubicle a short time later, leaving Stryker to mutter over his litter of notes. Sleep did not come to him at once; a vague sense of something overlooked prodded irritatingly at the back of his consciousness, but it was not until drowsiness had finally overtaken him that the discrepancy assumed definite form.

He recalled then that on the first day of the Marco's planetfall one of the pink fishers had fallen from a casting ledge into the water, and had all but drowned before his fellows pulled him out with extended spear-shafts. Which meant that the fishers could not swim, else some would surely have gone in after him.

And the Marco's crew had explored Arz exhaustively without finding any slightest trace of boats or of boat landings. The train of association completed itself with automatic logic, almost rousing Farrell out of his doze.

"I'll be damned," he muttered. "No boats, and they don't swim. *Then, how the devil do they get out to that islet?*"

He fell asleep with the paradox unresolved.

Stryker was still humped over his records when Farrell came out of his cubicle and broke a packaged meal from the food locker. The visicom over the control board hummed softly, its screen blank on open channel.

"Gibson found his lost city yet?" Farrell asked, and grinned when Stryker snorted.

"He's scouring the daylight side now," Stryker said. "Arthur, I'm going to ground Gib tomorrow, much as I dislike giving him a direct order. He's got that phantom city on the brain, and he lacks the imagination to understand how dangerous to our assignment an obsession of that sort can be."

Farrell shrugged. "I'd agree with you offhand if it weren't for Gib's bullheaded habit of being right. I hope he finds it soon, if it's here. I'll probably be standing his watch until he's satisfied."

Stryker looked relieved. "Would you mind taking it tonight? I'm completely bushed after today's logging."

Farrell waved a hand and took up his magnoscanner. It was dark outside already, the close, soft night of a moonless tropical world whose moist atmosphere absorbed even starlight. He dragged a chair to the open port and packed his pipe, settling himself comfortably while Stryker mixed a nightcap before turning in.

Later he remembered that Stryker dissolved a tablet in his glass, but at the moment it meant nothing. In a matter of minutes the older man's snoring drifted to him, a sound faintly irritating against the velvety hush outside.

Farrell lit his pipe and turned to the inconsistencies he had uncovered. The Arzians did not swim, and without boats . . .

It occurred to him then that there had been two of the pink fishers on the islet each morning, and the coincidence made him sit up suddenly, startled. Why two? Why not three or four, or only one?

He stepped out through the open lock and paced restlessly up and down on the springy turf, feeling the ocean breeze soft on his face. Three days of dull routine logwork had built up a need for physical action that chafed his temper; he was intrigued and at the same time annoyed by the enigmatic relation that linked the Arzian fishers to the dragons and squids, and his desire to understand that relation was aggravated by the knowledge that Arz could be a perfect world for Terran colonization. That is, he thought wryly, if Terran colonists could stomach the weird custom pursued by its natives of committing suicide in pairs.

He went over again the improbable drama of the past three mornings, and found it not too unnatural until he came to the motivation and the means of transportation that placed the Arzians in pairs on the islet, when his whole fabric of speculation fell into a tangled snarl of inconsistencies. He gave it up finally; how could any Earthman rationalize the outlandish compulsions that actuated so alien a race?

He went inside again, and the sound of Stryker's muffled snoring fanned his restlessness. He made his decision abruptly, laying aside the magnoscanner for a hand-flash and a pocket-sized audicom unit which he clipped to the belt of his shorts.

He did not choose a weapon because he saw no need for one. The torch would show him how the natives reached the outcrop, and if he should need help the audicom would summon Stryker. Investigating without Stryker's sanction was, strictly speaking, a breach of Terran Regulations, but—

"Damn Terran Regulations," he muttered. "I've got to know."

Farrell snapped on the torch at the edge of the thorn forest and entered briskly, eager for action now that he had begun. Just inside the edge of the bramble he came upon a pair of Arzians curled up together on the mossy ground, sleeping soundly, their triangular faces wholly blank and unrevealing.

He worked deeper into the underbrush and found other sleeping couples, but nothing else. There were no humming insects, no twittering night-birds or scurrying rodents. He had worked his way close to the center of the island without further discovery and was on the point of turning back, disgusted, when something bulky and powerful seized him from behind.

A sharp sting burned his shoulder, wasp-like, and a sudden overwhelming lassitude swept him into a darkness deeper than the Arzian night. His last conscious thought was not of his own danger, but of Stryker—asleep and unprotected behind the *Marco's* open port. . . .

He was standing erect when he woke, his back to the open sea and a prismatic glimmer of early dawn rainbow shining on the water before him. For a moment he was totally disoriented; then from the corner of an eye he caught the pinkish blur of an Arzian fisher standing beside him, and cried out hoarsely in sudden panic when he tried to turn his head and could not.

He was on the coral outcropping offshore, and except for the involuntary muscles of balance and respiration his body was paralyzed.

The first red glow of sunrise blurred the reflected rainbow at his feet, but for some seconds his shuttling mind was too busy to consider the danger of predicament. *Whatever brought me here anesthetized me first*, he thought. *That sting in my shoulder was like a hypo needle.*

Panic seized him again when he remembered the green flying-lizards; more seconds passed before he gained control of himself, sweating with the effort. He had to get help. If he could switch on the audicom at his belt and call Stryker . . .

He bent every ounce of his will toward raising his right hand, and failed.

His arm was like a limb of lead, its inertia too great to budge. He relaxed the effort with a groan, sweating again when he saw a fiery half-disk of sun on the water, edges blurred and distorted by tiny surface ripples.

On shore he could see the *Marco Four* resting between thorn forest and beach, its silvered sides glistening with dew. The port was still open, and the empty carrier rack in the bow told him that Gibson had not yet returned with the scouter.

He grew aware then that sensation was returning to him slowly, that the cold surface of the audicom unit at his hip—unfelt before—

was pressing against the inner curve of his elbow. He bent his will again toward motion; this time the arm tensed a little, enough to send hope flaring through him. If he could put pressure enough against the stud . . .

The tiny click of its engaging sent him faint with relief.

"Stryker!" he yelled. "Lee, roll out—*Stryker!*"

The audicom hummed gently, without answer.

He gathered himself for another shout, and recalled with a chill of horror the tablet Stryker had mixed into his nightcap the night before. Worn out by his work, Stryker had made certain that he would not be easily disturbed.

The flattened sun-disk on the water brightened and grew rounder. Above its reflected glare he caught a flicker of movement, a restless suggestion of flapping wings.

He tried again. "Stryker, help me! I'm on the islet!"

The audicom crackled. The voice that answered was not Stryker's, but Gibson's.

"Farrell! What the devil are you doing on that butcher's block?"

Farrell fought down an insane desire to laugh. "Never mind that—get here fast, Gib! The flying- lizards—"

He broke off, seeing for the first time the octopods that ringed the outcrop just under the surface of the water, waiting with barbed tentacles spread and yellow eyes studying him glassily. He heard the unmistakable flapping of wings behind and above him then, and thought with shock-born lucidity: *I wanted a backstage look at this show, and now I'm one of the cast.*

The scouter roared in from the west across the thorn forest, flashing so close above his head that he felt the wind of its passage. Almost instantly he heard the shrilling blast of its emergency bow jets as Gibson met the lizard swarm head on.

Gibson's voice came tinnily from the audicom. "Scattered them for the moment, Arthur—blinded the whole crew with the exhaust, I think. Stand fast, now. I'm going to pick you up."

The scouter settled on the outcrop beside Farrell, so close that the hot wash of its exhaust gases scorched his bare legs. Gibson put out thick brown arms and hauled him inside like a straw man, ignoring the native. The scouter darted for shore with Farrell lying across Gibson's knees in the cockpit, his head hanging half overside.

Farrell had a last dizzy glimpse of the islet against the rush of green water below, and felt his shaky laugh of relief stick in his throat. Two of the octopods were swimming strongly for shore, holding the rigid Arzian native carefully above water between them.

"Gib," Farrell croaked. "Gib, can you risk a look back? I think I've gone mad."

The scouter swerved briefly as Gibson looked back. "You're all right, Arthur. Just hang on tight. I'll explain everything when we get you safe in the *Marco*."

Farrell forced himself to relax, more relieved than alarmed by the painful pricking of returning sensation. "I might have known it, damn you," he said. "You found your lost city, didn't you?"

Gibson sounded a little disgusted, as if he were still angry with himself over some private stupidity. "I'd have found it sooner if I'd had any brains. It was under water, of course."

In the *Marco Four*, Gibson routed Stryker out of his cubicle and mixed drinks around, leaving Farrell comfortably relaxed in the padded control chair. The paralysis was still wearing off slowly, easing Farrell's fear of being permanently disabled.

"We never saw the city from the scouter because we didn't go high enough," Gibson said. "I realized that finally, remembering how they used high-altitude blimps during the First Wars to spot submarines, and when I took the scouter up far enough there it was, at the ocean bottom—a city to compare with anything men ever built."

Stryker stared. "A marine city? What use would sea-creatures have for buildings?"

"None," Gibson said. "I think the city must have been built ages ago—by men or by a manlike race, judging from the architecture— and was submerged later by a sinking of land masses that killed off the original builders and left Arz nothing but an oversized archipelago. The squids took over then, and from all appearances they've developed a culture of their own."

"I don't see it," Stryker complained, shaking his head. "The pink fishers—"

"Are cattle, or less," Gibson finished. "The octopods are the dominant race, and they're so far above Fifth Order that we're completely out of bounds here. Under Terran Regulations we can't colonize Arz. It would be armed invasion."

"Invasion of a squid world?" Farrell protested, baffled. "Why should surface colonization conflict with an undersea culture, Gib? Why couldn't we share the planet?"

"Because the octopods own the islands too, and keep them policed," Gibson said patiently. "They even own the pink fishers. It was one of the squid-people, making a dry-land canvass of his preserve here to pick a couple of victims for this morning's show, that carried you off last night."

"Behold a familiar pattern shaping up," Stryker said. He laughed suddenly, a great irrepressible bellow of sound. "Arz is a squid's world, Arthur, don't you see? And like most civilized peoples, they're sportsmen. The flying-lizards are the game they hunt, and they raise the pink fishers for—"

Farrell swore in astonishment. "Then those poor devils are put out there deliberately, like worms on a hook—angling in reverse! No wonder I couldn't spot their motivation!"

Gibson got up and sealed the port, shutting out the soft morning breeze. "Colonization being out of the question, we may as well move on before the octopods get curious enough about us to make trouble. Do you feel up to the acceleration, Arthur?"

Farrell and Stryker looked at each other, grinning. Farrell said: "You don't think I want to stick here and be used for bait again, do you?"

He and Stryker were still grinning over it when Gibson, unamused, blasted the *Marco Four* free of Arz.

GREEN THUMB

CLIFFORD D. SIMAK

I HAD COME BACK from lunch and was watching the office while Millie went out to get a bite to eat. With my feet up on the desk in a comfortable position, I was giving considerable attention to how I might outwit a garbage-stealing dog.

The dog and I had carried on a feud for months and I was about ready to resort to some desperate measures.

I had blocked up the can with heavy concrete blocks so he couldn't tip it over, but he was a big dog and could stand up and reach down into the can and drag all the garbage out. I had tried putting a heavy weight on the lid, but he simply dragged it off and calmly proceeded with his foraging. I had waited up and caught him red-handed at it and heaved some rocks and whatever else was handy at him, but he recognized tactics such as these for what they were and they didn't bother him. He'd come back in half an hour, calm as ever.

I had considered setting a light muskrat trap on top of the garbage so that, when he reached down into the can, he'd get his muzzle caught. But if I did that, sure as hell I'd forget to take it out some Tuesday morning and the garbageman would get caught instead. I had toyed with the idea of wiring the can so the dog would get an electric shock when he came fooling around. But I didn't know how to go about wiring it and, if I did, ten to one I'd fix it up so I'd electrocute him instead of just scaring him off, and I didn't want to kill him.

I like dogs, you understand. That doesn't mean I have to like all dogs, does it? And if you had to scrape up garbage every morning, you'd be just as sore at the mutt as I was.

While I was wondering if I couldn't put something in a particularly tempting bit of garbage that would make him sick and still not kill him, the phone rang.

It was old Pete Skinner out on Acorn Ridge.

"Could you come out?" he asked.

"Maybe," I said. "What you got?"

"I got a hole out in the north forty."

"Sink-hole?"

"Nope. Looks like someone dug it out and carried off the dirt."

"Who would do that, Pete?"

"I don't know. And that ain't all of it. They left a pile of sand beside the hole."

"Maybe that's what they dug out of the hole."

"You know well enough," said Pete, "that I haven't any sandy soil. You've run tests enough on it. All of mine is clay."

"I'll be right out," I told him.

A county agent gets some funny calls, but this one topped them all. Hog cholera, corn borers, fruit blight, milk production records—any of these would have been down my alley. But a hole in the north forty?

And yet, I suppose I should have taken it as a compliment that Pete called me. When you've been a county agent for fifteen years, a lot of farmers get to trust you and some of them, like Pete, figure you can straighten out any problem. I enjoy a compliment as much as anybody. It's the headaches that go with them that I don't like.

When Millie came back, I drove out to Pete's place, which is only four or five miles out of town.

Pete's wife told me that he was up in the north forty, so I went there and found not only Pete, but some of his neighbors. All of them were looking at the hole and doing a lot of talking. I never saw a more puzzled bunch of people.

The hole was about 30 feet in diameter and about 35 feet deep, an almost perfect cone—not the kind of hole you'd dig with a pick and shovel. The sides were cut as clean as if they'd been machined, but the soil was not compressed, as it would have been if machinery had been used.

The pile of sand lay just a short distance from the hole. Looking at it, I had the insane feeling that, if you shoveled that sand into the hole, it would exactly fit. It was the whitest sand I've ever seen and, when I walked over to the pile and picked up some of it, I saw that it was clean. Not just ordinary clean, but *absolutely* clean—as though laundered grain by grain.

I stood around for a while, like the rest of them, staring at the hole and the pile of sand and wishing I could come up with some bright idea. But I wasn't able to. There was the hole and there was the sand. The topsoil was dry and powdery and would have shown wheelmarks or any other kind if there'd been any. There weren't.

I told Pete maybe he'd better fence in the whole business, because the sheriff or somebody from the state, or even the university, might want to look it over. Pete said that was a good idea and he'd do it right away.

I went back to the farmhouse and asked Mrs. Skinner to give me a couple of fruit jars. One of them I filled with a sample from the sand pile and the other with soil from the hole, being careful not to jolt the walls.

By this time, Pete and a couple of the neighbors had gotten a wagonload of fence posts and some wire and were coming out to the field. I waited and helped unload the posts and wire, then drove back to the office, envying Pete. He was satisfied to put up the fence and let me worry about the problem.

I found three fellows waiting for me. I gave Millie the fruit jars and asked her to send them right away to the Soils Bureau at the State Farm Campus. Then I settled down to work.

Other people drifted in and it was late in the afternoon before I could call up the Soils Bureau and tell them I wanted the contents of the two jars analyzed. I told them a little of what had happened, although not all of it for, when you tried to put it into words, it sounded pretty weird.

"Banker Stevens called and asked if you'd drop by his place on your way home," Millie told me.

"What would Stevens want with me?" I asked. "He isn't a farmer and I don't owe him any money."

"He grows fancy flowers," said Millie.

"I know that. He lives just up the street from me."

"From what I gathered, something awful happened to them. He was all broken up."

So, on the way home, I stopped at the Stevens place. The banker was out in the yard, waiting for me. He looked terrible. He led me around to the big flower garden in the back and never have I seen such utter devastation. In that whole area, there wasn't a single plant alive. Every one of them had given up the ghost and was lying wilted on the ground.

"What could have done it, Joe?" asked Stevens and the way he said it, I felt sorry for him.

After all, those flowers were a big thing in his life. He'd raised them from special seed and he'd babied them along, and for anybody who is crazy about flowers, I imagine they were tops.

"Someone might have used some spray on them," I said. "Almost any kind of spray, if you didn't dilute it enough, would kill them."

Out in the garden, I took a close look at the dead flowers, but nowhere could I see any sign of the burning from too strong a spray.

Then I saw the holes, at first only two or three of them, then, as I went on looking, dozens of them. They were all over the garden, about an inch in diameter, for all the world as if someone had taken a broomstick and punched holes all over the place. I got down on my knees and could see that they tapered, the way they do when you pull weeds with big taproots out of the ground.

"You been pulling weeds?" I asked.

"Not big ones like that," said the banker. "I take good care of those flowers, Joe. You know that. Keep them weeded and watered and cultivated and sprayed. Put just the right amount of commercial fertilizer in the soil. Try to keep it at top fertility."

"You should use manure. It's better than all the commercial fertilizer you can buy."

"I don't agree with you. Tests have proved . . ."

It was an old argument, one that we fought out each year. I let him run on, only half listening to him, while I picked up some of the soil and crumbled it. It was dead soil. You could feel that it was. It crumbled at the lightest touch and was dry, even when I dug a foot beneath the surface.

"You water this bed recently?" I asked.

"Last evening," Stevens said.

"When did you find the flowers like this?"

"This morning. They looked fine last night. And now—" he blinked fast.

I asked him for a fruit jar and filled it with a sample of the soil.

"I'll send this in and see if there's anything wrong with it," I said.

A bunch of dogs were barking at something in the hedge in front of my place when I got home. Some of the dogs in the neighborhood are hell on cats. I parked the car and picked up an old hoe handle and went out to rescue the cat they seemed to have cornered.

They scattered when they saw me coming and I started to look in the hedge for the cat. There wasn't any and that aroused my curiosity and I wondered what the dogs could have been barking at. So I went hunting. And I found it.

It was lying on the ground, close against the lower growth of the hedge, as if it had crawled there for protection.

I reached in and pulled it out—a weed of some sort, about five feet tall, and with a funny root system. There were eight roots, each about an inch in diameter at the top and tapering to a quarter inch or so. They weren't all twisted up, but were sort of sprung out, so that there were four to the side, each set of four in line. I looked at their tips and I saw that the roots were not broken off, but ended in blunt, strong points.

The stalk, at the bottom, was about as thick as a man's fist. There were four main branches covered with thick, substantial, rather meaty leaves; but the last foot of the branches was bare of leaves. At the top were several flower or seed pouches, the biggest of them about the size of an old-fashioned coffee mug.

I squatted there looking at it. The more I looked, the more puzzled I became. As a county agent, you have to know quite a bit about botany and this plant was like none I had seen before.

I dragged it across the lawn to the toolshed back of the garage and tossed it in there, figuring that after supper I'd have a closer look at it

I went in the house to get my evening meal ready and decided to broil a steak and fix up a bowl of salad.

A lot of people in town wonder at my living in the old home-stead, but I'm used to the house and there seemed to be no sense in moving somewhere else when all it costs me is taxes and a little upkeep. For several years before Mother died, she had been quite feeble and I did all the cleaning and helped with the cooking, so I'm fairly handy at it.

After I washed the dishes, I read what little there was to read in the evening paper and then looked up an old text on botany, to see if I could find anything that might help identify the plant.

I didn't find anything and, just before I went to bed, I got a flashlight and went out, imagining, I suppose, that I'd find the weed somehow different than I remembered it.

I opened the door of the shed and flashed the light where I'd tossed the weed on the floor. At first, I couldn't see it, then I heard a leafy rustling over in one corner and I turned the light in that direction.

The weed had crawled over to one corner and it was trying to get up, its stem bowed out—the way a man would arch his back—pressing against the wall of the shed.

Standing there with my mouth open, watching it try to raise itself erect, I felt horror and fear. I reached out to the corner near-est the door and snatched up an axe.

If the plant had succeeded in getting up, I might have chopped it to bits. But, as I stood there, I saw the thing would never make it. I was not surprised when it slumped back on the floor.

What I did next was just as unreasoning and instinctive as reaching for the axe.

I found an old washtub and half filled it with water. Then I picked up the plant—it had a squirmish feel to it, like a worm—stuck its roots into the water, and pushed the tub back against the wall, so the thing could be braced upright.

I went into the house and ransacked a couple of closets until I found the sunlamp I'd bought a couple of years back, to use when I had a touch of arthritis in my shoulder. I rigged up the lamp and trained it on the plant, not too close. Then I got a big shovelful of dirt and dumped it in the tub.

And that, I figured, was about all I could do. I was giving the plant water, soil-food and simulated sunlight. I was afraid that, if I tried a more fancy treatment, I might kill it, for I hadn't any notion of what conditions it might be used to.

Apparently I handled it right. It perked up considerably and, as I moved about, the coffee-cup-sized pod on the top kept turning, following every move I made.

I watched it for a while and moved the sunlamp back a little, so there'd be no chance of scorching it, and went back into the house.

It was then that I really began to get bone-scared. I had been frightened out in the shed, of course, but that had been shock. Now, thinking it over, I began to understand more clearly what sort of creature I'd found underneath the hedge. I remember I wasn't yet ready to say it out loud, but it seemed probable that my guest was an alien intelligence.

I did some wondering about how it had gotten here and if it had made the holes in Banker Stevens' flowerbed and also if it could have had anything to do with the big hole out in Pete Skinner's north forty.

I sat around, arguing with myself, for a man just does not go prowling around in his neighbor's garden after midnight.

But I had to know.

I walked up the alley to the back of the Stevens house and sneaked into the garden. Shielding the flashlight with my hat, I had another look at the holes in the ruined flowerbed. I wasn't too surprised when I saw that they occurred in series of eight, four to the side—exactly the kind of holes the plant back in my toolshed would make if it sank its roots into the ground.

I counted at least eleven of those eight-in-line sets of holes and I'm sure that there were more. But I didn't want to stick around too long, for fear Banker Stevens might wake up and ask questions.

So I went back home, down the alley, and was just in time to catch that garbage-stealing dog doing a good job on the can. He had his head stuck clear down into it and I was able to sneak up behind him. He heard me and struggled to get out, but he'd jammed himself into the can. Before he could get loose, I landed a good swift kick where it did maximum good. He set some kind of canine speed record in getting off the premises, I imagine.

I went to the toolshed and opened the door. The tub half full of muddy water was still there and the sunlamp was still burning— but the plant was gone. I looked all over the shed and couldn't find it. So I unplugged the sunlamp and headed for the house.

To be truthful, I was a little relieved that the plant had wandered off.

But when I rounded the corner of the house, I saw it hadn't. It was in the window box, and the geraniums I had nursed all spring were hanging limply over the side of the box.

I stood there and looked at it and had the feeling that it was looking back at me.

And I remembered that not only had it had to travel from the toolshed to the house and then climb into the window box, but it had had to open the toolshed door and close it again.

It was standing up, stiff and straight, and appeared to be in the best of health. It looked thoroughly incongruous in the window box—as if a man had grown a tall stalk of corn there, although it didn't look anything like a stalk of corn.

I got a pail of water and poured it into the window box. Then I felt something tapping me on the head and looked up. The plant had bent over and was patting me with one of its branches. The modified leaf at the end of the branch had spread itself out to do the patting and looked something like a hand.

I went into the house and up to bed and the main thing I was thinking about was that, if the plant got too troublesome or dangerous, all I had to do was mix a strong dose of commercial fertilizer or arsenic, or something just as deadly, and water it with the mixture.

Believe it or not, I went to sleep.

Next morning, I got to thinking that maybe I should repair the old greenhouse and put my guest in there and be sure to keep the door locked. It seemed to be reasonably friendly and inoffensive, but I couldn't be sure, of course.

After breakfast, I went out into the yard to look for it, with the idea of locking it in the garage for the day, but it wasn't in the window box, or anywhere that I could see. And since it was Saturday, when a lot of farmers came to town, with some of them sure to be dropping in to see me, I didn't want to be late to work.

I was fairly busy during the day and didn't have much time for thinking or worrying. But when I was wrapping up the sample of soil from the banker's garden to send to the Soils Bureau, I wondered if maybe there wasn't someone at the university I should notify. I also wondered about letting someone in Washington know, except I didn't have the least idea whom to contact, or even which department.

Coming home that evening, I found the plant anchored in the garden, in a little space where the radishes and lettuce had been. The few lettuce plants still left in the ground were looking sort of limp, but everything else was all right. I took a good look at the plant. It waved a couple of its branches at me—and it wasn't the wind blowing them, for there wasn't any wind—and it nodded its coffee-cup pod as if to let me know it recognized me. But that was all it did.

After supper, I scouted the hedge in front of the house and found two more of the plants. Both of them were dead.

My next-door neighbors had gone to a movie, so I scouted their place, too, and found four more of the plants, under bushes and in corners where they had crawled away to die.

I wondered whether it might not have been the plant I'd rescued that the dogs had been barking at the night before. I felt fairly sure it was. A dog might be able to recognize an alien being where a man would be unable to.

I counted up. At least seven of the things had picked out Banker Stevens' flowerbed for a meal and the chemical fertilizer he used had killed all but one of them. The sole survivor, then, was out in the garden, killing off my lettuce.

I wondered why the lettuce and geraniums and Stevens' flowers had reacted as they did. It might be that the alien plants produced some sort of poison, which they injected into the soil to discourage other plant life from crowding their feeding grounds. That was not exactly far-fetched. There are trees and plants on Earth that accomplish the same thing by various methods. Or it might be that the aliens sucked the soil so dry of moisture and plant-food that the other plants simply starved to death.

I did some wondering on why they'd come to Earth at all and why some of them had stayed. If they had traveled from some other planet, they must have come in a ship, so that hole out in Pete's north forty might have been where they stopped to replenish their food supply, dumping the equivalent of garbage beside the hole.

And what about the seven I had counted?

Could they have jumped ship? Or gone on shore leave and run into trouble, the way human sailors often do?

Maybe the ship had searched for the missing members of the party, had been unable to find them, and had gone on. If that were so, then my own plant was a marooned alien. Or maybe the ship was still hunting.

I wore myself out, thinking about it, and went to bed early, but lay there tossing for a long time. Then, just as I was falling asleep, I heard the dog at the garbage can. You'd think after what had happened to him the night before, that he'd have decided to skip that particular can, but not him. He was rattling and banging it around, trying to tip it over.

I picked a skillet off the stove and opened the back door. I got a good shot at him, but missed him by a good ten feet. I was so sore that I didn't even go out to pick up the skillet, but went back to bed.

It must have been several hours later that I was brought straight up in bed by the terror-stricken yelping of a dog. I jumped out and ran to the window. It was a bright moonlit night and the dog was going down the driveway as if the devil himself were after him. Behind him sailed the plant. It had wrapped one of its branches around his tail and the other three branches were really giving him a working over.

They went up the street out of sight and, for a long time after they disappeared, I could hear the dog still yelping. Within a few minutes, I saw the plant coming up the gravel, walking like a spider on its eight roots.

It turned off the driveway and planted itself beside a lilac bush and seemed to settle down for the night. I decided that if it wasn't good for anything else, the garbage can would be safe, at least. If the dog came back again, the plant would be waiting to put the bee on him.

I lay awake for a long time, wondering how the plant had known I didn't want the dog raiding the garbage. It probably had seen—if that is the proper word—me chase him out of the yard.

I went to sleep with the comfortable feeling that the plant and I had finally begun to understand each other.

The next day was Sunday and I started working on the greenhouse, putting it into shape so I could cage up the plant. It had found itself a sunny spot in the garden and was imitating a large and particularly ugly weed I'd been too lazy to pull out.

My next-door neighbor came over to offer free advice, but he kept shifting uneasily and I knew there was something on his mind.

Finally he came out with it. "Funny thing—Jenny swears she saw a big plant walking around in your yard the other day. The kid saw it, too, and he claims it chased him." He tittered a little, embarrassed. "You know how kids are."

"Sure," I said.

He stood around a while longer and gave me some more advice, then went across the yard and home.

I worried about what he had told me. If the plant really had taken to chasing kids, there'd be hell to pay.

I worked at the greenhouse all day long, but there was a lot to do, for it had been out of use ten years or more, and by nightfall I was tuckered out.

After supper, I went out on the back stoop and sat on the steps, watching the stars. It was quiet and restful.

I hadn't been there more than fifteen minutes when I heard a rustling. I looked around and there was the plant, coming up out of the garden, walking along on its roots.

It sort of squatted down beside me and the two of us just sat there, looking at the stars. Or, at least, I looked at them. I don't actually know if the plant could see. If it couldn't, it had some other faculty that was just as good as sight. We just sat there.

After a while, the plant moved one of its branches over and took hold of my arm with that hand-like leaf. I tensed a bit, but its touch was gentle enough and I sat still, figuring that if the two of us were to get along, we couldn't start out by flinching away from one another.

Then, so gradually that at first I didn't notice it, I began to perceive a sense of gratitude, as if the plant might be thanking me. I looked around to see what it was doing and it wasn't doing a thing, just sitting there as I was, but with its "hand" still on my arm.

Yet in some way, the plant was trying to make me understand that it was grateful to me for saving it.

It formed no words, you understand. Other than rustling its leaves, it couldn't make a sound. But I understood that some system of communication was in operation. No words, but emotion—deep, clear, utterly sincere emotion.

It eventually got a little embarrassing, this non-stop gratitude.

"Oh, that's all right," I said, trying to put an end to it. "You would have done as much for me."

Somehow, the plant must have sensed that its thanks had been accepted, because the gratitude wore off a bit and something else took over—a sense of peace and quiet.

The plant got up and started to walk off and I called out to it, "Hey, Plant, wait a minute!"

It seemed to understand that I had called it back, for it turned around. I took it by a branch and started to lead it around the boundaries of the yard. If this communication business was going to be any good, you see, it had to go beyond the sense of gratitude and peace and quiet. So I led the plant all the way around the yard and I kept thinking at it as hard as I could, telling it not to go beyond that perimeter.

By the time I'd finished, I was wringing wet with effort. But, finally, the plant seemed to be trying to say okay. Then I built up a mental image of it chasing a kid and I shook a mental finger at it. The plant agreed. I tried to tell it not to move around the yard in daylight, when people would be able to see it. Whether the concept was harder or I was getting tired, I don't know, but both the plant and I were limp when it at last indicated that it understood.

Lying in bed that night, I thought a lot about this problem of communication. It was not telepathy, apparently, but something based on mental pictures and emotions.

But I saw it as my one chance. If I could learn to converse, no matter how, and the plant could learn to communicate something beyond abstracts to me, it could talk to people, would be acceptable and believable, and the authorities might be willing to recognize it as an intelligent being. I decided that the best thing to do would be to acquaint it with the way we humans lived and try to make it understand why we lived that way. And since I couldn't take my visitor outside the yard, I'd have to do it inside.

I went to sleep, chuckling at the idea of my house and yard being a classroom for an alien.

The next day, I received a phone call from the Soils Bureau at the university.

"What kind of stuff is this you're sending us?" the man demanded.

"Just some soil I picked up," I said. "What's wrong with it?"

"Sample One is all right. It's just common, everyday Burton County soil. But Sample Two, that sand—good God, man, it has gold dust and flakes of silver and some copper in it! All of it in minute particles, of course. But if some farmer out your way has a pit of that stuff, he's rich."

"At the most, he has twenty-five or thirty truckloads of it."

"Where'd he get it? Where'd it come from?"

I took a deep breath and told him all I knew about the incident out at Pete's north forty.

He said he'd be right out, but I caught him before he hung up and asked him about the third sample.

"What was he growing on that ground?" the man asked baffledly. "Nothing I know of could suck it that clean, right down to the bare bone! Tell him to put in a lot of organic material and some lime and almost everything else that's needed in good soil, before he tries to use it."

The Soils people came out to Pete's place and they brought along some other men from the university. A little later in the week, after the papers had spelled out big headlines, a couple of men from Washington showed up. But no one seemed able to figure it out and they finally gave up. The newspapers gave it a play and dropped it as soon as the experts did.

During that time, curiosity seekers flocked to the farm to gape at the hole and the pile of sand. They had carried off more than half the sand and Pete was madder than hell about the whole business.

"I'm going to fill in that hole and forget all about it," he told me, and that was what he did.

Meanwhile, at home, the situation was progressing. Plant seemed to understand what I had told him about not moving out of the yard and acting like a weed during the daytime and leaving kids alone. Everything was peaceable and I got no more complaints. Best of all, the garbage-stealing dog never showed his snout again.

Several times, during all the excitement out at Pete's place, I had been tempted to tell someone from the university about Plant. In each case, I decided not to, for we weren't getting along too well in the talk department.

But in other ways, we were doing just fine.

I let Plant watch me while I took an electric motor apart and then put it together again, but I wasn't too sure he knew what it was all about. I tried to show him the concept of mechanical power and I demonstrated how the motor would deliver that power and I tried to tell him what electricity was. But I got all bogged down with that, not knowing too much about it myself. I don't honestly think Plant got a thing out of that electric motor.

With the motor of the car, though, we were more successful. We spent one whole Sunday dismantling it and then putting it back together. Watching what I was doing, Plant seemed to take a lot of interest in it.

We had to keep the garage door locked and it was a scorcher of a day and, anyhow, I'd much rather spend a Sunday fishing than tearing down a motor. I wondered a dozen times if it was worth it, if there might not be easier ways to teach Plant the facts of our Earth culture.

I was all tired out and failed to hear the alarm and woke up an hour later than I should. I jumped into my clothes, ran out to the garage, unlocked the door and there was Plant. He had parts from that motor strewn all over the floor and he was working away at it, happy as a clam. I almost took an axe to him, but I got hold of myself in time. I locked the door behind me and walked to work.

All day, I wondered how Plant had gotten into the garage. Had he sneaked back in the night before, when I wasn't looking, or had he been able to pick the lock? I wondered, too, what sort of shape I'd find the car in when I got home. I could just see myself working half the night, putting it back together.

I left work a little early. If I had to work on the car, I wanted an early start.

When I got home, the motor was all assembled and Plant was out in the garden, acting like a weed. Seeing him there, I realized he knew how to unlock the door, for I'd locked it when I left that morning.

I turned on the ignition, making bets with myself that it wouldn't start. But it did. I rode around town a little to check it and there wasn't a thing wrong with it.

For the next lesson, I tried something simpler. I got my carpentry tools and showed them to Plant and let him watch me while I made a bird house. Not that I needed any more bird houses. The place already crawled with them. But it was the easiest, quickest thing I could think of to show Plant how we worked in wood.

He watched closely and seemed to understand what was going on, all right, but I detected a sadness in him. I put my hand on his arm to ask him what was the matter.

All that I got was a mournful reaction.

It bewildered me. Why should Plant take so much interest in monkeying around with a motor and then grieve at the making of a bird house? I didn't get it figured out until a few days later, when Plant saw me picking a bouquet of flowers for the kitchen table.

And then it hit me.

Plant was a plant and flowers were plants and so was lumber, or at least lumber at one time had been a plant. And I stood there, with the bouquet dangling in my hand and Plant looking at me, and I thought of all the shocks he had in store for him when he found out more about us—how we slaughtered our forests, grew plants for food and clothing, squeezed or boiled drugs from them.

It was just like a human going to another planet, I realized, and finding that some alien life form grew humans for food.

Plant didn't seem to be sore at me nor did he shrink from me in horror. He was just sad. When he got sad, he was the saddest-looking thing you could possibly imagine. A bloodhound with a hangover would have looked positively joyous in comparison.

If we ever had gotten to the point where we could have really talked—about things like ethics and philosophy, I mean—I might have learned just how Plant felt about our plant-utilizing culture. I'm sure he tried to tell me, but I couldn't understand much of what he was driving at.

We were sitting out on the steps one night, looking at the stars. Earlier, Plant had been showing me his home planet, or it may have been some of the planets he had visited. I don't know. All I could get were fuzzy mental pictures and reactions. One place was hot and red, another blue and cold. There was another that had all the colors of the rainbow and a cool, restful feel about it, as if there might have been gentle winds and fountains and birdsongs in the twilight.

We had been sitting there for quite a while when he put his hand back on my arm again and he showed me a plant. He must have put considerable effort into getting me to visualize it, for the image was sharp and clear. It was a scraggy, rundown plant and it looked even sadder than Plant looked when he got sad, if that is possible. When I started feeling sorry for it, he began to think of kindness and, when he thought of things like kindness and sadness and gratitude and happiness, he could really pour it on.

He had me thinking such big, kindly thoughts, I was afraid that I would burst. While I sat there, thinking that way, I saw the plant begin to perk up. It grew and flowered and was the most beautiful thing I had ever seen. It matured its seeds and dropped them. Swiftly, little plants sprang from the seeds and they were healthy and full of ginger, too.

I mulled that one over several days, suspecting I was crazy for even thinking what I did. I tried to shrug it off, but it wouldn't shrug. It gave me an idea.

The only way I could get rid of it was to try it out.

Out in back of the toolshed was the sorriest yellow rose in town. Why it clung to life, year after year, I could never figure out. It had been there ever since I was a boy. The only reason it hadn't been dug up and thrown away long ago was that no one had ever needed the ground it was rooted in.

I thought, if a plant ever needed help, that yellow rose was it.

So I sneaked out back of the toolshed, making sure that Plant didn't see me, and stood in front of that yellow rose. I began to think kindly thoughts about it, although God knows it was hard to think kindly toward such a wretched thing. I felt foolish and hoped none of the neighbors spotted me, but I kept at it. I didn't seem to accomplish much to start with, but I went back, time after time. In a week or so, I got so that I just naturally loved that yellow rose to pieces.

After four or five days, I began to see some change in it. At the end of two weeks, it had developed from a scraggy, no-account bush to one that any rose fancier would have been proud to own. It dropped its bug-chewed leaves and grew new ones that were so shiny, they looked as if they were waxed. Then it grew big flower buds and, in no time at all, was a blaze of yellow glory.

But I didn't quite believe it. In the back of my mind, I figured that Plant must have seen me doing it and helped along a bit. So I decided to test the process again where he couldn't interfere.

Millie had been trying for a couple of years to grow an African violet in a flower pot at the office. By this time, even she was willing to admit it was a losing battle. I had made a lot of jokes about the violet and, at times, Millie had been sore at me about it. Like the yellow rose, it was a hard-luck plant. The bugs ate it. Millie forgot to water it. It got knocked onto the floor. Visitors used it for an ashtray.

Naturally, I couldn't give it the close, intensive treatment I'd given the rose, but I made a point to stop for a few minutes every day beside the violet and think good things about it and, in a couple of weeks, it perked up considerably. By the end of the month, it had bloomed for the first time in its life.

Meanwhile, Plant's education continued.

At first, he'd balked at entering the house, but finally trusted me enough to go in. He didn't spend much time there, for the house was too full of reminders that ours was a plant-utilizing culture. Furniture, clothing, cereal, paper—even the house itself—all were made of vegetation. I got an old butter tub and filled it with soil and put it in one corner of the dining room, so he could eat in the house if he wanted to, but I don't remember that he even once took a snack out of that tub.

Although I didn't admit it then, I knew that what Plant and I had tried to do had been a failure. Whether someone else might have done better, I don't know. I suspect he might have. But I didn't know how to go about getting in touch and I was afraid of being laughed at. It's a terrible thing, our human fear of ridicule.

And there was Plant to consider, too. How would he take being passed on to someone else? I'd screw up my courage to do something about it, and then Plant would come up out of the garden and sit beside me on the steps, and we'd talk—not about anything that mattered, really, but about happiness and sadness and brotherhood, and my courage would go glimmering and I'd have to start all over again.

I've since thought how much like two lost children we must have been, strange kids raised in different countries, who would have liked to play together, except neither knew the rules for the other's games or spoke the other's language.

I know . . . I know. According to common sense, you begin with mathematics. You show the alien that you know two and two are four. Then you draw the Solar System and show him the Sun on the diagram and then point to the Sun overhead and you point to Earth on the diagram, then point to yourself. In this way, you demonstrate to him that you know about the Solar System and about space and the stars and so on.

Then you hand him the paper and the pencil.

But what if he doesn't know mathematics? What if the two-plus-two-makes-four routine doesn't mean a thing to him? What if he's never seen a drawing? What if he can't draw—or see or hear or feel or think the way you do?

To deal with an alien, you've got to get down to basics.

And maybe math isn't basic.

Maybe diagrams aren't.

In that case, you have to search for something that is.

Yet there must be certain universal basics.

I think I know what they are.

That, if nothing else, Plant taught me.

Happiness is basic. And sadness is basic. And gratitude, in perhaps a lesser sense. Kindness, too. And perhaps hatred—although Plant and I never dealt in that.

Maybe brotherhood. For the sake of humanity, I hope so.

But kindness and happiness and brotherhood are awkward tools to use in reaching specific understanding, although in Plant's world, they may not be.

It was getting on toward autumn and I was beginning to wonder how I'd take care of Plant during the winter months.

I could have kept him in the house, but he hated it there.

Then, one night, we were sitting on the back steps, listening to the first crickets of the season.

The ship came down without a sound. I didn't see it until it was about at treetop level. It floated down and landed between the house and toolshed.

I was startled for a moment, but not frightened, and perhaps not too surprised. In the back of my head, I'd wondered all the time, without actually knowing it, whether Plant's pals might not ultimately find him.

The ship was a shimmery sort of thing, as if it might not have been made of metal and was not really solid. I noticed that it had not really landed, but floated a foot or so above the grass.

Three other Plants stepped out and the oddest part of it was that there wasn't any door. They just came out of the ship and the ship closed behind them.

Plant took me by the arm and twitched it just a little, to make me understand he wanted me to walk with him to the ship. He made little comforting thoughts to try to calm me down.

And all the time that this was going on, I could sense the talk between Plant and those other three—but just grasping the fringe of the conversation, barely knowing there was talk, not aware of what was being said.

And then, while Plant stood beside me, with his hand still on my arm, those other plants walked up. One by one, each took me by the other arm and stood facing me for a moment and told me thanks and happiness.

Plant told me the same, for the last time, and then the four of them walked toward the ship and disappeared into it. The ship left me standing there, watching it rise into the night, until I couldn't see it any longer.

I stood there for a long time, staring up into the sky, with the thanks and happiness fading and loneliness beginning to creep in.

I knew that, somewhere up there, was a larger ship, that in it were many other Plants, that one of them had lived with me for almost six months and that others of them had died in the hedges and fence corners of the neighborhood. I knew also that it had been the big ship that had scooped out the load of nutritious soil from Pete Skinner's field.

Finally, I stopped looking at the sky. Over behind the toolshed, I saw the whiteness of the yellow rose in bloom and once again I thought about the basics.

I wondered if happiness and kindness, perhaps even emotions that we humans do not know, might not be used on Plant's world as we use the sciences.

For the rose bush had bloomed when I thought kindly thoughts of it. And the African violet had found a new life in the kindness of a human.

Startling as it may seem, foolish as it may sound, it is not an unknown phenomenon. There are people who have the knack of getting the most out of a flowerbed or a garden. And it is said of these people that they have green thumbs.

May it not be that *green thumbness* is not so much concerned with skill or how much care is taken of a plant, as with the kindliness and the interest of the person tending it?

For eons, the plant life of this planet has been taken for granted. It is simply there. By and large, plants are given little affection. They are planted or sown. They grow. In proper season, they are harvested.

I sometimes wonder if, as hunger tightens its grip upon our teeming planet, there may not be a vital need for the secret of *green thumbness*.

If kindness and sympathy can cause a plant to produce beyond its normal wont, then shouldn't we consider kindness as a tool to ward off Earth's hunger? How much more might be produced if the farmer loved his wheat?

It's silly, of course, a principle that could not gain acceptance.

And undoubtedly it would not work—not in a plant-utilizing culture.

For how could you keep on convincing a plant that you feel kindly toward it when, season after season, you prove that your only interest in it is to eat it or make it into clothing or chop it down for lumber?

I walked out back of the shed and stood beside the yellow rose, trying to find the answer. The yellow rose stirred, like a pretty woman who knows she's being admired, but no emotion came from it.

The thanks and happiness were gone. There was nothing left but the loneliness.

Damned vegetable aliens—upsetting a man so he couldn't eat his breakfast cereal in peace!

TABBY
WINSTON MARKS

APRIL 18, 1956

DEAR BEN: It breaks my heart you didn't sign on for this trip. Your replacement, who *calls* himself an ichthyologist, has only one talent that pertains to fish—he drinks like one. There are nine of us in the expedition, and every one of us is fed up with this joker, Cleveland, already. We've only been on the island a week, and he's gone native, complete with beard, bare feet and bone laziness. He slops around the lagoon like a beachcomber and hasn't brought in a decent specimen yet.

The island is a bit of paradise, though. Wouldn't be hard to let yourself relax under the palms all day instead of collecting blisters and coral gashes out in the bright sun of the atoll. No complaints, however. We aren't killing ourselves, and our little camp is very comfortable. The portable lab is working out fine, and the screened sleeping tent-houses have solved the one big nuisance we've suffered before: *Insects.* I think an entomologist would find more to keep him busy here than we will.

Your ankle should be useable by the time our next supply plane from Hawaii takes off. If you apply again at the Foundation right now I'm sure Sellers and the others will help me get rid of Cleveland, and there'll be an open berth here.

Got to close now. Our amphib jets off in an hour for the return trip. Hope this note is properly seductive. Come to the isles, boy, and live!—Cordially, Fred

MAY 26, 1956

DEAR BEN: Now, aren't you sorry you didn't take my advice?!!!! I'm assuming you read the papers, and also, that too tight a censorship hasn't clamped down on this thing yet. Maybe I'm assuming too much on the latter. Anyhow, here's a detailed version from an actual eyewitness.

That's right! I was right there on the beach when the "saucer" landed. Only it looked more like a king-size pokerchip. About six feet across and eight inches thick with a little hemispherical dome dead center on top. It hit offshore about seventy-five yards with a splash that sounded like a whale's tail. Jenner and I dropped our seine, waded to shore and started running along the beach to get opposite it. Cleveland came out of the shade and helped us launch a small boat.

We got within twenty feet of the thing when it started moving out, slowly, just fast enough to keep ahead of us. I was in the bow looking right at it when the lid popped open with a sound like a cork coming out of a wine bottle. The little dome had split. Sellers quit rowing and we all hit the bottom of the boat. I peeked over the gunwale right away, and it's a good thing. All that came out of the dome was a little cloud of flies, maybe a hundred or so, and the breeze picked them up and blew them over us inshore so fast that Cleveland and Sellers never did see them.

I yelled at them to look, but by then the flies were in mingling with the local varieties of sudden itch, and they figured I was seeing things. Cleveland, though, listened with the most interest. It develops that his specialty *is* entomology. He took this job because he was out of work. Don't know how he bluffed his way past the Foundation, but here he is, and it looks like he might be useful after all.

He was all for going ashore, but Sellers and I rowed after the white disk for awhile until it became apparent we couldn't catch it. It's a good thing we didn't. A half hour later, Olafsen caught up to it in the power launch. We were watching from shore. It was about a half mile out when Ole cut his speed. Luckily he was alone. We had yelled at him to pick us up and take us along, but he was too excited to stop. He passed us up, went out there and boom!

It wasn't exactly an A-bomb, but the spray hit us a half mile away, and the surface wave swamped us.

Sellers radioed the whole incident to Honolulu right away, and they are sending out a plane with a diver, but we don't think he'll find anything. Things really blew! So far we haven't even found any identifiable driftwood from the launch, let alone Ole's body or traces of the disk.

Meanwhile, Cleveland has come to believe my story, and he's out prowling around with an insect net. Most energy he's shown in weeks.

May 28—Looks like this letter will be delayed a bit. We are under quarantine. The government plane came this morning. They sent along a diver, two reporters and a navy officer. The diver went down right away, but it's several hundred feet deep out there and slants off fast. This island is the tip of a sunken mountain, and the diver gave up after less than an hour. Personally I think a couple of sharks scared him off, but he claims there's so much vegetable ruck down there he couldn't expect to find anything smaller than the launch's motor.

Cleveland hasn't found anything unusual in his bug net, but everyone is excited here, and you can guess why.

When the "saucer" reports stopped cold about a year ago, you'll remember, it made almost as much news for a while as when they were first spotted. Now the people out here are speculating that maybe this disc thing came from the same source as the *saucers*, after they had a chance to look us over, study our ecology and return to their base. Cleveland is the one who started this trend of thought with his obsession that the flies I reported seeing are an attack on our planet from someone out in space.

Commander Clawson, the navy officer, doesn't know what to think. He won't believe Cleveland until he produces a specimen of the "fly-from-Mars", but then he turns around and contradicts himself by declaring a temporary quarantine until he gets further orders from Honolulu.

The reporters are damned nuisances. They're turning out reams of Sunday supplement type stuff and pestering the devil out of

Sparks to let them wire it back, but our radio is now under navy control, too.

Sure is crowded in the bunk-house with the six additional people, but no one will sleep outside the screen.

MAY 29—Cleveland thinks he has his specimen. He went out at dawn this morning and came in before breakfast. He's quit drinking but he hasn't slept in three days now and looks like hell. I thought he was getting his fancy imagination out of the bottle, but the soberer he got the more worried he looked over this "invasion" idea of his.

Now he claims that his catch is definitely a sample of something new under our particular sun. He hustled it under a glass and started classifying it. It filled the bill for the arthropods, class Insecta. It looked to me, in fact, just like a small, ordinary blowfly, except that it has green wings. And I mean *green*, not just a little iridescent color.

Cleve very gently pulled one wing off and we looked at it under low power. There is more similarity to a leaf than to a wing. In the bug's back is a tiny pocket, a sort of reservoir of the green stuff, and Cleve's dissection shows tiny veins running up into the wings. It seems to be a closed system with no connection with the rest of the body except the restraining membrane.

Cleveland now rests his extraterrestrial origin theory on an idea that the green stuff is chlorophyll. If it is chlorophyll, either Cleve is right or else he's discovered a new class of arthropods. In other respects the critter is an ordinary biting and sucking bug with the potentials of about a deerfly for making life miserable. The high-power lens showed no sign of unusual or malignant microscopic life inside or out of the thing. Cleve can't say how bad a bite would be, because he doesn't have his entomologist kit with him, and he can't analyze the secretion from the poison gland.

The commander has let him radio for a botanist and some micro-analysis equipment.

Everyone was so pitched up that Cleve's findings have been rather anti-climactic. I guess we were giving more credence to the space-invader theory than we thought. But even if Cleve has proved it, this fly doesn't look like much to be frightened over. The reporters are clamoring to be let loose, but the quarantine still holds.

JUNE 1—By the time the plane with the botanist arrived we were able to gather all the specimens of *Tabanidae viridis* (Cleveland's designation) that he wanted. Seems like every tenth flying creature you meet is a green "Tabby" now.

The botanist helped Cleve and me set up the bio kit, and he confirmed Cleve's guess. The green stuff is chlorophyll. Which makes Tabby quite a bug.

Kyser, the youngest reporter, volunteered to let a Tabby bite him. It did without too much coaxing. Now he has a little, itchy bump on his wrist, and he's happily banging away at his typewriter on a story titled, "I Was Bitten by the Bug from Space!" That was hours ago, and we haven't learned anything sinister about the green fly except that it does have a remarkable breeding ability.

One thing the reporter accomplished: we can go outside the screened quarters now without wondering about catching space-typhus.

JUNE 2—The quarantine was probably a pretty good idea. Cleve has turned up some dope on Tabby's life cycle that makes us glad all over that we are surrounded by a thousand miles of salt water. Tabby's adult life is only a couple of days, but she is viviparous, prolific (some thousand young at a sitting), and her green little microscopic babies combine the best survival features of spores and plankton, minus one: they don't live in salt water. But they do very well almost anyplace else. We have watched them grow on hot rocks, leaves, in the sand and best of all, filtered down a little into the moist earth.

They grow incredibly fast with a little sun, so the chlorophyll is biologically justified in the life-cycle. This puzzled us at first, because the adult Tabby turns into a blood-sucking little brute. Deprived of any organic matter, our bottled specimens die in a short time, in or out of the sunlight, indicating the green stuff doesn't provide them with much if any nourishment after they are full-grown.

Now we are waiting for a supply of assorted insecticides to find the best controls over the pests. The few things we had on hand worked quite well, but I guess they aren't forgetting our sad experience with DDT a few years back.

The Tabbies now outnumber all the other insects here, and most outside work has been halted. The little green devils make life miserable outside the tent-houses. We have built another screened shelter to accommodate the latest arrivals. We are getting quite a fleet of amphibian aircraft floating around our lagoon. No one will be allowed to return until we come up with all the answers to the question of controlling our insect invasion.

Cleveland is trying to convince Sellers and the commander that we should get out and send in atomic fire to blow the whole island into the sea. They forwarded his suggestion to the U.N. committee which now has jurisdiction, but they wired back that if the insect is from space, we couldn't stop other discs from landing on the mainlands. Our orders are to study the bug and learn all we can.

Opinion is mixed here. I can't explain the flying disc unless it's extraterrestrial, but why would an invader choose an isolated spot like this to attack? Cleve says this is just a "test patch" and probably under surveillance. But why such an innocuous little fly if they mean business?

The newsmen are really bored now. They see no doom in the bugs, and since they can't file their stories they take a dim view of the quarantine. They have gotten up an evening fishing derby with the crew members of the planes. Have to fish after dusk. The Tabbies bite too often as long as the sun is up.

Cleve has turned into a different man. He is soft-spoken and intense. His hands tremble so much that he is conducting most of his work by verbal directions with the botanist and me to carry them out. When his suggestion about blowing up the atoll was turned down he quit talking except to conduct his work. If things were half as ominous as he makes out we'd be pretty worried.

JUNE 4—The spray planes got here and none too soon. We were running out of drinking water. The Tabbies got so thick that even at night a man would get stung insane if he went outside the screen.

The various sprays all worked well. This evening the air is relatively clear. Incidentally, the birds have been having a feast. Now the gulls are congregating to help us out like they did the Mormons in the cricket plague. The spiders are doing all right for themselves, too. In fact, now that we have sprayed the place the spiders and their confounded webs are the biggest nuisance we have to contend with. They are getting fat and sassy. Spin their webs between your legs if you stand still a minute too long. Remind me of real estate speculators in a land boom, the little bastardly opportunists. As you might gather, I don't care for brothers Arachnidae. They make everyone else nervous, too. Strangely, Cleveland, the entomologist, gets the worst jolt out of them. He'll stand for minutes at the screen watching them spin their nasty webs and skipping out to de-juice a stray Tabby that the spray missed. And he'll mutter to himself and scowl and curse them. It is hard to include them as God's creatures.

Cleve still isn't giving out with the opinions. He works incessantly and has filled two notebooks full of data. Looks to me like our work is almost done.

AUGUST 7, YEAR OF OUR LORD 1956—To whom it will never concern: I can no longer make believe this is addressed to my friend, Ben Tobin. Cleveland has convinced me of the implications of our tragedy here. But somehow it gives me some crazy, necessary ray of hope to keep this journal until the end.

I think the real horror of this thing started to penetrate to me about June 6. Our big spray job lasted less than 24 hours, and on that morning I was watching for the planes to come in for a second try at it when I noticed the heavy spider webbing in the upper tree foliage. As I looked a gull dove through the trees, mouth open, eating Tabbies. Damned if the webs didn't foul his wings. At first he tore at them bravely and it looked like he was trying to swim in thin mud—sort of slow motion. Then he headed into a thick patch, slewed around at right angles and did a complete flip. Instantly three mammoth spiders the size of my fist pounced out on him and trussed him up before he could tear loose with his feet.

His pitiful squawking was what made me feel that horror for the first time. And the scene was repeated more and more often. The planes dusted us with everything they had, and it cut down the Tabbies pretty well again, but it didn't touch the spiders, of course.

And then our return radio messages started getting very vague. We were transmitting Cleve's data hourly as he compiled it, and we had been getting ordinary chatter and speculation from the Honolulu operator at the end of our message. That stopped on the sixth of June. Since then, we've had only curt acknowledgements of our data and sign-offs.

At the same time, we noticed that complete censorship on news of our situation and progress apparently hit all the long-wave radio broadcasts. Up to that time the newscasts had been feeding out a dilute and very cautious pablum about our fight against Tabby. Immediately when we noticed this news blind spot Cleve went all to pieces and started drinking again.

Cleve, Sellers and I had the lab tent to ourselves, having moved our bunks in there, so we got a little out of touch with the others. It wasn't the way Sellers and I liked it, but none of us liked the trip from lab to living quarters any more, although it was only fifty feet or so.

Then Sparks moved in, too. For the same reason. He said it was getting on his nerves running back and forth to the lab to pick up our outgoing bulletins. So he shifted the generator, radio gear and all over to a corner of the lab and brought in his bunk.

By the tenth of June we could see that the spraying was a losing battle. And it finally took the big tragedy to drive home the truth that was all about us already. When the crew got ready to go out to their planes on the eleventh, everyone except the four of us in the lab tent was drafted to help clear webs between the tents and the beach. We could hear them shouting from tent to tent as they made up their work party. We could no longer see across the distance. Everywhere outside, vision was obscured by the grayish film of webs on which little droplets caught the tropical sun like a million tiny mirrors. In the shade it was like trying to peer through thin milk, with the vicious, leggy little shadows skittering about restlessly.

As usual in the morning, the hum of the Tabbies had risen above the normal jungle buzzing, and this morning it was the loudest we'd heard it.

Well, we heard the first screen door squeak open, and someone let out a whoop as the group moved out with brooms, palm fronds and sticks to snatch a path through the nightmare of spider webs. The other two doors opened and slammed, and we could hear many sounds of deep disgust voiced amid the grunts and thrashings.

They must have been almost to the beach when the first scream reached us. Cleve had been listening in fascination, and the awful sound tore him loose of his senses. He screamed back. The rest of us had to sit on him to quiet him. Then the others outside all began screaming—not words, just shattering screams of pure terror, mixed with roars of pain and anger. Soon there was no more anger. Just horror. And in a few minutes they died away.

Sellers and Sparks and I looked at each other. Cleve had vomited and passed out. Sparks got out Cleve's whiskey, and we spilled half of it trying to get drinks into us.

Sparks snapped out of it first. He didn't try to talk to us. He just went to his gear, turned on the generator and warmed up the radio. He told Honolulu what had happened as we had heard it.

When he finished, he keyed over for an acknowledgment. The operator said to hold on for a minute. Then he said they would *try* to dispatch an air task force to get us off, but they couldn't be sure just when.

While this was coming in Cleve came to his senses and listened. He was deadly calm now, and when Honolulu finished he grabbed the mike from Sparks, cut in the TX and asked, "Are they landing discs on the mainlands?"

The operator answered, "Sorry, that's classified."

"For God's sake," Cleve demanded, "if you are ready to write us off you can at least answer our questions. Are there any of the green sonsofbitches on the mainland?"

There was another little pause, and then, "Yes."

That was all. Sparks ran down the batteries trying to raise them again for more answers, but no response. When the batteries went dead he checked the generator that had kicked off. It was out of gasoline. The drums were on the beach. Now we were without lights, power and juice for our other radios.

We kept alive the first few days by staying half drunk. Then Cleve's case of whiskey gave out and we began to get hungry. Sparks and Sellers set fire to one of our straw-ticking mattresses and used it as a torch to burn their way over to the supply tent about thirty feet away. It worked fairly well. The silky webs flashed into nothing as the flames hit them, but they wouldn't support the fire, and other webs streamed down behind the two. They had to burn another mattress to get back with a few cases of food.

Then we dug a well under the floor of our tent. Hit water within a few feet. But when we cut through the screen floor it cost us sentry duty. We had to have one person awake all night long to stamp on the spiders that slipped in around the edge of the well.

Through all of this Cleveland has been out on his feet. He has just stood and stared out through the screen all day. We had to force him to eat. He didn't snap out of it until this morning.

Sparks couldn't stand our radio silence any longer, so he talked Sellers into helping him make a dash for the gas drums on the beach. They set fire to two mattresses and disappeared into the tunnel of burned webs that tangled and caved in behind them.

When they were gone, Cleveland suddenly came out of his trance and put a hand on my shoulder. I thought for a moment he was going to jump me, but his eyes were calm. He said, "Well, Fred, are you convinced now that we've been attacked?"

I said, "It makes no sense to me at all. Why these little flies?"

Cleve said, "They couldn't have done better so easily. They studied our ecology well. They saw that our greatest potential enemy was the insect population, and the most vicious part of it was the spider. *Tabanidae viridis* was not sent just to plague us with horsefly bites. Tabby was sent to multiply and feed the arachnids. There are durable species in all climates. And if our botanist were still alive he could explain in detail how long our plant life can last under this spider infestation.

"Look for yourself," he said pointing outside. "Not only are the regular pollenizing insects doomed, but the density of those webs will choke out even wind pollinated grains."

He stared down our shallow well hole and stamped on a small, black, flat spider that had slithered under the screening. "I suppose you realize the spiders got the others. Down here in the tropics the big varieties could do it by working together. Sellers and Sparks won't return. Sounds like they got through all right, but they'll be bitten so badly they won't try to get back."

And even as he spoke we heard one of the aircraft engines start up. The sound was muffled as under a bed quilt.

Cleve said, "I don't blame them. I'd rather die in the sun, too. The beach should be fairly clear of webs. We've got one mattress left. What do you say?"

He's standing there now holding the mattress with the ticking sticking out. I don't think one torch will get us through. But it will be worth a try for one more look at the sun.

THE NIGHT OF HOGGY DARN
R. M. MCKENNA

RED-HAIRED FLINTER COLE sipped his black coffee and looked around the chrome and white tile galley of Space Freighter *Gorbals*, in which he was riding down the last joint of a dogleg journey to the hermit planet of New Cornwall.

"Nothing's been published about the planet for the last five hundred years," he said in a nervous, jerky voice. "You people on *Gorbals* at least *see* the place, and I understand you're the only ship that does."

"That's right, twice every standard year," said the cook. He was a placid, squinting man, pink in his crisp whites. "But like I said, no girls, no drinks, nothing down there but hard looks and a punch in the nose for being curious. We mostly stay aboard, up in orbit. Them New Cornish are the biggest, meanest men I ever did see, Doc."

"I'm not a real doctor yet," Cole said, glancing down at the scholar grays he was wearing. "If I don't do a good job on New Cornwall I may never be. This is my Ph. D. trial field assignment. I should be *stuffing* myself with data on the ecosystem so I can ask the right questions when I get there. But there's nothing!"

"What's a pee aitch dee?"

"That's being a doctor. I'm an ecologist—that means I deal with everything alive, and the way it all works in with climate and geography. I can use *any* kind of data. I have only six months until *Gorbals* comes again to make my survey and report. If I fumble away my doctorate, and I'm twenty-three already. . . ." Cole knitted shaggy red eyebrows in worry.

"Well hell, Doc. I can tell you things like, it's got four moons and only one whopper of a continent and it's low grav, and the forest there you won't believe even when you see it—"

"I need to know about *stompers*. Bidgrass Company wants Belconti U. to save them from extinction, but they didn't say what the threat is. They sent travel directions, a visa and passage scrip for just one man. And I only had two days for packing and library research, before I had to jump to Tristan in order to catch this ship. I've been running in the dark ever since. You'd think the Bidgrass people didn't really care."

"Price of stomper egg what it is, I doubt that," the cook said, scratching his fat jaw. "But for a fact, they're shipping less these days. Must be some kind of trouble. I never saw a stomper, but they say they're big birds that live in the forest."

"You see? The few old journal articles I did find, said they were flightless bird-homologs that lived on the plains and preyed on the great herds of something called darv cattle."

"Nothing but forest and sea for thousands of miles around Bidgrass Station, Doc. Stompers are pure hell on big long legs, they say."

"There again! *I* read they were harmless to man."

"Tell you what, you talk to Daley. He's cargo officer and has to go down with each tender trip. He'll maybe know something can help you."

The cook turned away to inspect his ovens. Cole put down his cup and clamped a freckled hand over his chin, thinking. He thought about stomper eggs, New Cornwall's sole export and apparently, for five hundred years, its one link with the other planets of Carina sector. Their reputedly indescribable flavor had endeared them to gourmets on a hundred planets. They were symbols of conspicuous consumption for the ostentatious wealthy. No wonder most of the literature under the New Cornwall reference had turned out to be cookbooks.

Orphaned and impecunious, a self-made scholar, Cole had never tasted stomper egg.

The cook slammed an oven door on the fresh bread smell.

"Just thought, Doc. I keep a can or two of stomper egg, squeeze it from cargo for when I got a passenger to feed. How'd you like a mess for chow tonight?"

"Why not?" Cole said, grinning suddenly. "Anything may be data for an ecologist, especially if it's good to eat."

The stomper egg came to the officers' mess table as a heaped platter of bite-sized golden spheres, deep-fried in bittra oil. Their delicate, porous texture hardly required chewing. Their flavor was like—cinnamon? Peppery sandalwood? Yes, yes, and yet unique. . . .

Cole realized in confusion that he had eaten half the platterful and the other six men had not had any. He groped for a lost feeling—was it that he and the others formed a connected biomass and that he could eat for all of them? Ridiculous!

"I'm a pig," he laughed weakly. "Here, Mr. Daley, have some."

Daley, a gingery, spry little man, said "By me" and slid the platter along. It rounded the table and returned to Cole untouched.

"Fall to, Doc." Daley said, grinning.

Cole was already reaching . . . lying in his stateroom and he *was* the bunk cradling a taut, messianic body flaming with imageless dreams. He dreamed himself asleep and slept himself into shamed wakefulness needing coffee.

It was ship-night. Cole walked through dimmed lights to the galley and carried his cup of hot black coffee to main control, where he found Daley on watch, lounging against the gray enamel computer.

"I feel like a fool," Cole said.

"You're a martyr to science, Doc. Which reminds me, Cookie told me you got questions about Bidgrass Station."

"Well, yes, about stompers. What's wiping them out, what's their habitat and life pattern, oh anything."

"I learned quick not to ask about stompers. I gather they're twenty feet high or so and they're penned up behind a stockade. I never saw one."

"Well dammit! I read they couldn't be domesticated."

"They're not. Bidgrass Station is in a clearing the New Cornish cut from sea to sea across a narrow neck of land. On the west is this stockade and beyond it is Lundy Peninsula, a good half-million square miles of the damndest forest ever grew on any planet. That's where the stompers are."

"How thickly settled is this Lundy Peninsula?"

"Not a soul there, Doc. The settlement is around Car Truro on the east coast, twelve thousand miles east of Bidgrass. I never been there, but you can see from the air it isn't much."

"How big a city is Bidgrass? Does it have a university?"

Daley smiled again and shook his head. "They got fields and pastures, but it's more like a military camp than a town. I see barracks for the workers and egg hunters, hangars and shops, a big egg-processing plant and warehouses around the landing field. I never get away from the field, but I'd guess four, five thousand people at Bidgrass."

Cole sighed and put down his cup on the log desk.

"What is it they import, one half so precious as the stuff they sell?"

Daley chuckled and rocked on his toes. "Drugs, chemicals, machinery parts, hundreds of tons of Warburton energy capsules. Pistols, blasters, cases of flame charge, tanks of fire mist—you'd think they had a war on."

"That's no help. I'll make up for lost time when I get there. I'll beat their ears off with questions."

Daley's gnomish face grew serious. "Watch what you ask and who you ask, Doc. They're suspicious as hell and they hate strangers."

"They need my help. Besides, I'll deal only with scientists."

"Bidgrass isn't much like a campus. I don't know, Doc, something's wrong on that planet and I'm always glad to lift out."

"Why didn't you and the others eat any of that stomper egg?" Cole asked abruptly.

"Because the people at Bidgrass turn sick and want to slug you if you mention eating it. That's reason enough for me."

Well, that was data too, Cole thought, heading back to his stateroom.

Two days later Daley piloted the cargo tender down in a three-lap braking spiral around New Cornwall. Cole sat beside him in the cramped control room, eyes fixed on the view panel. Once he had the bright and barren moon Cairdween at upper left, above a vastly curving sweep of sun-glinting ocean, and he caught his breath in wonder.

"I know the feeling, Doc," Daley said softly. "Like being a giant and jumping from world to world."

Clouds obscured much of the sprawling, multi-lobed single continent. The sharpening of outline and hint of regularity Cole remembered noting on Tristan and his own planet of Belconti, the mark of man, was absent here. Yet New Cornwall, as a human settlement, was two hundred years older than Belconti.

The forests stretched across the south and west, broken by uplands and rain shadows, as the old books said. He saw between cloud patches the glint of lakes and the crumpled leaf drainage pattern of the great northeastern plain but, oddly, the plain was darker in color than the pinkish-yellow forest. He mentioned it to Daley.

"It's flowers and vines and moss makes it that color," the little man said, busy with controls. "Whole world in that forest top—snakes, birds, jumping things big as horses. Doc, them trees are *big*."

"Of course! I read about the epiphytal biota. And low gravity always conduces to gigantism."

"There's Lundy," Daley grunted, pointing.

It looked like a grinning ovoid monster-head straining into the western ocean at the end of a threadlike neck. Across the neck Bidgrass Station slashed between parallel lines of forest edge like a collar. Cole watched it again on the landing approach, noting the half-mile of clearing between the great wall and the forest edge, the buildings and fields rectilinear in ordered clumps east of the wall, and then the light aberration of the tender's lift field blotted it out.

"Likely I won't see you till next trip," Daley said, taking leave. "Good luck, Doc."

Cole shuffled down the personnel ramp, grateful for the weight of his two bags in the absurdly light gravity. Trucks and cargo lifts were coming across the white field from the silvery warehouses along its edge. Men also, shaggy-haired big men in loose blue garments, walking oddly without the stride and drive of leg muscles. Their faces were uniformly grim and blank to Cole, standing there uncertainly. Then a ground car pulled up and a tall old man in the same rough clothing got out and walked directly toward him. He had white hair, bushy white eyebrows over deep-set gray eyes, and a commanding beak of a nose.

"Who might you be?" he demanded.

"I'm Flinter Cole, from Belconti University. Someone here is expecting me."

The old man squinted in thought and bit his lower lip. Finally he said, "The biologist, hey? Didn't expect you until next *Gorbals*. Didn't think you could make the connections for this one."

"It left me no time at all to study up in. But when species extinction is the issue, time is important. And I'm an ecologist."

"Well," the old man said. "Well, I'm Garth Bidgrass."

He shook Cole's hand, a powerful grip quickly released.

"Hawkins there in the car will take you to the manor house and get you settled. I'll phone ahead. I'll be tied up checking cargo for a day or two, I expect. You just rest up awhile."

He spoke to the driver in what sounded like Old English, then moved rapidly across the field toward the warehouses in the same strange walk as the other men. As far as Cole could see, he did not bend his knees at all.

Hawkins, also old but frail and stooped, took Cole's bags to the car. When the ecologist tried to follow him he almost fell headlong, then managed a stiff-legged shuffle. Momentarily he longed for the Earth-normal gravity of Belconti and the ship.

They drove past unfenced fields green with vegetable and cereal crops, and fenced pastures holding beef and dairy cattle of the old Earth breeds. It was a typical human ecosystem. Then they passed a group of field workers, and surprise jolted the ecologist. They were huge—eight or nine feet tall, both men and women, all with long hair and some of them naked. They did not look up.

Cole looked at Hawkins. The old man glared at him from red-rimmed eyes and chattered something in archaic English. He speeded up, losing the giants behind a hedge, and the manor house with the palisade behind it loomed ahead.

The great fence dwarfed the house. Single baulks of grassy brown timber ten feet on a side soared two hundred feet into the air, intricately braced and stayed. High above, a flyer drifted as if on sentry duty. Half a mile beyond, dwarfing the fence in its turn, arose the thousand-foot black escarpment of the forest edge.

The manor house huddled in a walled garden with armed guards at the gate. It was two-storied and sprawling, with a flat-roofed watch tower at the southeast corner, and made of the same glassy brown timber. Hawkins stopped the car by the pillared veranda where a lumpy, gray, nondescript woman waited. Cole got out, awkwardly careful in the light gravity.

The woman would not meet his glance. "I'm Flada Vignoli, Mr. Bidgrass's niece and housekeeper," she said in a dead voice. "I'll show you your rooms." She turned away before Cole could respond.

"Let me carry the bags, I need to," he said to Hawkins, laughing uncertainly. The old man hoisted his skinny shoulders and spat.

The rooms were on the second floor, comfortable but archaic in style. The gray woman told him that Hawkins would bring his meals, that Garth Bidgrass would see him in a few days to make plans, and that Mr. Bidgrass thought he should not go about unescorted until he knew more about local conditions.

Cole nodded. "I'll want to confer with your leading biologists, Mrs. Vignoli, as soon as I can. For today, can you get me a copy of your most recent biotic survey?"

"Ain't any biologists, ain't any surveys," she said, standing in the half-closed door.

"Well, any recent book about stompers or your general zoology. It's important that I start at once."

The face under the scraggly gray hair went blanker still. "You'll have to talk to Mr. Bidgrass." She closed the door.

Cole unpacked, bathed, dressed again and explored his three rooms. Like a museum, he thought. He looked out his west windows at the palisade and forest edge. Then he decided to go downstairs, and found his door was locked.

THE NIGHT OF HOGGY DARN

The shock was more fear than indignation, he realized, wondering at himself. He paced his sitting room, thinking about his scholarly status and the wealth and power of Belconti, until he had the indignation flaming. Then a knock came at the door and it opened to reveal old Hawkins with a wheeled food tray.

"What do you mean, locking me in?" Cole asked hotly.

He pushed past the food tray into the hall. Hawkins danced and made shooing motions with his hands, chattering shrilly in the vernacular. Cole walked to the railing around the stairwell and looked down. At the foot of the stair a giant figure, man or woman he could not say, sat and busied itself with something in its lap.

Cole went back into his room. The food was boiled beef, potatoes and beets, plain but plentiful, plus bread and coffee. He ate heartily and looked out his windows again to see night coming on. Finally he tried the door and it was not locked. He shrugged, pushed the food tray into the hall and closed the door again. Then he shot the inside bolt.

In bed, he finally dropped off into a restless, disturbed sleep.

Emboldened by morning and a hearty tray breakfast, Cole explored. He was in a two-floor wing, and the doors into the main house were locked. Through them he heard voices and domestic clatter. Unlocked across the second-floor hall was another suite of rooms like his own. Downstairs was still another suite and along the south side a library. The door into the garden was locked.

My kingdom, Cole thought wryly. Prisoner of state!

He explored the library. Tristanian books, historical romances for the most part, none less than three hundred years old. No periodicals, nothing of New Cornwall publication. He drifted from window to window looking out at the formal garden of flower beds, hedges and white sand paths. Then he saw the girl.

She knelt in a sleeveless gray dress trimming a hedge. Her tanned and rounded arms had dimpled elbows, he noted. She turned suddenly and he saw, framed by reddish-brown curls, her oval face with small nose and firm chin. The face was unsuitably grave and the eyes wide.

She was not staring at his window, Cole decided after a qualm, but listening. Then she rose, picked up her basket of trimmings and glided around the corner of the house. Before he could pursue her plump vision to another window, a man appeared.

He looked taller than Cole and was built massively as a stone. Straight black hair fell to his shoulders, cut square across his forehead and bound by a white fillet. Under the black bar of eyebrow the heavy face held itself in grim, unsmiling lines. He moved with that odd, unstriding New Cornish walk that suggested tremendous power held in leash.

Cole crossed the hall and watched the blue-clad form enter a door in the wing opposite. The girl was nowhere. Again Cole felt a twinge of fear, and boiled up anger to mask it.

Inside looking out, he thought. Peeping like an ecologist in a bird blind!

When Hawkins brought lunch Cole raged at him and demanded to see Garth Bidgrass. The old man chattered incomprehensibly and danced like a fighting cock. Thwarted, the ecologist ate moodily and went down to the library. The garden was empty and he decided on impulse to open a window. A way of retreat, but from what and to where, he wondered as he worked at the fastenings. Just as he got it free, a woman stooped through the library door. She was at least seven feet tall.

Cole stood erect and held his breath. Not looking at him, the woman dropped to her knees and began dusting the natural wood half-paneling that encircled the room between bookcases. She had long blonde hair and a mild, vacant face; she wore a shapeless blue dress.

"Hello," Cole said.

She paid no attention.

"Hello!" he said more sharply. "Do you speak Galactic English?"

She looked at him out of empty blue eyes and went back to her work. He went past her gingerly and up to his room. There he wrote a note to Garth Bidgrass, paced and fanned his indignation, tore up the note and wrote a stronger one. When Hawkins brought his dinner, Cole beat down his chattering objections and stuffed the note into the old man's coat pocket.

"See that Bidgrass gets it at once! Do you hear, at once!" he shouted.

After nightfall, nervous and wakeful, Cole looked out on the garden by the pale light of two moons. He saw the girl, wearing the same dress, come out of the opposite wing, and decided on impulse to intercept her.

As he climbed through the library window he said to himself, "Anything may be data to an ecologist, especially if it's pretty to look at."

He met her full face at the house corner and her hands flew up, fending. She turned and he said, "Please don't run away from me. I want to talk to you."

She turned back with eyes wide and troubled, in what nature had meant to be a merry, careless face.

"Do you know who I am?" he asked.

She nodded. "Uncle Garth says I'm not to talk to you." It was a little girl's voice, tremulous.

"Why? What am I, some kind of monster?"

"N-no. You're an outworlder, from a great, wealthy planet."

"Belconti is a very ordinary planet. What's your name?"

"I'm Pia—Pia Vignoli." The voice took on more assurance, but the plump body stayed poised for flight.

"Well I'm Flinter Cole, and I have a job to do on this planet. It's *terribly* important that I get started. Will you help me?"

"How can I, Mr. Cole? I'm nobody. I don't know anything." She moved away, and he followed, awkwardly.

"Girls know all sorts of things that would interest an ecologist," he protested. "Tell me all you know about stompers."

"Oh *no!* I mustn't talk about stompers."

"Well talk about nothing then, like girls do," he said impatiently. "What's the name of that moon?" he pointed overhead.

Tension left her and she smiled a little. "Morwenna," she said. "That one just setting into Lundy Forest is Annis. You can tell Annis by her bluish shadows that are never the same."

"Good girl! How about the other two, the ones that aren't up?"

"One's Cairdween and the other, the red one—oh, I daren't talk about moons either."

"Not even *moons?* Really, Miss Vignoli—"

"Let's not talk at all. I'll show you how to walk, you do look so funny all spraddled and scraping your feet. I was born off-planet and I had to learn it myself."

She showed him the light down-flex of the foot that threw the body more forward than up, and he learned to wait out the strange micropause before his weight settled on the other foot. With a little practice he got it, walking up and down the moonlit path beside her in an effortless toe dance. Then he learned to turn corners and to jump.

"Pia," he said once. "Pia. I like the sound, but it doesn't suit this rough planet."

"I was born on Tristan," she murmured. "Please don't ask—"

"I won't. But no reason why I can't talk. May I call you Pia?"

He described Belconti and the university, and his doctorate, at stake in this field assignment. Suddenly she stopped short and pointed to where a red moon lifted above the dark cliff of the eastern forest.

"It's late," she said. "There comes Hoggy Darn. Good night, Mr. Cole."

She danced away faster than he could follow. He crawled back through his window in the reddish moonlight.

Next afternoon Cole faced Garth Bidgrass in the library.

The old man sat with folded arms, craggy face impassive. Cole, standing, leaned his weight on his hands and thrust his sharp face across the table. His freckles stood out against his angry pallor, and sunlight from the end window blazed in his red hair.

"Let me sum up," he said, thin-lipped. "For obscure reasons I must be essentially a prisoner. All right. You have no education here, no biologists of any kind. All right. Now here is what they expect of me on Belconti: to rough out the planetary ecosystem, set up a functional profile series for the stomper and its interacting species, make energy flow charts and outline the problem. If my report is incorrect or incomplete, Belconti won't send the right task group of specialists. Then you spend your money for nothing and I lose my doctorate. I must have skilled helpers, a clerical staff, *masses* of data!"

"You've said all that before," Bidgrass said calmly. "I told you, I can provide none of that."

"Then it's hopeless! Why did you ever send for an ecologist?"

"I sent for help. Belconti sent the ecologist."

"Help me to *help* you, then. You must try to understand, Mr. Bidgrass, science can't operate in a vacuum. I can't work up a total planetary biology. I must start with that data."

"Do what you can for us," Bidgrass said. "They won't blame you on Belconti when they know and we won't blame you here if it doesn't help."

Cole sat down, shaking his head. "But Belconti won't count it as a field job, not in ecology. You *will* not understand my position. Let me put it this way: suppose someone gave you a hatchet and told you, only one man, to cut down Lundy Forest?"

"I could start," the old man said. His eyes blazed and he smiled grimly. "I'd leave my mark on one tree."

Colt felt suddenly foolish and humbled.

"All right," he said. "I'll do what I can. What do you think is wiping out the stompers?"

"I know what. A parasite bird that lays its eggs on stomper eggs. Its young hatch first and eat the big egg. The people call them piskies."

"I'll need to work out its life cycle, look for weak points and natural enemies. Who knows a lot about these piskies?"

"I know as much as anybody, and I've never seen a grown one. We believe they stay in the deep forest. But there are always three to each stomper egg and they're vicious. Go for a man's eyes or jugular. Egg hunters kill dozens every day."

"I'll want dozens, alive if possible, and a lab. Can you do that much?"

"Yes. You can use Dr. Rudall's lab at the hospital." Bidgrass stood up and looked at his watch. "The egg harvest should start coming in soon down at the plant and there may be a dead pisky. Come along and see."

As Hawkins guided the car past a group of the giant field workers, Cole felt Bidgrass' eyes on him. He turned, and the old man said slowly, "Stick to piskies, Mr. Cole. We'll all be happier."

"Anything may be data to an ecologist, especially if he overlooks it," Cole murmured stubbornly.

Hawkins cackled something about "Hoggy Darn itha hoose" and speeded up.

In the cavernous, machinery-lined plant Cole met the manager. He was the same powerful, long-haired man Cole had seen in the garden. "Morgan." Bidgrass introduced him with the one name, adding, "He doesn't use Galactic English."

Morgan bent his head slightly, unsmiling, ignoring Cole's offered hand. His wide-set eyes were so lustrously black that they seemed to have no pupils, and under the hostile stare Cole flushed angrily. They walked through the plant, Morgan talking to Bidgrass in the vernacular. His voice was deep and resonant, organ-like.

Bidgrass explained to Cole how stomper egg was vac-frozen under biostat and sealed in plastic for export. He pointed out a piece of shell, half an inch thick and highly translucent. From its radius of curvature Cole realized that stomper eggs were much larger than he had pictured them. Then someone shouted and Bidgrass said a flyer was coming in. They went out on the loading dock.

The flyer alongside carried six men forward of the cargo space and had four heavy blasters mounted almost like a warcraft. As the dock crew unloaded two eggs into dollies, other flyers were skittering in, further along the dock. Bidgrass pointed out to Cole on one huge four by three-foot egg the bases of broken parasite eggs cemented to its shell. Through a hole made by piskies, the ecologist noted that the substance of the large egg was a stiff gel. Morgan flashed a strong pocket lamp on the shell and growled something.

"There may be a pisky hiding inside," Bidgrass said. "You are lucky, Mr. Cole."

Morgan stepped inside and returned almost at once wearing goggles and heavy gloves, and carrying a small power saw, He used the light again, traced an eight-inch square with his finger, and sawed it out. The others, all but Cole, stood back. Morgan pulled away the piece and something black flew up, incredibly swift, with a shrill, keening sound.

Cole looked after it and Morgan struck him heavily in the face, knocking him to hands and knees. Feet stamped and scraped around him and Cole saw his own blood dripping on the dock. He stood up dazed and angry.

"Morgan saved your eye," Bidgrass told him, "but the pisky took a nasty gouge at your cheekbone. I'll have Hawkins drive you to the hospital—you wanted to meet Dr. Rudall anyway."

Cole examined the crushed pisky on the way to the hospital. Big as his fist, with a tripartite beak, it was no true bird. The wings were flaps of black skin that still wrinkled and folded flexibly with residual life. It had nine toes on each foot and seemed covered with fine scales.

Dr. Rudall treated Cole's cheek in a surprisingly large and well-appointed dressing room. He was a gray, defeated-looking man and told Cole in an apologetic voice that he had taken medical training on Planet Tristan many years ago . . . out of touch now. His small lab looked hopelessly archaic, but he promised to biostat the dead pisky until Cole could get back to it.

Hawkins was not with the ground car. Cole drove back to the plant without him. He wanted another look at the mode of adhesion of pisky egg on stomper egg. He drove to the further end of the plant and mounted the dock from outside, to freeze in surprise. Twenty feet away, the dock crew was unloading a giant.

He was naked, strapped limply to a plank, and his face was bloody. Half his reddish hair and beard was singed away. Then a hand hit Cole's shoulder and spun him around. It was Morgan.

"Clear out of here, you!" the big man said in fluent, if plain, Galactic English. "Don't you ever come here without Garth Bidgrass brings you!" He seemed hardly to move his lips, but the voice rumbled like thunder.

"Well," thought Cole, driving back after Hawkins, "datums are data, if they bite off your head."

"For your own safety, Mr. Cole, you must not again leave the company of either Hawkins or Dr. Rudall when you are away from the house," Bidgrass told Cole the next morning. "The people have strange beliefs that would seem sheer nonsense to you, but their impulsive acts, if you provoke them, will be unpleasantly real."

"If I knew their beliefs I might know how to behave."

"It is your very presence that is provoking. If you were made of salt you would have to stay out of the rain. Here you are an outworlder and you must stay within certain limits. It's like that."

"All right," Cole said glumly. He worked all day at the hospital dissecting the pisky, but found no parasites. He noted interesting points of anatomy. The three-part beak of silicified horn was razor sharp and designed to exert a double shearing stress. The eye was triune and of fixed focus; the three eyeballs lay in a narrow isosceles triangle pattern, base down, behind a common triangular conjunctiva with incurved sides and narrow base. The wings were elastic and stiffened with a fan of nine multi-jointed bones that probably gave them grasping and manipulating power in the living organism. None of it suggested the limit factor he sought.

Dr. Rudall helped him make cultures in a sterile broth derived from the pisky's own tissues. In the evening a worker from the plant brought eleven dead piskies and Cole put them in biostat. He rode home with Hawkins to his solitary dinner feeling he had made a start.

Day followed day. Cole remained isolated in his wing, coming and going through his back door into the garden. He became used to the mute giant domestics who swept and cleaned. Now and then he exchanged a few words with the sad Mrs. Vignoli, Pia's mother, he learned, or with old Bidgrass, in chance meetings. He watched Pia through his windows sometimes and knew she fled when he came out. There was something incongruous in the timid wariness with which her plump figure and should-be-merry face confronted the world.

Once he caught her and held her wrist. "Why do you run away from me, Pia?"

She pulled away gently. "I'll get you in trouble, Mr. Cole. They don't trust me either. My father was a Tristanian."

"Who are *they?*"

"Just they. Morgan, all of them."

"If we're both outworld, we should stick together. I'm the loneliest man on this planet, Pia."

"I know the feeling," she said, looking down.

He patted her curls. "Let's be friends then, and you help me. Where do these giant people come from?"

Her head jerked up angrily. "That has nothing to do with your work! I'm inworld too, Mr. Cole. My mother is of the old stock."

Cole let her go in silence.

He began working evenings in the lab, losing himself in work. Few of the blue-clad men and women he encountered would look at him, but he sensed their hostile glances on the back of his neck. He felt islanded in a sea of dull hatred. Only Dr. Rudall was vaguely friendly.

Cole found no parasites in hundreds of dissected piskies, but his cultures were frequently contaminated by a fungus that formed dark red, globular fruiting bodies. When he turned to cytology he found that what he had supposed to be an incredibly complex autonomic nervous system was instead a fungal mycelium, so fine as to be visible only in phase contrast. He experimented with staining techniques and verified it in a dozen specimens, then danced the surprised Dr. Rudall around the lab.

"I've done it! One man against a planet!" he chortled. "We'll culture it, then work up mutant strains of increasing virulence—oh for a Belconti geno-mycologist now!"

"It's not pathogenic, I'm afraid," Dr. Rudall said. "I . . . ah . . . read once, that idea was tried centuries ago . . . all the native fauna have fungal symbiotes . . . protect them against all known pathogenic microbiota . . . should have mentioned it, I suppose. . . ."

"Yes, you should have told me! My God, there go half the weapons of applied ecology over the moon . . . my time wasted . . . *why* didn't you tell me?" The ecologist's sharp face flushed red as his hair with frustrated anger.

"You didn't ask . . . hardly know what ecology means . . . didn't realize it was important . . ." the old doctor stammered.

"*Everything* is important to an ecologist, especially what people won't tell him!" Cole stormed.

He tried to stamp out of the lab, and progressed in a ludicrous bouncing that enraged him even more. He shouted for Hawkins and went home early.

In his rooms he brooded on his wrongs for an hour, then went downstairs and thundered on the locked door into the main house, shouting Garth Bidgrass' name. The sounds beyond hushed. Then Garth Bidgrass opened the door, looking stern and angry.

"Come into the library, Mr. Cole," he said. "Try to control yourself."

In the library Cole poured out his story while Bidgrass, standing with right elbow resting atop a bookcase, listened gravely.

"You must understand," Cole finished, "to save the stompers we must cut down the piskies. Crudely put, the most common method is to find a disease or a parasite that affects them, and breed more potent strains of it. But that won't work on piskies, and I could have and should have known that to begin with."

"Then you must give up?"

"*No!* Something must prey on them or their eggs in their native habitat, a macrobiotic limit factor I can use. I must learn the adult pisky's diet; if its range is narrow enough that can be made a limit factor."

The old man frowned. "How would you learn all this?"

"Field study. I want at least twenty intelligent men and a permanent camp somewhere in Lundy Forest."

Bidgrass folded his arms and shook his head. "Can't spare the men. And it's too dangerous—stompers would attack you day and night. I've had over two hundred egg hunters killed this year, and they're trained men in teams."

"Let me go out with a team then, use my own two eyes."

"Men wouldn't have you. I told you, they're superstitious about outworlders."

"Then it's failure! Your money and my doctorate go down the drain."

"You're young, you'll get your doctorate another place," the old man said. "You've tried hard, and I'll tell Belconti that." His voice was placating, but Cole thought he saw a wary glint in the hard gray eyes.

Cole shrugged. "I suppose I'll settle in and wait for *Gorbals*. But I've had pleasanter vacations."

He turned his back and scanned the shelves ostentatiously for a book. Bidgrass left the room quietly.

It was a boring evening. Pia was not in the garden. Cole looked at the barrier and the incredible cliff of Lundy Forest. He would like to get into that forest, just once. Hundred and fifty days before *Gorbals* . . . *why* had they ever sent for him? They seemed to be conspiring to cheat him of his doctorate. They had, too. . . . Finally he slept.

He woke to a distant siren wail and doors slamming and feet scraping in the main house. Dressing in haste, he noted a red glow in the sky to southward and heard a booming noise. In the hall outside his room he met Pia, face white and eyes enormous.

"Stomper attack!" she cried. "Come quickly, you must hide in the basement with us!"

He followed her into the main house and downstairs to where Mrs. Vignoli was herding a crowd of the giant domestics down a doored staircase. The giant women were tossing their heads nervously. Several were naked and one was tearing off her dress. Cole drew back.

"I'm an ecologist, I want to see," he said. "Stompers are data."

He pushed her gently toward the women and walked out on the front veranda. From southward came an incredibly rich and powerful chord of organ music, booming and swelling, impossibly sustained. Old Hawkins danced in the driveway in grotesque pointed leaps, shrieking "Hoosa maida! Hoosa maida!" Overhead the moons Cairdween, Morwenna and Annis of the blue shadows were arranged in a perfect isosceles triangle, narrow base parallel to the horizon. It stirred something in Cole, but the swelling music unhinged his thought. With a twinge of panic he turned, to find Pia at his elbow.

"They're after me, after us," she cried against the music.

"I must see. You go find shelter, Pia."

"With you I feel less alone now," she said. "One can't really hide, anyway. Come to the watch tower and you'll see."

He followed her through the house and up two flights to the roof of the tower on the southeast corner. As they stepped into the night air, the great organ sound enwrapped them, and Cole saw the southern sky ablaze, with flyers swooping and black motes hurtling through the glare. Interwoven pencils of ion-flame flickered in the verging darkness and the ripping sound of heavy blasters came faintly through the music.

A hundred-yard section of the barrier was down in flames, and the great, bobbing, leggy shapes of stompers came bounding through it while others glided down from the top. Flyers swarmed like angry bees around the top of the break, firing mounted blasters and tearing away great masses of wood. The powerful chord of music swelled unendurably in volume and exultant richness until Cole cried out and shook the girl.

"It plucks at my backbone and I can't think! Pia, Pia, what *is* that music?"

"It's the stompers singing," she shouted back.

He shook his head. Bidgrass Station seethed, lights everywhere, roads crowded with trucks. Around the base of the breakthrough a defense perimeter flared with the blue-violet of blasters and the angry red of flame guns. As Cole watched it was overrun and darkened in place after place, only to reform further out as reserves came into action. Expanding jerkily, pushed this way and that, the flaming periphery looked like a fire-membrane stressed past endurance by some savage contained thing. With a surge of emotion Cole realized it was men down there, with their guns and their puny muscles and their fragile lives against two-legged, boat-shaped monsters twenty feet high.

"Sheer power of biomass," he thought. "Even their shot-down bodies are missiles, to crush and break." A sudden eddy in the flaming defense line brought it to within half a mile of the house. Cole could see men die against the glare, in the great music.

The girl pressed close to him and whimpered, "Oh, start the fire mist! Morwenna pity them!" Cole put his arm tightly around her.

A truck convoy pulled up by the manor house and soldiers were everywhere, moving quickly and surely. A group hauled a squat, vertical cylinder on wheels crashing through the ornamental shrubbery. Violet glowing metal vaning wound about it in a double helix.

"It's a Corbin powercaster," Pia shouted into Cole's ear. "It broadcasts power to the portable blasters so the men don't need to carry pack charges or lose time changing them."

Cole looked at the soldiers. The same big men he saw every day, the same closed and hostile faces, but now a wild and savage joy shone in them. This was their human meaning to themselves, their justification. The red boundary roared down on them, they would be dying in a few minutes, but they were braced and fiercely ready.

The music swelled impossibly loud and Cole knew that he too was going to die with them, despised outworlder that he was. He hugged the girl fiercely and tried to kiss her.

"Let me in your world, Pia!" he cried.

She pulled away. "Look! The fire mist! Oh thank you, good Morwenna!"

He saw it, a rose pink paled by nearer flame, washing lazily against the black cliff edge of Lundy Forest. It grew, boiling up over the barrier in places, spilling through the gap, and the great, agonizing chord of music muted and dwindled. The flame-perimeter began shrinking and still the fire mist grew, staining the night sky north and south beyond eye-reach. The song became a mournful wailing and the soldiers in the garden moved forward for the mopping up.

"Pia, I've got to go down there. I've got to see a stomper close up."

She was trembling and crying with reaction. "I think they'll be too busy to mind," she said. "But don't go too far in . . . Flinter."

He ran down the stairs and through the unguarded gate toward the fought-over area. Wounded men were being helped or carried past him, but no one noticed him. He found a stomper, blaster-torn but not yet dead, and stopped to watch the four-foot tripart beak snap feebly and the dark wings writhe and clutch. The paired vertical eyelid folds rolled apart laterally to reveal three eyes under a single triangular conjunctiva, lambent in the flame-shot darkness. Soldiers passed unheeding while Cole stood and wondered. Then a hand jerked violently at his arm. It was Morgan.

Morgan wordlessly marched him off to a knot of men nearer the mopping up line and pushed him before Garth Bidgrass. Sweat dripped from flaring eyebrows down the grim old face, and over a blistered right cheek. A heavy blaster hung from the old man's body harness.

"Well, Mr. Cole, is this data?" he asked dourly. "Have you come out to save stompers?"

"I wish I could have saved men, Mr. Bidgrass. I wanted to help," Cole said.

"Another like this and you may have to," Bidgrass said, less sharply. "It was close work, lad."

"I can help Dr. Rudall. You must have many wounded."

"Good, good," the old man said approvingly. "The men will take that kindly and so will I."

"One favor," Cole said. "Will you have your men save half a dozen living stompers for me? I have another idea."

"Well, I don't know," Bidgrass said. "The men won't like it . . . but a few days, maybe . . . yes, I'll save you some."

"Thank you, sir." Cole turned away, catching a thick scowl from Morgan. Overhead the three moons were strung in a ragged line across the sky, and Hoggy Darn was rising.

Cole worked around the clock at the hospital, sterilizing instruments and helping Dr. Rudall with dressings. He was surprised to see other doctors, many nurses, and numerous biofield projectors as modern as any on Belconti. Some of the wounded were women. All of them, wounded and unwounded, seemed in a shared mood of exaltation. He caught glimpses of Pia, working too. She seemed less poised for flight, tired but happy, and she smiled at him.

After three days Cole saw his stompers in a stone-floored pen at the slaughter house. Earth breed cattle lowed in adjacent pens. Four stompers still lived, their bodies blaster torn and their legs crudely hamstrung so they could not stand. They lay with heads together and the sun glinted on the blue-black, iridescent scales covering the domed heads and long necks.

Three shock-headed butchers stood by, assigned to help him.

Their distaste for Cole and the job was so evident that he hurried through the gross dissection of the two dead stompers at one end of the same pen. After an hour he thought to ask, as best he could, whether the living stompers were being given food and water. When one man understood, black hatred crossed his face and he spat on Cole's shoe. The ecologist flushed, then shrugged and got on with the job.

It brought him jarring surprises culminating in a tentative conclusion late on the second day. Then the situation began to fall apart. Working alone for the moment, Cole opened the stomach of the second stomper and found in it half-digested parts of a human body. Skull and humerus size told him it was one of the giants.

First pulling a flap of mesentery over the stomach incision, Cole went into the office and phoned Dr. Rudall to come at once. Coming out, he heard angry shouts and saw two of his helpers running to join the third, who stood pointing into the carcass. Then all three seized axes, ran across the pen and began hacking at the necks of the living stompers.

The great creatures boomed and writhed, clacking their beaks and half rising on their wings, unable to defend themselves. The butchers howled curses, and the stompers broke into a mournful wailing harmonized with flesh-creeping subsonics. Cole shouted and pleaded, finally wrested an axe from one and mounted guard over the last living stomper. He stood embattled, facing a growing crowd of butchers from the plant, when Dr. Rudall arrived.

"Dr. Rudall, explain to these maniacs why I must keep this stomper alive!" he cried angrily.

"I'm sorry, Mr. Cole, they will kill it in spite of you."

"But Garth Bidgrass ordered—"

"In spite of him. There are factors you don't understand, Mr. Cole. You are yourself in great danger." The old doctor's hands trembled.

Cole thought rapidly. "All right, will they wait a day? I want tissue explants for a reason I'll explain later. If you'll help me work up the nutrient tonight—"

"Our pisky nutrient will work. We can take your samples within the hour. Let me call the hospital."

He spoke rapidly to the glowering butchers in the vernacular, then hurried into the building. An hour later the stomper was dead, and Hawkins drove Cole and the doctor back to their lab with the explants.

"I've almost got it," Cole said happily. "Several weeks and two more bits of information and I'll tell you. In spite of all odds, one man against a planet—this will found my professional reputation back on Belconti."

Once again Cole faced Garth Bidgrass across the round table in the library. This time he felt vastly different.

"The piskies are really baby stompers," he said, watching the craggy old face for its reaction. It did not change.

"I suspected it when I saw how the smaller eggs fused with the large egg, with continuous laminae," Cole went on. "There was the morphological resemblance, too. But when I dissected two mature stompers I found immature eggs. Even before entry into the oviduct what you call pisky eggs are filamented to the main body of cytoplasm."

Disappointingly, Bidgrass did not marvel. He squinted and cocked his head. Finally he said, "Do you mean the piskies lay their eggs internally in the stompers?"

"Impossible! I made a karyotype analysis of pisky and stomper tissue and they are identical, I tell you. My working hypothesis for now is that pisky eggs are fertilized polar bodies. It's not unknown. But that the main body should be sterile and serve as an external food source—that's new, I'm sure. That will get my name in the journals all through Carina sector."

He could not help smiling happily. Bidgrass bit his lower lip and stared keenly, not speaking. Cole became nettled.

"I hope you see the logic," he said. "What threatens your stompers is harvest pressure from your own egg hunters. Stop it for a few decades, or set aside breeding areas, and you can have a whole planetful again."

The old man scowled and stood up. "We'll not stop," he said gruffly. "There are still plenty of stompers. Remember last month." He walked to the end window and back, then sat down again still looking grim.

"Don't be too sure," Cole objected. "I haven't finished my report. I made a Harvey analysis on the tissues of one stomper. It involves culturing clones, measuring growth rates and zones of migration and working out a complex set of ratios—I won't go into details. But when I fitted my figures into Harvey's formula it indicated *unmistakably* that the stompers have a critical biomass."

"What does that mean?"

"Think of a species as one great animal that never dies, of which each individual is only a part. Can you do that?"

"Yes!" the old man exploded, sitting bolt upright.

"Well, the weight of a cross-section of the greater animal at any moment in time is its biomass. Many species have a point or value of critical biomass such that, if it falls below that point, the greater animal dies. The species loses its will to live, decays, drifts into extinction in spite of all efforts to save it. The stomper is such a species, no doubt whatever. Do you see how the slaughter a month ago may *already* have extinguished them as a species?"

Bidgrass nodded, smiling grimly. His eyes held a curious light.

"Tell me, Mr. Cole, your Harvey formula—do *human beings* have a critical biomass?"

"Yes, biologically," Cole said, surprised. "But in our case a varying part of the greater animal is carried in our culture, our symbol system, and is not directly dependent on biomass. A mathematical anthropologist could tell you more than I can."

Bidgrass placed his hands palm down on the table and leaned back in sudden resolution.

"Mr. Cole, you force me to tell you something I had been minded to hold back. I already know a good part of what you have just told me. I *wish* to exterminate the stompers and I will do so. But I meant for you to go back to Belconti thinking it was the piskies."

Cole propped his chin on folded hands and raised his eyebrows. "I half suspected that. But I fooled you, didn't I?"

"Yes, and I admire you for it. Now let me tell you more. Stomper egg brings a very high price and I have kept it higher by storing large reserves. When it is known the stomper is extinct, the rarity value of my reserve will be enormous. It will mean an end of this harsh life for me and for my grandniece after me."

Cole's lip curled, and red mounted in the old man's face as he talked, but he went on doggedly.

"I want the pisky theory and the news of stomper extinction to be released through Belconti University. The news will spread faster and be more readily believed and I will avoid a certain moral stigma—"

"And now I've crossed you up!"

"You can still do it. I can ease your conscience with a settlement of—say—five thousand solars a year for life."

Cole leaped up and leaned across the table.

"No!" he snapped. "Old man, you don't know how ecologists feel about the greed-murder of species. What I *will* do is work through Belconti on your government at Car Truro, warn it that you are about to destroy an important planetary resource."

Bidgrass stood up too, scowling darkly red.

"Not so fast, young fellow. I have copies of your early notes in which you call the piskies the critical limit factor in stomper extinction. Almost three hundred people were killed in that stomper attack, and you could easily have been one of them. If you had, I would naturally have reported it via the next *Gorbals* to Belconti and sent along your notes to date—do you follow me?"

"Yes. A threat."

"A counter-threat. Think it over for a few days, Mr. Cole."

Cole sat glumly in his room waiting for his dinner and wondering if it would be poisoned. When old Hawkins tapped, he pulled open the door, only to find Pia instead with a service for two. She was rosy and smiling in a low-cut, off-shoulder brown dress he had not seen before.

"May I eat dinner with you tonight, Flinter?" she asked.

"Please do," he said, startled. "Am I people now, or something?"

"Uncle Garth says now that you know—" She broke off, blushing still more.

"I don't like what I know," he said somberly, "but it's not you, Pia. Here, let me."

He pulled the cart into the room and helped her set the things on his table. Pia *was* lovely, he decided, wanting to caress the smooth roundness of her shoulders and dimpled arms. When she sat across the small table from him he could not help responding to the swell of her round breasts barely below the neckline. But her manner seemed forced and she looked more frightened than ever.

"You look like a little rabbit that knows it's strayed too far from the woods, Pia. What *are* you always afraid of?"

Her smile faded. "Not because I'm too far from the woods," she said. "What's a rabbit? But let's not talk about fear."

They talked of food and weather through a more than usually elaborate dinner. There was a bottle of Tristanian *kresch* to follow it. Cole splashed the blue wine into the two crystal goblets, gave her one and held up his own.

"Here's to the richest little girl on Tristan someday," he said, half mockingly.

Tears sprang to her eyes. "I don't want to be rich. I just want a home away from New Cornwall, just anywhere. I was born on Tristan. Oh Flinter, what you must think—" She began crying in earnest.

He patted her shoulder. "Forgive me for a fool, Pia. Tell me about Tristan. I had only one day there, waiting for *Gorbals'* tender."

She spoke of her childhood on Tristan, and the tension eased in both. Finally she proposed a picnic for the next day, the two of them to take a sports flyer into the forest top. He agreed with pleasure and squeezed her hand in saying good night.

She squeezed back a little. But she still looked frightened.

Next day Pia wore a brief yellow playsuit, and Cole could not keep his eyes off her. When he was loading the picnic hamper into the small flyer before the main hangar, she suddenly pressed close to him. He followed her wide-eyed gaze over his right shoulder and saw Morgan bulking darkly ten feet away.

"Hello there, Mr. Morgan," Cole said into the impassive face under the black bar of eyebrow.

Morgan rumbled in vernacular and walked on. His lips did not move.

"You're afraid of Morgan," Cole said when he had the flyer aloft and heading east.

"He's a bard. He has a power," she said. "Today, let's forget him."

Cole looked back at the bulk of Lundy Peninsula, swelling lost into blue-green distance from the narrow isthmus. The straight slash of Bidgrass Station from sea to sea looked puny beside the mighty forest towering on either side. Then Pia had his arm and wanted him to land.

He grounded on a pinkish-green mass of lichen several acres in area. Pia assured him it would support the flyer, reminding him of the planet's low gravity.

The resilient surface gave off a fragrance as they walked about on it. In a sea all around their island, branches of the great forest trees thrust up, leafy and flowering and bedecked with a profusion of epiphytal plants in many shapes and colors. Bright-hued true birds darted from shadow into sunlight and back again, twittering and crying.

"It's beautiful," he said. And so was Pia, he thought, watching her on tiptoe reaching to a great white flower. The attractive firmness of her skin, the roundness and dimpling, *ripeness*, that was the word he wanted. And her eyes.

"Pia, you're not frightened any more!"

It was true. The long-lashed brown eyes were merry as nature meant them to be.

"It's peaceful and safe," she said. "When I come to the forest top I never want to go back to Bidgrass Station."

"Too bad we must, and let's pretend we don't," he said, pointing to a cluster of red-gold fruits. "Are those good to eat?"

"Too good. That's the trouble with New Cornwall."

"What do you mean?"

"Race you back to the flyer," she cried, and danced away, bare limbs twinkling in the sunlight. He floundered after.

The lunch was good and she had brought along the rest of the bottle of *kresch*. They sipped it seated beside the flyer while she tried to teach him New Cornish folk songs. Her small, clear singing blended with that of the birds around them.

"I catch parts of it," he said. "As an undergraduate a few years ago I studied the pre-space poets. I can read Old English, but it is strange to my ear."

"I could teach you."

"I love one wry-witted ancient named Robert Graves. How does it go: *If strange things happen where she is*—no, I can't recall it now."

"I could write the songs out for you."

"The beauty is in you and your voice. Just sing."

She sang, something about a king with light streaming from his hair, coming naked out of the forest to bring love into his kingdom. Small white clouds drifted in the blue sky, and blue Annis slept just above the rustling branches that guarded the secret of their island. He listened and watched her.

She was softly rounded as the clouds, and her clustered brown curls made an island of the vivid face expressing the song she sang so bird-like and naturally. She was vital, compact, self-closed, perfect—like one of the great flowers nodding in the breeze along the island shore—and his heart yearned across to her.

"Pia," he said, breaking into the song, "do you really want to get away from New Cornwall?"

She nodded, eyes suddenly wide, lips still parted.

"Come with me to Belconti then. Right now. We'll cross to Car Truro and wait there for *Gorbals*."

The light dimmed in her face. "Why Car Truro?"

"Pia, it's hard to tell you. I'm afraid of your great-uncle . . . I want to contact the planetary government."

"It's no good at Car Truro, Flinter. Can't you just come back to Bidgrass Station and . . . and . . . do what Uncle Garth wants?"

He could barely hear the last.

The fear was back in her eyes.

"Do you know what he wants?"

"Yes." The brown curls drooped.

Cole stood up. "So *that's* the reason—well, I'll not do it, do you hear? Garth Bidgrass is an evil, greedy old man and maybe it runs in the blood."

She jumped up, eyes more angry now than fearful. "He is not! He's trying to save you! He's good and noble and . . . and *great!* If you only knew the truth—Morwenna forgive me!" She clapped her hand to her mouth.

"*Tell* me the truth then, since I'm still being made a Belconti fool of. What is the truth?"

"I've said too much. Now I'll have to tell Uncle Garth—" She began crying.

"Tell him what? That I know he's a liar? That you failed as a—" He could not quite say the word.

"It's true I was supposed to make you love me and I tried and I can't because . . . because . . ." she ended in incoherent sobbing.

Cole stroked her hair and comforted her. "I've been hasty again," he apologized. "I'm still running in the dark, and that makes for stumbles. Let's go back, and I'll talk to your great-uncle again."

In the morning Garth Bidgrass, looking tired and stern, invited Cole to breakfast with the family. Cole had never been in the large, wood-paneled room overlooking the south garden through broad windows. Pia was subdued, Mrs. Vignoli strangely cheerful. The meal, served by a giant maid, was the customary plain porridge and fried meat.

The women left when the maid cleared the table. Bidgrass poured more coffee, then leaned back and looked across at Cole.

"Mr. Cole, I did you a wrong in having you sent here. I kept you in the dark for your own protection. Can you believe that?"

"I can believe that you believe it."

"You came too soon. You were too curious, too smart. I have had to compound that wrong with others to Pia and my own good name."

Cole smiled. "I know I'm curious. But why can't I know—"

"You can, lad. You've nosed through to it and I'll tell you if you insist. But it will endanger you even more and I wish you would forego it."

Cole shook his head. "I'm an ecologist. If I have the big picture, maybe I can help."

"I thought you'd say that. Well, history first, and settle yourself because it *is* a big picture and not a pretty one. This planet was settled directly from Earth in the year 145 After Space, almost eight hundred years ago. It seemed ideal—native protein was actually superior to Earth protein in human metabolism. Easy climate, geophysically stable, no diseases—but planetology was not much of a science in those days.

"The colony won political independence in 202 A.S. It had a thriving trade in luxury foods, mostly stomper egg concentrates—freight was dear then. Settlements radiated out from Car Truro across the plains. Food was to be had for the taking in the mild climate and it was a kind of paradise. *Paradise!*"

The old man's voice rang hard on the last word and Cole stiffened. Bidgrass went on.

"Early in the third century our social scientists began to worry about the unnatural way the culture graded from the complexity of Car Truro to a simple pattern of mud huts and food gathering along the frontiers. Children of successive generations were taller than their parents and much less willing or able to use symbols. By the time a minority decided the trend should be reversed, the majority of the people could not be roused to see a danger."

"Earth life is normally resistant to low-grav gigantism," Cole said. "I wonder—"

"It was all the native foods they ate, but mainly stomper egg. There are more powerful and quicker-acting substances in the forest fungi, but then the population was all in the eastern grasslands, where the stompers ranged."

"I read they were a plains animal."

"Yes, and harmless too, except for their eggs. Well, the minority set up a dictatorship and began cultivating Earth plants and animals. They passed laws limiting the mechanical simplicity of households and regulating diets. They took children from subnormal parents and educated and fed them in camps. But the normals were too few and the trend continued.

"Shortly after mid-century the population reached the edge of the southern forest, and there many were completely wild. They drifted along the forest edge naked, without tools or fire or language or even family groupings. Their average stature was nearly eight feet. The normals knew they were losing. Can you imagine how they *felt*, lad?"

Cole relaxed a little. "Ah . . . yes, I can . . . I imagine the fight was inside them, too."

Bidgrass nodded. "Yes, they were all tainted. But they fought. They asked Earth for help and learned that Earth regarded them as tyrants oppressing a simple, natural folk. The economy broke down and more had to be imported. The only way to pay was in stomper egg exports. In spite of that, in about the year 300, they decided to restrict the stompers to the western part of the grasslands, thousands of miles beyond the human range.

"The egg hunters began killing piskies and grown stompers. They killed off the great, stupid herds of darv cattle on which the stompers fed. The stompers that survived became wary and hostile, good at hiding and fierce to attack. But killing off the eastern darv herds broke them and in a generation they vanished from the eastern plains. Things seemed to improve and they thought the tide was turned. Then, in the year 374, came what our bards now call the Black Learning."

"Bards?" Cole said. He drained his coffee cup.

"Morgan could sing you this history to shiver the flesh on your bones," the old man said, pouring more coffee. "What I am telling you is nowhere written down, but it is engraved in thousands of hearts. Well, to go on.

"We knew some of the stompers had gone into the southern forest—you see, they have to incubate their eggs in direct sunlight and we kept finding them along the forest edge. But we had assumed they were eating the snakes and slugs and fungi native to the forest floor. Now we learned that a large population of wild humans had grown up unknown to us in the deep forest—and the stompers were eating them.

"You have seen our forests from a distance, lad. Do you realize how impossible it is to patrol them? We hadn't the men, money or machines for it. We appealed, and learned we would get no help from any planet in Carina sector except for pay. But the egg market fell off, and our income with it. Ships did come, however, small ones in stealth, to ground along the forest edge and capture the young women of the wild people."

Cole struck the table. "How rotten . . . !" His voice failed.

Bidgrass nodded. "We call that the Lesser Shame. The young women were without personality or language, yet tractable and responsive to affection. They were flawless in health and physique, and eight feet tall. They could be sold for fantastic prices on loosely organized frontier planets and yes, even to Earth, as we learned. Something dark in a man responds to that combination. You feel it as I speak—no, don't protest, I know. We had long had that trouble among our own people."

"Did my own people of Belconti—" Again Cole's voice failed. He brushed back his red hair angrily.

"Belconti was new then, still a colony. Well, that was the *help* we got. We hadn't the power to fight stompers, let alone slave raiders. But the Galactic Patrol was just getting organized and the sector admiral agreed to keep a ship in orbit blockading us. We broke off all contact except with Tristan, and the Patrol let only one freight line come through to handle our off-planet trade. It was then we began to hate the other planets. We call it the Turning Away.

"Now we are forgotten, almost a myth. The Patrol ship has been gone since two hundred years ago. But we remember."

"I wish I'd known this," Cole said. "Mr. Bidgrass, things are greatly changed in Carina sector—"

Bidgrass held up his hand. "I know, lad. That's why you're here, and I'll come to it. But let me go on. Early in the fifth century we decided to exterminate the stompers altogether and in two decades killed off all the darv cattle. But the stompers went into the forests in the south and west and from there came out to raid the plains. Not to kill, but to carry off normal and semi-wild people into the forest for breeding stock. A stomper's wing is more flexible than a hand. One of them can carry half a dozen men and women and run a thousand miles in a day. Some fungi in the forest can dull a man in an hour and take his mind in a week. Few who were carried in ever came out again.

"This went on, lad, for *centuries*. From our fortified towns and hunting camps we ranged along the forest edge like wolves. The stompers must lay their eggs in direct sunlight. That forced them out where we could get at them, into clearings and uplands and along the forest edge. We killed all we could.

"We found rhythms in their life pattern keyed to our four moons. When the three lady moons form a tall triangle, the stompers group in the open to mill and dance and sing. About every three months this happens over several days and in old times it was the peak raid season. It was also our chance to kill. The people call the configuration the House of the Maidens."

Cole nodded vigorously. "I remember that. Strange how lunar periodicity is bionative in every planet having a moon."

"It saved us here, praise Morwenna, but once almost destroyed us. There is a longer, sixty-two year cycle called the Nights of Hoggy Darn. Then the red moon passes through the House of the Maidens and the stompers go completely berserk. The first one after the war was joined fully, in 434, caught us unprepared and cost us more than three-fourths of our normal population in the week that we remember as the Great Taking. We were thrown back into Car Truro for decades and the stompers came back on the plains. They snatched people from the streets of Car Truro itself. That we call the Dark Time."

The old man's craggy face shadowed with sorrow and he sighed, leaning back. Cole opened his mouth but Bidgrass leaned forward again, new, fierce energy in his voice.

"We rallied and came back. We fought from the air and killed them in large numbers when we caught them in the open on Maiden nights. We drove them back off the plains and harried them along the forest edges and in the upland clearings where they came to lay eggs. We gathered all the eggs we could find. They defended their eggs and caused us steady losses. But we fought.

"We built our strategy on the Maidens and in time we drove the enemy out of the southern forest and into the west. Then we crowded him into Lundy Peninsula, made it a sanctuary for a hundred years to draw him in. When I was your age we fought out the last Nights of Hoggy Darn a few miles east of here. Ten years later we finished Bidgrass Station and the barrier and the continent was free of stompers."

Cole shifted his chair to get the sun off his neck. "I hardly know what to say," he began, but Bidgrass raised his hand.

"I've more to tell you, that you must know. By the late seventh century things were normal around Car Truro as regards regression. We began a pilot program of reclamation. The egg hunters captured wild people along the forest edge, still do. But some are beyond saving, and those they kill. We have to pen them like animals at first, but they can be trained to work in the fields, and for a long time now we have had few machines except what we need for war. Their children, on an Earth diet, come back toward normal in size and intelligence. The fourth and fifth generations are normal enough to join in the war. But war has always come first and we have never been able to spare many normals for reclamation work.

"Even so, ex-wilds make up more than half our normal population now. That's about forty thousand; there are nearly a hundred thousand on the reclamation ladder, mostly around Car Truro. The ex-wilds have a queer, poetic strain, and mainly through them we've developed a sort of religion along the way. It helps the subnormals who are so powerfully drawn to run back to the forests. It's a strange mixture of poetry and prophecy, but it's breath of life to the ex-wilds. I guess I pretty well believe it myself and even you believe some of it."

Cole looked his question, hitching his chair nearer the table.

"Yes, your notion of the greater animal, critical biomass, that you spoke of. We speak of Grandfather Stomper and we are trying to kill him. He is trying to enslave Grandfather Man. The whole purpose and meaning of human life, to an ex-wild, is to kill Grandfather Stomper and then to reclaim Grandfather Man from the forest. You would have to hear Morgan sing it to appreciate how deeply they feel that, lad."

"I feel it, a little. I understand Morgan now, I think. He's an ex-wild, isn't he?"

"Yes, and our master bard. In some ways he has more power than I."

Cole got up. "Mind if I pull a curtain? That sun is hot."

"No, go ahead. Our coffee is cold," the old man said, rising too. "I'll ask for a fresh pot."

Seated again in the shaded room, Bidgrass resumed, "There's not much more. After the barrier was up it seemed as if Grandfather Stomper knew his time was running out. Don't laugh now. Individual stompers don't have intelligence, symbol-using, that is, as far as we know. But they changed from plains to forest. They learned to practice a gruesome kind of animal husbandry—oh, I could tell you things. *Something* had to figure it out."

"I'm not laughing," Cole said. "You're talking sound ecology. Go on."

"Well, they began laying eggs right along the barrier and didn't try to defend them. We picked up hundreds, even thousands, every day. The people said Grandfather Stomper was trying to make peace, to pay rent on Lundy Forest. And maybe he was.

"But we spat in his face. We gathered his tribute and still took all the eggs we could find in the inland clearings. We killed every stomper we saw. Then, for the first time I think, Grandfather Stomper knew it was war to the death. He began to fight as never before. Where once a stomper would carry a captured egg hunter a hundred miles into the forest and turn him loose, now it killed out of hand. They began making mass attacks on the station and they didn't come to capture, they came to kill. So it has gone for forty years now."

The old man's voice changed, less fierce, more solemn. He sat up straight.

"Lundy Forest is near eight hundred thousand square miles. No one knows how many millions of wild humans are in it or how many scores of thousands of stompers. But this I knew long before you came to tell me about critical biomass: Grandfather Stomper is very near to death. He ruled this planet for a million years and he fought me for near a thousand, but his time is come.

"Don't laugh, lad, at what I am about to say now. Mass belief, blind faith over centuries of people like our ex-wilds and semi-wilds, can do strange things. To them and even to myself I represent Grandfather Man, and from them a power comes into me that is more than myself. I know in a direct way that in the Nights of Hoggy Darn to come I will at long last kill Grandfather Stomper and the war will be won. That time is only eight weeks away."

"Then I'll still be here. Grand— Mr. Bidgrass, I want to fight with you."

"You may and welcome, lad. Must, even, to redeem yourself. Because, for what you know now, your life is forfeit if the ex-wilds suspect."

"Why so? Are you not *proud—*" Cole half stood and Bidgrass waved him down.

"Consider, lad. For centuries across the inhabited planets people of wealth and influence have been eating stomper egg, serving it at state banquets. But now you know it is human flesh at one remove. How will they feel toward us when they learn that?"

"How should they feel? Man has to be consumed at some trophic level. His substance is as much in the biogeochemical cycles as that of a pig or a chicken. I suppose we *do* feel he should cap the end of a food chain and not short-cycle through himself, but I'm damned if I'm horrified—"

"Any non-ecologist would be. You know that."

The giant maid came in with a pot of coffee and clean cups. Bidgrass poured and both men sipped in silence. Then Bidgrass said slowly, "Do you know what the people here call outworlders? Cannibals! For centuries we have had the feeling that we have been selling our own flesh to the outworlds in exchange for the weapons to free Grandfather Man."

He stood up, towering over Cole, and his voice deepened.

"It has left hone-deep marks: of guilt, for making the outworlders unknowing cannibals; of hatred, because we feel the outworlds left us no choice. And shame, lad, deep, deep shame, more than a man can bear, to have been degraded to food animals here in our forests and across the opulent tables of the other planets. Morgan is only second-generation normal—his father was killed beside me, last Hoggy Darn. If Morgan knew you had learned our secret he would kill you out of hand. I could not stop him. Do you understand now why we didn't want you until next *Gorbals?* Do you see into the hell you have been skating over?"

Cole nodded and rubbed his chin. "Yes, I do. But I don't despise Morgan, I think I love him. On Belconti, Grandfather Man is mainly concerned to titillate his own appetites, but here, well . . . how do I feel it? . . . I think what you have just told me makes me more proud to be a man than I have ever been before. I will carry through the deception of Belconti University with all my heart. Can't Morgan understand that?"

"Yes, and kill you anyway. Because you *know*. You will not lightly be forgiven that."

Cole shook his head helplessly. "Well *dammit* then—"

"Now, now, there's a way out," Bidgrass said, sitting down again. "The prophecies all foretell a change of heart after Grandfather Stomper dies. They speak of joy, love, good feeling. Morgan did agree to your coming here—he wants to hide the past as much as I do and he could see the value of my plan. In the time of good feeling I hope he will accept you."

"I hope so too," Cole said. "Morgan is a strange man. Why is Pia so afraid of him?"

"I'll tell you that, lad—maybe it will help you to appreciate your own danger. Some few of us are educated on Tristan. Twenty-three years ago my younger brother took my niece Flada there. She ran away and married a Tristanian named Ralph Vignoli. My brother persuaded them to come back and live at our installation there, and Ralph swore to keep secret the little he knew.

"The ex-wilds of New Cornwall kept wanting Ralph to come here so they could be sure of the secret. He kept refusing and finally they sent an emissary to kill him. My brother was killed protecting him. I stepped in then with a compromise, persuaded Ralph to come here for the sake of his wife and daughter. Pia was seven at the time.

"Ralph was a good man and fought well in battles, but two years later Morgan and some others came to the house in my absence and took him away. They took him to a clearing in Lundy Forest, where the stompers come to lay eggs, stripped off his clothing and left him. That was so the stompers would not take him for an egg hunter and kill him outright, but would carry him into the forest like they do with strayed wild stock. Morgan said the command came to him in a dream.

"I think Pia feels she is partly responsible for Ralph's death. I think she sometimes fears Morgan will dream about her, her Tristanian blood. . . ."

"Poor Pia," Cole said softly. "These *years* of grief and fear. . . ."

"They'll be ended come Hoggy Darn again, Morwenna grant. Don't you grieve her with your death too, lad. Stay close to the house, in the house."

Bidgrass rose and gulped the last of his coffee standing.

"I must go, I'm late," he said, more cheerfully than Cole had ever heard his voice. "I have a conference with General Arscoate, our military leader, whom you'll meet soon."

He went out. Cole went out too, thoughts wrestling with feelings, looking for Pia.

In the days that followed Cole took his meals with the family except when there were guests not in Bidgrass' confidence. The doors into the main house remained unlocked and he saw much of Pia, but she seemed unexpectedly elusive and remote. Cole, busy with his report to Belconti University, had little time to wonder about it.

He faked statistics wholesale and cited dozens of nonexistent New Cornish authorities. To his real data indicating critical biomass he added imaginary values for the parameters of climate, range, longevity, fertility period, and Ruhan indices to get an estimated figure. Then he faked field census reports going back fifty years, and drew a curve dipping below critical ten years before his arrival. He made the latest field census show new biomass forty-two percent below critical and juggled figures to make the curve extrapolate to zero in twelve more years.

It pained him in his heart to leave out the curious inverse reproduction data. But it was a masterpiece of deception that should put the seal on his doctorate, and because it reported the extinction of a planetary dominant, he knew it would make the journals and the general news all through the sector.

The night he finished it, working late in the library, Pia brought him milk and cookies and sat with him as he explained what he had done.

"It's right," he defended himself to her against his scholar's conscience. "Humans on New Cornwall are a threatened species too. The secret must be hidden forever."

"Yes," she agreed soberly. "I think if all the sector knew, the ex-wilds would literally die of shame and rage. Being wild is not so bad, but that other!" She shuddered under her gray dress.

"Pia, sometimes I feel you're still avoiding me. Surely now it's all right and genuine between us."

She smiled sadly. "I'll bring you trouble, with Morgan. Father came to New Cornwall because of me."

"But I didn't. I've been thinking I may *stay*, partly because of you. You've been afraid so long it's habitual."

"Strangely, Flinter, I don't feel it as fear any more. It's like bowing with sadness, my strength to run is gone. My old dreams—Morgan coming for me—I have them every night now."

"Morgan! Always Morgan!"

She shook her head and smiled faintly. "He has a dark, poetic power. He is what he is, just like the stompers. I feel . . . not hate, not even fear . . . a kind of *dread*."

He stroked the back of her hand and she pulled it away.

"An old song runs through my head," she went on. "A prophecy that Grandfather Stomper cannot be killed while outworld blood pumps through any heart on the planet. I feel like my own enemy, like . . . like your enemy. You should not have come until next *Gorbals*. Flinter, *stay away from me!*"

He talked soothingly, to little avail. When they parted he said heartily, "Forget those silly prophecies, Pia. I'll look out for you."

Privately, he wondered how.

Cole sat beside Pia and across the food-laden table from General Arscoate, a large pink-faced man in middle life.

"It's an old and proven strategy, Mr. Cole," the general explained. "When Hoggy Darn starts we will harass the enemy from the air in all but one of the fourteen sizable open spaces in Lundy Forest. That one is Emrys Upland, the largest. They will concentrate in Emrys, more each night, until the climactic night of peak frenzy. Then we come down with all the men and women we can muster and we kill. We may go on killing stragglers for years after, but Grandfather Stomper will die on that night."

"Why not kill from the air?"

"More firepower on the ground. I can only lift ninety-four flyers all told. But I will shuttle twenty thousand fighting men into Emrys in an hour or two on the big night."

"So quickly? How can you?" Cole laid down his fork.

"They will be waiting in the forest top all around the periphery, in places where we are already building weapons dumps. In the first days of harrying, we will stage in the fighters."

"Morgan will visit each group in the forest top and sing our history," Bidgrass said from the head of the table. "On the evening of the climactic night, as Hoggy Darn rises, they will take a sacramental meal of stomper egg. At no other time is it eaten on this planet."

Mrs. Vignoli looked down. "Garth!" Arscoate said.

"The lad must know, must take it with us," Bidgrass said. "Lad, the real reason for not killing from the air is that the people *need* to kill personally, with their feet on the ground. So our poetry has always described that last, great fight. I must *personally* kill Grandfather Stomper."

Cole toyed with his knife. "But he is only a metaphor, a totem image—"

"The people believe in an actual individual who is the stomper counterpart of Garth here," the general broke in. "You know, Mr. Cole, the stompers we kill ordinarily are all females. The males are smaller, with a white crest, and they keep to the deep forest except on Hoggy Darn nights. Maybe the frenzy then has something to do with mating—no one knows. But Garth will kill the largest male he can find. The people, and I expect Garth and I, as well, are going to believe that he has killed Grandfather Stomper in person."

The general sipped water and looked sternly over his glass at Cole. Cole glanced at Pia, who seemed lost in a dream of her own, not there to them.

"I see. A symbol," he agreed.

"Not the less real," Arscoate said tartly. "Symbols both mean and are. Garth here is a symbol too and that is why, old as he is, he must be in the thick of it. He is like the ancient battle flags of romantic pre-space history. People before now have actually seen Grandfather Stomper. I am not a superstitious backworlder, Mr. Cole, but—"

Cole raised a placatory hand. "I know you are not, general. Forgive me if I seemed to suggest it."

"Let's have wine," Bidgrass said, pushing back his chair. "We'll take it in the parlor and Pia can sing for us."

When General Arscoate said good-night he told Cole not to worry, that he would have reliable guards at the manor gate during Garth Bidgrass' absence in Car Truro.

"I meant to tell you and Pia in the morning, lad," Bidgrass said. "Arscoate and I must go to Car Truro. There's heartburning there over who gets to fight and who must stay behind. It will be only two days."

Cole felt uneasy all day. He spent most of it writing the covering letter for his report and phrasing his resignation from the university field staff. He wrote personal letters to his uncle and a few friends. After dinner he finally signed the official letters and took the completed report to Bidgrass' desk. Then he went to bed and slept soundly.

Pia wakened him with frantic shaking.

"Dress quickly, Flinter. The guard at the gate was just changed and it's not time."

She darted out to the hall window while he struggled with clothing, then back again.

"*Quickly*, darling! Morgan's crossing the garden, with men. Follow me."

She led him through the kitchen and out a pantry window, then stooping along the base of a hedge to where a flowering tree overshadowed the garden wall.

"I planned this, out of sight of guard posts, when I was a little girl," she whispered. "I always knew—over, Flinter, quickly!"

Outside was rough ground, a road, a wide field of cabbages and then the barrier. Veiled Annis rode high and bluish in the clear sky. They crossed the field in soaring leaps, and shouts pursued them. The girl ran north a hundred yards behind the shadowy buttresses and squeezed through a narrow crack between two huge timber baulks. Cole barely made it, skinning his shoulders.

"I found this too when I was a little girl," Pia whispered. "I had to enlarge it when my hips grew, but only just enough. Morwenna grant they're all too big!"

"Morgan is, for sure," Cole said, rubbing his shoulder. "Pia, I *hate* to run."

"We must still run. My old plan was to reach here unseen, but now they know and they'll come over the wall in flyers. We'll have to hide in the thick brush near the forest edge until Uncle Garth returns."

She pulled a basket out of the shadows.

"Food," she said. "I brought it last night."

He carried the basket and they raced across the half-mile belt to concealment among high shrubbery and enormous mounds of fungi. Flyers with floodlights came low along the wall and others quartered the clearing. Cole and Pia stole nearer to the forest edge, into its shadow. They did not sleep.

Once he asked; "How about stompers?"

"They're a chance," she whispered. "Morgan's *sure*."

With daylight they saw four flyers patrolling instead of the usual one. At their backs colossal blackish-gray, deeply rugose tree trunks eighty feet in diameter rose up and up without a branch for many hundreds of feet. Then branches jutted out enormously and the colorful cascade of forest-top epiphytes came down the side and hung over their heads a thousand feet above.

Pia opened the food basket and they ate, seated on a bank. She wore her brown dress, her finest, he had learned, and she had new red shoes. She was quiet, as if tranced.

Cole remembered the picnic on the forest top, the secret island of beauty and innocence, and his heart stirred. He saw that the food basket was the same one. He did not tell her his thoughts.

They talked of trivial things or were silent for long periods. He held her hand. Once she roused herself to say, "Tomorrow, about this time, Uncle Garth will come looking for us." Shortly after, she gasped and caught his arm, pointing.

He peered, finally made a gestalt of broken outlines through the shrubbery. It was a stomper, swinging its head nervously.

"It smells us," she whispered. "Oh Flinter, forgive me darling. Take off your clothes, *quickly!*"

She undressed rapidly and hid her clothes. Cole undressed too, fear prickling his skin, remembering what Bidgrass had told him. The stomper moved nearer in a crackle of brush and stopped again.

Man and girl knelt trembling under a fan of red-orange fungus. The girl broke off a piece and motioned the man to do the same.

"When it comes, pretend to eat," she breathed, almost inaudibly. "Don't look up and don't say a word. Morwenna be with us now."

The stomper's shadow fell across them. The man's skin prickled and sweat sprang out. He looked at the girl and she was pale but not tense, munching on her piece of fungus. She clicked her teeth faintly and he knew it was a signal. He ate.

The stomper lifted the man by his right shoulder. It was like two fingers in a mitten holding him three times his own height off the ground. He saw the beak and the eye and his sight dimmed in anguish.

Then the right wing reached down and nipped the left shoulder of the rosy girl-body placidly crouching there. It swung her up to face the man momentarily under the great beak and the tricorn eye, and their own eyes met.

Very faintly she smiled and her eyes tried desperately to say, "I'm sorry" and "Goodbye, Flinter." His eyes cried in agony "No! No! I will not have it so!"

Then the two-fingered mitten became a nine-fingered mitten lapping him in darkness that bounced and swayed and he knew that the stomper was running into Lundy Forest. The wing was smooth and warm but not soft, and it smelled of cinnamon and sandalwood. The odor overpowered him and the man lapsed into stupor.

The man woke into a fantastic dream. Luminous surfaces stretched up to be lost in gloom, with columns of darkness between. The spongy ground on which he lay shone with faint blue light. Luminous, slanting walls criss-crossed in front of him. Close at hand, behind and to the right, enormous bracket fungi ascended into darkness in ten-foot steps that supported a profusion of higher order fungi in many bizarre shapes.

He stood up and he was alone.

He climbed over a slanting root-buttress and saw her lying there. He called her name and she rose lightly and came to him. Radiant face, dimpled arms, round breasts, cradling hips: *his* woman. They embraced without shame and she cried thanks to Morwenna.

He said, "People have come out of the forest. What are the rules?"

"We must eat only the seeds of the pure white fungus—that's the least dangerous. We must walk and walk to keep our bodies so tired and hungry that they use it all. We must keep to a straight line."

"We'll live," he said. "Outside among our people, with our minds whole. We'll alternate left and right each time we round a tree, to hold our straight line. We'll come out somewhere."

"I will follow. May Morwenna go with us."

The fantastic journey wound over great gnarled roots and buttresses fusing and intermingling until it seemed that the root-complex was one unthinkably vast organism with many trunks soaring half-seen into endless darkness. Time had no feeling there. Space was a bubble of ghostly light a man could leap across.

Could leap and did, over and over, the woman following. The man climbed a curiously regular, whitish root higher than his head and it writhed. Then, swaying back along its length, came a great serpent head with luminous ovoid eyes. While the man crouched in horror, waving the woman back, the monstrous jaws gaped and the teeth were blunt choppers and grinders, weirdly human looking. They bit hugely into a bracket fungus and worried at it. Man and woman hurried on.

Strength waned. The woman fell behind. The man turned back to her and the light was failing. The blue mold was black, the luminous panels more ghostly.

"It's night. Shall we sleep?" he asked.

"It's just come day," the woman said, pointing upward.

He looked up. Far above, where had been gloom, hung a pinkish-green, opalescent haze of light. Parallel lines of tree trunks converged through it to be lost in nebulosity.

"Daylight overpowers the luminous fungi," she said.

"We sleep, then walk again. Shall we find food?"

"No. We must always go to sleep hungry so we will wake again."

They looked, until tired out, for a place of shelter.

They slept, locked together in the cranny of a massive buttress. The man dreamed of his tame home-world.

He woke again into nightmare. In a twenty-foot fan-grove of the white fungus they combed handfuls of black spores out of gill slots. The birdshot-sized spores had a pleasant, nutty flavor.

With the strength more walking. *Use it, use it, burn the poison.* Day faded above, and luminous night below came back to light the way. A rocky ledge and another, and then a shallow ravine with a black stream cascading. They drank and the man said, "We'll follow it, find an upland clearing."

They heard rapid motion and crouched unbreathing while a stomper minced by up ahead. It had a white crest.

On and on, fatigue the whip for greater fatigue and salvation at the end of endurance. They passed wild humans. A statuesque woman with dull eyes and yellow hair to her ankles, placidly feeding. Babies big as four-year-old normals, by themselves, grazing on finger-shaped fungi. An enormous human, fourteen feet tall, fat-enfolded, too ponderous to stand even in low gravity, crawling through fungus beds. The man could not tell its sex.

On and on, sleep and eat and travel and sleep, darkness above or darkness below, outside of time. The stream lost, found again, sourcing out finally under a great rock. And there, lodged in a black sandbank, the man found a human thigh bone half his own height. He scoured off the water mold with sand. He was armed.

The man walked ahead clutching his thigh bone, and the woman followed. They slept clasped together naked all three, man, woman, and thigh bone.

Stompers passed them and they crouched in sham feeding. The man prayed without words, *both or neither*. And hatred grew in him.

Snakes and giant slugs and the beautiful, gigantic, mindless wild humans, again and again, a familiar part of nightmare. The fat and truly enormous humans; and the man learned they had been male once. He remembered from far away where time was linear the voice of Grandfather Man: *Some are beyond saving, and those they kill.*

And a stomper passed, white crested, and far ahead a human voice cried out in wordless pain and protest. The man was minded to deviate from his line for fear of what they might see, but he did not. When they came on the boy, larger than the man but beardless and without formed muscles, the man looked at the tears dropping from the dull eyes and the blood dropping from the mutilation and killed him with the thigh bone. *Some are beyond saving.* And the hatred in him flamed to whiteness.

On and on, day above and day below in recurrent clash of lights. A white crested stomper paused and looked at them, crouched apart and trembling. The man felt the deepest, most anguished fear of all and beneath it, hatred surged until his teeth ached.

On and on. The man's stubble softened into beard, his hair touched his ears. On and on.

The land sloped upward and became rocky. The trees became smaller and wider spaced so that whole trunks were visible and the light of upper day descended. A patch of blue sky, then more as they ran shouting with gladness, and a bare mountain crest reared in the distance.

They embraced in wild joy and the woman cried, "Thank you, oh *loveliest* Morwenna!"

"Pia, we're human again," Cole said. "We're back in the world. And I love you."

Fearful of stompers, they moved rapidly away from the forest over steadily rising ground. The growth became more sparse, the ground more rocky, and near evening they crossed a wide moorland covered with coarse grass and scattered blocks of stone. Ahead a long, low fault scarp bounded it and there they found a cave tunneled into the rock, too narrow for a stomper. At last they felt safe. Morwenna rode silvery above the distant forest.

Water trickled from the cave which widened into a squared-off chamber in which the water spilled over the rim of a basin that looked cut with hands. Underfoot were small stone cylinders of various lengths and as his eyes adjusted Cole saw that they were drill cores.

"Prospectors made this," he told Pia, "in the old, innocent days when they still hoped to find heavy metals." Then he saw the graven initials, T.C.B., and the date, 157 A.S.

They ate red berries growing in their dooryard, gathered grass for a bed and slept in a great weariness.

Next day and the next they ate red berries and fleshy, purple ground fruits and slept, gaining strength. Secure in their cave mouth they watched stompers cross the moorland. When night fell they gazed at the bunched moons, but the three Maidens did not quite form a house and Hoggy Darn was still pursuing them.

"A few days," Pia said.

"If this isn't Emrys Upland, Arscoate will kill us with fire mist."

She nodded.

More stompers crossed the moorland, some wilily crested. They moved there randomly at night and from the forest came a far-off sound of stompers singing. The Maidens formed a house and Hoggy Darn grazed the side of it before they fled. To south and west faint rose glowed in the night sky.

"Fire mist," Pia said. "The nights of harrying have begun. Oh Flinter, if this is really Emrys Upland it will be perfect."

"What will?"

"You—us—oh, I can't say yet."

"Secrets, Pia? Still secrets? Between us?"

"You'll know soon, Flinter. I mustn't spoil it."

The love in her eyes was tinged with a strangeness. She sought his arms and hid her face in his shoulder.

Stompers on the moorland all day so they dared not leave the cave. Flyers streaking high overhead, scouting.

"Pia, I believe this is Emrys Upland. I'll help after all with the great killing."

"You will help, Flinter."

"Afterward I'll take you to Belconti."

"We will never see Belconti, Flinter."

The strangeness in her eyes troubled him. He could not kiss it away.

Stompers crowding the moorland all night with their dancing, their vast singing coming to the cave from all round the compass. Rose banks distant in the night sky and Hoggy Darn crossing the House of the Maidens. Red Hoggy Darn, still lagging, still not catching it perfectly upright. The strangeness of Pia. The waiting, clutching a polished thigh bone.

At last the night when the mighty war song of the stompers went up unbearably, as the man had heard it that once before, and fire mist boiled along the distant mountains. Flyers shuttled across the sky, dropped, rose again. Blasters ripped the night with ion-pencils. Hoggy Darn gleamed redly on the threshold of the House of the Maidens that stood almost upright and perfect with silvery Morwenna at the vertex. Flyers blasted clearings in the throng of stompers, and grounded. Men boiled out of them, setting up Corbin powercasters here, there, another place, fighting as soon as their feet hit ground. The man stood up and brandished the thigh bone.

"I must go down and fight. Wait here."

"I must go too," the girl said calmly.

"Yes, you must," he agreed. "Come along."

Stompers rushed by them and bounded over their heads and did not harm them. Blaster-torn stompers fell heavily beside them, threshing and snapping, and they were not touched. Men lowered weapons to point at the man and girl, shouting to one another out of mazed faces silently in the whelming music of the stomper chorus. Man and girl walked on.

Unharmed through the forest of singing, leaping shapes, hand in hand through a screen of fighting men that parted to admit them, they walked into the light of a glowing Corbin where a tall, gaunt old man stood watching their approach. The feeling of exalted unreality began to lift from Cole.

"Grandfather, give us blasters," he shouted. "We want to fight."

"The power is on you, lad, and you only half know it," the old man shouted back. "Stand here by the Corbin. Your fight is not yet." Tears stood in the fierce old eyes.

Across the moorland the fighting raged. Islands of men and women grouped round their Corbins held back the booming, chaotic sea of stompers that surged against them from all sides. Dikes of dead and dying grew up, men and stompers mingled. The flyers shuttled down and up again and more islands of men took shape. Hoggy Darn crossed the threshold and the savage war song of the stompers shook the night sky.

In a lull Morgan came in to the Corbin to change the wave track on his blaster. His face was a mask of iron joy and his eyes blazed.

"Morgan, if we are both alive after, I will kill you!" Cole shouted.

"No," Morgan rumbled. "You have been into the forest and come out again. It took you three weeks. It took me three hundred years. Clasp hands, my brother in hatred."

"Yes, brother in hatred." The exalted unreality began coming back strongly. "I want a blaster!" he howled at Morgan.

"No, brother in hatred, your fight is not yet." Morgan rejoined the battle, the ring of men standing braced in blaster harness fifty yards away, ripping down with interweaving ion-pencils the great forms leaping inward. Man and girl held hands and watched.

To the left trouble came to a nearby island. Stompers converged from all sides, abandoning the other attacks, impossibly many. They overran the defenders, attacking not them but the power-caster behind them, and piled up until the Corbin's blue-violet glare was hidden. A great blossoming of flame tore the pile of stompers apart, but the Corbin was dark.

"They blew out the power banks," Pia said. "They've never known to do that before. Now the men still living have only pack charges."

It was a new tactic, a death-hour flash of insight for Grandfather Stomper. Across the moor, island after island went dark and the war song grew in savage exultation, but the man thought it dwindled in total volume. Then it was their own turn.

Cole and Pia crouched away from the Corbin in the lee of a stone block and two still-twitching stompers. Beside them Morgan and Bidgrass fired steadily at the shapes hurtling above. When the Corbin blew, a wave of stinking heat rolled over them. All around, survivors struggled to their feet, using flame pistols to head-shoot wounded stompers, digging out and connecting emergency pack charges to their blasters. They were pitifully few and their new, dark island was thirty feet across.

The moor seemed dark with only the red of flame pistols and the violet flickering of power pack blasters. It seemed to heave randomly like a sluggish sea with the seen struggles of dying stompers and the felt struggles of lesser human bodies. Thinned now, stompers attacked singly or in small groups. Blasters flickered and ripped and went darkly silent as power packs discharged. The red of short-range flame pistols replaced them. But across the fault scarp ridge the tumult swelled to new heights and Corbin after Corbin there flamed out of existence in a bloom of rose-purple against the skyline.

In a lull Bidgrass shouted to Morgan, "That's costing them more than they have to give, over there. Listen. Can you hear it?"

"Yes, Father in Hatred." Morgan said. "They will break soon."

"Yes, when Arscoate lays the fire mist. They will come through here. I have one charge left."

"I have two, Father in Hatred. Change packs with me."

Cole found his voice and his senses once more.

"I must find a weapon! Grandfather, give me your flame pistol!"

"Soon, lad. Soon now. Let the power take you," the old man soothed.

Stompers streamed over the moor again and the fighting flared up. The war song beat against the man's ears so that he drew the girl nearer and shook the thigh bone. Blaster fire flickered out altogether and the red blooming of flame pistols weakened. But more and more stompers streamed past without attacking. Then the man saw fire mist plume lazily in the east, point after point coalescing all along the forest edge.

"Now!" shouted a great voice beside him. "Now, lad!"

It was old Bidgrass, striding out like a giant, blaster leveled in its carrying harness.

The shout released Cole and he saw it far off, coming down the scrap rubble to the moor. Huger than any, white crest thirty feet above the ground, Grandfather Stomper. The war song roared insanely over the moor. Hoggy Darn gleamed heart-midst of the three lady moons.

The grim old man aimed and fired. The great bird-shape staggered and came on, left wing trailing. The old man waited until it was nearly on top of him and fired again. The stomper jerked its head and the bolt shattered the great tripart beak but did not kill it. With the right mitten-wing it reached down and swung its adversary twenty feet up, held him and haggled at him with its stumps of beak.

The old man's free right arm flailed wildly. Cole beat the stomper's leg with the thigh bone and howled in hatred. Then he saw the flame pistol lying where it had fallen from the holster. He picked it up, but the power was on him again and he did not use it. He hurled the thigh bone at the stomper's head, diverting it for a second, and tossed the pistol to old Bidgrass. He knew they could not fail.

The old man caught the pistol. When the great head swung back he held the muzzle against the tricorn eye and fired. Red plasma-jet burned into the brain behind it. The stomper bounded once in the air, dropped its slayer, ran three steps and collapsed.

The stomper song changed suddenly. It became a mournful lament, a dying into grieving subsonics. Cole knew that note. He had heard it from the stompers in the stone-floored pen when the butchers were hacking off their heads. He knew that Grandfather Stomper was dead forever, after seven hundred years of war.

Flyers crossed above, blasters were still at work across the ridge, but the war was ended. The power, whatever that sense of exalted unreality might be, left Cole; and he felt naked and ridiculous and wondered what he was doing there. Then he saw the girl bending above Garth Bidgrass and regained control of himself.

The strong old man was smiling wearily.

"We've won the war, lad," he said. "The next task is yours."

"I'll help you," Cole said.

"You'll lead. Oh, I'll live, but not for long. Centuries ago, lad, there was a prophecy, and until tonight people like myself and Arscoate thought it was only poetry, however literally Morgan and the other ex-wilds took it."

"What was it?"

"It foretells that on the night Grandfather Stomper shall die the new Grandfather Man will come naked out of the forest with his beautiful wife and armed with a thigh bone, and that he will lead us in the even greater task of reclamation that comes after. Your ritual title of address is 'Father in Love,' lad, and I'm just a broken old man now. Take up the burden."

Cole's throat swelled, choking speech for a moment.

"I can start," he said.

THE BOTTICELLI HORROR
LLOYD BIGGLE, JR.

EVEN FROM A THOUSAND FEET the town of Gwinn Center, Kansas, looked frightened.

The streets were deserted. The clumsy ground vehicles that crept along the twisting black ribbon of roadway miles beyond the town were headed south, running away. Stretched across the rich green of the cultivated fields was a wavering line of dots. As John Allen slanted his plane downward the dots enlarged and became men who edged forward doggedly, holding weapons at the ready.

The town was not completely abandoned. As Allen circled to pick out a landing place he saw a man dart from one of the commercial buildings, run at top speed along the center of a street, and with a final, furtive glance over his shoulder, disappear into a house. None of this surprised Allen. The message that had been plunked on his desk at Terran Customs an hour and a half before was explanation enough. The lurking atmosphere of terror, the fleeing townspeople, the grim line of armed men—Allen had expected all of that.

It was the tents that puzzled him.

They formed a square in a meadow near the edge of town, a miniature village of flapping brown and green canvas. Allen's message didn't account for the tents.

He circled again, spotted a police plane that was parked on one of the town's wider streets. A small group of men stood nearby in the shadow of a building. Allen completed his turn and pointed the plane downward.

Dr. Ralph Hilks lifted his nose from the scientific journal that had claimed his entire attention from the moment of their takeoff and peered down curiously. "Is this the place? Where is everyone?"

"Hiding, probably," Allen said. "Those that haven't already left."

"What are the tents?"

"I haven't any idea."

Hilks grunted. "Looks as if we've been handed a hot one," he said and returned to his reading.

Allen concentrated on the landing. They floated straight down and came to rest beside the police plane with a gentle thud.

Hilks closed his journal a second time. "Nice," he observed.

Allen cut the motor. "Thanks," he said dryly. "It has the new-type shocks."

They climbed out. The little group of men—there were four of them—had turned to watch them land. Not caring to waste time on formalities, Allen went to meet them.

"Allen is my name," he said. "Chief Customs Investigator. And this—" He paused until the pudgy, slow-moving scientist had caught up with him. "This is Dr. Hilks, our scientific consultant."

The men squared away for introductions. The tall one was Fred Corning, State Commissioner of Police. The young man in uniform was his aide, a Sergeant Darrow. The sturdy, deeply tanned individual with alert eyes and slow speech was Sheriff Townsend. The fourth man, old, wispy, with startlingly white, unruly hair and eyeglasses that could have been lifted from a museum, was Dr. Anderson, a medical doctor. All four of them were grim, and the horror that gripped the town had not left them unmarked, but at least they weren't frightened.

"You didn't waste any time getting here," the commissioner said. "We're glad of that."

"No," Allen said. "Let's not waste time now."

"I suppose you want to see the—ah—remains?"

"That's as good a place to start as any."

"This way," the commissioner said.

They moved off along the center of the street.

The house was one of a row of houses at the edge of town. It was small and tidy-looking, a white building with red shutters and window boxes full of flowers. The splashes of color should have given it a cheerful appearance, but in that town, on that day, nothing appeared cheerful.

The yard at the rear of the house was enclosed by a shoulder-high picket fence. They paused while the commissioner fussed with the fastener on the gate, and Dr. Hilks stood gaping at the row of houses.

The commissioner swung the gate open and turned to look at him. "See anything?"

"Chimneys!" Hilks said. "Every one of these dratted buildings has its own chimney. Think of it—a couple of hundred heating plants, and the town isn't large enough for one to function efficiently. The waste must be—"

The others moved through the gate and left him talking to himself.

At the rear of the yard a sheet lay loosely over unnatural contours. "We took photographs, of course," the commissioner said, "but it's so incredible—we wanted you to see—"

The four men each took a corner, raised the sheet carefully, and moved it away. Allen caught his breath and stepped back a pace.

"We left—things—just as they were," the commissioner said. "Except for the child that survived, of course. He was rushed—"

At Allen's feet lay the head of a blonde, blue-eyed child. She was no more than six, a young beauty who doubtless had already caused romantic palpitations in the hearts of her male playmates.

But no longer. The head was severed cleanly just below the chin. The eyes were wide open, and on the face was a haunting expression of indescribable horror. A few scraps of clothing lay where her body should have been.

A short distance away were other scraps of clothing and two shoes. Allen winced as he noticed that one shoe contained a foot. The other was empty. He circled to the other side, where two more shoes lay. Both were empty. Hilks was kneeling by the pathetic little head.

"No bleeding?" Hilks asked.

"No bleeding," Dr. Anderson said hoarsely. "If there had been, the other child—the one that survived—would have died. But the wounds were—cauterized, you might say, though I doubt that it's the right word. Anyway, there wasn't any bleeding."

Dr. Hilks bent close to the severed head. "You mean heat was applied—"

"I didn't say heat," Dr. Anderson said testily.

"We figure it happened like this," the commissioner said. "The three children were playing here in the yard. They were Sharon Brown, the eldest, and her little sister Ruth, who was three, and Johnnie Larkins, from next door. He's five. The mothers were in the house, and no one would have thought anything could possibly happen to the kids."

"The mothers didn't hear anything?" Allen asked.

The commissioner shook his head.

"Strange they wouldn't yell or scream or something."

"Perhaps they did. The carnival was making a powerful lot of noise, so the mothers didn't hear anything."

"Carnival?"

The commissioner nodded at the tents.

"Oh," Allen said, looking beyond the fence for the first time since he'd entered the yard. "So that's what it is."

"The kids were probably standing close together, playing something or maybe looking at something, and they didn't see the—see it—coming. When they did see it they tried to scatter, but it was too late. The thing dropped on them and pinned them down. Sharon was completely covered except for her head. Ruth was covered except for one foot. And Johnnie, maybe because he was the most active or maybe because he was standing apart a little, almost got away. His legs were covered, but only to his knees. And then—the thing ate them."

Allen shuddered in spite of himself. "Ate them? Bones and all?"

"That's the wrong word," Dr. Anderson said. "I would say—*absorbed* them."

"It seems to have absorbed most of their clothing, too," Allen said. "Also, Sharon's shoes."

The commissioner shook his head. "No. No shoes. Sharon wasn't wearing any, and it left the others' shoes. Well, this is what the mothers found when they came out. They're both in bad shape, and I doubt that Mrs. Brown will ever be the same again. We don't know yet whether Johnnie Larkins will recover. We don't know what the aftereffects might be when something like that eats part of you."

Allen turned to Hilks. "Any ideas?"

"I'd like to know a little more about this thing. Did anyone catch a glimpse of it?"

"Probably a couple of thousand people around here have seen it," the commissioner said. "Now we'll go talk to Bronsky."

"Who's Bronsky?" Allen asked.

"He's the guy that owned it."

They left Dr. Anderson at the scene of the tragedy to supervise whatever was to be done with the pathetic remains. The commissioner led the way through a rear gate and across the meadow to the tents.

Above the entrance a fluttering streamer read, JOLLY BROTHERS SHOWS. They entered, with Hilks mopping his perspiring face and complaining about the heat, Allen looking about alertly, and the others walking ahead in silence.

Allen turned his attention first to the strange apparatus that stood in the broad avenue between the tents. He saw miniature rocket ships, miniature planes, miniature ground cars, and devices too devious in appearance to identify, but he quickly puzzled out the fact that a carnival was a kind of traveling amusement park.

Hilks had paused to look at a poster featuring a row of scantily clad young ladies. "They look cool," he muttered, mopping his face again.

Allen took his arm and pulled him along. "They're also of unmistakable terrestrial origin. We're looking for a monster from outer space."

"This place is something right out of the twentieth century," Hilks said. "If not the nineteenth. Ever see one before?"

"No, but I've seen stuff like this in amusement parks. I guess a carnival just moves it around."

Sheriff Townsend spoke over his shoulder. "This carnival has been coming here every year for as long as I can remember."

They passed a tent that bore the flaming title, EXOTIC WONDERS OF THE UNIVERSE. The illustrations were lavishly colored and immodestly exaggerated. A gigantic flower that Allen recognized as vaguely resembling a Venusian Meat-Eater was holding a struggling rodent in its fangs. A vine, also from Venus, was in hot pursuit of a frantic young lady it had presumably surprised in the act of dressing. The plants illustrated were all Venusian, Allen thought, though the poster mentioned lichens from Mars and a Luna Vacuum Flower.

"That isn't the place," the commissioner said. "There isn't anything in there but plants and rocks."

"I'd like to take a look," Allen said. He raised the tent flap. In the dim light he could see long rows of plastic display cases, each tagged with the bright yellow import permit of Terran Customs.

"I'll take another look later, but things seem to be in proper order," he said.

They moved on and stopped in front of the most startling picture Allen had ever seen. A girl arose genie-like from the yawning opening of an enormous shell. Her shapely body was—perhaps—human. Tentacles intertwined nervously where her hair should have been. Her hands were webbed claws, her facial expression the rigid, staring look of a lunatic, and her torso tapered away into the sinister darkness of the shell's interior.

"This is it," the commissioner said.

"*This?*" Allen echoed doubtfully.

"That's one of the things it did in the act."

Hilks had been staring intently at the poster. Suddenly he giggled. "Know what that looks like? There was an old painting by one of those early Italians. Da Vinci, maybe. Or Botticelli. I think it was Botticelli. It was called 'The Birth of Venus,' and it had a dame standing on a shell in just about that posture—except that the dame was human and not bad-looking. I wonder what happened to it. Maybe it went up with the old Louvre. I've seen reproductions of it. I may have one at home."

"I doubt that it has much bearing on our present problem," the commissioner said dryly.

Hilks slapped his thigh. "Allen! Some dratted artist has a fiendish sense of humor. I'll give you odds this thing comes from Venus. It'll have to. And the painting was called, 'The Birth of Venus.' From heavenly beauty to Earthly horror. Pretty good, eh?"

"If you don't mind—" the commissioner said.

They followed him into the tent. Allen caught a passing glimpse of a sign that read, "Elmer, the Giant Snail. The World's Greatest Mimic." There was more, but he didn't bother to read it. He figured that he was too late for the show.

Bronsky was a heavy-set man of medium height, with a high forehead that merged with the gleaming dome of his bald head. His eyes were piercing, angry. At the same time he seemed frightened.

"Elmer didn't do it!" he shouted.

"So you say," the commissioner said. "This is Chief-Inspector Allen. And Dr. Hilks. Tell them about it."

Bronsky eyed them sullenly.

"Do you have a photograph of Elmer?" Allen asked.

Bronsky nodded and disappeared through a curtain at the rear of the tent. Allen nudged Hilks, and they walked together toward the curtain. Behind it was a roped-off platform six feet high. On the platform was a shallow metal tank. The tank was empty.

"Where Elmer performed, no doubt," Allen said.

"Sorry I missed him," Hilks said. "I use the masculine gender only as a courtesy due the name. We humans tend to take sex for granted, even in lower life forms, and we shouldn't."

Bronsky returned and handed Allen an envelope. "I just had these printed up," he said. "I think I'll make a nice profit selling them after the act."

"If I were you," Allen said, "I'd go slow about stocking up."

"Aw—Elmer wouldn't hurt nobody. I've had him almost three years, an' if he'd wanted to eat somebody he'da started on me, wouldn't he? Anyway, he won't even eat meat unless it's ground up pretty fine, an' he don't care much for it then. He's mostly a vegetarian."

Allen took out the glossy prints and passed the top one to Hilks.

"Looks a little like a giant conch shell," Hilks said. "It's much larger, of course. What did it weigh?"

"Three fifty," Bronsky said.

"I would have thought more than that. Has it grown any since you got him?"

Bronsky shook his head. "I figure he's full grown."

"He came from Venus?"

Bronsky nodded.

"I don't recall any customs listing of a creature like this."

Allen was studying the second print. It resembled—vaguely—the painting on the poster. The shell was there, as in the first photo, and protruding out of it was the caricature of a shapely Venus. The outline was hazy but recognizable.

The other photos showed other caricatures—an old bearded man with a pipe, an elephant's head, an entwining winged snake, a miniature rocket ship—all rising out of the cavernous opening.

"How do you do it?" Hilks asked.

"I don't do it," Bronsky said. "Elmer does it."

"Do you mean to say your act is genuine? That the snail actually forms these images?"

"Sure. Elmer loves to do it. He's just a big ham. Show him anyone or anything, and the first thing you know he's looking just like that. If you were to walk up to him, he'd think it over for a few seconds and then he'd come out looking pretty much like you. It's kind of like seeing yourself in a blurred mirror. I use that to close my act—I get some guy up on the stage and Elmer makes a pretty good reproduction of him. The audience loves it."

Hilks tapped the photo of the distorted Venus. "You didn't find a live model for that."

"Oh, no," Bronsky said. "Not for any of my regular acts. I got a young artist fellow to make some animated film strips for me. I project them onto a screen above the stage. The audience can't see it, but Elmer can. He makes a real good reproduction of that one—the snake hair twists around and the hands make clawing motions at the audience. It goes over big."

"I'll bet," Hilks said. "What does Elmer use for eyes?"

"I don't know. I've wondered about that myself. I've never been able to find any, but he sees better than I do."

"Is it a water creature or a land creature?"

"It doesn't seem to make much difference to him," Bronsky said. "I didn't keep him in water because it'd be hard to tote a big tank of water around. He drank a lot, though."

Hilks nodded and called the commissioner over. "Here's how I see it. Superficially, Elmer resembles some of the terrestrial uni-valve marine shells. That's undoubtedly deceptive. Life developed along different lines on Venus, and up until now we've found no similarity whatsoever between Terran and Venusian species. That doesn't mean that accidental similarities can't exist. Some of the Terran carnivores produce an acid that etches holes in the shells of the species they prey on. Then there's the common starfish, which paralyzes its victim with acid and then extrudes its stomach outside its body, wraps it around the victim, and digests it. Something like that must have happened to the kids. An acid is the only explanation for the effect of cauterization, and the way their bodies were—absorbed, the doctor said, a very good word—means that the digestive agent has a terrifying corrosive potency. The only puzzling thing about it is how this creature could move fast enough to get clear of the tent and all the way over to that house and surprise three agile children. Frankly, I don't understand how it was able to move at all, but it happened, and it isn't a pleasant thing to think about."

"How did Elmer get away?" Allen asked Bronsky.

"I don't know. We'd just finished a show, and I closed the curtains and saw the people out of the tent, and then I went back to the stage and he was gone. I didn't know he could move around. He never tried before."

"No one saw him after that?" Allen asked the commissioner.

The commissioner shook his head.

"May I see Elmer's license?" Allen asked Bronsky.

Bronsky stared at him. "Elmer don't need no license!"

Allen said wearily, "Section seven, paragraph nine of the Terran Customs Code, now ratified by all world governments. Any extra-terrestrial life form brought to this planet must be examined by Terran Customs, certified harmless, and licensed. Terran Customs may, at its discretion, place any restrictions it deems necessary upon the custody or use of such life. Did Elmer pass Terran Customs?"

Bronsky brightened. "Oh. Sure. This guy I bought Elmer from, he said all that stuff was taken care of and I wouldn't have any trouble."

"Who was he?"

"Fellow named Smith. I ran into him in a bar in San Diego. Told him I was in show business, and he said he had the best show on Earth in his warehouse. He offered to show it to me, and I walked into this room where there wasn't nothing but a big shell, and the next thing I knew I was looking at myself. I knew it was a natural. He wanted twenty-five grand, which was all the money I had, and I wrote him a check right on the spot. The very next day Elmer and I were in business, and we did well right from the start. As soon as I got enough money together to have the film strips made we did even better. I got a receipt from this guy Smith, and he certified that the twenty-five grand included all customs fees. It's in a deposit box in Phoenix."

"Did Smith give you a Terran Customs license for Elmer?"

Bronsky shook his head.

Allen turned away. "Place this man under arrest, Commissioner."

Bronsky yelped. "Hey—I haven't done anything! Neither has Elmer. You find him and bring him back to me. That's your job."

"My job is to protect the human race from fools like you."

"I haven't done anything!"

"Look," Allen said. "Ten, twelve years ago there was a serious famine in Eastern Asia. It took all the food reserves of the rest of the world to keep the populations from starving. There was no harvest of cereal crops for two years, and it all happened because a young space cadet brought home a Venusian flower for his girl. It was only a potted plant—nothing worth bothering customs about, he thought. But on that plant were lice, Venusian lice. Not many Venusian insects would thrive in Earth's atmosphere, but these did, and they had the food supplies of Japan and China ruined before we knew they were around. By the time we stopped them they were working into India and up into the Democratic Soviet. We spent a hundred million dollars, and finally we had to import a parasite from Venus to help us. That parasite could eventually do as much harm as the lice. It'll be decades before the whole mess is cleaned up.

"We have dozens of incidents like this every year, and each one is potentially disastrous. Even if Elmer didn't kill those kids, he could be carrying bacteria capable of decimating the human race. This is something for you to think about in the years to come. The minimum prison term for having unlicensed alien life in your possession is ten years. The maximum is life."

Bronsky, stricken silent, was led away by Sergeant Darrow.

"Do you suppose there really was a Smith?" the commissioner asked.

"It's likely. There've been a lot of Smiths lately. It was a mistake for the government to dump those surplus spaceships on the open market. A lot of retired spacers picked them up expecting to make a fortune freighting ore. They couldn't make expenses, so some of them took to smuggling in anything they could pick up, figuring that there'd be a nice profit in souvenirs from outer space. Unfortunately, they were right. Who's this?"

A dignified, scholarly looking man entered the tent and stood waiting by the entrance.

"Did you want something?" the commissioner asked.

"I'm Professor Dubois," the man said. "You probably don't remember me, but a short time ago you were asking if anyone had seen that perfidious snail. I haven't seen it, but I can tell you one of the places it went. It broke open one of my display cases and ate an exhibit."

"Ah!" Allen exclaimed. "You'll be from the Exotic Wonders of the Universe. You say the snail ate one of the 'Wonders'?"

"I don't know what else would have wanted it that badly."

"What was it?"

"Venusian moss."

"Interesting. The snail's been on Earth nearly three years, and it probably missed its natural diet. Let's have a look."

A plastic display case at the rear of the tent had been ripped open. Inside lay a bare slab of mottled green rock—Venusian rock.

"When did it happen?" Allen asked.

"I couldn't say. Obviously at a time when the tent was empty."

"None of your customers noticed that a Wonder was missing?"

He shook his head. "They'd think the rock was the exhibit. It's about as interesting as the moss. There wasn't much to it but the color scheme—yellows and reds and blacks with a kind of a sheen."

"And so friend Elmer likes moss. That's an interesting point, since Bronsky claims the snail was by preference a vegetarian. Thank you for letting us know. If you don't mind, we'll take charge of this display case. We might be able to let you have it back later."

"It's ruined anyway. You're welcome to it."

"Would you look after it, Commissioner? Just see that no one touches it until our equipment arrives. I want a close look at some of these Wonders."

The commissioner sighed. "If you say so. But I can't help thinking you two aren't acting overly concerned about this thing. You've been here the best part of two hours, and all you've done is walk around and look at things and ask questions. I've got three hundred men out there in the fields, and what we're mostly worried about is how we're supposed to handle this snail if we happen to catch him."

"Sorry," Allen said. "I should have told you. I have five divisions of army troops being flown in. They're on their way. The corps commander will place this entire county under martial law as soon as he touches down. Another five divisions are under stand-by orders for use when and if the general thinks he needs them. We have a complete scientific laboratory ordered, we've drafted the best scientists we can lay our hands on, and we're reserving one of the Venus frequencies for our own use in case we need information from the scientific stations there. Alien life is unpredictable, and we've had some bitter experiences with it. And—yes, you might say we're concerned about this."

From somewhere in the darkness came the snap of a rifle, and then another, and finally a rattling hum as the weapon was switched to full automatic.

"I didn't expect that," Allen said.

"Why not?" Hilks asked.

"These are regular troops. They shouldn't be shooting at shadows."

"Maybe word got around about what happened to the kids."

"Maybe." Allen went to the door of their tent. Corps Headquarters was a blaze of light; the remainder of the encampment was dark, but the men were stirring nervously and asking one another about the shooting. The full moon lay low on the horizon, silhouetting the orderly rows of tents.

"What were you muttering about just now?" Allen asked.

"I'm still trying to figure out how Elmer got his six-foot shell from one tent to another, and smashed that display, and ate the moss, and got himself across fifty yards of open ground and over a fence into that yard and grabbed off the kids before they saw him coming, and then got clean away. It's enough to make a man mutter."

"It was a much better trick than that," Allen said. "He also did it without leaving any marks. You'd think an object that large and heavy would crush a blade of grass now and then, but Elmer didn't. Which really leaves only one explanation."

"The damned thing can fly."

"Right," Allen said.

"How?"

"It's the world's greatest mimic. Bronsky says so. When it feels like it, it can make like a bird."

Hilks rejected the suggestion profanely. "It must be jet-propelled," he said. "Our own squids can do it in water. It's theoretically possible to do it in air, but in order to lift that much weight, it'd have to pump—let's see, cubic capacity, air pressure—what are you doing?"

"Going back to bed. I'd like to get some sleep, but between the army's shooting and your snoring—did you send a message to Venus?"

"Yes," Hilks said. "I asked for Elmer's pedigree."

"I'll give you two-to-one Venus has never heard of him."

Hilks reflected. "I think fifty-to-one would be fairer odds."

Allen closed his eyes. Hilks continued to mutter. He would not be able to sleep until he had reduced the jet-propelled Elmer to a satisfactory mathematical basis. Allen considered it a waste of time. He had no faith in Earth mathematics when applied to alien life forms.

Hilks turned on a light. A moment later his portable computer hummed to life. Allen turned over and kicked his blanket aside. The night was distressingly warm.

Footsteps crunched outside their tent. A tense voice snapped, "Allen? Hilks?"

"Come in," Allen said. Hilks continued to mutter and to punch buttons on the computer.

The tent flap zipped open, and a very young major stood blinking in at them. "General Fontaine would like to see you."

"Do we have time to dress, or is the general in a hurry?"

"I'd say he's in a powerful hurry."

Allen pulled on his dressing gown and slipped on a pair of shoes. Hilks was out of the tent ahead of him, shuffling along in his pajamas. The camp seemed suddenly wide awake, with voices coming from every tent.

They found General Fontaine in his operations headquarters pacing up and down in front of a map board. An overlay of colored scribbles identified troop positions. The general had aged several years since that afternoon. Obviously he had not been to bed, and he wore the weary, frustrated look of a man who has just realized that he might not get to bed.

"I've lost a man," he announced to Allen.

"How?" Allen asked.

"He's disappeared."

"Without a trace?"

"Not exactly," the general said. "He left his shoes."

Despite strict orders that sentries were to stand duty in pairs, the missing man, Private George Agazzi, had been posted alone on the edge of a small wood. Nearby sentries heard him shout a challenge and then open fire. They could not leave their posts to investigate, but Agazzi's sergeant was on the spot within minutes.

A patrol searched the wood and found no trace of the missing man. Reinforcements were called out, and the search was expanded. Half an hour later a staff officer found Agazzi's rifle, sundry items of equipment, and his shoes in tall grass less than six feet from his post. None of the searchers had seen them.

"Want to have a look?" the general asked.

Hilks shook his head. "In the morning, perhaps. We've already seen something similar, and I doubt that there's anything to be learned there tonight. Perhaps you'd better put three men on a post."

"You think this snail got Agazzi?"

"I'm sure of it."

"He wasn't the best-disciplined soldier in my corps, but he was tough, and he knew how to handle himself. He fired a full clip of atomic pellets, and that would make mincemeat out of any snail. It doesn't make sense. I'd be inclined to think he's gone A.W.O.L. if it weren't for one thing."

"Right," Hulks said. "He wouldn't have left his shoes."

They returned to their tent, and Allen lay awake with the camp stirring around him and sifted through the few facts he had collected. He could not fit them together. He examined each one carefully, testing it, pushing it aside, trying it again. Either he desperately needed more facts, or—could it be that he already had too many?

Patrols passed their tent, and occasionally the soldiers' muttered remarks were sharp enough to be understood. "How often does this thing get hungry?" one wanted to know. Allen wished he knew the answer. He lay awake until dawn.

Allen had worn his facts threadbare, and he could think of only one avenue of exploration still open to him. He had to interview young Johnnie Larkins, who had, through chance or agility, lost only his legs to the thing from Venus. Allen fervently hoped he had lived to tell about it.

General Fontaine established a "Contaminated Zone" centering about the town of Gwinn Center. The first problem, as he saw it, was to contain the thing within this zone. The second problem was to find it and destroy it.

He ringed the zone with armed men and attempted to move all civilians out. Some of the carnival people and a few other crotchety individuals refused to go, one of them being Dr. Anderson. Allen advised against the use of force, so the general contented himself with gloomily forecasting their probable fate and allowed them to remain.

Allen found Dr. Anderson in his home, which was also his office. The front room was a waiting room furnished with comfortable, antique-looking chairs. On the door to the inner office a small sign read, "Doctor is in. Please be seated." Allen ignored it and knocked firmly on the door.

Dr. Anderson emerged with a scowl of stern disapproval on his wrinkled face. "Oh," he said. "It's you. What d'ya want?"

Allen told him. The doctor's scowl deepened, and he said, "Office hours. I couldn't leave before noon, and I'd have to be back by two."

"I rather doubt that you'll be having any patients this morning, Doctor. Gwinn Center's population has been reduced to something like two dozen and all of them are staying home."

"Matter of principle," the doctor said.

"If this mess isn't cleared up, you may never have any patients. I'm hoping that the boy can help us."

Dr. Anderson stroked one withered cheek and continued to scowl. Finally, with an abrupt motion, he turned to the sign on the door and reversed it. "Doctor is out," it read.

"I'll get my hat," he said.

They walked out to the street together, and Allen handed the doctor into his plane. He turned for a last look about the abandoned town and felt a twinge of alarm as somewhere far down the street a door slammed. "There should be troops stationed in town," he told himself. "I'll speak to the general about it."

They flew south. The doctor continued to grumble until Allen patiently explained a second time that the boy would undoubtedly feel more comfortable answering questions with a familiar face present, and then he sulkily settled down to watch the scenery.

Langsford was a modern city, with tall apartment buildings rising from its park-like residential sections. The hospital was part of a vast service complex at the center of the city, a low, web-like structure with narrow, sprawling wings. All of the inner rooms opened into plastic-domed parks.

They found the boy outside his room laughing gaily, a squirrel perched on each arm of his powered chair and a flock of brightly colored birds fluttering about him. The birds flew into a nearby tree when they approached. The squirrels remained motionless.

"Hello, Johnnie," Dr. Anderson said.

The boy smiled at the doctor and then turned large, brown, extremely serious eyes on Allen.

"Found yourself a couple of pets, I see," the doctor said.

"They're my friends," Johnnie said and ceremoniously offered each squirrel a nut.

"Mr. Allen wants to ask you some questions about your accident. Do you feel like talking about it?"

"I don't know much about it," the boy said.

"Can you tell me what happened?" Allen asked.

The boy shook his head. "We were playing. Sharon and Ruthie and me. Then it grabbed me. I couldn't get away. It hurt."

"What did it look like?"

"A rug," the boy said.

Allen pondered that. "What sort of rug?"

"A real pretty rug. It was sailing through the air, and it landed on us."

"What color was it?"

The boy hesitated. "Lots of colors."

Allen scratched his head and tried to envision a sailing, multi-colored rug. "A big rug?" he asked.

"Real big."

"As big as a blanket?"

The boy frowned. "Not a real big blanket, I guess."

Dr. Anderson spoke in a low voice. "You can pinpoint the size by the area it covered."

Allen didn't agree, but he smiled and continued his questions. "How high did it fly, Johnnie?"

"Don't know," the boy said.

"Was it attached to something?"

The boy looked puzzled.

"I mean, was it fastened onto something?"

"Don't know."

"Okay, Johnnie. We want to try and catch that rug before it hurts someone else. You've been a help. If you should remember anything else about it, you tell your doctor, and he'll see that I'm told."

They walked away and left the boy with the motionless squirrels.

"Dratted waste of time," Dr. Anderson said.

"Perhaps. There's the matter of colors to consider. Could Elmer make himself different colors? The photos I saw were black and white."

"He could," the doctor said.

"You're sure about that?"

"I was one of the people he did an imitation of. This fellow Bronsky called me up on that platform. I only went out of curiosity. Then that dratted snail did an imitation of me. Made me feel like a dratted fool. But I was wearing a black suit and a red necktie, and it didn't have any trouble with those colors. Showed me wearing a black suit and a red necktie."

"Then that part is all right. As for the part about flying through the air—I wonder if it can come out of its shell and fly around. That would—perhaps—explain things."

"Don't see what there is to be explained," the doctor grumbled. "Catch the thing and do away with it before it eats someone else. Explain about it afterward if you think you have to."

The doctor had nothing more to say, not even when Allen landed him back in Gwinn Center. He shrugged off Allen's thanks and marched resolutely through his front door. Through the window Allen saw him reverse the sign to read, "Doctor is in. Please be seated." He disappeared into his inner office and closed the door firmly.

When Allen got back to base camp he found that the laboratory plane had arrived, a gigantic old converted transport. The scientists Hilks had requisitioned had also begun to report, but many of them would have little to do until someone brought in Elmer, dead or alive, for them to work on.

Hilks had set up an office for himself in what had been the navigation room, and he looked thoroughly at home as he waved a cigar with one hand and a piece of paper with the other.

"The trouble is," Hilks announced to Allen, "all the experts we need are on Venus, because if they stayed here they'd have so little Venusian life to study that they wouldn't be experts. And if we were to ask them to dash back here to help us cope with one so-called snail, they'd laugh us right out of the Solar System. Did you get anything?"

"Maybe," Allen said. He transferred a pile of books from a chair to the table and seated himself. "Elmer is more talented than we'd thought. He decks himself out in technicolor. The doctor saw him on display and verifies that. And the injured boy says Elmer looked like a pretty rug flying through the air."

"We figured he had to fly," Hilks said.

"Yeah. But that youngster is no dunce, and if he saw a big shell come whizzing through the air, I don't think he'd call it a rug."

"What do you want us to do?"

"We've got to come up with something that'll help Fontaine capture it and keep it captured."

"Uh huh," Hilks said, scowling. "I've been studying the report on Private Agazzi. He did empty a full clip at whatever it was he saw, and his officer thinks he was a good enough shot to hit what he aimed at. Add the fact that while you were gone a patrol spotted Elmer skimming across a field. They called it skimming. He vanished into a large grove of trees, and I do mean vanished. The general had a regiment standing by for just that contingency, and he dropped them around the grove in nothing flat. That was two hours ago, and they still haven't found anything."

"Are any of them missing?"

Hilks shook his head. "Maybe Elmer hasn't had time to get hungry again. We've come up with a thought that's somewhat less than pleasant. Elmer might be able to reproduce all by himself, and if he likes Earth enough to start populating the planet with baby snails, this continent could become a rather unpleasant place to live."

"Have you come up with anything at all?"

"Sure. One of the boys has designed a nifty steel net to be dropped out of a plane—if Elmer is ever spotted from a plane. We're also working on some traps, but it's a little hard to decide what to use for bait, since the only thing Elmer seems to like to eat is people. We might ask for volunteers and put cages inside the traps. Touchy proposition, we don't know what sort of a cage would keep Elmer out, just as we also don't know what sort of trap would keep him in."

"Did you do anything with that plastic display case Elmer broke into?" Allen asked.

"No," Hilks said. "I had it brought over here, but I completely forgot about it. Let's go look at it now. Meyers, find someone who knows something about Venusian moss and fungus and related subjects. Since Elmer likes that particular moss enough to break a display case to get it, maybe we could use it for bait."

"Never mind," Allen said. "We're slipping on this thing, Hilks. That exhibit was licensed, so Terran Customs will have a complete file on it. I'll ask for a report."

Allen copied the license number and called his office from the plane's communications room, using his own emergency channel. Ten minutes later he bounded wildly into Hilks's office.

"What's the matter?" Hilks demanded.

"Everything. Get this Professor Dubois over here and fast. That exhibit was never registered. The license is a forgery."

The professor waved his arms excitedly. "I never dreamed!" he exclaimed. "I have been extremely careful with all of my exhibits. It does not pay not to be careful. But you must admit that the license looks genuine."

"You say you bought the exhibit on the West Coast," Allen said. "Tell us about it."

"Let's see—it was maybe three years ago. I was showing in up-state California. Fellow came in one day and said he was breaking up his own exhibit and had a few things left to sell. He made them sound good, and I went all the way to San Diego to see what he had. It really wasn't bad stuff—it would have been a good basic collection for someone starting out, but there wasn't anything there that would have helped my collection. I took that one because I hated to waste a trip and he made me a good price. And it was a pretty thing."

"Could you describe this man?"

"I doubt it. It's been a long time. His name? Oh—that I remember. It was Smith."

"Describe this 'moss' again, please."

"Well, like I said, it was pretty stuff. Vivid colors, red and black and yellow and white without any special pattern. It had a nice sheen to it—looked like a hunk of thick blanket."

"Or a hunk of rug?" Allen suggested.

"Well, yes. I suppose you could say rug."

Allen backed over to a chair and sat down heavily. "The fact that it was small and thick means nothing. 'Thick' things some-times unfold into objects many yards square. Hilks, take a look at that case. Take a good look. I want to know if it was smashed by something breaking into it, or by something breaking out of it."

Hilks bent over the case. "It bulges," he announced. "If the snail could apply suction, it might have made it bulge this way."

Allen went to have a look. "The sides bulge, too," he said. "It looks as though something inside applied force in all directions, and the top gave first."

Hilks nodded slowly. "Yes, it does look that way. Without a demonstration to the contrary by the snail, I'd say that something broke out of here."

Allen returned to his chair. For twenty years he had been studying Venus and all things Venusian, assimilating every scrap of information and every report that came his way. Now he could rearrange his facts, and this time he could make them fit.

"Ever hear of a Venusian Night Cloak?" he asked.

They shook their heads.

"You have now. Tell General Fontaine to call off his snail hunt. This problem may be a lot worse than we'd thought."

They sat around a table in the large upper room of the lab plane—Allen, Hilks, General Fontaine, and Professor Dubois. Hilks's scientists had crowded into the room behind them.

Allen started the projector. The screen erupted a Venusian jungle, its blanched vegetation having a revolting, curdled appearance through the steaming mist. The camera shifted upward, taking in a square of greenish sky. In the distance, just above the seething treetops, appeared a blob of color. It enlarged slowly as it sailed toward them, a multicolored flat surface that rippled and twisted and curled in flight.

"That's it!" the professor exclaimed. "The markings are just like my moss."

It came on until it filled the screen. Suddenly it plummeted away, and the camera followed it until it disappeared into the jungle.

Allen switched off the projector. "Officially that's the closest anyone has gotten to one," he said. "Now we know otherwise. My feeling is that a number of scientists missing and presumed dead in the Great Doleman Swamp got rather too close to a Night Cloak."

The professor looked stricken. "This—my moss—killed those innocent children?"

"None of our facts fit the snail. All of them fit the Night Cloak."

"Why do they call it a Night Cloak?" the general asked.

"It was first observed at night, and it seems most active then. It grows to an enormous size, and as far as anyone on Venus knows—and don't forget there's a lot of the planet to be explored yet—it is found only in the Great Doleman Swamp. That's the reason so little is known about it. A jungle growing in a swamp isn't the easiest place for field work, and a Venusian jungle is impossible. Stations on the edge of the swamp occasionally observe the Night Cloaks, but always from a distance. They seem to be a unique life form, and the scientists were naturally curious about them. Twice expeditions were sent out to capture a specimen, and both parties disappeared without a trace. No one thought to blame the Night Cloaks—there are enough other things in that swamp that can do away with a man, especially some of the giant amphibians.

"This film strip was shot by a lucky pilot who happened to be hanging motionless over the swamp. A Night Cloak won't approach a moving plane. The scientific reports contain little but speculation. Frankly, gentlemen, we already know more about the Night Cloak than Venus does, and we're going to have to learn in a hurry something Venus hasn't discovered in a hundred years of field work: How to catch one."

"This fellow Smith caught one," Professor Dubois said.

"It was obviously a young one, and it's possible that they have periods of dormancy when one could be picked up easily—fortunately for Smith. Something about being transported and placed in Earth's atmosphere kept it dormant. It's our misfortune that it didn't die."

General Fontaine was drumming on the table with his fingers. "You say we know more about them than Venus knows. Just what do we know?"

"We know that you can't shoot one. Private Agazzi probably punched a lot of holes in it, but how would you aim at vital organs of a creature thirty feet square and who knows what fraction of an inch thick? We know that it has strength. It broke that plastic display case apart. We know a few unpleasant things about its diet and how it ingests food. We even know that its victims are likely to leave their shoes behind, which may or may not be a vital bit of information. And we know that our contaminated zone isn't worth a damn because a Night Cloak can fly right over the ground troops and probably already has."

"I'll have to call up all the planes I can get ahold of," the general said. "I'll have to reorganize the ground troops so I can rush them in when the thing is sighted."

"Excuse me, sir," said the young scientist named Meyers. "What was that you said a moment ago about shoes?"

"Just a little peculiarity of our Night Cloak," Allen told him. "It will totally consume a human body, and it doesn't mind clothing, but shoes absolutely do not appeal to it. It eats the feet and stockings right out of them, sometimes, but it leaves the shoes. I don't know what it means, but it's one positive thing we do know."

"Just a moment," Meyers said. He pushed his way out of the room and ran noisily down the stairway. He returned waving a newspaper. "I picked this up when I came through Langsford this morning," he said.

He passed the paper to Allen, who glanced at the headline and shrugged. "Monster still at large."

"That isn't exactly news to us," General Fontaine said.

"It's down at the bottom of the page," Meyers said. "A woman went for a walk last night and disappeared. They found her handbag in a park on the edge of Langsford, and a short distance away they found her shoes."

The general sucked in his breath sharply and reached for the paper. Hilks leaned back, folded his hands behind his head, and looked at the ceiling.

"Langsford," Allen said slowly. "Forty miles. But it also got Private Agazzi last night."

"If we make this public, it'll start a panic," General Fontaine said. "We'll have to evacuate the eastern half of the state. And if we don't make it public—"

"We'll have to make it public," Allen said.

"I'll have to order in my five reserve divisions. I'll need them for police work, and I'll need their transport to get the people out. God knows how far that thing may have gone by now."

"Message from Venus," a voice called. It was handed to Hilks, who read it and tossed it onto the table disgustedly.

"I asked Venus about the mollusk. They've checked all their records, and as far as they know it has no Venusian relatives. They ask, please, if we will kindly send it along to them when we're finished with it, preferably alive. They'd like to study it."

General Fontaine got to his feet. "Shall I take care of the news release?" he asked Allen.

"I'll handle it," Allen said and reached for a piece of paper. He studied a map for a moment, and then he wrote, "Notice to the populations of Kansas, Oklahoma, Arkansas, Missouri, Iowa, Nebraska, and Colorado."

For five days Allen sat at a desk in the lab plane answering inquiries, sifting through reports and rumors, searching vainly for a fact, an idea, that he could convert into a weapon. The lab's location was changed five times and he hardly noticed the moves.

The list of victims grew with horrifying rapidity. A farmer at work in his fields, a housewife hurrying along a quiet street to visit a friend, a sheriff's deputy investigating a report of looting in an abandoned town, an off-duty soldier who left his bivouac area for reasons best known to himself—Allen compiled the list, and Hilks added the shoes to his collection.

"This may not be the half of it," Allen said worriedly. "With so many people on the move, it'll be weeks before we get reports on everyone that's missing."

General Fontaine's Contaminated Area doubled and tripled and tripled again. On the third day the Night Cloak was sighted near the Missouri-Kansas border, and the populations of four states were in panicky flight.

That same night old Dr. Anderson got a call through to Allen from Gwinn Center. "That dratted thing is fussing around my window," he said.

"That can't be," Allen told him. "It was sighted two hundred miles from there this afternoon."

"I'm watching it while I talk to you," the doctor said.

"I'll send someone right away."

They found Dr. Anderson's shoes near a broken window, directly under the sign that read, "Doctor is in."

The next morning an air patrol sighted an abandoned ground car just across the Missouri border. It landed to investigate and found mute evidence of high tragedy. A family of nine had been fleeing eastward. The car had broken down, and the driver got out to make repairs. At that moment the horror had struck. In and around the car were nine pairs of shoes.

Hilks was losing weight, and he had also lost much of his good-natured nonchalance. "That thing can't travel that fast," he said. "The car must have been sitting there for a couple of days."

"Fontaine has traced it," Allen told him. "The family left home yesterday afternoon, and it'd have reached the place the car was found about ten o'clock last night."

"That's when the doctor called."

"Right," Allen said.

Lieutenant Gus Smallet was one small cog in the enormous observation grid General Fontaine hung over eastern Kansas and western Missouri. His plane was a veteran road-hopper, a civilian model pressed into service when the general received emergency authority to grab anything that would fly. It was armed only with a camera that Smallet had supplied himself.

Smallet flew slowly in a straight line, his plane being one of a vast formation of slow-moving observation planes. It was his third day on this fruitless search, his third day of taking off into the pre-dawn darkness and flying until daylight faded, and he was wondering which he would succumb to first, fatigue or boredom. His head ached. Other portions of his anatomy ached worse, especially that which had been crushed against an uncomfortable, thinly padded seat for more hours than

Smallet cared to remember. His movements had become mechanical, his thoughts had long since taken flight to other, more pleasant subjects than a Venusian Night Cloak, and he had stopped asking himself whether he would recognize the damned thing if he happened to see it.

Suddenly, against the dark green of a cluster of trees, he glimpsed a fleck of color. He slipped into a shallow dive, staring hypnotically as the indistinct blur grew larger and took on shape.

A bellow from his radio jolted Smallet back to reality. His sharp-eyed commanding officer, whose plane was a speck somewhere on the horizon, was telling him to stop horsing around and keep his altitude.

"I see the damned thing!" Smallet shouted. "I see—"

What he did see so startled him that he babbled incoherently and did not realize until afterward that he had instinctively flipped the switch on his camera. It was well that he had done so. His story was received with derision, and his commanding officer sniffed his breath suspiciously and muttered words that sounded direly like *Courts-Martial.*

Then the developed film was brought in, and what Smallet had seen was there for all to gape at.

Not one Night Cloak, but five.

It was dark by the time the transports started pouring ground troops into the area. They lost seven men that night and saw nothing at all.

Solly Hertz was an ordnance sergeant with ability and imagination. So when Hertz told his captain that he wanted to go to division headquarters to discuss an idea he had about these Night Cloak things, the captain paled at the thought of losing the one man who could keep his electronic equipment operating. He confined Hertz to the company area and mopped his brow over the narrow margin of his escape.

Hertz went A.W.O.L., by-passed division and corps and army, and invaded the sanctuary of the supreme air commander. That much-harassed general encountered Hertz through the accident of seeing a squad of military police leading him away. Fortunately he had enough residual curiosity to inquire about the offense and ask Hertz what he wanted.

"One of your guys sees one of these Night Cloaks," Hertz said. "What's he supposed to do about it?"

"Blast it," the general said promptly.

"Won't do any good," Hertz said. "Slugs and shrapnel just punch holes in it, and that don't bother it none. And a contact fuse wouldn't even go off when it hit. It's like shooting at tissue paper."

"You think you can do something about that?" the general asked.

"I got an atomic mini-rocket with a proximity fuse. It'll trigger just before it hits the thing. It'll *really* blast it."

"You're sure it won't go off at the wrong time and cost me a pilot?"

"Not the way I got it fixed."

"How many have you got?"

"One," Hertz said. "How many do you want?"

"Just for a starter, about five thousand. Tell me what you need and get to work on it."

Captain Joe Carr took off the next morning equipped with two of Hertz's rockets. Before he entered his plane he crossed fingers on both hands and spat over his left shoulder. And once inside the plane he went through a brisk ceremony of clicking certain switches on and off with certain predetermined fingers. Having thus dutifully sacrificed to the goddess of luck, he was not at all surprised an hour later when he sighted a Night Cloak.

It was a big one. It was enormous, and Carr glowed with satisfaction as he made a perfect approach, fired one rocket, and circled to see if another was needed.

It was not. The enormous, rippling surface was suddenly seared into nothingness—almost. The rocket hit it dead center, and when Carr completed his turn he saw the Night Cloak looking, as he said later, like the rind off a piece of bologna.

But even as he yelped news of his triumph into the radio, the rind collapsed crazily and parted, and four small, misshapen Night Cloaks flew gently downward to disappear into the trees.

Private Edward Walker was thinking about shoes. Night Cloaks never ate shoes. Flesh and bones and clothing and maybe even metal, but not shoes. That was official.

"All right," Walker told himself grimly. "If one of those things comes around here, I'll kick the life out of it."

He delivered a vicious practice kick and felt very little the better for it; and the truth was that Private Edward Walker had excellent reason for his uneasiness.

His regiment was deployed around a small grove of trees. Two Night Cloaks had been sighted entering the trees. The place had been kept under observation, and as far as anyone knew they were still there, but the planes hovering overhead, and the cautious patrols of lift-equipped soldiers that looped skittishly over the grove, from one side to the other, had caught no further glimpse of them.

Walker had put in an hour of lift-patrolling himself, and he hadn't liked it. He had the uncomfortable feeling, as he floated over the trees and squinted down into the shadows, that someone was using him for bait. This was maybe excusable if it promised to accomplish anything, but so far as anyone knew these Cloaks had the pernicious habit of taking the bait and never getting caught. The casualty list was growing with appalling speed, the Cloaks were getting fat—or at least getting bigger—and not one of them had been destroyed.

But the brass hats had tired of that nonsense and decided to make a stand. This insignificant grove of trees could well be the Armageddon of the human race.

Walker's captain had been precise about it. "If these things go on multiplying, it means the end of humanity. We've got to stop them, and this is the place and we're the guys to do it."

The men looked at each other, and a sergeant was bold enough to ask a question. "Just how are we going to knock them off?"

"They're working that out right now," the captain said. "I'll let you know as soon as I get the Word."

That had been early morning. Now it was noon, and they were still waiting for the Word. Private Walker felt more like bait with each passing minute. He looked again at his indestructible shoe leather. "I'll kick the life out of them," he muttered.

"Walker!" his sergeant bellowed. "You going off your nut? Sit down and relax."

Walker walked toward the sergeant. "It's true, isn't it? That business about the Cloaks not eating shoes?"

Sergeant Altman took a cautious glance at his own shoes and nodded.

"Shoes are made out of leather," Walker said. "Why don't we make us some suits out of leather? And gloves, too?"

The sergeant scratched his head fretfully. "Let's talk to the captain."

They talked to the captain. The captain rushed the two of them off to see a colonel, and in no time at all they were in the hallowed presence of a general, a big, intense man whose glance chilled Walker to the soles of his feet and who paced irritably back and forth while Walker stammered his fanciful question about leather suits and gloves.

When he finished, the general stopped pacing. "Congratulations, Private Walker," he said. "Someone should have thought of this three weeks ago, but no one did. It's men like you who make our army great. I'll see that you get a medal for this, and I'll also see that you get all the leather you want."

They saluted and turned away, both of them stunned at the realization that they'd been granted the honor of testing Walker's idea. It didn't help when they heard the general say, just before they passed out of hearing, "Darned silly notion. Do you think it'd work?"

Dusk was dropping down on them when the "leather" arrived. Walker slipped on a leather jacket and boots that reached his knees. He wrapped pieces of leather around his upper legs and tied them on with strips of leather. He fashioned a rough leather skirt for himself, ignoring the snickers of those watching. Five others did the same—three privates, the sergeant and the captain. The captain tossed leather hats to them, and gloves, and Walker carefully worked the sleeves of his jacket down into the gloves.

"All right," the captain said. "This will have to do. If it works they'll design a one-piece leather suit with something to protect the face, but we'll have to show them that it works. Let's get in there before it's too dark to see."

The grove was already ringed with lights that laced the half-darkness with freakish shadows as far as they were able to penetrate. The captain arranged them in a tight formation, himself in the lead and the sergeant bringing up the rear. A quick glance to see that all was ready, a nod, and they worked their way forward.

After an advance of ten yards the captain held up his hand. They stopped, and Walker, in his position on the right flank, looked about uneasily—up, down, sideways. A light breeze stirred the treetops high overhead. From the sky came the hollow buzz of a multitude of planes. The noise had a remote, unreal quality.

The captain signaled, and they moved on. Someone stumbled and swore, and the captain hissed, "Silence!"

They reached the far side of the grove and turned back. The tension had lifted somewhat; they spread out and began to walk faster. Walker suddenly realized that he was perspiring under the leather garments, that his inner clothing was sopped with sweat.

"I could do with a bath," he muttered, and the captain silenced him with a wave of his hand.

At the center of the grove they wheeled off at an angle. Walker became momentarily separated from the others when he detoured around a dense clump of bushes. There was a warning shout, and as he whirled the Night Cloak was upon him.

He shielded his face with one arm and swung a clenched fist. His hand punched a gaping hole, and he withdrew it and swung again. There was almost no resistance to his blows, and he riddled the pulsating, multicolored substance that draped over him. He had a momentary feeling of exultation. The leather worked. It was protecting him, and he would fix this Cloak but good. He punched and clawed and tore, and huge pieces came away in his grasp. Someone was beside him trying to tear the Cloak away, and he had a glimpse of a furious battle with the other Night Cloak taking place a short distance away. Then he was completely enveloped, and he screamed with agony as a searing, excruciating pain encircled one knee and then the other. There were several hands fumbling about him, now, pulling shreds of Night Cloak from his struggling body. He raised both arms to protect his face and became aware for the first time of a vile odor. Then the thing flowed, slithered around his arms and found his face, and he lost consciousness.

He awoke gazing at the restful pale gray ceiling of a hospital.

Someone in the next bed chuckled. "Came around, did you? It's about time."

He turned. Sergeant Altman sat on the edge of the bed grinning broadly. Both of his wrists were bandaged; otherwise he seemed unhurt. "How do you feel?" he asked.

Walker felt the bandage that covered most of his face. "It hurts like the devil," he said.

"Sure. You got a good stiff dose of it, too—around your knees and on your face. But the doc says you'll be as good as new after some skin grafts, and you're a lot better off than Lyle. It didn't get your eyes."

"What happened?" Walker asked.

"Well, the leather works good. None of us got hurt except where we weren't protected or where the Cloaks could get underneath the leather. So now they'll be making those one-piece leather suits with maybe a thick plastic to protect the face. All of us are heroes, especially you."

"What happened to the Cloaks?"

"Oh, we tore them into about a hundred pieces each."

Walker nodded his satisfaction.

"And then," Altman went on, "the pieces flew away."

Hilks had a scientific headquarters set up near what had been a sleepy little town north of Memphis. It was a deserted town, now, in a deserted countryside where no living thing moved, and the bustling activity around the lab plane seemed strangely inappropriate, like a frolic at a funeral.

John Allen dropped his plane neatly into a vacant spot among the two dozen planes that were parked nearby. He stood looking at the lab plane for a moment before he walked toward it, and when he did move it was with the uncertain step of an outsider who expects at any moment to be ordered away.

At this moment the Night Cloaks were, as a general had put it that very morning, none of his business.

Two weeks previously his assignment had been cancelled and his authority transferred to the military high command. It was not to be considered a demotion or a reprimand, his superiors told him. On the contrary, he would receive a citation for his work. His competence, and his years of devotion to duty, had enabled him to quickly recognize the menace for what it was and take the best possible action. He had identified the Night Cloak on the sketchiest of evidence, and no one could suggest anything that he should have done but didn't.

But control of the investigation was passed to the military because the Night Cloaks had assumed the dimensions of a national catastrophe that threatened to become international. The nation's top military men could not be placed under the orders of a civilian employee of an extra-national organization.

"Can I continue the investigation on my own?" Allen demanded.

"Take a vacation," his chief said with a smile. "You've earned it."

So Allen had taken vacation leave and immediately returned to the zone of action. Unfortunately, he was temperamentally unsuited to the role of observer. He made suggestions, he criticized, and he attempted to prod the authorities into various kinds of action, and that morning a general had ordered him out of the Contaminated Zone and threatened to have him shot if he returned.

The lab plane was inside the Contaminated Zone, but word of Allen's banishment seemed not to have reached it. A few scientists recognized him and greeted him warmly. He went directly to Hilks's office, and there he found Hilks sitting moodily at his desk and gazing fixedly at a bottle that stood in front of him.

Allen exclaimed, "Where did you get it?"

In the bottle lay a jagged fragment, splotched red and yellow and black, that twisted and curled and uncurled.

"Didn't you hear about the great leather battle?" Hilks asked.

"I heard," Allen said.

"Great fight while it lasted. One small infantry patrol managed to convert two Cloaks into about a hundred cloaks, and this thing—" He nodded at the bottle. "This thing got left behind. It was only an inch long and a quarter of an inch wide, and it was too small to fly. I think one of the men must have stepped on the edge of a Cloak and pinched it off. Anyway, it was found afterward, so we've been studying it. I started feeding it insects, and then I gave it a baby mouse, and the thing literally grows while you watch it. Now it's grown big enough to fly, so I've stopped feeding it."

"But this is just what you needed!" Allen exclaimed. "Now you can find a way to wipe the things out!"

"Yeah? How? We've tried every poison we could think of, not to mention a nitric acid solution that Ferguson dreamed up. It seems to like the stuff. We've tried poison gases, including some hush-hush things the military flew in. You can see how healthy it looks. Now I have my entire staff trying to think up experiments, and I'm just sitting here hating the thing."

"Anything new from Venus?"

"Yeah. They found a cousin of Elmer the snail, so they kindly let us know that we could keep ours. Good joke, eh? I sent them my congratulations and told them the Night Cloaks have already eaten Elmer. Since the Cloaks absorb bones, they probably can absorb snail shells, too. Elmer's kind may be one of their favorite foods."

"What does Venus have to say about the Night Cloaks?"

"Well, they're very interested in what we've been able to tell them, and they thank its for the information. They're going to keep their research teams out of the Great Doleman Swamp until we can tell them how to cope with the things. Other than that, nothing."

"Too bad. I'd hoped they might know something."

"It's a lot worse than you realize. Venus has been so damned smug about the whole catastrophe that some of our politicians have decided to resent that. There's a movement afoot to ban travel to Venus and close down all the Venusian scientific stations. The other planets may be next, and then perhaps even the moon. After triumphantly moving out across the Solar System and hopefully taking aim at the stars, man crawls ignominiously back into his shell. Some of the pessimists think it may take us generations to handle the Cloaks, and in the meantime the Mississippi basin will become uninhabitable as far north as Minnesota and perhaps above the Canadian border in summer. Whatever happens, I'm betting that the well-dressed man will be wearing a lot of leather. The well-dressed woman, too. Do you have any bright ideas for us to work on?"

"I ran out of bright ideas on the third day," Allen said.

"If your mind isn't occupied with anything else, you might work on this one: Where are all the Night Cloaks?"

"The military seems to be keeping good track of them. That's one thing it does well."

"We have a rough tabulation of the minimum number that should be around, and we have records of all of the sightings. As far as we can tell, about ninety per cent have disappeared."

"We figured they had periods of dormancy."

"Sure. But if they're going dormant on us, why hasn't someone found a dormant Night Cloak somewhere? We're worried because we have no notion of what their range is. If they ever get established in the Central and South American jungles, it will take us generations to root them out."

"Do you mind if I hang around?" Allen asked. "The last friend I had on the general staff just ordered me out of the Contaminated Zone, but I don't think he'll come here looking for me."

Hilks grinned. "What have you been up to?"

"I keep giving advice even when I'm not supposed to. I raised a ruckus because I didn't see much sense in picking Night Cloaks apart just to make more and smaller Night Cloaks. And then they were designing a new leather uniform to be used in Cloak hunting, and I suggested that instead of wearing such ghastly uncomfortable armor they just give everyone a bath in tannic acid, or whatever the stuff is they use to make leather, and soak their clothing in it at the same time. That was when he threw me out. He said he had ten million scientists telling him what to do, and he had to put up with them, but he didn't have to put up with me. So—what's the matter?"

"Tannic acid?" Hilks said.

"Isn't that the stuff? Probably it'd dry up or evaporate or something and not work anyway, but I thought—"

Hilks was already on his way to the door. "Meyers!" he shouted. "Get your crew in here. We have work to do."

By coincidence Allen entered the room first. The general, looking up sharply from his desk, flushed an unhealthy crimson and leaped to his feet. "You! I told you—"

Hilks stepped around Allen. "Meet my assistant," he said. "Name of Allen."

The general sat down again. "All right. I have my orders. Hilks and three assistants. I have the protective clothing ready for you, and I have a place picked out for you and a patrol to take you there."

"Good," Hilks said. "Let's get going."

"My orders also say that I'm to satisfy myself as to the soundness of whatever it is you propose to do."

"We've developed a spray we'd like to try out on the Cloaks," Hilks said.

"What'll it do to them?"

"You know we have a specimen to work on? The spray seems to anesthetize it. Of course there's a difference between spraying a Cloak sliver in a bottle and spraying a full-sized Cloak in open air."

"You really don't know, then."

"Of course not. That's why we're making the experiment."

"You're asking me to risk the lives of my men—"

"Nope. All we want them to do is show us where the Night Cloaks are and get out of the way. I'm not even risking the lives of my own men. Allen and I will do the testing."

The general stood up. "Tell me. I'm not asking for a prediction, damn it. Do you think this stuff might work?"

"We've had a lot of disappointments, General," Hilks said. "We're fresh out of predictions. But yes, we think it just might work."

"And if it doesn't?"

"The scientific staff will have a couple of openings. That's not much of a risk for a general to take, is it?"

The general grinned. "You're brave men. Anything you want, take it. And—good luck!"

As Allen dropped the plane into the small clearing, the pine forest took on an unexpectedly gloomy aspect. "Cover us while we're dressing," Allen said. He and Hilks climbed out and quickly slipped into the leather suits.

Meyers and another young scientist named Wilcox watched them anxiously. "Wasn't there a better place than this?" Meyers asked.

Allen shook his head. "All the other locations are swampy. Night Cloaks seem to be attracted to swamps, but I'm not. Also, they only saw two of them in this area. Two are enough for beginners like Hilks and me."

"Sure you don't want us to come along?" Meyers asked, as they donned their spray tanks.

Hilks shook his head. "One of the problems has been the total absence of witnesses. If we'd known exactly what happened with each victim, maybe we'd have solved this long ago. You're our witnesses. You're to record everything we say, and we'll try to describe it so you can understand what's happening. If we don't come back, you'll know what went wrong."

Meyers nodded unhappily. They fastened their plastic face guards, picked up the spray guns, and waved a cheerful farewell.

"No undergrowth," Allen observed as they entered the trees.

"It's a Co-op Forest," Hilks said.

"That means we're trespassing."

"So are the Night Cloaks."

They walked briskly for a couple of miles, turned, and started to circle back. "Better check in with Meyers," Allen said. "He'll be turning somersaults."

Hilks switched on his radio. "Haven't seen a thing," he announced.

"Man, you must be blind!" Meyers blurted at them. "There was one right overhead when you started out. It followed you."

They turned quickly and stared upward. For a moment they saw only the cloudless sky through the treetops, and then a blur of color flashed past.

"Okay," Hilks said. "It's flying above the trees—waiting for reinforcements, maybe. We'll keep moving toward the plane. When they attack we'll put a couple of nice big trees at our backs so they won't be able to get at us from behind. If I can find a tree as big around as I am, that is."

"Keep your radios on," Meyers said.

"Right."

They moved at a steady pace, keeping close together and taking turns looking upward.

"Two of them, now," Hilks announced. "They're circling. They look like small ones."

Two minutes later it was Allen's turn. "I just counted three," he said. "No, four. They're coming down—*get ready!*"

The Cloaks dropped through the trees with amazing speed. They plummeted, and Allen, backing up to a tree, had no time for more than the split-second observation that they were unusually small, one being no more than a yard across. All four of them curved toward him. He gave the first one the spray at ten feet and then cut it off. The Cloaks were gone.

Hilks was chuckling as he talked with Meyers. "They got one whiff of the stuff and beat it."

"Now we won't know what'll happen to the one I sprayed," Allen said.

Hilks swore. "I didn't think about that. The most we can claim is that they don't particularly like the stuff."

"Don't be too sure," Allen said. "Here they come again."

They were wary. They dipped down slowly, circled, sailed in and out among the trees. Only the small one ventured close, and it shot upward when Allen gave it a blast of spray.

"For what it's worth," Allen said, "the small ones are hungrier than the big ones."

"It figures," Hilks said.

Meyers, sitting far away in the plane, made unintelligible noises.

The Cloaks did not return immediately. Allen and Hilks peered upward searchingly, and finally Allen asked, "What do we do now?"

"Add the score and go home, I suppose. The stuff doesn't have the punch we hoped for, none of them dropped unconscious at our feet, but at the same time we can claim a limited success. It drives them off, which is more than anything else was able to accomplish. We can develop pressurized containers for self-defense and put the chemists to work making the stuff more potent. Shall we go back?"

"Not yet," Allen said. "Here they come again."

They came, and they continued to come. They seemed not to have noticed Hilks in their first rushes, but now they divided their attention and swooped down in pairs again and again. They were coming closer before they turned upward, flying through the clouds of spray. Once the small one brushed against Allen.

"They can't be *that* hungry," Hilks said.

"No. They're angry. That's what the spray does to them. It maddens them. Are you listening, Meyers?"

"We'd better get moving," Hilks said. "The spray won't last forever. Let's leapfrog. I'll cover you, and then you cover me."

Meyers cut in. "If you can find a clearing, I'll pick you up."

"We'll let you know," Hilks said. "In the meantime, keep a close watch on the forest. With them on our backs we might miss your clearing."

"Right," Meyers said.

Allen made a short dash, placed a tree at his back, and turned to cover Hilks. The sudden movement seemed to infuriate the Cloaks. All four shot after Allen. Three of them turned away as he pointed the spray upward. The small Cloak hovered over him for a moment, taking the full, drenching blast. Then the pressure faded, the spray gun sputtered and cut off, and the Cloak fell upon Allen.

Allen thrust at it, but it encircled and clung to his arm. Hilks raced toward him, drenching both Allen and the Cloak with spray. Pain seared and stabbed at Allen's arm, and he staggered backward and fell. He must have blacked out, for he had no memory of the moment when the Cloak released him. He regained consciousness with Hilks standing over him and turning aside the Cloaks with blasts of spray. He pushed himself to a sitting position and stared down at the throbbing numbness that had been his arm.

"Are you all right?" Hilks asked anxiously. "Can you walk?"

"I—think so." Allen got up unsteadily. "My spray is gone."

"I know. You started before I did, but I can't have much left."

Allen was examining his arm.

"Bad?" Hilks asked.

"Clear to the bone in one place," Allen said. "Fortunately it's not bleeding."

"So we've learned another thing," Hilks said. "Even leather won't stop them when they're riled up or really hungry."

"Can we do anything?" Meyers asked.

"Just watch for us. We'll have to make a run for it. We'll start after their next rush. Ready?"

"Ready," Allen said.

They darted off through the trees.

But the Cloaks were after them in a fluttering rush. Hilks turned, warded them off, and they ran again.

"It's no good," Hilks panted. "My spray is almost finished. Not much pressure left. Any ideas?"

Allen did not answer. Hilks sprayed again, turned for another dash, and fell headlong over the protruding edge of a large rock. He scrambled to his feet and both of them stood staring, not at the circling Cloaks, but at the rock, which inexplicably humped up out of the ground and seemed to float away. After a dozen feet it bumped to the ground. Encrusted dirt fell away from it.

"The devil!" Allen breathed. "It's Bronsky's snail. And look at the size of it!"

"Here come the Cloaks," Hilks said. He aimed the spray gun.

But he did not use it. As the Cloaks dropped down through the trees, a tongue-like ribbon of flesh shot out from the enormous shell, broadened, folded back, and dropped to the ground with a convulsive shudder of satisfaction. And the Cloaks were gone.

They watched in fascination as the flesh heaved and twisted and finally subsided and began slowly to withdraw.

Meyers, screaming wildly into the radio, finally aroused them. "Are you all right?" he demanded.

"Sure," Hilks said. "Everything is all right now."

"What about the Cloaks?"

"They've just been eaten."

"What did you say? Beaten?"

"Eaten," Hilks said. "I have the picture now. All of it. How about you?"

Allen nodded. "The snail is the Cloak's natural enemy. Or the Cloak is its favorite food. This one was more or less happy with Bronsky until one day it smelled or otherwise sensed a Night Cloak in the vicinity. If we hadn't put an army to beating the woods and shooting at it, it probably would have eliminated the menace at once. As soon as we stopped bothering it, it started eating Cloaks, and it's been eating them ever since. That's where the missing Cloaks went. They aren't hibernating, or migrating, they're in the snail. Look how it's grown! How big did Bronsky say it was?"

"About six feet."

"It's ten feet now. At least. There's the answer to our Cloak problem. Forget the spray and the leather clothing. Clear everyone out and leave it to Elmer. Have Venus ship us the snail they have and as many more as they can find. Are you recording, Meyers?"

"Recording," Meyers said happily. "I got the whole thing. Just as the Cloaks were about to finish you off, that snail came galloping up and ate them."

"Not exactly," Allen said. "But close enough. What's Elmer doing now?"

"It sees us," Hilks said.

They watched. The pinkish flesh flowed out slowly, thickened, stood upright. Then, before their disbelieving eyes, it suddenly took shape and color and became the snaky caricature of a once-lovely Venus.

"Allen!" Hilks hissed. "That thing has a memory? It has the proportions wrong, but the image is still recognizable."

"It thinks we're an audience," Allen said. "So it's performing. Bronsky said it was just a big ham." He walked toward it.

"Watch yourself!" Hilks said sharply.

Allen ignored him. He approached the snail, stood close to it, looked up at the wreathing head of Venus.

The Venus collapsed abruptly. The flesh quivered, thrust up again, and became a hazy, misshapen caricature of John Allen, complete with face mask, wounded arm, and dangling spray gun. Somewhere behind him he heard Hilks choking with laughter. Allen ignored him. He extended his sound arm and solemnly shook hands with himself.

COACHWHIP PUBLICATIONS

COACHWHIPBOOKS.COM

zoologica
fantastica

ISBN 978-1-61646-163-8

Coachwhip Publications

Also Available

FLORA CURIOSA

CRYPTOBOTANY, MYSTERIOUS FUNGI,
SENTIENT TREES, AND DEADLY PLANTS IN
CLASSIC SCIENCE FICTION AND FANTASY

ISBN 978-1-61646-219-2

COACHWHIP PUBLICATIONS

COACHWHIPBOOKS.COM

BOTANICA DELIRA

MORE STORIES OF STRANGE,
UNDISCOVERED, AND MURDEROUS
VEGETATION

ISBN 978-1-61646-025-9

COACHWHIP PUBLICATIONS

ALSO AVAILABLE

ARBORIS MYSTERIUS

STORIES OF THE UNKNOWN AND UNDESCRIBED
FROM THE BOTANICAL KINGDOM

ISBN 978-1-61646-246-8

COACHWHIP PUBLICATIONS

COACHWHIPBOOKS.COM

ISBN 978-1-93058-528-7

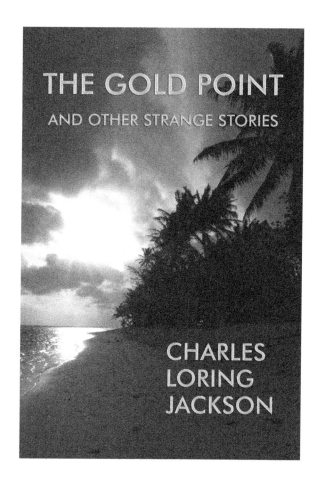

THE GOLD POINT

AND OTHER STRANGE STORIES

CHARLES
LORING
JACKSON

ISBN 978-1-61646-085-3